Also by L

THE CHRISTMAS FIX

LUCY SCORE

Bloom books

Published by Bloom Books, an imprint of Sourcebooks
P.O. Box 4410, Naperville, Illinois 60567-4410
(630) 961-3900
sourcebooks.com

Originally published in 2017 by That's What She Said, Inc.

Cataloging-in-Publication data is on file with the Library of Congress.

Printed and bound in the United States of America.
WOZ 10 9 8 7 6 5 4

To Quinn. You're going to be an amazing mom!

CHAPTER

1

C at stabbed the Answer button on her phone's screen while the makeup artist filled in her right eyebrow. "Hey, Laur. Tell me we're a go for shooting," Cat demanded.

"Put your eyebrow down, or I'm going to make you look like you have caterpillars crawling across your forehead," Archie warned her.

Cat wrinkled her nose at the makeup artist and smoothed the muscles of her forehead.

"Yeah, about that," Lauren began. "I don't think you're going to like this."

"They said *no*? Who in their right minds would say no to having their destroyed town rebuilt in time for Christmas for a network special?"

"I know," Lauren replied.

But Cat was on a righteous roll. "They don't have to wait for FEMA money, and we can guaran-damn-tee that their

Christmas Festival will happen *and* be bigger than ever. That's even more revenue for the town." Cat's voice echoed around the white walls of the hair and makeup room.

"I know. I know. Preaching to the choir, my friend," Lauren said.

"I shouldn't have gone straight to the network with this one. But who knew the town was run by a dumbass?" Cat lamented without moving her lips as Archie slathered gloss over them.

"Well, you see, Cat. I think it's a dumbass with a grudge. Apparently when you were in Merry for that episode of *Kings of Construction*, you ruffled some feathers."

"What exactly does that mean?" Cat demanded, drumming her freshly painted nails on the arm of the makeup chair.

"The city manager felt that the show turned his town into a circus."

Cat snorted. "We renovated the home of one of the town's most beloved families after they were hit by a drunk driver and nearly lost everything. That same house has two feet of standing water in it! I'm not going to just stand by and do nothing!"

"You sound mad."

"We saw the town. We were there. Half of Merry, Connecticut, was underwater two days ago," Cat argued.

"I know. I know. I was right there."

"Why in the hell would some city suit decide they don't need this?"

"Well, among a few other comments, the city manager's main refrain was he didn't want some network profiting off the trauma of his neighbors."

"As if I would let that happen!"

Archie poked Cat in the forehead with a makeup brush. "Stop it with the expressions until I get this shit on your face."

Cat stuck her tongue out at him but continued more calmly. "I want his phone number," she told Lauren.

"Are you sure that's a good idea? I mean, the guy still seems pissed about you and that bar fight when you were in town."

"*Bar fight?*" Cat's voice hit a high note that had Archie bobbling his makeup palette. "He's going to hold *that* against me? Obviously, he's never seen a bar fight before, or he doesn't believe a woman has the right to defend herself. Either way, I'm going to have to educate him."

"I don't know, Cat. He seems to think you're basically an Antichrist TV star who wants to swoop in and exploit his town's disaster for ratings."

"I hope you're paraphrasing."

Lauren laughed nervously. "To be fair, I think the guy is stressed to the breaking point. I mean, you saw how bad the damage was."

"Your pregnancy hormones are making you soft," Cat sighed. "Text me his number."

"Okay, but—"

"I'll handle this with tact," Cat promised. "I'm getting all the 'you're a big, stupid idiot' insults out now. Just don't say anything to the network yet about this city manager guy's refusal. We're doing a Christmas special, and it's going to be in Merry."

"Good luck. Please don't make him cry."

Cat disconnected and leaned back in her chair.

"You shouldn't yell at pregnant ladies," Archie commented, holding Cat's jaw in his hand as he swooped in with fake lashes. "Do not move a muscle."

"I wasn't yelling at Lauren. She allows me to freely express my displeasure at things that are stupid, like a city manager refusing what could be a golden ticket to saving his town's entire tourism income for the year."

"Uh-huh." His fingers deftly pressed the lashes in place.

"The town is devastated. Their huge moneymaker is the Christmas Festival every year, and government money isn't going to get them back on their feet by December."

"Mmm," Archie said, sweeping a bronzer into the hollows of her cheeks.

Cat's phone buzzed in her lap with a text from Lauren.

Lauren: "Here's his number. Noah Yates. Be nice!"

"Be nice," Cat mumbled.

"Stop pouting," Archie insisted. He swept the cape off her and angled her toward the mirror. "You're too gorgeous to be grumpy."

She eyed his handiwork in the mirror. She'd trudged into the studio still half-asleep with yesterday's hair spray wreaking havoc on her hastily tied ponytail, and now she looked like a cover-worthy model. Or at least a promo-worthy TV star.

"You're a freaking genius, Archie. You and your godlike hands and your magical potions."

"Nothing a gay man and his abiding love of Sephora can't fix." Archie checked his watch. "You've got five before they come pounding on the door demanding your hotness in front of the camera. Go make your call and eviscerate your city manager."

Cat blew him a kiss, careful not to smudge the violet lip gloss he'd so expertly applied to her mouth. "Will do."

She ducked out of the room into the hallway. They were shooting promos for her solo show's second season to run in magazines. Apparently, hosting a home renovation show when you were a woman called for her to be decked out in four-inch Jimmy Choos and a gorgeous, fitted dress the color of cranberries. She didn't mind it. If some designer duds—that she was totally keeping after the shoot—caught the eye of an audience and made even one little girl think that maybe she could wield a sledgehammer or a circular saw, then Cat considered her work done.

If people wanted to keep putting her in the pretty Barbie box, she was just going to keep cutting and smashing her way out over and over again until they learned their lesson. She may be pretty, but that didn't mean she was stupid or incapable or the slightest bit dependent on anyone. Catalina King had clawed her way up the ranks of reality TV to not just star in her own show but produce it as well.

And there was nothing she loved more than a chance to use her face to make a difference. Sure, it opened her up to public scrutiny. Two weeks ago, on a whim, she'd dyed her platinum locks a sexy caramel color with highlights. Twitter had lost its damn mind. People were still debating whether blond was better.

Cat took the attention in stride. Her life was perfect. A challenging job, a jet-setting lifestyle, a never-ending parade of new, interesting men available for casual consumption, and a project in the new year that would take her beyond TV stardom into something that really mattered.

But between now and then stood Merry.

She dialed Yates and tapped out an impatient beat with the toe of her shoe as the phone rang. After a handful of rings, it went to voicemail. She disconnected and called back.

"This is Noah," the man on the other end barked.

"Mr. Yates," Cat began. "This is Catalina King."

She heard an honest-to-God growl from the other end of the call. "I don't have time for this," he snapped.

"Frankly, Mr. Yates, your town doesn't have time."

Cat heard conversation happening in the background.

"Listen, whoever the hell you are," Noah snapped. "I'm trying to dry out an entire town here and figure out exactly how extensive the damage is. I've got people who might not be able to return to their homes for months and a town that is losing hope. We don't need some TV show coming in and churning out some sob story for ratings and advertising."

"What *do* you need?" Cat asked coolly.

"I need you to take no for an answer so I can get back to work. You're taking up time that I need to dedicate to more important things."

"Then maybe next time, don't answer the phone," she suggested sarcastically.

"Great idea," he snapped back.

"Before you continue your tirade, think about what you're turning down here. We're offering you a chance to rebuild quickly. The chance to get Merry back on its feet in time for Christmas. I know how much money comes into your town between Thanksgiving and New Year's Eve. We can help make sure that the park is up and running—"

"We don't need your bullshit pity, and I sure as hell don't need some reality TV star prancing around breaking her nails and punching my residents in the face while turning my town into some sideshow. We're good. We don't need you." And with, that he disconnected the call.

Cat took a deep breath and glared down at her phone. Noah Yates had no idea who he just pissed off. But he sure as hell was going to find out. She was going to save Merry's Christmas whether Noah wanted her to or not.

"Cat?" A production assistant poked her head out of a doorway. "The photographer's ready for you."

The real question was: Was Noah Yates ready for her?

CHAPTER 2

Four days earlier

The clouds, a dull gray swirl, twisted and roiled over Cat's head as she marched down Broadway. Both the hurricane above and the woman below moved with purpose. The heels of her fawn-colored boots clicked out a staccato rhythm on the cement as leaves and the occasional Manhattan debris darted in front of her on the wind.

"I'm not going to be late," she sighed into her phone and quickened her pace.

"You already are," her assistant, the very adorable and very British Henry, answered in his clipped accent.

"Five minutes," she scoffed, rolling her eyes behind her oversize sunglasses. "That's on time for me." She was perpetually ten minutes late to everything. It wasn't because she enjoyed making people wait or even that she liked to make an entrance—though she did. It was that a bit of fame overcomplicated everything. Leaving events and appointments was never as quick as it used to be. TV stars couldn't just wave goodbye and duck into a car. There was small talk and photos and the occasional autograph.

She was still getting used to it, though she was certainly better suited to it than her twin brother. Gannon couldn't stand the fuss and hadn't looked back after leaving the "biz" a year ago. But Cat loved it, thrived on it.

She was officially the highest paid star on the Reno and Realty Network, counting both those with vaginas *and* penises. Her new show was the network's version of a blockbuster. The second season was in postproduction, and she had her fingers in a few side projects and endorsement deals to keep her busy between filming. Life was pretty freaking perfect.

"How did the branding meeting go?" Henry asked, all efficiency. She could practically hear his fingers hovering over his ever-present iPad keyboard.

"Duluth wants to expand the line. We're looking at bringing in a few more feminine colors, and they're considering my idea to rework a few of the favorite men's pieces with more female-friendly tailoring."

"They're happy with the sales?"

Cat could hear the smirk in Henry's voice.

"Yes, they seemed rather pleased with selling out of product in less than two weeks."

"Are they planning to restock before Christmas?"

"Already done," Cat laughed. "The new catalog goes out in a week."

"Good. Text me the drafts of the adverts you're supposed to be reviewing, and I'll make sure nothing is grossly misspelled and that you don't look like a grinning idiot in them."

"You're a good man, Henry." *He knew her so well.*

"I'd be a better one if I could get you to your appointments on time," he grumbled.

"I can literally see the restaurant from here," she lied, hustling around a dog walker. The man's jaw dropped open with recognition, and he nearly stepped on a Pomeranian.

Cat wiggled her fingers in his direction and hurried on.

"I realize this is just lunch with your agent, but I'm trying to train you to have better habits."

Cat snorted. "Good luck with that. Now, go fuss over someone else."

"Don't forget you've got a phone interview at two and a mani at four."

Cat's nails were usually destroyed during filming. Home renovation, even for the cameras, was a dirty business. In the off-season, she treated herself to shiny, pretty nails.

"Then you've got that cocktail thing—"

"I already know you programmed each and every one of those things into my calendar."

"It never hurts to remind you. And I can hear you making that face at me right now," Henry told her.

"Smart-ass," Cat said, unscrewing her face. "Thank you for your obsessive attention to detail. Now, I need you to stop talking my ear off so I can get to my lunch before this hurricane opens up on us and wrecks my hair."

"By the time you get there, it will be high tea, and we're only supposed to see about three inches of rain. Farther north is going to take the brunt." Henry was a fount of knowledge. "I hope you remembered your umbrella."

"Bye, Henry," Cat sang. She disconnected from her snarky assistant and stowed her phone in her bag. She pursed her lips, ran a hand down her artful over-the-shoulder braid, and smoothed her features into an impassive mask.

A handful of photographers milled about, huddling deeper into their jackets and staring at their phones, in front of the very bohemian, very popular Courtyard Restaurant and Lounge. They were always here, capturing the occasional celebrity on their way to a posh lunch or for pricey cocktails on the sunken patio. It would be the former for Cat today as the outer edge of Hurricane Veronica lumbered its way up the coast.

"Cat! Cat!"

Cat's lips curved in the slightest hint of a smile. It wasn't that long ago that they had no idea who she was. Sure, they'd snapped a few pictures on her way in because she dressed nicely enough to be "someone." But now they knew her name. It was a reminder of how far she'd come in the last few years. It was this side of five years ago that she and her brother had been desperate to save the family business, and now strangers with cameras clamored for her picture.

"Who are you meeting, Cat?"

"Where'd you get the boots, gorgeous?"

"Smile pretty for me, baby."

"Sorry, gentlemen," she said with an apologetic grin. "Running late!"

Their comments followed her inside as the hostess stood stalwart guardian between the restaurant's diners and those outside wanting a piece of them.

"Catalina, lovely to have you with us again." The hostess offered the perfunctory celebrity greeting.

"Thank you. I've been dreaming about your kale salad all day." It was a lie. Cat had been fantasizing about Courtyard's very thick, very juicy bacon cheeseburger. But there was a price to pay to look the way she looked on camera. The days of eating whatever she wanted and drinking as much as she could were tapering off. Thirty-two meant making more good choices than bad, a sacrifice that she was constantly reminding herself was worth it in the long run.

Her heels clicked on the tile floor as the hostess led her back into the restaurant and heads turned in her direction. She was used to it by now…mostly. Dark bamboo lined the walls and kitschy chandeliers threw off dim pools of light. High-backed tufted leather booths offered diners a modicum of privacy. For those who preferred to be seen, there was a selection of high-top tables clustered around the sleek bar.

The hostess led her to a booth under a folksy painting of a rooster.

"Catalina King, you always know how to make an entrance," her agent, Marta, sighed. She rose and gave Cat a kiss on each cheek.

"You should talk," Cat teased, taking in Marta's curve-hugging white dress and glossy black hair. The former Mexican soap star turned producer's ex-wife had carved out a very profitable niche as a fierce agent to Broadway stars and TV talent. Her cavernous three-bedroom Upper West Side apartment and Bentley were proof of a never-quit work ethic.

They slid into the booth, and Cat ordered a flat water.

"First thing first," Marta said, her accent lightly tinging her words. "How's it working out with Henry?"

Cat leaned back against the booth. "He's perfect, and you're a diabolical genius for suggesting I steal him from that bitchsicle." Meeghan Traxx was an asshole of epic proportions. The woman was a fellow Reno and Realty star but had the personality of a cactus and the soul of a dementor. The woman had trolled Cat's brother and his wife every chance she got. And Cat took great pleasure in stealing the woman's abused assistant from her.

"You were a year late on the assistant front," Marta pointed out. "You keep trying to do it all yourself, and you'll end up combusting."

"I should have listened to you a long time ago," Cat admitted. She was a control freak. But she liked it that way. No one was going to be as invested in her career, in her brand, in her plans as she was—no matter how much she paid them. Though now that she had Henry handling more mundane matters, she'd really begun to make progress on her pet project.

The server returned with Cat's drink, and they placed their orders. Cat sighed internally when she ordered the kale salad.

"So what do you have for me?" Cat asked. Marta and Cat both shared an appreciation for business first, another reason they got along so well.

"Yet another magazine cover offer," Marta said, booting up her tablet and taking out her stylish reading glasses.

"Topless?"

"Of course."

"Pass," Cat said, sipping her water.

"They promised it would be—and I quote—'most tasteful,'" Marta added.

"These girls are worth more than a magazine cover," Cat said, pointing at her chest with both index fingers.

"It would be great exposure—no pun intended—leading up to your second season."

Cat shook her head. "Not happening. I'm not hitting any long-term goals by flashing my tits to twentysomethings."

Marta moved on without breaking her stride. "The network wants to offer you a Christmas special."

"Isn't it a little late in the game for a Christmas special?" Cat glanced out the window at the worsening October weather. "The other networks probably filmed theirs months ago."

"They found more money in the budget and want to add a special starring you and Drake Mackenrowe."

"Drake? Interesting."

They paused their conversation long enough to thank the waitress for their figure-friendly salads.

"Things ended well with you two, didn't they?" Marta asked, stabbing her fork into a piece of broiled chicken.

Cat and Drake had shared a very pleasant month-long relationship two years ago. Technically, "relationship" made it sound more serious than it had been. They were never in the same place long enough for more than a series of one-night stands and had parted as friends. They'd managed to stir the pot by showing up to a red-carpet function together, but—try as the suits had—the relationship hadn't stuck.

It had been a temporary good time, one Cat had no regrets about. She'd never worked with Drake before but couldn't see a reason why it would be a problem now. He was a nice guy and would have no problems with her calling the shots.

"It ended well," Cat said, spearing an unsatisfying leaf of kale. As soon as the show's promo shoot was done this week, she was treating herself to a pizza. A whole one. And an entire bottle of wine. She'd invite Paige, her sister-in-law, and they could get sloppy drunk together. "What kind of special?"

"They're thinking a neighbor-versus-neighbor decorating contest," Marta told her.

Cat wrinkled her nose. "Ugh. Not interested."

"Their offer is reasonably generous," Marta said, naming a figure that stilled Cat's fingers on her fork. But her time was valuable, and if she was going to shift focus from the balls she was currently juggling, it needed to interest her.

"Don't they get that viewers are tired of competition? What about something with actual feelings and Christmas spirit?"

"I don't think you're going to get something with generosity and human kindness out of network television," Marta quipped.

"My plate is full enough already. I'm not interested in adding another project unless they're open to a show that would actually benefit something besides their bank accounts. It's the holidays, for Christ's sake."

"And that's exactly what I told them," Marta announced smugly.

Cat smiled. "You know me so well."

"That's what you pay me quite well for."

Cat contemplated her salad for a quiet moment. "Isn't Christmas supposed to be about more than advertising and competition?"

"Not in show business."

CHAPTER

3

D ad!"
    Noah winced at his daughter's near shriek. "Hang on a sec, Dave," he said, covering the mouthpiece of his office phone as Sara burst into his office with all the overwhelming energy of a twelve-year-old. "I'm on the phone, Sar."

She rolled her dark eyes at him and flopped down in his visitor's chair, slouching until her chin touched her chest. She was wearing the yellow sweater she'd lobbied her mother for and a chunky turquoise necklace.

"Let's keep the old high school as a plan A for the shelter. It's already got the empty space, and we won't have to waste time and energy clearing it out. Check with the fire station and see how many cots and blankets they have, and we'll figure out where we can get more." He hung up and gave his daughter his full attention. "Why aren't you in school, young lady?"

"Daaaad! The hurricane?" Sara pointed out the third-floor

window where rain was already falling. "They let us out early so we could get home safely and help bat on the hatches." She kicked her pink-and-yellow rain boots out and crossed them at the ankle.

"Batten down the hatches," Noah corrected automatically, shuffling papers of town business that he could afford to set aside while dealing with what looked as though it would be a direct hit from a Category 2 hurricane. And with the Connecticut River in their backyard, they were facing some serious flooding.

"Whatever. If you give me money, I'll grab some stuff at the market."

Noah rose, automatically reaching for his wallet. "Can you let me know what the bread and water aisles look like?" He'd already put out an informational sheet on provisions and emergency procedures to the town. But Merry, Connecticut, was traditionally overly optimistic when it came to nearly everything. Being city manager here was both a constant joy and battle trying to get residents to understand the less-than-positive consequences of their choices.

"I'll text you," Sara said, hopping to her feet and snatching the cash out of his hand.

"I have to finish up a few things here. Meet me at home in an hour?"

Sara was too busy texting to respond.

Noah covered the phone screen with his palm. "Excuse me, daughter."

With a dramatic sigh, she tucked her phone back into her backpack. "Bread and water aisle. Be home in an hour. I got it, Dad. You're the one who's always late."

She spoke the truth. It seemed that his job was never done.

"Watch the bucket," he warned, sidestepping a snowman tin one of the residents had donated to help catch the leaks that had begun plaguing the ceiling of his shabby office last spring. Town hall was in dire need of a facelift. "Is your mom ready for the storm?" he asked her as he walked her to the door, skimming a hand over her ponytail. "Is she okay with you staying with me?"

She swung the doeskin tail out of his grasp and shrugged. "I guess."

He added it to the long list of rejections a father of a twelve-year-old suffered.

"Did she get my memo?"

Sara rolled her eyes. "Dad, why don't you ask her? You have her number. I gotta go."

"Be safe," he called after her.

"I'm getting donuts," she yelled from the stairs.

Noah ran his hand through his curling hair and watched her skip down the stairs. Sometimes it baffled him that he'd known his daughter for all of her twelve years yet at times they were complete strangers. He was officially one of those dads who didn't "get it." Sara had gone from his adorable princess who raced down the stairs to greet him every day to the fiercely independent near teen who now seemed to care more about magazines and reality TV than being a well-rounded human.

He still caught glimpses of the little girl who captured his heart about two seconds after she was born. But most hours of the day were now spent in a constant battle of homework and parental nudging to make good life choices. He loved her more than anything in the world. He'd do whatever it took to protect Sara from bad decisions and frivolous diversions. Even if it meant she was constantly annoyed with him.

Noah's desk phone rang again, and a second later, his cell phone echoed it. He sighed. He had less than twelve hours to make sure every one of Merry's citizens was safe before

Hurricane Veronica made landfall. He rubbed his tired eyes under his glasses. It was going to be a long night.

———————

Sara's gaze wandered to the living room windows where the incessant rain pelted. The roar of the storm surrounded them, and Noah wished he would have gotten the roof redone like he'd planned this summer. The three-story Victorian monstrosity on the hill was too big for just the two of them. Six bedrooms, five bathrooms in dire need of updating, and two freaking formal parlors. Purchasing it had been a whim, despite the fact that Noah never had whims. But in the midst of a polite divorce, he and Sara had spotted the for-sale sign one day. She'd fallen in love with the fanciful mess in a way that only an imaginative six-year-old could.

Noah blamed Sara's princess phase and his desire to ease the transition to two separate families for the choice of real estate. Not that he minded the house. Its creaky, crooked doors, cozy nooks, and football field–sized kitchen had a certain charm, a character that made it impossible not to like.

However, the projects that he'd promised himself he'd tackle had taken a back seat to raising his daughter and keeping his town under control.

A town now under siege by a hurricane that seemed hell-bent on swamping them.

"House wins," Noah said, drawing Sara's attention back to their game.

She glared at his cards, adding them up in her head. "Cheater! You busted. *I* win!"

Noah grinned and ruffled her hair. He'd taught her blackjack back in the day to help sharpen her math skills, and she'd become quite quick with the cards. He hoped it wouldn't someday come back to bite him in the ass.

"Dad, I'm quitting college to become a blackjack dealer on a cruise ship."

"So how's school going? Are you still having trouble with fractions?"

Sara flopped over backward to sprawl across the rug. "Dad, can we *please* talk about normal stuff for once?"

Noah frowned. "School's normal. Isn't it?"

Sara's sigh of frustration was Emmy-worthy. "Dad, you treat every conversation like some chance for a life lesson. Can't you just be *human* every once in a while?"

"I'm your father," he reminded her. "It's my job to make sure—"

"Yeah, yeah. That I don't destroy my future by making bad decisions now." She parroted his own words back at him with more than a hint of sass. "I get it, but why can't we talk about other things too?"

"Like what?"

"Like how about this giant hurricane that's drowning Merry? How are we going to help people and fix stuff? What's going to happen to the Christmas Festival? Or why haven't you dated anyone in forever?"

"Geez, kid. I thought we'd wade into real stuff with a talk about favorite cheeses or something."

"Cheddar. Next," Sara deadpanned from the floor. She was wearing the ridiculous mermaid-scale pajamas he'd gotten her for Christmas the previous year. Mellody, his ex-wife, had helpfully sent him the link, suggesting their daughter would love them.

Noah cleared his throat.

In so many ways, Sara was still a little girl. He'd thought he'd been protecting her by keeping her out of storm prep. "Well, there's going to be flooding. We know that for sure. I'm worried about how much the water will rise overnight. The lower end of town by the park is going to have the most damage, and the fire department contacted everyone there to make sure they know that the old high school will be open as a shelter."

Sara sat up and slumped against the ottoman.

"Are you worried?" Sara asked, her pretty brown eyes assessing.

He hesitated for a second. "Yeah. Are you?" A gust of wind rattled the front window.

"Yeah."

"We're going to be fine—"

"I'm not worried for us. We might have a leaky roof and stuff, but we're on a hill. I'm worried about April. She lives across from the park. And what about Mrs. Pringle? She's all alone in a wheelchair. Remember how bad her basement flooded this spring?"

Noah sighed. He'd stopped by Mrs. Pringle's house on his way home and begged her for a solid ten minutes to let him take her to the high school. He'd even offered up a guest room in his house. At eighty-one, the woman was impossibly stubborn. He'd made sure her name was at the top of the fire department's welfare checklist for the morning.

"If people are in trouble, Sar, we'll help. That's the best thing about Merry. We're all in this together. We're going to be okay, and that means we can help everyone else who needs it."

She weighed his words and stared into the flames of the fireplace behind him.

"Okay. Now, why aren't you dating?"

"Where is this coming from?"

"Mom's engaged to Ricky."

Noah rolled his eyes. He was well aware that his ex-wife was getting remarried. And to be fair, he had no complaints about her choice in husband—besides a grown man still going by the name "Ricky." He seemed nice enough and certainly treated both Mellody and Sara well. As long as Sara didn't suddenly start calling Ricky "Dad," Noah planned to have a polite relationship with the man.

"What does your mom being engaged have to do with anything?"

Sara gave a one-shoulder shrug. "I thought maybe you were still, like, pining over her or something."

"Did you think we were going to get back together?" he asked, a headache forming between his eyes at the thought of his daughter being disappointed.

"Geez. No. I just think that Mom's happy now. But you're not. So why don't you go find someone who makes you happy?"

"People don't make other people happy," Noah pointed out.

"Life lesson." Sara stabbed her pointer finger at him accusingly.

"Sorry." Noah hid his smile.

"You never have fun, Dad. I worry about you."

"I have plenty of fun," he argued.

"No. You don't. You work, and you lecture me, and you worry about stuff. Zero. Fun. Ever. I kinda wonder if maybe you don't know how to have fun."

Noah did the only thing a father could do when faced with such an accusation. He hit his daughter in the face with a pillow.

CHAPTER

Cat finished up the email and pushed away from the workstation in her apartment. Rain, a deluge of it, made it impossible to see through her fourth-floor windows. The edges of Hurricane Veronica were doing their best to remind New York City that no one messed with Mother Nature. She couldn't imagine what a direct hit would look like.

The TV screen mounted on the wall flickered, catching her attention. She picked up the remote and turned the volume up.

"Hurricane Veronica has made landfall over Long Island and continues to head for the Connecticut coast."

Cat squinted at the screen, stepped closer. "Crap," she muttered. Right between New Haven and New London, directly in the path of the tropical bitch, was Merry.

She grabbed her phone and scrolled through her contacts until she found Kathy Hai.

"Kathy?" Cat said as soon as she heard the woman's voice.

"Cat? I can't hear you very well. Reception's spotty."

"Are you guys okay? I just saw on the news that you're in for some rain."

Kathy's laugh was forced. "Oh, just a little sprinkle. Nothing to worry about." Cat heard static, and then Kathy's voice came through clearer. "Sorry. I had to come upstairs. I didn't want April to hear me freak out over the phone."

"Oh geez. Are you guys okay?"

"Jasper and I are debating whether we should go to the shelter."

"Kathy, you live eye level to a river that's about to be raging. Get the hell out of there."

"I know, but I'll be worried about the house the whole time."

"You can rebuild a house," Cat reminded her.

"Yeah, but not as nice as you can." Kathy gave a sad laugh. "This place is our home, and you made it that way for us."

"I'll be up with my tools and my brother if need be," Cat promised.

"You're a good person, Cat King," Kathy told her.

"Yeah, well, let's just make sure you're a safe, dry person. I'll call you guys tomorrow and make sure you weren't total idiots who decided to stay home."

Kathy's reply was cut off by static, and the line went dead.

Cat looked back at her computer, at the pile of work waiting for her, and then at the TV screen. The Hai family was one of her favorites from the show. A few years back, their car had been hit by a drunk driver. A hit-and-run. Between the medical bills and not working, the Hais had come within weeks of losing their home. *Kings of Construction* had swooped in, not only renovating the home but paying off the mortgage, and the town had chipped in with a generous donation to help with the family's remaining medical bills. Since then, the Hais were back on their feet, and Cat stayed in touch with the family, even managing to get together once a year or so.

The town of Merry itself was postcard adorable. No box stores graced the town limits. The downtown was all mom-and-pop shops, kids walking home from school, and waving neighbors. Merry's fame came from its Christmas Festival. The entire town decked its halls to the nines and hosted late-shopper nights. Every year, they transformed the park into a winter wonderland with three acres of Christmas lights viewed from the country club's borrowed fleet of golf carts. There were hot chocolate and kettle corn stands, handmade crafts, and an entire Santa's village. On Christmas Eve, the town could rival the North Pole in festivity. If you lived within one hundred miles of Merry, you went there for Christmas Eve. It was part of thousands of families' Christmas traditions.

Where would they go this year? Cat wondered.

She picked up her phone again, dialed.

"Hey!" Her sister-in-law's cheery greeting was undercut by Gabby's squeal of delight or frustration. The one-year-old certainly had gotten the volume from the King side of the family.

"Hey, Paige. I just talked to Kathy Hai," Cat said, cutting to the chase.

"Oh! How is she? How's April?" Paige asked. Cat's sister-in-law had an uncanny memory for the families they'd featured on all four seasons of *Kings of Construction*.

"It was hard to hear her over the hurricane bearing down on her."

"Oh no! I haven't caught up on the news. Are they going to be okay?"

Cat blew out a frustrated sigh. "I don't know. I mean, it's a direct hit."

"And their house is across from the park," Paige said, getting the gist.

"And the river."

"If they need anything at all, you know you can count on Gannon and me."

"Thanks. I think I just want someone else to worry about them with me."

"Consider me your partner in concern," Paige promised. "How's Operation School Days coming?"

Cat flopped down on her overstuffed sofa and turned off the TV. "I'm not on speakerphone, am I?"

"No."

"Good. Because I'm so fucking pumped about it. I think I just found my ideal facilities manager, and I've got a few lines on some other VIP staff. And I'm dying to talk about it. But until I have a location, what am I going to say?"

"That you're an amazing woman who is going to train other amazing women to work in trades and run their own businesses?" Paige suggested.

"Aww. You're pretty amazeballs yourself, Paigey. How's my beautiful niece?"

"Big, bad, and beautiful. Just like her daddy and her aunt."

"What's next on your busy filmmaker schedule?" Paige had gotten her start behind the camera in reality television. She'd worked her way up to director and had started her own production studio that developed documentaries. Her first documentary, on women in the television industry, had opened eyes across the country to double standards and inequalities. The Reno and Realty Network—probably fearful that Paige would take aim at them specifically—had started a program to advance women behind the camera and put in place an equal pay policy.

Paige filled Cat in on the particulars of her latest project. "But listen, when this school thing pans out, I'd be interested in documenting it."

"Really?" Cat kicked her legs up over the arm of the couch. "Like a day in the life?"

"I'm thinking following the first class to graduation and then beyond."

"You must have a lot of faith in me."

"In the words of Gannon King, 'I'd be a fucking moron not to.'"

"Yeah, that sounds about right. Is my uglier, older half around?" Gannon and Cat were twins born two minutes apart. Neither of them was hard on the eyes, and their sincere brotherly-sisterly angst had won the hearts of viewers everywhere. The reality TV world was still mourning the fact that Gannon had gone back to managing their grandfather's construction business.

"He's putting Gabby down, but he'll want to know about the Hais."

"I'll call him tomorrow once I know how they fared."

"Okay. If they need anything at all, let us know. I'm serious. I've got some time between now and the end of the year. And I know Gannon will juggle things to make time."

"Will do, sis. Thanks."

They ended the call, and Cat listened to the unceasing rain while staring up at her ceiling. She'd been in this space for five years now. Everything in the two-bedroom Brooklyn apartment was exactly the way she wanted it. The teal textured walls of the master bedroom. The refinished hardwood. The kitchen had taken her eight weeks of her own labor to get just perfect. Everything in it was just perfect, right down to the custom-sized claw-foot tub in the bathroom.

It made her antsy.

Cat would never consider herself a settler-downer. Sure, Gannon made it look appealing with his smart-ass, beautiful wife and their gush-worthy baby girl in their gorgeous brownstone six blocks away. But that wasn't for Cat. The idea of walking in the same door every day to the same man? It gave her the heebie-jeebies. Life was too big and bright for that. Maybe later. Maybe when she hit her midforties, she'd change her mind. But for now, she loved her life just the way it was. Traveling light and not having to consider anyone else's feelings or opinions on decisions. She went where she wanted when she wanted, slept with men without strings or guilt, and designed her space to exactly suit her tastes.

Maybe it was time to move on and find a new real estate project to satisfy her wanderlust?

She thought of the Hais and felt a stab of guilt. Here she was mentally whining to herself about living in the same perfect property for too long, and her friends were in danger of losing their home. It's not like the network would swoop in a second time to rebuild their home—

Cat's feet hit the floor as she propelled herself into a seated position.

Maybe they would...

CHAPTER

5

"Holy. Shit."

Cat muttered the pronouncement as she sat on the tailgate of a pickup truck and pulled on a pair of her father's hip waders. The muddy, murky floodwaters lapped at the stack of sandbags some enterprising employee had thought to set up in the grocery store parking lot.

After her epiphany the night before, she hadn't slept. There was too much planning to do. She'd swung by her parents' empty house at midnight and raided her father's fishing gear while talking her favorite location manager into an early-morning road trip. They'd left Brooklyn in one of the Kings Construction pickups at dawn and headed north in the rain.

The trip had taken hours longer than usual with road closures and Lauren's frequent pee breaks. The system, now downgraded to an annoying tropical storm, had pushed farther inland, which meant more flooding would be likely for the coastal areas as rivers and creeks pushed their overflow to the ocean.

Cat had parked the pickup in a half-flooded grocery store parking lot where a dozen other civilian vehicles towing boats and carting kayaks were lining up. They'd heard on the radio that New Haven had gotten quite a bit of water too, and that was where most of the help was focused.

Merry was on its own.

The river had overflowed its banks and taken up residence in the lower end of downtown. But the stalwart New England community was ready to save its own ass.

"You're not going out there," Lauren announced, tossing her hair over her shoulder. The woman was seven months pregnant and in no condition to physically stop Cat.

"Lauren, Lauren, Lauren," Cat tsked. "If I don't go out there, how will we know how extensive the damage is? This is our chance to put together a real Christmas special here. Something that means something. The network needs to know what a hot mess we've got on our hands, or they'll never agree to it. And Merry will miss out on its biggest source of revenue."

"Hell to the no." Lauren shook her head and crossed her arms over her baby bump. "If the insurance company finds out that your fine ass went into waist-deep floodwaters, you'll have bigger problems than Christmas decorations."

They watched as a pickup truck backed a trailer hauling two Jet Skis into the murky water.

Lauren shook her head. "I can't believe we're watching someone launch Jet Skis from a ShopRight."

Cat spotted a flat-bottomed boat trolling down what yesterday had been a street and used her taxi whistle to catch the man's attention. She waved and he changed directions.

"You are going to get me fired, and then this baby won't be able to go to college!" Lauren wailed.

"You're not getting fired. No one's going to know. I'm just going to take a little boat tour, and you're going to document whatever damage you can from safety."

"I'm going with you," Lauren said stubbornly.

"You and I both know your wife is one of the scariest women on the planet. If she found out I let your pregnant ass get on a fishing boat and go trolling through floodwaters, she'd murder me. Stay!"

Cat hooked a leg over the bow of the boat and clambered aboard.

———

Stuart was a middle-aged man of few words. He piloted the small boat down flooded town streets with close-mouthed determination. *Just another fishing trip for him*, Cat thought. He had no idea who she was, just that she was some crazy woman who showed up to a flood with a small cooler of sandwiches and water and a thermos of coffee. She was just another volunteer to him, and she was happy to keep it that way.

Cat was incognito in her ball cap and layers.

She'd recorded the canoe rescue of a young mother, her little boy, and a bedraggled cat from their flooded home. And Cat had taken dozens of photos of floodwaters and damage. She'd coaxed Stu—Cat had no idea if he minded her calling him that—to float them through the park in hopes of getting close to the Hai house. The park itself was completely submerged. The tree... The tree that had been decorated and lit every Christmas season for the past fifty years was broken, listing on its side in the ice-cold, debris-filled water.

There'd be no Christmas Festival here. Unless the network

put their money where their mouth was. If the suits didn't jump on this as the most epic Christmas special ever—well, that wasn't going to happen. She'd make sure of it.

Mindful of the current, Stu didn't venture too far into the park. Instead, he motored up Mistletoe Avenue. The Hai house, a cute bungalow that Cat had personally helped renovate from top to bottom, was sitting in three feet of water. The finished basement would be a complete loss, and the first floor would need new drywall, new floors, and new molding, but barring a further freak act of nature, it would be livable again.

They weren't there. The sign on the front door said so. And Cat wondered who had the forethought to ask residents to post whether their homes were empty, saving rescuers time.

She snapped away pictures, video. Whatever it would take to convince the network to send her back to this tiny town.

Cat stowed her phone in her rain slicker and began scanning neighboring windows for movement. Burrowing deeper into her slicker, she shivered. She could see puffs of her own breath, silvery clouds in the frigid air. The floodwaters were even more dangerous with their arctic temperatures.

She spotted movement up ahead. Arms waved from the covered porch of a cottage halfway down the block. Cat signaled Stu, and they chugged up the street. A family of four clutching garbage bags and one another waded out to greet them.

A woman, a complete stranger, handed Cat her most precious possession, her baby girl. "Thank you," the woman whispered through chattering teeth as her husband boosted her aboard.

Cat bit her lip and nodded briskly. She handed the baby back and plucked the little boy off his father's shoulders.

"Hey there, buddy. Ready for a boat ride?"

He grinned up at her, too innocent to understand their circumstances.

"I like boats!" he announced.

Cat offered her hand to the dad and helped haul him into the boat. He picked up his son and put his arm around his wife, pulling her into his side.

"Where we takin' 'em?" Stu wanted to know. It was the first full sentence he'd spoken to her.

Shit. When had she become the boss? "Let's go back to the grocery store. There's food there, cars. It'll be easier for everyone to find a ride."

Stu grunted and gunned the outboard motor.

The little boy clapped his gloved hands as they cruised through muddy water down the ruined street.

———

Cat had lost count of how many people they'd hauled to safety. Her phone had died hours ago and was left to charge in the truck. Lauren, a natural organizer, had set up a receiving area of sorts for people in the parking lot of the grocery store. The store itself had opened its doors and was grilling hot dogs and hamburgers and handing out bottled water and sports drinks to everyone who was in need. Donations of blankets and socks, dog and cat food, and other necessities were being sorted and distributed.

As if to add insult to injury, the tail end of the storm had stalled over Merry. The winds were calmer now, but the rain fell steadily, soaking rescuers and their precious cargo to the bone. It was a deep-down chill that made Cat wonder if she'd ever feel warm again.

They'd all become immune to the rain. Now that the worst had passed, now that their town was underwater, a little rain was the least of their worries.

Cell service was nonexistent, which added another jagged

layer to the frustration everyone was feeling. Friends and relatives worried about Merry residents were convening in clumps at the edges of the floodwaters. Lauren pressed them all into duty, giving everyone a task.

Cat made sure her friend had a sandwich and a chair before shoving off again with Stu.

She waved as they chugged away from the parking lot. They'd teamed up with two other boats and, between the three tiny vessels, had nearly cleared Mistletoe Avenue and Holly Alley. There were two more homes to clear before they could move on to another street.

CHAPTER

6

Noah squinted against the wind and the rain and fought to keep the bow of the canoe pointed in the right direction. He'd slogged through eighteen inches of water to meet up with his fire chief, who couldn't verify if any of his crew had made it to Mrs. Pringle's house. A neighboring town's search and rescue team was on its way, but with water still rising in the downtown, Noah wasn't taking any chances.

He'd left Sara in the house with the dozen displaced neighbors they'd opened the doors to. A veritable river separated them from the old high school building that was acting as a shelter. Sara was more than happy to play hostess, and he'd left her making her "famous tuna salad" for their new roommates.

He'd liberated a canoe from the back of a neighbor's garage and pushed off into the murk and mud. Mrs. Pringle's home was only five blocks over, an easy walk on a pretty day.

However, paddling through debris and current slowed him down considerably.

His hands were white knuckled on the oar as the rain and cold bit at every gap in his rain jacket and pants. The water was higher and faster on the lower end of town, and he lost valuable time when the current plowed him through a hedgerow.

He hoped to God that Mrs. Pringle had been talked into going to a neighbor's house. But the woman was beyond stubborn. Round and soft, she fit the grandmother type to a T. Her hair still had more black than silver in it, and she always wore a hat to church on Sundays. Her vocabulary was sprinkled with southernisms like "lawd a' mercy!" Everyone loved her. Hell, Noah adored her, and she doted on Sara as if she was one of her eleven grandbabies. There were always cookies in her house, always a donation ready for whoever knocked on her door selling candles or candy. She was everyone's granny.

She'd been wheelchair-bound for about ten years now. Volunteers from town had gotten together to build the ramp in front of the house she shared with Mr. Pringle. Noah remembered helping. He'd been twenty-two. Fresh out of college and juggling a wife, a new career as a public servant, and his toddler.

He spotted the house coming up on his right. The current was moving fast here, and he wished he'd tracked down someone with a fishing boat. Best case scenario, he'd find that Mrs. Pringle had moved to higher ground to wait out the storm. Worst case scenario? He had no idea how he was going to get a two-hundred-pound—not that he'd ever say that guesstimate to her face—wheelchair-bound woman into a canoe, but he'd figure it out.

Fixing problems was his superpower.

Noah lined up the nose of the canoe with the visible part of Mrs. Pringle's white picket fence gate and paddled hard, his muscles bunching and screaming under the duress. He hit the gate hard enough that it opened and the canoe scraped through, landing with a dull thud against the house.

The impact nearly toppled him into the water, and Noah vowed if he ever attempted a water rescue again, it would be with at the very least a more stable kayak. The front porch itself was underwater, and Noah had to scramble out of the canoe into thigh-deep water to get to the front door. He fastened the canoe's lead rope to one of Mrs. Pringle's porch columns and pounded on the front door.

"Miz Pringle!"

He banged again and then pressed his face to the glass.

Mrs. Pringle was sitting in her wheelchair at the foot of the stairs she hadn't used in a decade, wearing a pink rain slicker and holding a container of cookies. She was up to her knees in water.

She waved cheerfully.

"Fuck me," Noah muttered, yanking the front door open.

"Hal-le-lu-jah, Noah. I sure am happy to see your handsome face."

"Miz Pringle." Noah sloshed toward her. "What in the ever-living hell am I going to do with you? You've got to be freezing."

She pushed her thick glasses up her nose and gave him a smile. "Why, Noah Yates. I know you don't mean to swear in front of a lady, do you?"

"No, ma'am." Noah grabbed the handles of her wheelchair and started to push her toward the door.

"The water was only ankle deep until about half an hour ago, and then, my goodness, it just started pouring in!"

"You're going to get yourself a case of hypothermia." Or worse if he'd waited just half an hour more.

Mrs. Pringle wasn't concerned. "I knew you'd be coming along any minute now to rescue me just like a handsome white knight. Wait now! We can't go without my belongings." She pointed toward the garbage bags on the third step that the water was just beginning to lick at.

"Are you absolutely sure you need all this?"

She gave him a steely-eyed glare.

"Okay. All right. Just checking."

She refused to let him wheel her out until he'd loaded the bags into the canoe. Only then did she give him the royal nod.

The bags took up more room in the canoe than he'd hoped. And there was still the problem of the wheelchair and its occupant.

"Well, Mr. Manager, what are you gonna do now?" she asked, more amused than terrified.

Noah shook his head. Merry residents had a little too much faith in one another. They forgot to be worried or scared, assuming that their neighbors would always have their back. And now, here he was holding a wheelchair as floodwaters swirled around his knees, hoping for a fucking Merry miracle.

The whistle, shrill and loud, cut through the wind.

"Need a hand?"

The voice was his salvation. It was a woman in a bright yellow slicker holding a small fishing boat in place by clinging to the top of Mrs. Pringle's picket fence.

"Hallelujah," Mrs. Pringle sang.

"Don't hallelujah until our asses are safe and dry," Noah suggested.

"Honey, after this hurricane ends, we're gonna have a talk about your vo-*cab-u*-lary!"

"Yes, ma'am. But for now, I need you to stay right here."

She harrumphed, and Noah positioned her against the front door before slogging his way toward the boat. The icy water didn't even register anymore. He was beyond numb.

"Nice day," the woman in the yellow slicker commented.

"Just beautiful," he said, grabbing onto the fence. "I got a wheelchair-bound eighty-year-old and a canoe."

"Well, fuck," the woman swore ripely. "Stu? Wheelchair."

The man at the motor grunted. He seemed unimpressed with the circumstances. "Gonna hafta float her out," he said finally. He fished out a rope from the bottom of the boat and tossed one end to Noah. "You take this end and tie it around her. We'll reel ya in."

Noah clamped a hand around the rope and trudged back through the waters to Mrs. Pringle, who was entirely too cheerful about the situation. "Ready for your ride, Miz Pringle?"

She nodded. "Let's do this."

He took her down the first of the steps backward, hoping to God she and the chair would float rather than sink like a stone.

She floated, sort of. But the current was strong, and it took every ounce of Noah's strength to keep her on course, head above water. They were both going to die of hypothermia if he couldn't get her someplace warm and dry fast.

The woman in the boat made a grab for Mrs. Pringle's arm. Through his rain-smeared glasses, Noah couldn't see much of her other than her height and general bedraggledness. But there was no way she was going to muscle the very solid Mrs. Pringle into the boat.

"Stu, I need your ass up here," she yelled over her shoulder.

Mrs. Pringle tut-tutted. "You young'uns and your language."

"Sorry, ma'am, but it's bound to get worse before it gets better," the woman said with a quick grin beneath the brim of her ball cap.

The man Noah presumed to be Stu grimaced as he lashed another rope around the picket fence to hold the boat in place.

"Shoulda gone fishin' in Canada when I had the chance," he muttered under his breath. Pissed off but surefooted, Stu climbed his way to the woman. He took one look at Mrs. Pringle and swiped the hat off his head. "Gonna take more than the two of us."

No shit, Sherlock.

"Now, I *know* you aren't calling me fat," Mrs. Pringle huffed, haughty even in floodwater up to her chest.

"What if we put the chair in first and then I boost her up to you?"

"Sounds good to me," the woman said. "Ma'am, can you hang on to the side of the boat?"

"I sure can. I go to physical therapy twice a week. I can bicep curl five pounds."

Noah kept one arm around Mrs. Pringle's waist while she grabbed on to the boat. "Ready?"

"Ready as I'll ever be." She curled her fingers tighter, and Noah pushed and pulled the chair out from under her. He muscled it up one-handed until one of the handles popped out of the water. His biceps screamed until Stu grabbed the arm of the chair and hauled it aboard.

Noah ran through his list of things he was going to do when the hurricane was over. *Hug my daughter. Shower. Put on dry socks. Eat a steak. Sleep for twenty-four hours.*

But first he had to get Mrs. Pringle on that boat.

"Current's picking up," Stu observed. He sounded like he was describing the night's dinner specials.

Noah was well aware of the current. The water rushing around his legs and waist was pulling on him like a riptide. Debris and flotsam smacked into him with alarming and painful frequency.

He hefted, and they hauled. Together they managed to

wrangle Mrs. Pringle over the side of the boat. She landed unceremoniously, and the boat slashed gracelessly back to an even keel. Noah was just reaching for the hand the woman in the yellow raincoat offered when something big and unwieldy hit him with the force of a speeding truck.

He saw the tattoo on the inside of her wrist. A tiny hammer. And then the water closed over his head. His legs swept out from under him. He was an idiot. He was going to drown in water the color of chocolate milk. Sara was going to grow up without him. He'd miss her graduation. What if she went to the wrong college? Picked the wrong guy? What if she never outgrew her obsession with clothes and boys and gossip?

It wasn't his life that flashed before his eyes. It was Sara's. Maybe because she'd been right. He wasn't happy. He had no idea what fun was. And now he'd never get the chance to find out.

Something grabbed him. A strong hand, a glimpse of tattoo. It got a fistful of hood and neck, and the icy waters released him. It was the woman, the line of her jaw tense as she strained to drag his ass over the side of the boat.

"Lean!" she yelled.

Stu and Mrs. Pringle leaned hard to the other side as she pulled him higher. Noah found his footing again and, with one last burst of strength, boosted himself over the edge. He landed in the bottom of the boat, the woman collapsing next to him.

"We good?" Stu grumbled from the back.

Noah was too tired to open his eyes, so he settled for nodding. He was going to hug the hell out of Sara and add an entire pizza to that list.

"We're good. Get us the hell out of here, Stu, before we all become fish bait," the woman next to him called.

"Thanks," Noah gasped.

"No problem."

"You all want some cookies?" Mrs. Pringle asked as they chugged away from Mistletoe Avenue.

CHAPTER

7

Present

That son of a bitch Noah Yates *made* her resort to this. She had to bring in the big guns since he couldn't be bothered to take her calls anymore. Except that one time that he answered with a curt "Stop. Calling. Me."

Cat drummed her fingers in time to the blaring beat of Bon Jovi as she headed north to Merry for the second time in a week. Not only did she have the blessing of the network for this special but also their throbbing hard-on for the idea. They saw schmaltz and advertising dollars, a multi-episode arc of pure profit. She saw a chance to save Christmas for an entire town. Drake was committed to costarring. Sponsors were lining up.

The only thing she needed was a yes from an asshole.

She took the exit for Merry, steering the SUV she'd rented around piles of still-soggy trash arranged at the curb in front of nearly every home. For some, renovations had started immediately. Others needed more time to process. Soon, they'd have volunteers to help where they could, replacing insulation and drywall, ripping out old carpet, laying new.

Cat turned onto the main street, a road that only days ago had been underwater. Storefronts showed the water damage, but there were people, still smiling, still waving. And that was the appeal of Merry. That was why they needed camera crews here now, shooting B-roll and capturing the post-flood, pre-reno. This was what people cared about seeing.

She'd enjoyed the week they spent here with the show a few years ago, getting to know the town and its residents. She'd never known a community to be so protective and supportive of their own.

She came to a stop in front of the diner. Sunshine's was where locals gathered for breakfast and strong cups of coffee seven days a week. The cook and owner, Reggie, sprinkled a bit of his Jamaican roots into every traditional diner dish. Cat had been especially fond of the banana fritter pancakes.

But the diner as she'd known it was gone. In its place was a muddy hull of a building. People still gathered there, she noted. Reggie was serving up coffee and donuts from a folding card table in front of the building.

The steadfast New England spirit. She could respect that.

Cat eased down the block to the three-story brick building that housed Merry's police station, community room, and city manager's office. The building, marred by a line of mud demarking the flood level, was remarkably intact.

She turned off the SUV and flipped down the visor mirror to check her reflection. She'd gone all out in the weaponry department. A subtle smoky eye, bright red lips, perfectly coiffed ponytail. She was dressed casually in leg-hugging jeans and a gray sweater. One did not strut onto the scene of a disaster in four-inch stilettos and a miniskirt.

43

She'd taken a rash of shit from Gannon when he found out she'd "fucking frolicked through hurricane floodwaters." Her brother wasn't exactly thrilled when she mentioned that was exactly why she hadn't told him in the first place.

And she had a feeling she'd be taking another rash of shit from the man three floors up in a minute. But she was prepared. Catalina King didn't back down from challenges. No, she pounded and sawed her way through them and then flipped them the bird once she was on the other side.

She slid out of the SUV and marched up the stairs to the building's glass doors. It smelled like all old buildings. A little musty, a little dusty, with a hint of polished wood.

Noah Yates's office was on the top floor, and Cat used all three flights to walk herself through her argument. A King by birth, she mostly resorted to yelling or—if the situation called for it—throwing something that would make a satisfying smash. She had a feeling that wouldn't work with Mr. We Don't Need Your Help.

The desk outside his office was empty and the door open. Cat took it as an implied welcome. The office itself was empty, but judging by the wallet on the desk, Cat assumed its occupant and his stubborn streak would be returning shortly.

Papers littered the desk and credenza but in a seemingly chaotic sort of organization. Buckets in varying sizes sat under weak spots in the drop ceiling, catching the occasional drip. The carpet was old and stained, and the coffeepot looked as though it had been purchased in the 1980s.

The windows overlooked Main Street and the evidence of the town's trauma. A constant reminder of the work that needed to be done.

Cat snooped around the desk and picked up a framed photo. Noah, who she hadn't had the misfortune to meet when she'd been in town shooting before, appeared to be a good-looking man. The glasses gave him a hint of nerd, but the dark, tousled hair and happy grin upped the appeal. The girl next to him had mischief and magic written in her pretty brown eyes.

Cat wondered if he was as hard-assed a father as he was town manager.

She'd looked up her show notes and discovered that Mr. Yates had been on vacation with his daughter the week they'd shot here in Merry. He'd cut his vacation short when he got word of her "confrontation" with one of the townsfolk in the one and only bar during her birthday celebration. When he'd shown up on set, she'd been sleeping off a hangover in her trailer.

A production assistant and the field producer were able to talk him down and get him off set before Cat could blow up on him. She didn't care how beloved Handsy McGrabber was in the town of Merry. Her ass was off-limits, *especially* after an ignored verbal warning. She'd given the drunken grabber one chance to keep his beefy hands to himself, and when he paid her no heed and went for the gold, she'd clocked him in the face maybe just a little harder than she should have. But in her defense, she was six or seven sheets to the wind, and her tolerance for bullshit was at an all-time low.

She didn't overdo it as much anymore. Sure, she still enjoyed a good time. But she was a little more careful when it came to weighing the consequences. Especially since hangovers had stopped being inconveniences and turned into raging days of wishing for a swift death.

Yates's desk phone rang, and the blinking red light told her there were already several voicemail messages awaiting him.

"Can I help you?" He stood in the open doorway in jeans and a fleece. His hair, a dark brown, was longer on top than it had been in the photo, curling just a little. His eyes, a bright, sharp green, crinkled a little at the corners behind those glasses that were actually pretty sexy in real life. He had broad shoulders and, from what Cat could see under the layers, a very athletic body.

Cat set the photo back in its place and flashed him her most winning smile. "I think I should be asking you that."

His eyes narrowed and a deep line appeared between his brows.

She walked around his desk and extended her hand. "Cat King."

"Fuck." He muttered the oath and sidestepped her to dump his messenger bag on the desk.

"It's lovely to meet you too," Cat said.

"Look, *Cat* or whatever 'I'm so sexy' name you go by for work, why don't you just do us both a favor and sashay on out of here. I've got work to do, and none of that involves letting a camera crew victimize my town."

"No one is looking to victimize anyone," Cat argued, hands landing on her hips. "I'm offering you help. Financial and otherwise. Can your town afford to skip Christmas this year?"

"What Merry can and can't afford is none of your business."

"Well, that's just bullshit," Cat shot back. "I have friends who live here. Friends who could use a hand putting their lives back together again, and I'm not going to walk away from that."

"Then send them a damn gift card and leave me the hell out of it."

"I have the resources to get this entire town back on its feet and ready for Christmas. To walk away from that is irresponsible and downright idiotic."

46

"Being a reality TV star, I'd think that would be your life's mantra."

Cat's eyebrows winged up. So Mr. Manager wanted to play dirty. Good. She didn't mind getting dirty.

"You're really willing to pass up the opportunity to rebuild and still host your Christmas Festival just because you don't like me? Is that really in the best interest of your town?"

"I don't like what you stand for. Profiting off the misfortune of others? Selling a front-row seat to it and then disappearing as soon as the cameras are off? Yeah," he scoffed. "You shouldn't be lecturing me on the best interests of others."

"You're behaving like an ass right now."

He came around the desk to stand toe-to-toe with her. "Frankly, I don't care. My town is wading out of the worst natural disaster it's ever seen. I'm on the phone twenty-four hours a day with insurance companies and the state and concerned citizens who can't even drink the water yet, let alone go home and start to rebuild. You'll excuse me if I don't jump at the chance to add to the circus. We're a family in Merry, and you and your reality show don't belong."

Cat didn't back down. She never did. At five foot nine, she could be just as imposing as the tall jackass in front of her.

"I wonder what your neighbors would think if they could hear you turning down help for them. Do you think they'd be so quick to dismiss the offer? Think about it. A show leading up to Christmas Eve and the big reveal of the day Merry came back to life. That kind of publicity doesn't just go away. Next year, your festival will be even bigger. More tourism dollars, happier residents."

Noah's eyes flashed. "Get out of my office, Cat, and don't come back."

He was backing her toward the door, and Cat let him. She

was going to take an extreme amount of pleasure in emotionally eviscerating him in just a few short hours.

"I have a feeling you're going to regret this," she promised with a wide grin.

"Wanna bet?"

He slammed the door in her face, and Cat skipped her way downstairs. She was going to grind Noah Yates into a bloody pulp and tap-dance on his remains. And then she was going to fix his town.

CHAPTER

8

Noah fought off the encroaching headache with sheer stubbornness. It was already dark, and Sara had called him twice to see if he'd be home for dinner. He blamed Catalina King and her sneak attack on him in his own office for it.

The woman was a viper. Sniffing around for ratings. It was people like her that he needed to keep Sara away from. His daughter already spent way too much time with fashion magazines and reality TV shows that glamorized pretty over smart and wealth over worth.

He didn't feel equipped to battle the sexist, demeaning messages Sara and her friends were bombarded with every single day. He had to admit he'd never paid much attention to such things until he held his daughter in his arms. Then *everything* took on a new meaning.

He had promised that little pink bundle that he'd make

sure she understood she could be anything she wanted to be as long as she was strong, independent, and smart.

Women like Cat? They were walking self-esteem diminishers. Those long, long legs? All that honey-blond hair? The high cheekbones and the delicate hollows of her face? He could see why she and TV found each other. Technically, she was beautiful. Stunning even. But that was only on the outside. He knew enough about Cat and her industry to keep her far away from Sara.

Sara. Crap. He looked at his watch.

He was supposed to be home already. She was helping some of their temporary tenants cook a "flood feast." The dozen people now taking up residence in their house had emptied their thawed freezers and had been cooking all day.

He grabbed his phone and his messenger bag.

Noah: I'm late! I'm sorry! I'm the worst dad in the history of dads. Leaving now and sprinting.
Sara: *eye roll* I knew you would be. That's why I gave you a fake time. Dinner won't be ready for another half hour.
Noah: You're diabolical.

She responded with a Dr. Evil GIF that had Noah rolling his eyes. At least he had time for his customary evening coffee now. He locked the door to his office and hustled down the stairs. Merry and Bright was a cozy bakery and café that specialized in year-round Christmas desserts and good coffee. Usually he stopped at Reggie's for his first morning caffeine fix and Merry and Bright in the evenings on his way home.

Noah headed north. The chill in the air was edging toward frosty. Halloween was two days away, and he'd already canceled trick-or-treat night and the parade. He had a disappointed town on his hands, but there was no way they'd be able to clean up enough of the mess to clear the parade route, let alone let kids tromp around through half-frozen mud in superhero masks.

No. Halloween was one holiday Merry would have to give up this year. Most likely it wouldn't be the only one. Noah hated to think of his town without Christmas, but it was becoming clear that the money and hands they needed for a miracle weren't going to come fast enough.

He zipped his fleece against the night chill and raised a hand at the couple who greeted him from their front porch. This side of town had been spared, thankfully. And they'd been more than willing to make room for their less lucky neighbors in guest rooms and living rooms.

He sighed, his breath coming out in a silvery cloud. He loved this town. He hated being the bearer of bad news, but they needed to know sooner rather than later that there would be no Christmas Festival this year.

The glow of the café warmed him with a Pavlovian response. The smell of fresh cookies and hot coffee greeted Noah as he pushed open the door that always ground out the first few chords of "Jingle Bells."

"Evenin', Noah. You're running late." Freddy Fawkes, the café's co-owner greeted him from behind the register. Freddy bore an uncanny resemblance to the lean, ruddy-cheeked Santa Claus that he did his best to maintain. He and his wife, Frieda, claimed that the secret to their twenty-seven-year marriage and business partnership was that Frieda came in to bake and open the shop by six every morning, and Freddy took over after lunch and worked until closing.

"Long day," Noah said, scanning the display case. "Can I get two dozen pecan rolls to go and a coffee?"

Freddy's wintery white eyebrows rose. "You must have quite the crowd over there."

Noah gave the man a tired smile. "I'm happy we have the room to offer."

Freddy puttered around behind the counter, readying Noah's order.

Noah felt a twinge between his shoulder blades. A tickle. A looming shadow of doom.

He already knew who it was before he turned around.

"Well, well. We meet again." Cat smiled that canary-eating grin at him. She was sitting with April Hai, hot chocolates, and a Merry and Bright cookie sampler between them.

"Hi, Mr. Yates," April said cheerfully. She was a tiny little thing with stick-straight, jet-black hair handed down from her Japanese and Vietnamese parents. She smiled up at him winningly. "Did you hear the good news?"

Noah had no desire to hear any good news associated with Cat. He sent the woman a sharp look just to let her know. "No, I didn't, April. What's up?"

"Cat says she's going to fix my house and the diner and the park so we don't have to miss Christmas!" April bounced in her chair, fueled by sugar and happiness.

"Is she now?"

"Don't be modest," April sighed. The kid had the vocabulary of a college senior at a decent university. "She told me it was all your idea. We all knew you'd find a way to fix everything!"

Just what the hell was he supposed to do now? Tell April that the answer was no and crush her kid-holiday dreams?

Cat ran her tongue over her teeth and sat there smugly, daring him to say it.

"Cat says the festival is going to be even bigger this year! Can you believe it?" April bumped the cookie plate in her excitement and nearly sent it flying. "I thought this was going to be the worst thing ever, but it's going to be superlative!" She jumped out of her chair and hugged Noah around the waist.

Damn it. Damn it. Damn it.

"I hate you," he mouthed to Cat, not caring that he was behaving like an immature junior high schooler.

She blew him a kiss.

"April, do you mind if I borrow Cat for a minute?"

"Oh, sure! I'm sure you have a lot of plans to facilitate."

He grabbed Cat by the arm and dragged her out the front door. The bells jingled happily behind them.

"That was the lowest, most underhanded manipulation—"

"I wouldn't have had to bring in the big guns if you would have listened to reason," she pointed out, yanking her arm out of his grasp.

"Since when is reality television the voice of reason?" He was practically shouting now. He didn't know what it was about this woman, but she had the uncanny knack of raising his blood pressure to apoplectic levels.

"Have you ever even watched my show?"

"I saw the episode you shot here. The whitewashed version of the truth. You made the Hais look like helpless victims."

"Hey!" She stepped in on him, obviously taking offense. "I would never do that. The Hais are some of the strongest, most resilient people I know. I would never let them be painted in a negative light."

"Aren't you too busy with your photo shoots and your bar fights to really pay attention to what's going on on set?"

"You're an ass, Yates. But I'm still going to help your town, and guess what? I'm going to rub your face in it every step of the way," Cat snapped back. They were toe-to-toe again in battle stances.

"I don't like you."

"Good, because the feeling is beyond mutual." She drilled a finger into his chest.

"I hate everything that you stand for." He grabbed her finger, held it.

"Yeah? And I hate that you'd let your personal feelings stand in the way of the good of your town. So I guess we're even."

She had a cocky damn mouth on her.

"It's my job to protect these people."

Cat scoffed. "You make it sound like I'm coming in to rape and pillage."

"You might as well be. You're using this as fodder for public consumption. My friends and neighbors have been devastated, and you're going to shove cameras in their faces and make money off it," he snapped.

"I don't give a flying fuck what you think of me and my show. What I think we both can agree on is we want that little girl in there to have a home to go home to."

"The Hais can have a home without you."

"I have the budget for April's house, Reggie's diner, *and* the park. I can also bring in an army of volunteers to help with the other buildings and homes. I've got the money and the resources. You just have to say yes," she said.

Noah swiped a hand over the back of his neck, fighting the tension that coiled there. He was good and fucked. There'd be no money from the state until mid-December at the earliest. Contractors were already in short supply with the bulk of the rebuilding happening in New Haven. Merry was looking at a desolate year end at best. No festival, no tourism revenue, and cleanup that would take them months and months into the new year.

He swore under his breath, hating himself.

"What about decorations?" he asked. "If you want us to have a Christmas festival worthy of national television, we're going to need all new stuff for downtown and the park."

"Done. Is that a yes?"

She was too smug, too sure of herself. She had him over a fucking barrel, and she knew it.

"Look, I'll even throw in some kind of bullshit producer's credit so you'll at least have the chance to view footage before it airs," Cat offered. "That way, there won't be any surprises."

"I want a say in what airs."

She was shaking her head. "Not happening. Take the deal, Noah. I'm not going to screw over your town. In fact, I'm going to make it my goal to have you feeling like the world's biggest jackass for dragging your feet by Christmas Eve."

She stared at him. She could smell the victory like a shark circling an easy prey. He wanted to tell her no. Wanted to personally escort her out of town. But the town needed her money more than it needed his righteousness.

Noah nodded. Once. "Fine. But if you step one foot over any line, I'll make your life miserable."

She grinned, a sharp feline smile that any other man would have found sexy as hell. Noah found it evil. She offered him her hand, and with reluctance, he took it and shook. The spark that he felt ride up his arm? That was his body warning him away from the evil before him.

"I'll have cameras here tomorrow, so you might want to spread the word. If you need any help acting like a human being, let me know, and I'll have marketing write up a script for you."

She turned and strutted back into the restaurant, her glossy hair bobbing in its tail. He stared after her and clenched his hand into a fist.

Noah had just made a deal with the devil herself.

CHAPTER

9

Eight weeks to Christmas Eve

Cat, with the network's blessing and sense of urgency, mobilized an army in less time than it took most people to pack for vacation. By morning, she had a small camera crew rolling through Merry, scouting locations and shooting cleanup. She had PAs calling local news stations looking for any flood footage the show could use.

Cat shoved the first story editor on location out the door with a preliminary list of interviewees and the task of figuring out which stories would be followed on the five-episode arc.

The first of the RVs the cast and crew would be staying in were setting up camp in the side parking lot of the grocery store. Noah had signed the permits himself, which Cat considered a personal victory. He'd been a tougher nut to crack than she thought. Though why a city manager would balk at having a TV show with deep pockets finance most of a town's rebuilding budget was beyond her.

She'd enjoyed making him squirm with the adorably verbose April. No man who loved his daughter could say no to a little face calling him a hero. Cat 1, Noah 0.

She only hoped he'd crawl off to lick his wounds and leave her the hell alone for the rest of the shoot. They had eight weeks to craft the story, rebuild a town, and air the finale live on Christmas Eve. If Noah knew what was good for him and his town, he'd stay out of her way. But there was nothing Cat loved more than a good challenge.

She let the RV door slam behind her as she stepped down onto the asphalt of the parking lot. Her list was eighteen miles long, and she was going to start knocking items off it.

"Hey there, Madam Producer."

Cat spun around.

"Well, if it isn't my gorgeous and deeply talented sister-in-law!" She grabbed Paige for a hard hug.

"For now, I'm your gorgeous and deeply talented director."

Cat pushed her back a step. "No! The network said they were sending Martinez!"

Paige pushed her short dark waves out of her face. "They were until I volunteered my time for free."

Cat felt tears prick at her eyes. "You didn't. You noble shithead!"

Paige nodded, grinning wider. "It's a good cause, and my next project doesn't ramp up until January."

"You didn't have to, but I'm so damn glad you did," Cat said, clearing the emotion that lodged in her throat. "What about Gannon and Gabby?"

"We're a mobile family," the deep raspy voice, as familiar as her own, announced over her shoulder.

"Shut the front door!" Cat launched herself at her brother. Gannon King, handsome as a devil and prickly as

57

a cactus, was dressed for work in worn jeans and boots that should have seen the inside of a trash bin months ago. He wore a Kings Construction fleece and a ball cap. He hugged her back, hard.

"Gotta make sure my idiot sister doesn't go floundering through any more floods."

Cat snorted and punched him in the chest. "Like you wouldn't have done the same thing."

"And you would have been just as pissed at me for not inviting you."

He had a point.

"Where's Gabby?" A devastated town and TV set was no place for her niece.

"We called in a favor," Paige said. "Your parents flew back from Florida. We're renting a place about ten miles from here. I'm not sharing an RV with our daughter and my in-laws. They're ecstatic about the grandparenting emergency."

"Mom and Dad are here?"

"Mom left strict orders for you to carve out an hour for dinner tonight," Gannon warned her.

Angela King was a pushover as an Italian grandmother, but *no one* said no to her when it came to food. "I've got a lot going on here, but I'll do my best," Cat sighed, mentally rearranging her evening.

Gannon eyed the activity around them. "I'll mention that it would be really helpful if she brought dinner here tonight."

"I'd appreciate that."

"Got something you'll appreciate even more than dinner." Gannon jerked his thumb over his shoulder. "Brought a couple of reinforcements with us."

He'd brought her a crew. Men she'd known for half her life who had stuck with them after their grandfather's death when payroll had been late and jobs scarce. They whistled their patented "Cat call" that one of the jokers had invented years ago to entertain her when she was a kid. She opened her arms to them.

"What the hell are you jokers doing here?" Her budget was cringing, but having a Kings crew already familiar with the world of reality TV? It would be worth it.

"They're volunteering too," Gannon said, scratching the back of his head.

"The fuck they are," Cat said succinctly.

"They're going to swap out with the rest of the guys. Three days on set, three days back home."

"I can't ask them to do that," Cat argued.

"It's done. Besides, banner year for Kings Construction," Gannon reminded her. "Word may have leaked about those bonuses we decided on."

"Let's fight about this later," Cat said. She had too much other shit on her plate.

"Where we startin', Cat?" Flynn, Gannon's best friend and favorite foreman, demanded, tossing his hammer in the air and catching it neatly in his tool belt.

She crossed to him.

"Geez, Flynn. How many hours wasted on job sites did it take you to master that?" Cat asked, slapping the man on the shoulder.

His grin was quick. "Your brother bet me a burger and a beer I couldn't get it before the end of a workday." He patted his belly in satisfaction. "That burger was worth the bruises."

"Well, gentlemen, why don't you go grab yourselves some coffee and donuts and get ready for a briefing? We're gonna start with either demo or park cleanup. So I hope you brought your muscles."

They flexed for her, as she knew they would, flannel and Henleys stretched over both muscles and beer guts. Cat laughed. Surrounded by family, she suddenly felt like she was home.

———

Cat rapped her knuckles on Noah's open door and braced herself for a fight. "Got a minute?"

He looked up from his desk, shrugged. "Does it matter if I do? Or are you just going to drag a kindergarten class in here to cry until I give you whatever you want?"

"Try to not be an ass for five minutes, and I'll get out of your hair," Cat suggested, walking in and sitting in one of his visitor chairs without an invitation.

"What can I do for you today, Lucifer?" Noah asked, folding his hands on his desk.

"You're going to have to try harder than that if you want to insult me," Cat warned him. "We're going to need a headquarters. The RV park at the ShopRight isn't going to cut it. For one, we need heat. For two, we're going to need all the other comforts of home: electricity, internet, bathrooms."

"And you want me to build you what? A five-star hotel with conference space?"

God, he pissed her off. And sooner or later, she was going to have to teach Noah what the consequences were when he poked the bear.

"I'm thinking more along the lines of the old high school. It's empty and, from what the locals tell me, has more than enough space for what we need."

"It also costs the town astronomical amounts of money in terms of heating and electricity," Noah said.

"We're prepared to rent it for the duration of the shoot,"

Cat said coolly. She named a figure and had the satisfaction of seeing surprise flash across his face before he frowned again.

"I'd have to check with the town council."

Cat dropped her head against the back of her chair and stared up at the ceiling. "Matters of public facility rental are deemed the responsibility of the city manager, and unless the title painted on your door is a joke, you're the stubborn jackass who gives the okay."

"If you're looking for me to commit wholeheartedly to selling out my town for the sake of ratings, you might as well hold your damn breath because it's not going to happen."

Cat stood and rested her fingertips on his desk.

"I've had just about enough of your holier-than-thou attitude—"

"Excuse my interruption."

Cat flopped back down in her chair. "Noah Yates, this is Paige King, director of *The Selling Out of Merry*—working title of course. Paige, this is Noah, stubborn ass."

She ignored Paige's sharp look in her direction. She'd dealt with Paige and Gannon sniping at each other for a year before they decided to play nice. She figured Paige wouldn't mind being on the other side for once.

"Noah, it's great to see you again. I was with the show two years ago when we were here for the Hai family, and your community really made an impression on all of us. My husband had to turn away volunteers for his crew."

Cat watched Noah shift uncomfortably in his seat. "Uh, thanks. Please, sit." He gestured toward the other empty chair.

Cat rolled her eyes at the suddenly solicitous bastard.

"Oh, I can't stay, and neither can Cat." Paige glared in her direction until Cat rose from the chair and crossed her arms. "What I'd like to do is invite you to our briefing. We're sitting down with your county's emergency services chief and waste management to get everyone on the same page. We don't want to be stepping on any toes while we're here, and we'd like to fill any gaps you have in the cleanup process so we can begin renovations immediately. I know you've probably got a full calendar dealing with the city end of things, but if you can spare an hour, I think we'll all be better prepared and have a clearer idea of what our roles are."

"I'd appreciate that, Mrs. King."

Cat glared at him. "I was going to invite him to the meeting," she muttered to Paige.

Paige grinned. "Of course you were. Gannon was looking for you. He went through the Hais' house and has a preliminary list of concerns. Can you go track him down ASAP?"

Cat shot Noah one last dirty look. He met her scowl for scowl. "I'll see you outside," she told Paige and strode out.

CHAPTER 10

Noah watched Cat go. He felt like he'd gotten in a few good shots, felt a little raw in some of the spots she'd poked. But fighting with her was better than any shot of espresso. It made him feel awake, focused, energized. And it gave him something to do with the ball of nervous energy that had lodged itself in his gut the moment the first raindrop had fallen on Merry.

"Noah, I'd like to be candid with you, if I may," Paige said, sinking into the chair Cat had just vacated.

He spread his hands. "By all means."

"I can't imagine how upsetting the past week has been for you. It would be devastating for anyone who cares about their community to watch it be destroyed. And I understand how important the Christmas Festival is for Merry. I also know better than most how ugly reality television can be. You can trust me—and Cat. We don't do drama for ratings. We're going to give you your town back in one piece in time for Christmas. But we can't do it without your cooperation."

Noah sighed and rose. He opened the mini fridge behind his desk and took out a Coke. "Want one?"

"I'll take a water if you've got one."

Paige seemed like an upstanding person, even if she did work in TV. She was earnest and smart, and she didn't waste her time trying to enhance her already striking natural beauty. She seemed sincere, and he felt the slightest bit embarrassed that she'd caught him and Cat sniping at each other.

"I'll be frank too. I've been very open about my feelings toward your industry. The last time the show was here, the whole town went star crazy, and Cat lived up to the hype by breaking the nose of one of our citizens when she'd had a few too many out on the town. I don't like what she stands for." He raised his hand when Paige moved to interrupt. "That being said, I'm not blind. We need your help if we're going to get through this. Waiting for state or federal money would take forever, and even if we had the money for rebuilding, we don't have access to crews."

"I'm just asking you to be open-minded about the process. I can't promise that we won't disrupt your town because we both know that's impossible. But I can promise you we'll do everything in our power to keep the story sincere and real."

"And you'll keep Cat out of trouble?"

Paige laughed. "I'm not sure where you got this impression of Cat, but it's going to be very entertaining to me to watch you figure out how wrong you are about her. She's fiercely loyal, and I've never known anyone with a more generous heart."

Noah blinked. That was *not* the viciously beautiful woman who sashayed into his office and called him a jackass.

"Agree to disagree."

Paige grinned. "I'll see you at the meeting. I promise you're not going to regret this."

———

"What are your thoughts about this whole TV thing?" Velma Murdock, town council member and owner of the recently flooded laundromat and Merry's two hot chocolate stands, demanded as she slid into his SUV.

Noah pulled away from the curb and headed toward the old high school. He weighed his words carefully. "I have my reservations."

"Of course," Velma nodded.

"What 'of course'?"

Velma patted his arm and flipped down the visor to check her fluffy blond hair that she'd religiously styled like a football helmet for the last twenty or so years. "Noah, you're a very cautious man."

"Which is why I'm good at my job," he pointed out.

"Which is why you're very good at your job. You're a professional worrier. You worry so much that none of the rest of us have to. I'm asking you if you think this whole show thing will be good for the town."

He sighed. He had the unfair reputation of being Mr. No. But when his townspeople wanted to spend twelve percent of their annual budget on new reindeer light cutouts for the lampposts, he was the voice of reason. The crusher of dreams.

But their noses light up red!

"I'm withholding judgment," he told Velma. "But I will say, at this point, we don't have any other option. All our eggs are in this basket. If we don't have that influx of cash at the end of the year like we're used to, it could be catastrophic."

Velma nodded, flipping the visor back up. "Well, let's go let a TV show save our collective ass."

He pulled into the old high school parking lot, noting the fleet of other vehicles already parked. Production vans, construction trucks, a handful of rental vehicles. It looked like Cat had called in her own personal army.

Paige's words played back to him. He felt he was a good judge of risk. And his risk meter was screaming warnings at him where Cat was concerned. There was no way he was lowering his defenses around the woman. He wasn't putting the fate of Merry in the hands of a vapid TV star who cared more about her appearance than she did the welfare of his friends and neighbors. No, he was going to watch Catalina King like a hawk.

———

The woman was a four-star general. At least that was the impression she'd forced on him at the meeting in an old science lab. Noah had expected Cat to sit back and file her nails or not even be present. He hadn't expected her to take point, pacing in front of the small, hodgepodge crowd of city council, production staff, and county services. And he certainly hadn't expected her to casually mention that she was producing the series. He wanted that information to make him even more nervous. But he was too busy feeling a little shell-shocked at just exactly how well she knew Merry and its current predicament.

She'd marched them all through a potential timeline, fielding questions and making adjustments accordingly while keeping everyone present focused on the end goal: the Christmas Festival. Noah itched for a shot of caffeine while he digested the information. Velma listened intently next to him.

"Excuse me, Ms. King?" Elroy Leakhart, the balding school principal and Noah's cochair for the Christmas Festival, raised his hand.

"Cat," Cat reminded him.

"Right. Cat." Elroy squinted through his thick glasses. "When do you think we'll be able to open the Christmas Festival? This seems like an awful lot of work to get done."

"You're right. It is," Cat told him. "Even if everything goes perfectly, with a timeline this tight, we aren't going to have the park and the rest of the downtown up and functioning by December 1," Cat said. "We could cut projects and focus more on the park, but that would mean that Sunshine's Diner doesn't get rebuilt or the Hais' house isn't touched or the dozens of other flooded homes don't get the help they need."

She scanned the room, those gray-green eyes landing on Noah and holding briefly before moving on.

"By my estimates, we'll be able to open the festival on Christmas Eve."

Murmurs rose around the room. Noah felt simultaneously smug and sick. He knew she was promising more than she could deliver. Now everyone else would see it too. Condensing a month-long holiday extravaganza into a day? It wouldn't even be worth putting up the decorations.

"I know. I know. It's not nearly enough time. But what we're lacking in time, we'll make up for in planning, outreach, and marketing. This show will be airing four of the five episodes leading up to the Christmas Eve reveal. That's going to draw its own crowd, and I have some ideas on how to maximize the festival, including running it into New Year's Day and calling on some of our bigger sponsors to partner with us for the festival itself."

The murmurs quieted down. Noah glanced around him. People still looked nervous, but they wanted to believe her. They wanted to believe that she was here to help because she cared.

"I won't go over the plans now for the sake of brevity as I know all your plates are already overflowing. But I promise you,

I will make this worth your time. Together, we'll find a way to bring in the money you need. Now, if anyone has any specific questions, you'll find my cell number on the packets we handed out earlier," Cat told the crowd.

Who was this woman who fielded questions about production logistics, emergency management, and craft service?

Sadie, the county's chief of emergency services, who looked as though she hadn't slept more than two hours since the flooding started, was smiling at Cat as if she were the embodiment of salvation. Velma nodded thoughtfully to his right as Cat wrapped up the meeting, a slight smile curving her lips.

"It's all going to be okay, Noah," Velma said. "You made the right call."

He had no idea what magic spell Cat had woven to give them confidence. He was far from convinced. Sure, she was prepared and far more knowledgeable than he had expected, but it would take more than a detailed timeline and a pretty printed packet to put his faith in her.

The meeting was breaking up around them. "I'm going to clarify a few points with her," he announced, pushing his stool back from the lab table.

"Be nice," Velma cautioned him. "I'll catch a ride home with Sadie so I can insist she takes the night off. She looks like she's ready to drop on her face."

The meeting broke up, and Noah took his chance cornering Cat.

"Problem, Yates?" she asked without looking up as she tucked papers into her leather portfolio.

"I'm interested in hearing your plans for increasing revenue for the festival when the timeline is abbreviated."

"You mean you're dying to poke holes in my plans with your 'no' stick," she corrected him.

He saw it in her eyes. The same exhaustion he'd seen in the mirror. Just a flash of it before she straightened her shoulders and glared at him.

"I have legitimate questions," he insisted.

She glanced down at her watch. "I've gotta go, but I can carve out fifteen tomorrow around eleven. I'll go over the plan with you, and then you can poke all the holes in it you want."

"Fifteen minutes?" He found it hard to believe that a TV star's schedule was as packed as his own before shooting even began.

"Take it or leave it."

"Eleven here," he agreed.

"Don't bring your attitude," she said snidely.

"I'll try not to interrupt your time with your manicurist," he shot back.

"Your insults need work," Cat said.

The corner of his mouth turned up. "I'm tired. Off my game. I'll insult you properly tomorrow."

"Looking forward to it." Her voice was thick with sarcasm. But there was just a hint of sparkle in her eyes. Were they hazel? There was something vaguely familiar about those eyes. Something that tugged at him.

"If you're done staring at me, I have work to do," she said.

"You have something in your teeth," Noah announced and walked away grinning while she swore and dug a mirror out of her bag.

CHAPTER
11

Cat's trailer was full to bursting with bodies, and it smelled like garlic and bubbly marinara. She was in heaven.

"I can't believe you guys are all here," she sighed. Cat swooped in, pretending to steal Gabby's baby bite of breadstick. The little girl crowed her pleasure at the joke and shook her dark curls at Aunt Cat.

"No! Mine!"

"I see she's a King through and through," Cat and Gannon's mother, Angela, said wryly. She slapped her husband of thirty-four years as he tried to snatch a fourth lemon ricotta cookie.

"She gets her bossiness from her mother," Gannon insisted, leaning in to kiss the frown off Paige's mouth.

Figure be damned. There was no way Cat could say no to her mother's cooking. It had been a blessing to her waistline when her parents had made the part-time move to Florida a few years back. Then she only had to contend with Noni's bimonthly carb-filled dinners. A few truly torturous personal training sessions took care of that. Though she still fantasized about the day when her time in front of the camera was over and an extra five pounds wouldn't spark pregnancy rumors on Twitter.

Cat placed a smacking kiss on Gabby's round cheek and patted her father on the thigh. They were crowded around the minuscule dining table in her trailer. Their empty plates had made it as far as a stack at the center of the table, but no one was in any hurry to start the cleanup or the inevitable goodbyes.

"I don't know how you juggle all these projects on your plate," Angela sighed to her daughter. "Pop's business, your show, the clothing line, and now a Christmas special. You're gonna get wrinkles and gray hair and be unemployable," she teased.

Cat laughed. "I like being busy. And I have a very good dermatologist and colorist. So unemployment is a few years away."

"When does your very handsome costar get here?" her mother asked, wriggling her dark eyebrows. Angela King had a soft spot for the elegantly attractive Drake Mackenrowe.

"Drake gets in tomorrow," Cat said, mentally calling up the information. Drake would arrive with Henry by noon. Following a briefing, she'd give Drake the afternoon to get comfortable in his new digs before dragging him around town so he could get the lay of the land.

"Speaking of handsome men, Noah Yates isn't hard on the eyes," Paige commented.

Gannon shot his wife a feigned glare of jealousy and nudged her with his beefy elbow. Much to his embarrassment, he'd been named Sexiest Reality TV Star by a well-known magazine. Gannon favored his mother in traditional Italian looks. Cat took after her blond, mostly German father.

Paige snickered. "Not for me. For a certain single TV star we both know and love."

Cat scoffed. "The man is a monster, and he's made it very clear that he hates me."

"No one can hate you, pumpkin," Pete King chimed in with oblivious fatherly confidence.

"I don't know. I think it's more sparks than abject hatred," Paige cut in.

Cat rolled her eyes. "Ugh. Please. You're going to make me throw up the six pounds of fettuccine I just ate."

Her dad patted her absently on the back.

"Tell me more about this handsome man who hates our Cat," Angela demanded, plucking Gabby up and settling her granddaughter on her lap.

"I happened to walk in on a verbal sparring match, and you could have started a forest fire from the smolder that was in that room," Paige continued as if Cat weren't sitting two feet away from her.

"You're blinded by love for this big lug," Cat countered, poking her brother in the shoulder. "You don't know what it looks like when two people hate each other."

Gannon and Paige shared a smug look.

"Noah Yates hates my guts and is watching my every move to see if I'm going to destroy his town."

"He has very strong feelings about you," Paige conceded. "And he has no idea who you really are. Did you even tell him you donated your salary back to the show budget?"

Cat gave a shrug. "Why would I want to disprove his theory of me being a money-hungry hellbitch?"

"Does he know you were here dragging people out of the flood the day after the storm passed?" Gannon asked.

"You were *what*?" Angela screeched.

Cat threw a chunk of bread at her brother. "Thanks a lot, Gann."

She winced as her mother launched into her version of an Italian opera, loudly asking the heavens why she was cursed with such pigheaded children.

Gabby covered her ears with her little hands.

"You pull anyone out?" Pete asked quietly. Where Angela was loud and vibrant and likely to drown you in love and carbs, Pete was the silent supportive type.

Cat nodded. "Got a few people out. I borrowed your waders."

"Seams hold up okay?"

"Worked great."

He nodded his approval. "Good."

Angela was winding down her tirade, bouncing Gabby on her hip now.

"I don't mind allowing Noah to keep his wrong impression of me."

"We all know how you love it when people underestimate you," Gannon chimed in with a swift grin.

Cat smiled deviously. "Believe me, the only thing that is going to give me greater pleasure than returning the Hais to their house will be rubbing Noah's nose in transforming his town. I'm going to show that weasel-faced asshole just what a reality TV star can accomplish."

"Handsome weasel face," Paige corrected.

Cat groaned. "Fine. He's good-looking. Too bad he's a candy-coated jackass."

"Your auntie needs to mind her language, doesn't she, Gabby girl?" Angela cooed at the little girl in her arms.

Cat sat shoulder to shoulder with Reggie the diner owner as she went over some very preliminary designs for the diner renovation. They were crowded around a folding table that had been liberated from one of the school's unlocked supply closets.

"We've got room to squeeze in an extra booth here in the back corner, or I can give you a second station for your waitstaff," Cat said, pointing at the floor plan on the screen. "That way, they won't have to pile up behind the counter to ring up orders."

"They'd love you forever for that." Reggie grinned his blindingly white smile. His voice carried the singsong accent of his Jamaican home.

"Okay, we'll go with the server station, and I'll add some shelves so they can stock supplies, and maybe we can even squeeze in a second drink fountain for refills."

Reggie nodded his head as if to a beat only he could hear. "This is good, Cat. Really good."

Cat rolled her shoulders. She'd been going strong since six that morning and was hoping caffeine and a salad could carry her through the afternoon. "I want you to be happy with this. So if there's something you don't like about the design or later on when we get to the colors and finishes, you speak up. This is your business, your livelihood. You make the calls."

"You do this for me, and you'll get free breakfast for the rest of your life in Merry," Reggie promised.

"Can you add something to the menu that won't balloon me up to four hundred pounds but still tastes good?" Cat teased, thinking of her beloved banana fritter pancakes.

"I'll make a special dish just for you," Reggie promised, leaning back and crossing his arms over his striped rugby shirt.

"Then you've got yourself a deal," Cat laughed. "So you get

back to work, and I'll spend some time with the crew finalizing the construction plans. I'll get them to you, and if your city manager signs off on the outside changes, we should be good to go. In the meantime, I'll have a crew over there to help with the initial cleanup."

She thought she'd done an excellent job of covering up the bitterness in the words "city manager." For the most part, Cat prided herself on being a consummate professional.

"You're an angel, Catalina," Reggie sang.

"Says the man who makes pancakes from heaven," Cat quipped.

Her gaze slid to the doorway at the sound of the knock. The smile vanished from her face when she spotted Noah leaning against the doorframe. "I'm early," he said. He was wearing jeans, an oxford shirt, and a soft gray pullover sweater. He held two coffees in one hand.

She glanced at the time on the laptop in front of her. "Not by much. Reggie and I were just finishing up here."

"Thank you again, Cat," Reggie said, ignoring her proffered hand and pulling her in for a hug. They rocked side to side for a moment, and Cat forgot about the cloud of doom lurking in the doorway.

She pulled back from Reggie's embrace and looked him square in the eye. "We're going to make this better than okay," she promised him.

"You already have. Be seein' you."

"Bye, Reg."

He paused in the door to offer Noah a slap on the shoulder. "Be good to my friend Cat," he told Noah. "She's gonna fix us all up."

Cat watched Reggie leave, taking all the good vibes out of the room with him.

"You're making some big promises to these people," Noah ventured.

Cat stared at him coolly. "I never promise more than I can deliver."

He grunted. "The meeting yesterday," he began. "You running this project isn't what I expected."

She fluttered her lashes at him. "Because I'm just a pretty face?"

"Yeah," he said without a hint of embarrassment. "A pretty face who makes a living in front of the camera."

"I'm more than just my face, Noah. And the more is what gets shit done."

Noah eyed her warily. "I guess we'll see. I brought you a coffee. Not to be nice but because it's polite."

She made a grab for the cup he offered. "I'm accepting your thoughtless gift not because I think you're generous but because I need caffeine to survive."

"Coffee truce." Noah nodded.

"For the next fifteen minutes."

"I can be polite for fifteen minutes."

"I guess we'll see," she said, turning his own words against him. "So you had questions about the Christmas Festival itself."

"Yes. Namely how you expect to make up an entire month of tourism revenue in just a day. You're not exactly Santa Claus."

"No, but I am a very organized, very dedicated miracle worker. No one says no to me." She shifted into business mode. She'd spent her entire career dealing with men who underestimated her. She'd always proven them wrong before, and she'd pull out all the stops here in Merry just to wipe that doubting smirk off Noah's face.

Cat called up a document on the laptop and sent it to the dinosaur of a printer she'd found in the school's abandoned office and lugged back into the classroom she considered her temporary office. The show's budget was so strained that the addition of a new printer could implode the whole damn thing.

"This is a draft of the plan," she said, handing him the sixteen pages. "I'll refine it more this week before finalizing. So if there's something in there that's an issue, I need to know ASAP."

"And if I have a problem with something, you'll do what?"

"Listen politely to your concerns and take great pleasure in explaining to you why everything will work in terms a three-year-old could grasp."

"Are you trying to make me take my coffee back?"

"Mine," she said, her fingers tightening on the cup. "Here are the highlights. Thanks to the attention from the show as well as a series of Facebook ads and geographically targeted social media posts, we'll remind everyone in the tristate area about the festival. We'll be shooting, a lot of it B-roll—in layman's terms, supplemental footage like crowd shots, downtown video that gets cut into the main interviews and filming."

"You think people will want to come to the festival just to be on TV?" he asked.

Cat grinned. "Uh, yeah. Supporting a great cause that we've spent four weeks selling them on and the chance to be in the finale? You're going to have thousands of people show up here on Christmas Eve."

Noah harrumphed and continued skimming the pages.

"Marketing is going to design posts for all your vendors and retail shops who utilize social media so Merry can help us spread the word. I've already spoken to several store and restaurant owners who say they've been bombarded with messages and emails from past visitors. We can leverage that interest by guiding those visitors to the show and reminding them that this is going to be one hell of a holiday party that no one wants to miss."

"That actually isn't a horrible idea," Noah admitted.

"Of course it isn't."

"What about Christmas Eve?"

"Christmas Eve is going to be business as usual for Merry and a clusterfuck of epic proportions for the crew. We're going to be shooting the tree lighting in the park, one-on-ones with both Merry citizens and outsiders, the band and dancing, Santa Claus." She rattled off the scenes they'd already decided to focus on.

Noah raised a finger. "About the tree lighting."

She interrupted. "I know. The tree that's been decorated for fifty years went to tree heaven in the storm. I'm working on it. We're hoping to make Christmas Eve a mega event that will attract people from all over. It's a feel-good story and they're going to know that every dollar they spend on hot chocolate and presents and cookies is going right back into Merry's economy."

"It's still not going to be close to what we'd bring in during a normal year."

"Which is why the week after Christmas is going to be huge. The lights in the park will be accompanied by fireworks every night, and we've got confirmations from three musical artists that I'm not allowed to name yet due to current negotiations who will be performing concerts in your park that week. We're going to fill the heart of every Grinch viewer with so much Christmas spirit, Merry will be synonymous with Christmas for the next five years."

Noah paged through the report, frowning.

"I hate to admit it, but—"

"Yeah, I am that awesome," Cat said, cutting him off. She

checked her watch and downed the rest of her coffee. "I've got somewhere to be. You hang on to that, and if you have any notes or ideas that won't piss me off, email me."

The corner of his mouth turned up. "Because it'll be harder for us to fight over email?"

"Hopefully," she said with a wry smile of her own.

"I think we did okay today."

"Fair warning, Yates. The further we get into this process, the more sleep-deprived I become. And when that happens, I'm going to be a lot more likely to dump hot coffee on your crotch."

"I'll make sure to only supply you with iced coffee."

Cat shook her head. "I'm sorry. Did Noah 'Let Me Piss on Your Parade' Yates just make a joke?"

He leveled his gaze at her. "Maybe you're not as vapid and self-obsessed as I assumed you were. And if you're not, then maybe I don't have to be quite as hard on you."

"That's a lot of maybes."

He stacked the papers together and slid them into his messenger bag. "I'll let you get back to it then."

She nodded, already reaching for her phone. "Thanks for the coffee," Cat said.

"Thanks for the time." He paused just inside the door and glanced back at her. "You know I don't really want you to fail, right?"

She did know, and that was the only reason why she hadn't kicked his ass yet. "I know. You're just trying to protect your town from the boogeyman."

Noah nodded. "I am. And I'll do whatever it takes."

Cat met his gaze. "So will I."

CHAPTER

12

Noah crossed the parking lot, heading in the direction of his SUV. He thought the meeting had gone well and experienced a sliver of relief at the fact that Cat actually had a plan in place for drawing the much-needed crowds to Merry. Whether or not it would work remained to be seen.

One thing that was uncomfortably clear was that the more competent and efficient Cat appeared to be, the more attractive he found her. Which was inconvenient at best and downright stupid at worst.

While Noah was willing to be just slightly more open-minded when it came to the woman, he wanted to make sure he kept his guard up. He needed to be ready to handle things when this whole TV show thing imploded.

"Dad!"

He whirled around just as Sara ran full force into him.

"What are you doing here?" he asked, simultaneously

thrilled at the spontaneous hug and annoyed that his darling daughter wasn't in school.

"It's lunchtime. They let us leave school grounds, remember?"

Right. The school district's population was made up mostly of students who lived within town limits. Starting with junior high, students were allowed to leave for their lunch.

He didn't like it.

"Did you want to have lunch with me?" he asked, thrilled at the glimpse of his little girl.

"Uh, well, sure. But I saw in your calendar you had a meeting with…" Sara trailed off and took a deep breath. "Cat King," she said reverently.

His ego took the shot dead center. Of course Sara wanted to meet Cat. The woman stood for everything Sara worshipped: glitz, glamour, and fame.

"So can I meet her? I mean, will you introduce me?"

Noah's mind launched into overdrive. Was Cat the kind of celebrity who would be nice to kids? Did he really want Sara meeting a reality TV idol? And on the other hand, he'd be his kid's biggest hero for probably the entire holiday season if he could provide an introduction.

"Ohmygod! There she is," Sara hissed, half hiding behind him as Cat strode out of the building, staring at her phone in one hand and unlocking a vehicle with the other.

Shit.

He had to decide and fast.

"Uh, Cat? Do you have a second?" Noah called out.

She stopped and looked up with a frown. But when she spotted Sara literally clinging to Noah's arm, she broke into a smile. *A genuine one from the looks of it. Or she's a brilliant actress and wasting her time in reality television*, Noah thought with sharp realization. He put stock in judging people by the way they interacted with kids, his in particular.

"Sure," she said, crossing to them, her stride as impressive as if she were strutting down the catwalk instead of clomping across a parking lot in work boots.

"This is my daughter, Sara," Noah said, putting his hands on her shoulders and giving his daughter a little shove toward the star. "She appears to be a fan of yours."

"Hey, Sara," Cat said, offering her hand.

Sara shook it, eyes wide. Her mouth opened and closed several times before the words found their way out. And when they did, it was a tidal wave.

"Oh my God. I can't believe I'm meeting Catalina King. You are just the best! Your show is so great! I can't believe you're going to rebuild April's house again. Dad and I were on vacation last time when you were in town, so I didn't get to meet you. But April and I, we're BFFs, and that's just the coolest that you decided you'd drop what you're doing with your clothing line and stuff so you could come help her again."

Cat laughed, and Noah felt an uncomfortable warmth in his gut. He wasn't prepared to like the woman. He could grow to learn to maybe tolerate her, but liking her was impossible... even if she was looking at Sara like his daughter was the most interesting person on the planet.

"Wow. Well, thank you," Cat said, her hand still wrapped in Sara's death grip. "Your dad was pretty instrumental in all of us being here."

Sara's eyebrows winged up. "Seriously?" She looked back and forth between Cat and Noah, and Noah felt like a giant asshole.

"Sure. We wouldn't be able to be here fixing anything if it weren't for your dad."

Sara stared up at him with a look he hadn't seen in those

brown eyes since she was seven or eight. Hero worship. At this point, he didn't even care if Cat was doing it to goad him. He'd take every second of adulation he could get, knowing full well that the next time he questioned Sara on homework or eating vegetables, it would be gone in a wink.

"That is really cool, Dad," Sara said. "So, Cat. Do you want to come over for dinner sometime?"

Noah blinked and cleared his throat.

Cat looked up at him and grinned diabolically, knowing the last place Noah would want her was front and center in his dining room. "I would love to."

"Oh my God? Really? Because we have a lot of people staying with us who were displaced by the storm, and we do these really big meals every night, and it's fun. Like having a really big family!"

"You opened your home to your neighbors?" Cat asked Noah, raising a skeptical eyebrow.

"Yeah," Sara answered for him. "We have eight guests now. We call them guests so they don't feel bad that they can't stay in their own houses. We had twelve, but some of them went to stay with family. April and her mom and dad are staying with us, so you'll get to hang out with them if you come see me. We tried to get Mrs. Pringle to stay with us after Dad rescued her. But she's in a wheelchair, and she can't get around the house 'cause of all the stairs."

Noah was watching Cat's face and saw when the look of genuine surprise crossed it. "Mrs. Pringle?" Cat asked. "Wheelchair and cookies, right?"

"That's her," Sara grinned.

Cat looked up at Noah again, her expression unreadable. "Unbelievable," she murmured, shaking her head.

Noah was about to ask her what she found to be so

unbelievable when Sara launched into a recitation of everything she knew about Cat.

"You're two whole minutes younger than your brother, right?" Sara asked.

Cat, back to being amused, nodded.

"I wish I had a brother or a sister," Sara sighed. "But Mom and Dad had to get divorced, so that sucked."

Noah swiped a hand over his face, knocking his glasses askew. If he didn't get Sara back to school in the next four seconds, she'd spill all the family secrets and embarrassments to his potential enemy.

"Well, that's the nice thing about friends. You can be just as close to them as you can a brother or sister," Cat said wisely. "I bet you and April are practically sisters."

Sara brightened. "We really are! So when are you coming over? Tonight? Not today 'cause I have to go back to school. But tonight's good."

Cat laughed. "Well, what's for dinner?"

Sara whirled around. "Dad? Can we have pizza or something? Oh, wait. Cat likes kale salads and black bean soup," she recited. "Can we find that—"

Noah pressed a hand over his daughter's motor mouth. "Honey, I think we'd better check with the rest of our guests to make sure they're okay with more company, because I have a feeling Cat would like to bring a camera crew with her."

Cat was nodding. "I really, really would. Like a lot."

Great. Now his already overcrowded home was going to be under the scrutiny of a camera crew for a national audience.

Sara pulled his hand away and jumped up and down. "Will you ask them if it's okay? Will you, Dad?"

He sighed, gritting his teeth. "I guess."

"You'll let me know," Cat said. It wasn't a question.

Noah nodded briskly. "Now, if you'll excuse us, I should get this young lady back to school."

He was just about to pick Sara up and stuff her into his SUV before she could invite Cat to move in with them when a shiny black pickup truck rolled into the lot, windows down, music blaring.

Cat, arms in a V over her head, whooped out a welcome.

The truck squeaked to a stop, and two men bounded out, one short and dapper in trousers and a yellow checked shirt. The other was tall and broad and looked vaguely familiar. The tall one reached Cat first and swept her feet off the ground in a dramatic hug. He placed a loud kiss on her mouth before settling her back on the ground. "Hey, gorgeous."

He was tall and self-assured as if he'd had years of people telling him how great he was.

Noah felt instantly uncomfortable, and he wasn't sure why.

"Hey, yourself! I've missed your face," Cat laughed, cupping the man's face. He let her slide to the ground, and she leaned in and offered a one-armed hug to the second man. "Henry, I've been going crazy without you."

"Of course you have," he announced in a clipped British accent. "I hope you haven't cocked it all up already."

"Impressionable ears, Henry," Cat said, nodding in Sara's direction.

"Sorry, darling," Henry said, flashing a dazzling smile at Sara.

Sara giggled, and Noah noticed his daughter had a slightly dazed look like she was a concussion victim. The last thing he needed was men amping up Sara's recently acquired obsession with boys. He was about to drag her away when Cat twined her arm through the taller man's and led him over. "Sara, I'd like you to meet my friend Drake. He has his own show too."

Sara turned a shade of scarlet Noah hoped to never see on her face again.

"Hey, Sara. Nice to meet you." Drake—of course his name was Drake—squeezed Sara's arm in a friendly greeting. Noah didn't like it. He didn't like the guppy-fish look on his daughter's face, and quite frankly, he didn't care for the way Cat was glowing up at him either. *Get a freaking room.*

"Noah," he said by way of a greeting and gripped Drake's hand in a steely hold.

"Drake. Great to meet you. I'm excited to be working with this lovely lady again," Drake said, bringing Cat's knuckles to his lips.

Cat's phone chimed. She frowned at the screen and shook her head. "I know I'm late, Henry. Get out of my calendar, and stop texting me!"

Henry shrugged. "Why don't I come with you to meet the parks manager so you can fill me in on the way."

"Don't you want to settle in first?" Cat asked.

Henry snorted.

"Good, because I need you desperately," Cat said, cocking her head to the side. "Sara, Henry is my very British, very snooty assistant."

"Hi, Sara," Henry said, sparing her a wink.

Sara giggled and then couldn't seem to stop.

Noah felt like he should be covering Sara's ears. He was witnessing the flirty side of America's home renovation sweetheart, and he didn't care for it. Was she dating one of them? *Both* of them? Did it even matter?

One thing was clear, Cat wasn't the kind of role model he wanted Sara clinging to.

"Sara, it was great meeting you. Noah, let me know about tonight so I can have a small crew ready if it's a yes. You have my number?"

Noah nodded.

"Come on, Sar. Let's get you back to school," Noah insisted. Sara looked like she was going to argue, but when Drake and Henry winked at her and said their goodbyes, she lost the power of speech again. Noah half dragged, half carried her to the SUV and unceremoniously stuffed her inside.

"Oh my God, Dad. That was the most amazing moment of my life," she squealed. "Cat King! She's so gorgeous, and did you see those guys with her? She is literally the coolest, most beautiful person I've ever met in my life. Do you think both those guys are her boyfriends?"

Noah hit the brakes a little too hard as they rolled up to a stop sign. "Why would you think that would be cool?"

Sara gave him a sideways look. "I've seen *Sex and the City* reruns. Sometimes people don't want to be in a relationship. Sometimes they just want to have fun."

Noah wasn't sure who he wanted to curse more: Catalina King or Samantha Jones.

Hell would freeze over before he allowed Cat to parade into his house with a camera crew and her smoldering boyfriends who rendered his daughter speechless.

CHAPTER
13

That sneaky son of a bitch tried to weasel his way out of letting her into his house, just like Cat knew he would. The temporary coffee truce had been short-lived. Sure, it had held up long enough for him to introduce his daughter. Sara was bright, charming, and fun. The exact opposite of her shithead father.

Cat guessed the girl took after her mother.

Once Drake and Henry had made their grand entrance, Noah's pleasantries had turned off like the flipping of a switch.

He'd gone from grateful father to Judgy McJudgerson in the blink of an eye. The look he'd given her as he loaded Sara into his SUV? Oh, she knew that expression well enough. Judgment, swift and sure.

People often felt the urge to judge her. Her sex life (what a slut!), her wardrobe (designer dresses and flannels?), the way she interacted with people (too friendly or too uppity), all of it was fodder for public opinion. And Cat didn't give a good damn. She lived her life the way she chose.

She worked and played equally hard because otherwise, what was the point? She enjoyed casual sexual relationships with men she liked. And some days, she just felt like wearing fucking leggings and making a waiter blush.

She did things her way, which was why she was sitting at Noah's dining room table while he glowered at her. Cat had to admit, he fascinated her. How did a man take potshots at her one second and then nearly drown trying to save one of his neighbors? She'd been shocked when she realized they'd met before during the flood when she hauled his ass aboard. She'd keep that information to herself for now. And when it would give him the biggest punch in the gut, she'd drop that bomb on him.

Paige was explaining to the scowling Noah that she'd like to set up the one-on-ones in his front parlor. Meanwhile, a camerawoman, sound guy, and PA were already covering the worn rug and cozy furniture with a million feet of cords. And another half dozen people thundered up and down the stairs, poking their heads in to greet their host.

A fat cat named Felipe wound his way around her ankles, purring louder than a motorboat.

Kathy Hai, her stick-straight black hair tied back in a stubby tail, settled in at the cozy dining table next to Cat. "I can't believe we're back here again," she sighed.

Cat patted her friend's hand. "This sucks balls."

Kathy's smile was tired but broad. "I miss you and your inappropriate mouth."

"I missed you too, and now we've got the next eight weeks to enjoy each other's company again."

Jasper Hai skirted the table and handed Kathy a cup of tea.

Lines of tension were carved into his face. His jet-black hair was disheveled as if he'd been shoving both hands through it. Cat remembered the signs, remembered the strain he put himself under in times of crisis.

"You got a minute?" she asked Jasper, keeping her voice low.

It wasn't necessary to whisper, not with a dozen people roaming the first floor of Noah's house. She could understand the man's agitation. Not only did he have a few extra families crowding him in his own space, but he also had the better part of a reality TV show getting ready to happen in his living room.

"Ah, sure," Jasper said, scrubbing a hand through his hair.

He followed Cat down the hallway. The kitchen was full of people cooking and arguing good-naturedly. The sitting room or parlor had two teenagers in it battling it out on a video game. Finally, she found a room in the back of the house whose purpose Cat couldn't identify. Along the back wall between two windows was a bookcase stuffed with fiction hardbacks, the better part of the Sweet Valley High series, and magazines that ran the gamut from *Men's Health* to *Teen Vogue*. There was a suede beanbag the size of Rhode Island nestled in the corner. Two air mattresses occupied the far wall, and there was still room for a wardrobe that looked as though it weighed more than a car and could transport someone to Narnia.

"Uh, step into my office," Cat joked.

"Noah calls this his crap room," Jasper said with no hint of amusement in his soft voice.

Cat knew that tone, that look. He was a man exhausted. A man who felt like he was failing at caring for his family. They'd been down this road once before when his injuries had robbed him of his paycheck. This time, it had been Mother Nature, and that bitch Veronica had robbed them of their beautiful home.

But pity wouldn't fix anything.

"Jasper, I know you've got a lot going on right now. But I was wondering if you'd be able to help me out."

"Sure. What do you need?" Even exhausted and beaten down, Jasper was ready to lend a hand. It was the Merry spirit.

"It's a pretty big favor. We're low on labor." Technically, that wasn't a lie. Most construction firms in a two-hundred-mile radius were camped out in New Haven, which had gotten hit just as hard. The fact that Gannon had showed up with a Kings crew ready for action evened that out in Cat's mind. But Jasper didn't need to be privy to that.

"I know you're working full-time—" she began.

But he was shaking his head. "They cut me back to part-time just before…this."

Could the guy not catch a break? Cat silently cursed his employer and made a mental note to pay the company a little visit.

"Well, if you've got the time, I could use some labor. We can pay you, of course. It'll be some cleanup, a lot of hauling." Jasper's questionable talent with power tools was still fresh in Cat's mind. "And there's something else." She glanced over her shoulder.

"What?" Jasper reacted to her subterfuge.

"April's tree house."

"You're doing a tree house for her?"

"Actually, you are," Cat said.

Jasper straightened, his shoulders losing the slump. "Seriously? You want me to build it?"

Cat nodded, choosing her words carefully. "Gannon's going to do some plans, and I was hoping you could sit down with him and walk him through what April wants. Then you can take lead on it with a couple of helpers." A couple of helpers who kept him away from the sharp and the dangerous.

"That would be awesome." He nodded. "Yeah. I'd love to do it."

"Great," Cat said, feigning relief. "That's a lot off my mind. I'll give your number to my foreman, and he'll be in touch tomorrow. You just work what you can. I don't want you missing out on family time or taking more time off work. I know this is a stressful time for you guys."

"It's not so bad with good friends," Jasper said, nudging her with his elbow.

"You guys are going to get through this and come out even better."

"That's what you said last time," he reminded her.

"And *of course*, I was right, because I'm a celebrity genius."

"Is the tree house a surprise?" Jasper asked. "I mean, it would be cool if it was."

"Absolutely." Cat nodded. "We'll refer to it as the utility room around April."

"Diabolical." Jasper grinned. He held up a hand, and Cat slapped it.

"Team Utility Room."

Jasper returned to the dining room, and Cat took a moment to check her messages. With Henry here now, he was fielding a portion of them so she wasn't completely overwhelmed...yet. She could hear the team setting up the lights in the parlor for the first official rounds of one-on-ones and the thunder of footsteps overhead. It was a gorgeous house. She'd been surprised to see Noah had chosen something with so much character, history. She itched to get her hands on it, scrape the paint from the moldings, replaster the walls, bring the floors back to their glory days.

It would be a lucky contractor who got his or her hands on this place. One day, it would be a beautiful family home. A showcase, but a livable one. *Well, if the kitchen were redesigned.*

Put in an island, one big enough for one of those built-in banquettes. And the back porch—

"You do realize that putting a power tool in Jasper's hands is like begging him to slice off a limb, don't you?" Noah asked dryly from the doorway, yanking her from her renovation fantasies. "It might not be his own, but it's bound to happen."

"Oh, you're speaking to me again? How nice."

His green eyes hardened. "I'm only pointing out that he could get hurt. Though I'm sure that would play for the cameras."

Cat tossed her hair over her shoulder and arched an eyebrow. She wasn't going to let him get her into a screaming rage. Nope. It would probably piss him off even more if she kept her cool. No matter what it cost her.

"What are you doing here?" she asked, all peaches and cream with just a dash of arsenic. Her fingernails dug crescents into her palms.

"I *live* here."

No shit, Captain Obvious. "I meant, what are you doing lurking in the hallway?"

He entered the room, agitation pumping off him, and crossed to the bookcase. He adjusted a stack of hardbacks, a family photo, and gave a jerky shrug of his shoulders. "I don't know what I'm doing here. It's not even my home anymore. It used to be. Now I'm just lurking in corners while everyone else lives here. I even have a cat now." He pointed as Felipe strutted past the doorway. "He didn't belong to anyone before the flood. Had seven houses he'd visit like a time-share cat, and now he's decided this house is where he wants to settle down. I don't even like cats."

She wasn't going to feel sorry for him. *Nope. Ice queen mode engaged.*

93

"I feel like I'm failing them." Noah stuffed his hands in his pockets and stared unseeingly into his backyard.

His confession disengaged ice queen mode.

"Noah, don't be an idiot."

"We were unprepared for the flooding. We've got residents displaced from their homes. There's a possibility our major source of revenue will go bust. And I have to depend on *you* to fix it all."

She had a feeling that was the part he was most worried about. "You're not failing anyone. No town can be completely zipped up and prepared for eleven-plus inches of rain. It's not possible. Your residents are all going to get to go home. You'll get your house back. And the Christmas Festival will kick ass."

He didn't look convinced.

"This town? These people? It's my life and my livelihood. I grew up here. We'd be inventorying decorations by now, getting ready for the day after Thanksgiving. I can't imagine Merry without our Christmas. It…it was my favorite thing growing up."

"It's going to be different," Cat acknowledged, joining him at the window. "But different doesn't have to mean worse. If anything, it's going to mean a whole hell of a lot more to people after what you've all been through."

Noah sighed and said nothing.

"You're right to be skeptical, to be protective. Not every show that could have come in here would have Merry's best interests at heart. But we do. *I* do."

"I know what you were doing with Jasper," Noah admitted. "I get it, and it's nice of you."

"What? Trying to get him to saw off his own arm for ratings because his family doesn't have enough going on right now?"

"Sorry for that. I'm tired, stressed. I don't usually take it out on people, but for some reason, your mere existence pushes my buttons."

"Right back at you."

"I wonder if I'd feel the same way in different circumstances?" Noah posited. Felipe padded into the room and rubbed up against Noah's legs. Reluctantly, he bent to ruffle the cat's ears.

"You mean if you didn't have to watch me like a hawk to make sure I'm not ruining your town for advertising dollars?"

He straightened. "Pretty much, yeah."

His smile was wry, and when he looked at her like that, Cat felt a little hiccup zing through her blood. Noah Yates was a good-looking man. Too bad about the whole personality thing.

"Well, I guess we're never going to find out, are we? Now let's go get you miked."

"Miked? Oh no. I'm not participating." Noah shook his head.

Cat smiled and showed her teeth. "The handsome city manager opening his home to his neighbors and a stray cat? Oh yeah. You're participating. And you're going to hold Felipe in your lap."

CHAPTER

14

Six weeks to Christmas Eve

Well, it had happened. Just as he'd known it would. Noah slammed the phone down into the receiver. The first episode of *Merry's Christmas* had aired two days ago, and the calls hadn't stopped. Volunteers offering their time, contractors who suddenly found openings in their schedules, businesses hoping to give Merry residents discounts on this and that.

Cat King was hell-bent on turning his life, his nice quiet town, into a circus.

And now he was the one fielding all the calls. Well, that wasn't going to fly. He had a job to do, a town to provide for. Noah didn't need to be the network's answering service.

He shoved his arms into his coat. "I'm going out," he told his part-time secretary, Carolanne.

It was cold, and the forecast was calling for snow this week. But his anger, his sense of inconvenience kept him warm.

The field producer had decided to cc him on all shooting schedules so he knew where he could find Cat. Part of him recognized that he should be bringing the issue to the field producer or Paige. But he'd prefer to yell at Cat. It was more satisfying.

Noah decided to walk the four blocks to the park. He'd spent so many hours the past few days holed up in his office, the amount of cleanup progress surprised him. The buildings that had seen floodwaters licking at their foundations had all been power washed, and a temporary week-long parking restriction on the last three blocks of Main Street had allowed a team of street sweepers to clean up the leftover mud clogging gutters and curbs.

Window cleaners had made quick work of the entire downtown. The town was still devoid of any actual holiday decorations. While the bulk of the decorating didn't happen until Black Friday, there were still touches here and there that he missed. The storage shed that held most of the park's decorations had yielded the disappointing news that nearly every item had been damaged if not destroyed.

Cat hadn't seemed fazed by it, but Noah couldn't help but mourn the decades of history wiped out by relentless inches of black water.

There was a crew stacking drywall and materials in front of Reggie's diner. Cat and her ambitions. How were one woman and a tightly run crew or two going to turn a flooded park into a winter wonderland, return a destroyed diner into the breakfast mecca it had been, and redo half a dozen houses into livable homes, all in time for Christmas?

She wasn't. And that fact was plain as day. Cat King was getting people's hopes up, and they were only going to get crushed. It didn't matter how many volunteers showed up with cleaning supplies and tools. There was no way in hell that some pretty little actress could save his town.

And he'd be the one to pick up the pieces when she packed up and left town. He'd be the one sweating over budgets and bills, making the tough choices that needed to be faced.

Through his fog of anger, Noah waved at the handful of people who greeted him. Frieda Fawkes poked her head out of the hair salon to holler a hello, and Ismail Byler called a greeting over his newspaper from the bench in front of the insurance agency he'd run since 1967. Their cheerfulness grated. Noah knew they were weeks away from disappointment, and he wished he could prepare them for it.

He shoved his hands into his pockets and pressed on.

The park was a hive of activity. Landscaping crews were blowing in mulch to beds revitalized with new evergreens. A crew of cleaners was pressure washing the salvaged benches and trash receptacles. A tree surgeon was in the process of examining the remaining pines and hemlocks for damage.

They'd lost enough trees, buried enough sidewalks in mud, that North Pole Park seemed a foreign landscape to him. The river, calm again, had returned to its banks beyond the park and sparkled icily in the morning light, giving no hint of the destruction it was capable of.

It made him think of Cat. Beautiful, fun to look at, but dangerous beneath the surface.

Noah spotted the small village of production tents and pop-ups and headed in that direction. Picking his way over cables and boxes and leftover storm debris, Noah headed toward the voices. It sounded like a meeting was in progress.

He poked his head around the corner and spotted a handful of crew huddled together under a two-sided pop-up, clutching coffees and papers.

"Let's talk ratings." Paige's voice cut through the murmurings around her. She was sitting on the ground, leaning against

Cat, who looked as if she were asleep. Cat's back rested on the skinny leg of the tent. Her long, denim-clad legs were stretched out straight in front of her, a cup of something steaming between her knees. Her eyes were closed. Another woman in a powder-blue beanie leaned against her opposite side.

Everyone was yawning. *Must not be morning people*, Noah decided. Cat seemed like the type who would lounge about in bed until noon every day if given the chance.

Cat cracked open one eye. "Must you with the numbers? I'm too tired to comprehend."

Paige kicked her good-naturedly in the foot and rattled off a series of stats.

Cat's eyes were closed again. "I told you," she said smugly. "I told you this was going to strike a chord with a lot of people."

"Yeah, a lot of people who want to get on camera next to Cat and Mr. I Make Preteen Girls Giggle," Noah muttered under his breath.

"I'm very pleased with the numbers, and I have a feeling they're only going to go up from here. We could be looking at a big finale," Paige said.

"Color me shocked." Clearly Cat was gifted in sarcasm.

"I'm not the one who was arguing with you," Paige pointed out.

"No, that judgmental lout of a city manager was. But he's not here for me to be snarky to, so you'll have to do."

Noah decided to let Cat shove her foot further down her throat before alerting her to his presence.

"What is it with the war between you two?" the woman next to Cat demanded, shifting her head to rest on Cat's shoulder.

Cat gave a snort. "He's wrong, I'm right, and he's too

thickheaded to grasp that. And speaking of the thickheaded, stubborn ass, can we have a PA get in touch with him?"

Paige looked up from her notes. "Why? So you can deliver him a message of insults?"

"With ratings like that, I guarantee we're going to be looking at an influx of volunteers. And while we could use the help, I don't want Mr. No over there at town hall scaring them off with the 'we don't need anyone' spiel if they call him instead of us. We need all the hands we can get if we're going to make this park festival-worthy by Christmas Eve."

"I'll pick a PA to be point of contact and volunteer coordinator," Paige agreed. "We can get the number to Noah and his secretary so if anyone does call, they'll at least know where to forward them."

Noah felt a new rush of annoyance. She wasn't supposed to identify problems and fix them for him. He was supposed to be able to throw them in her face and then make her fix them.

He realized he was being petty and his behavior bore an unfortunate similarity to that of his preteen daughter when provoked. But Cat didn't exactly bring out the best in him.

"Now, here's something interesting," Paige said, pulling the cap down over her ears. "Literally fifty percent of all Instagram comments on the posts from episode one want to know if you and Drake are back together."

Noah held his breath and then immediately released it. What did he care who Cat dated? Or whatever. But still, he couldn't quite seem to get himself to interrupt them.

"I figured," Cat sighed. "I'll talk to Drake first, but we'll probably go with vague no comments for now. Might drum up some more interest."

Noah cringed. *What did that mean? Were they together or not?*

"We could take a few behind-the-scenes pics of you guys staring deeply into each other's eyes," the woman on Cat's left suggested.

"You're coming along nicely, Jayla," Cat teased. "Almost as diabolical as me."

"I love learning from the masters." Jayla grinned, pulling her gloves off to attack the bagel in her lap.

"Run it by Drake," Paige agreed. "Okay, moving on…"

Noah debated whether he should crash their meeting or just skulk on back to his office.

"Crap. One more thing," Cat said when Paige started to pack up her notes. "Do we have any room in the budget for a new roof?"

"How big?" Paige asked.

"Huge and inconvenient. Town hall is a hot mess. While Yates was bitching at me about our generosity and great ideas, I couldn't help but notice the half dozen buckets sitting around to catch leaks."

Noah took a step back. He felt the annoyance at her potential relationship status dull. *Damn it.* She wasn't supposed to be thoughtful. She was supposed to be a vapid, self-obsessed, train wreck of celebrity.

Town hall's roof was a year past dire. But without tapping into emergency reserves, there was no way to fund it without raising taxes. And that wasn't going to happen, especially not after what they'd been through with the storm and the flood. He'd resolved himself to working with buckets for at least another year. On the bright side, he probably wouldn't need a humidifier.

"I ran into Carolanne, Yates's secretary, at that damn cookie place that I can't stay away from. By the way, remind me to remind Henry to schedule me some training sessions or else I'm going to be wider than Santa by Christmas," Cat said. "Anyway, she said there's no funding for it. I know it's not a sexy project. But at least it would be one thing we wouldn't need to shoot."

Paige nodded thoughtfully. "If you're right, and we're on the verge of having a ton of volunteers and donations coming our way, we should be able to swing it. I agree that it's not sexy, and we don't need to cull out any shooting time. Maybe a drone shot for B-roll would work?"

"Awesome." Cat nodded. She picked up the cup between her legs and sipped.

"Interesting that you'd think to do something nice for your sworn enemy," Paige said slyly.

Noah took a step to the left so he was hidden behind a hastily tied tarp that cut the wind.

"I'm not doing something nice for Asshat Yates," Cat argued. "He's not the only one who works in that building."

"So you don't find him the least bit attractive?" Jayla asked through a bite of everything bagel.

"Shut up, Jayla," Cat snapped.

Jayla laughed. "Come on, Cat. Admit it. He's pretty easy on the eyes."

Noah felt his ears warm in embarrassment. He wasn't used to overhearing such things about himself. Conversations about him around Merry usually involved what project he'd just shot down and what initiatives he'd declined to pursue. This was new.

"Yeah? Well, too bad his personality is an arid desert of human feelings," Cat shot back.

That was more like it.

"You can admit he's handsome and still be mortal enemies," Paige pointed out.

"Can we please get back to work?" Cat groaned. "I'm exhausted already, and it's barely nine."

"No one twisted your arm to be here so early," Paige reminded her.

Cat yawned, and Noah caught a glimpse of her stretching her arms overhead. "Back to the agenda, ladies. I need some breakfast before the next scene."

"Next on the agenda is who's going to work with Drake about his wooden delivery?" Paige asked.

Noah peered around the tarp to see Paige and Jayla touch their fingers to their noses.

"Not it," Jayla proclaimed.

"Yep," Paige agreed.

"Damn it. I hate when you guys do that," Cat grumbled. "Fine. I'll talk to him. Again. He'll be fine. We just need him to be able to play off people on-screen. Let's give him to Mrs. Pringle and let her chase him around set for a day. He'll be fine."

"Ladies." Cat's assistant Henry appeared with a tray of coffees. They pounced on him like alley cats on a mouse. "No spilling!" he cautioned them, brushing at the sleeve of his coat. "This is Italian wool. Oh, hey, Noah."

All eyes turned to him, and Noah felt his face flush. He'd eased a little too far forward while they were calling him attractive. He shoved his hands in his pockets and tried to look as though he hadn't just been busted for eavesdropping.

"Uh, hi. I just got here," he lied.

Cat's eyes narrowed over her fresh coffee as she shot him a withering glare. "What can we do for you, *No*-ah? Did you decide to revoke our permits?"

"I wanted to come down and see if there's anything you guys need," he said, remembering to add an easy smile. There was nothing more in this world that he wanted than to wipe the smirk off her face.

He saw Paige rise and give Cat's boot a kick. "That's very kind of you, Noah. I think we're all set for the day. Did you get the shooting schedule for the week?"

He nodded, eyes still on Cat. "I did. Thanks for including me. It was helpful to know what to expect. Also, do you have anyone on your end coordinating volunteers? We've been getting some calls about the show, and we'd be happy to transfer them to the right contact."

Cat made a growling sound that had him grinning and Jayla scrambling to her feet. She put her five-foot-two self between Cat and Noah.

"That's very thoughtful of you," Jayla said, grabbing his arm and pulling him away from Cat. "Why don't you come with me, and I'll introduce you to…someone."

Noah raised his hand over his shoulder as Jayla dragged him out of the danger zone. "Bye, Cat."

CHAPTER

15

Cat pushed through the door of Merry and Bright, ignoring the jingle of bells. Instead she zoomed in on the scent of hot, fresh caffeine. It was eight a.m. on a Saturday, and for the second day in a row, she'd been up for nearly four hours, dragging debris and downed tree branches out of what was left of North Pole Park.

It was par for the course when it came to her jobs. As a general contractor, she knew how to do everything from demo to finish carpentry. As a TV star, she was used to long, monotonous hours. On a typical shoot, she worked like a dog for eight or ten days straight and then had a week or two off to sleep, eat, and get a half dozen massages. In Merry, she'd be pulling thirteen-and fourteen-hour days for three weeks.

Her new holiday plans included sleeping through Christmas.

"What the hell is a butterscotch latte?" she wondered out loud. And was it as carby as it sounded?

"Cat! Hey, Cat!"

Cat grinned at the frantically waving Sara Yates. Stylish as always, the girl was wearing a long flannel tunic over textured leggings. Her hair was pulled up on top of her head in a cute ballerina bun. She bore a striking resemblance to the woman next to her with a gingerbread man in her mouth.

"Come meet my mom," Sara said, waving her over.

The gingerbread feet fell out of the woman's mouth.

Cat abandoned her carb concerns for the moment and joined them.

"Cat, this is my mom, Mellody."

Mellody wiped her hands hastily on a napkin. "It's really nice to meet you, Cat. I've heard a lot about you from my daughter who rarely stops talking."

Sara grinned, unaffected by the comment.

"It's great to meet you, Mellody," Cat said, holding up her dirt-stained hands. "I'd shake but…"

"That's all right. I'm covered in icing and forbidden carbs that I'm not going to tell my personal trainer or the seamstress about," Mellody announced.

A kindred spirit in the carb department.

Cat grinned. "Sara's a pretty cool kid."

Mellody had rich, dark hair like Sara's and wide brown eyes. Cat could see more of Noah in Sara's nose and jawline. But she clearly got her pleasantness from her mother. "She is cool if I do say so myself. I hope my ex-husband isn't giving you a rough time while you're here."

"Why would Dad give Cat a hard time?" Sara wanted to know.

Mellody grinned at Cat in commiseration. "Oh, you know your father, sweetie. He likes to have everything a certain way."

"His?" Cat suggested.

"That's our Noah," Mellody laughed. "Don't let his stubbornness throw you. Deep down, under his crabby exterior, he's a wonderful man. Isn't he, Sara?"

"Well, he's no Drake or Henry." Sara sighed dreamily, and Cat laughed.

Mellody's phone rang from the depths of her purse. She dug for it. "Oh, crap. The venue. Please don't let this be bad news. Hello? Oh no."

Sara looked at Cat and whispered, "Mom's getting remarried. It's making her anxious." Sara circled a finger around her ear and then pointed at her mom.

Cat bit back a laugh. They listened to Mellody's side of the conversation, a series of "oh nos" and "what can we do about its?" followed by an "I'll be right there."

"Mom," Sara groaned when Mellody hung up. "We're supposed to have a girls' day. I don't want to go wherever you're freaking out about going."

"Sorry, kid. I don't think we have a choice. Your dad is working today, and the venue called. They had some water damage and need me to check out the secondary ceremony site."

Sara groaned again, melting to the table like a dejected pat of butter. "But it's an hour away!"

"Sara," Mellody said, going for stern but still sounding panicked. "You know how your dad and I feel about you being home alone by yourself for hours."

"I'm twelve, not four," Sara pointed out. "Besides, Dad's house is full of neighbors."

Mellody brightened. "Then maybe Kathy can watch you? You can hang out with April."

"Kathy and April are shopping to replace some of their stuff they lost in the flood. Ugh. This was supposed to be a fun day, Mom."

"Sara can come hang out with me on set for a bit if she wants—"

"Oh my God! Yes!" The acceptance was out of Sara's mouth before Cat could even finish the offer. "Yes! Yes! Yes!"

"If it's okay with your mom?" Cat finished.

"That would be amazing and save me from dragging Pouty MacGee around on a wasted girls' day," Mellody said, biting her lip. "Are you sure it wouldn't be any trouble?"

"Well, I'd have to put Sara to work. Getting coffee and donuts, maybe holding the boom for sound? The production assistants have lists a mile long with things that they need help with."

"Mom, please?" Sara squeezed her hands together under her chin. "This would be the most amazing girls' day present ever even though you bailed on me."

"Sure know how to make a mom feel special," Mellody groaned, poking Sara in the shoulder.

"Come on, Mom. You know what I mean. If I can't spend the day hanging out with you, maybe I could hang out with Cat. I might learn things about responsibility." Sara dangled that morsel in front of her mom.

"For the record, that argument would work better with your father. Cat, if you're absolutely positive she wouldn't be a bother…" Mellody looked at her pleadingly.

"I could use an extra set of hands on set. Let me give you my number in case you need to check in. We'll be filming at the diner all morning, and then we're touring the Hai house. Sara can be there for moral support for April."

Mellody looked elated as she entered Cat's number into her phone. "Thank you so much! You don't even know. And you." She pointed warningly at her daughter. "None of that really annoying squealing. Don't tackle any of Cat's costars and profess your love for them. Be helpful and quiet. Got it?"

Sara threw her arms around her mother. "You're, like, literally the best human being on the planet, Mom!"

Mellody pumped her fist in the air. "Score one for Mom!"

———

Sara turned out to be an excellent addition to the set. She ran water and coffee service for Reggie while field producer Jayla walked him, Cat, and Drake through the opening sequence. She stood guard next to the sawhorses and made sure no Merry residents accidentally walked onto the scene when shooting started. She even grabbed Cat a carrot and hummus snack to go along with her protein shake when they broke for a late lunch.

"You get yourself something?" Cat asked, slipping into a heavier jacket to ward off the chilly breeze. Her on-set wardrobe was a little too light. She made a mental note to switch off to her Duluth-branded coat for the shoot this afternoon.

Sara held up a panini and a Coke.

"Awesome. Let's eat." Cat led the girl to the curb so they could sit. "So what do you think so far?"

"I think your life is so cool, and there's a lot more that goes on behind the camera. Like everything takes forever. Seriously, how many times does it take Drake to say, 'We're going to get this done for you'?"

Cat snorted and took a long pull of unsatisfying smoothie.

"Drake's used to working with more of a scripted story," she explained. "It's a huge transition coming from 'read this, say this' to winging it. But we're on a tight timeline, and we need the before shots so we can jump right into construction."

Sara nodded and took a generous bite of sandwich. "Makes sense," she said through her full mouth. "You work a lot harder than I imagined. It's a lot less glamorous than I thought being a TV star would be."

Cat grinned. "It *is*, isn't it? But if something's worth doing, it's worth working really hard for."

"I like that. But I bet a lot of people don't realize how hard you work."

Cat shook her head, bit into a carrot. "They don't. But the point of working hard isn't really getting people to notice how hard you work. It's about giving it your all and being able to walk away with no regrets. Doing a good job shouldn't be so someone else tells you that you did good. It should be about you feeling good about your effort."

"That's deep." Sara grinned.

"It's all about effort, sacrifice, and reward," Cat said, straightening her legs out in front of her and brushing at some of the dirt streaks. "You have to decide how much you're willing to sacrifice and how much effort you're willing to put into something. And those two things usually add up to the reward you get."

"Give me an example," Sara demanded skeptically.

"Okay, sometimes it means enduring some pain now so you can enjoy yourself later." Cat wiggled her smoothie. "Now, I don't particularly like smoothies. I'd much rather eat three slices of greasy sausage and green pepper pizza. But part of my job involves me staying in shape—not just for looks, mind you. Beyond making good-for-you nutritional choices, you shouldn't be worried about food, weight, or diet. Got it?"

Sara nodded earnestly.

"In my case, I'm older than you, and my metabolism doesn't want me to eat pizza for lunch and fried chicken and mashed potatoes for dinner. Because I'll fall asleep in four seconds. So I'm choking down my carrots and hummus and this disgusting smoothie because I know that it will fuel me for the rest of the afternoon, and then I'm going to have a couple of glasses of adult beverage with my leftover fettuccine tonight. So I'm enduring a little pain now for a bigger payoff later."

Sara laughed.

"Ah, you laugh, but it applies to much bigger lessons. It's all about keeping your eyes on the prize."

"You grown-ups really like to deliver the life lessons, don't you?"

"Kid, if I had someone giving me this life lesson at your age, I'd be a lot further ahead. You should probably be taking notes."

Sara mimed scrawling frantic notes, looking enthralled, and Cat laughed.

Paige wandered over, her long legs wrapped in festive reindeer leggings to ward off the chill in the air. "Mind if I join you, ladies?" she asked, holding up a hoagie.

"Just the perfect woman to join the conversation," Cat announced. "Sara and I were just discussing hard work and dreams."

"Oh, my fave! What do you want to do with your life, Sara?" Paige asked.

"Mmm, well, I'm really into fashion." Sara shrugged. "But I think my dad wants me to find something serious to get excited about."

"Fashion can be serious," Cat argued.

"*Dad* doesn't think so. He's all like, 'Why don't you try accounting or neuroscience or physical therapy?'" Sara mimicked.

Cat snorted and Paige elbowed her in the side.

"Ouch! Fashion can be very serious. What parts of the industry do you like the most?" Cat asked, rubbing her ribs where Paige's bony elbow connected.

Sara furrowed her brow. "You know, it's not so much the

modeling that I like. It's like the stuff that goes into magazines and commercials and when you see someone wearing it on Instagram or TV."

"Ah, the branding." Cat nodded. "Fashion branding and marketing is a huge, *serious* industry."

Sara brightened. "Really?"

"There's so much more to fashion than just clothes and accessories. There's art and business and accounting and international relations." Cat counted each one off on her fingers. "It's a huge, important industry."

"My dad doesn't think so."

"Well, maybe your dad just doesn't understand how much work goes into fashion," Paige pointed out. "Sometimes it's our job to educate people on what they don't understand."

Noah Yates doesn't understand anything he doesn't want to, Cat thought uncharitably.

"What if they don't want to be educated?" Sara asked.

"Then you do it anyway and rub their faces in your success in a really graceful way," Cat told her.

CHAPTER

16

Noah glared at the message on his phone. He stabbed the Call button.

"Tell me you didn't leave our daughter in the care of a TV star," he growled. He heard what sounded like static from the other end. "Mellody, I know that's you blowing into the phone. Don't even try the tunnel trick on me."

His ex-wife and sort of friend sighed. "Noah, you make it sound like she's a porn star. I met Cat. She seemed like a reasonably responsible adult, more so than that babysitter you hired a few years ago who broke into our box of wine and passed out on the couch while our five-year-old watched *The Shining*."

"This is basically the same thing, but it's your fault this time."

"What's been going on with you? Since the flood, you've been wound tighter than a helicopter mom on the first day of kindergarten."

The truth of his ex-wife's words wasn't lost on him. "I just have a lot going on." He did, he reminded himself. The fact that his life flashed before his eyes as he envisioned muddy-brown waters closing over his head a half dozen times a day... well, that was a little distracting too.

He found himself fixating on that handful of seconds over and over again. And then the tattoo, the boat. Safety. The woman who'd dragged him out of the water like a half-drowned dog had very likely saved his life. And he had no idea who she was. A stranger he'd never forget. One he'd probably never get the chance to thank.

Noah blew out a breath. "I'm sorry. I'm just not Cat King's biggest fan. She's a reality TV celebrity. Is that really who we want our daughter spending time with?"

Mellody laughed. "It's a home renovation show, Noah, not *The Weird Housewives of Wherever*. She's nice, she's smart, and she volunteered. Sara would have been inconsolable for a week straight if I'd said no."

"I get that. It's just..."

"Noah. She's twelve, almost thirteen."

He could hear the gentle firmness in Mellody's tone. He'd heard it millions of times during the course of their relationship.

"We're going to have to start accepting that," Mellody continued. "She's old enough to stay home alone. She's old enough to pick her after-school activities. She's old enough to be her own person."

Logically, rationally, he got that. But when he looked at his little girl? He wasn't ready to release her into the world. She wasn't ready. *He* wasn't ready.

"I'll take it into consideration," Noah said grudgingly. There were reasons he was the way he was. Reasons he'd never really delved into with Mellody.

Mellody laughed. "You know this is a partnership, right?"

"I do vaguely recall it being something along those lines. But if I find our daughter in a tube top and big hair talking about manicures and greased-up pool boys, I'm blaming you forever."

He heard the distinct sound of fake static. "What's that? I can't hear you...going through...tunn—"

His ex-wife the comedian.

Noah tossed his phone on the seat next to him and headed toward Merry. He'd spent his lunch hour and the better part of his afternoon in New Haven meeting with state officials who marched through what aid Merry could and couldn't expect. There were dozens and dozens of federal programs that dealt with recovery. And now it was his job to parse through the thousand pages—barely an exaggeration—of resources and figure out which programs fit Merry's recovery needs and which ones they could qualify for.

It wasn't ideal, but at least Merry could count on something outside *A Soggy, Sad Christmas of Destruction* or whatever the hell moniker Cat's network decided on for the show.

He spotted the fleet of production vehicles parked all over Mistletoe Avenue. He could add parking etiquette to his list of issues to discuss with Cat, Noah decided as he slid out of the vehicle and slammed the door.

Tired and frustrated, he was spoiling for a fight, and he knew Cat would give him what he wanted.

He spotted that mass of caramel-colored hair spilling over a forest-green vest. She was sitting on the front porch steps next to April. Pretty as a picture, of course. Because that was what her life was. One big show for the cameras. His Sara was on April's other side, her slim arm around her friend's shoulder. April was crying.

What had been a slow, churning anger exploded into full-blown temper.

"Babe, it's okay to feel upset," Cat was saying to a twelve-year-old in her infinite TV star wisdom. "It's tough to see your house like this and watch your parents worry. But you know I've got your back, and Sara does too."

April nodded, tears still sliding down her round cheeks.

"It's gonna be okay," Sara announced confidently. "Cat's going to fix it all."

That unwavering faith in a woman who had just made her best friend cry for the cameras made him snap.

"Sara, go wait in the car," Noah snarled. His daughter's eyes widened, but she recognized the temper in his tone and, after squeezing April's arm one more time, hightailed it down the sidewalk.

"I need a moment," he said, pointing a finger at Cat.

She rose, and he thought she deliberately put herself between him and April as if *he* were the one the girl needed protection from.

"April, why don't you go on inside while I talk to Mr. Yates for a minute?"

April sniffled and nodded. "Okay." She plodded up the stairs and into her ruined house where the ruckus of an entire production team throbbed.

"What exactly is your problem?" Cat demanded, hands on hips. "Are my permits expired? Did I look at someone sideways? Did I get too much work done?"

"Don't give me that bullshit," Noah said coldly. "You're the one who just made a twelve-year-old cry for the cameras. How do you sleep at night? Doesn't it bother you? Using people to get where you want to go?"

"Excuse me?"

He saw fire ignite in those hazel eyes.

"You drag this kid through her soggy, moldy childhood home and make her cry on camera. Oh, I'm sure the heart-strings will be singing, but you just emotionally scarred a child. Where are her parents? Do they even know you have her?"

Cat stepped up to meet him, the toes of her dirty work boots brushing his loafers. "Do you see any fucking cameras out here?"

Noah blinked and spared a glance around the sidewalk. There was no camera crew, no sound guy with a boom, no director watching playback. He opened his mouth, but Cat held up a hand.

"Don't bother. There are no cameras out here because we took a break because April was feeling emotional. She *volunteered* to give the cameras a house tour. And yeah, I was all for it because the audience loved her two years ago, and she's only gotten cuter and smarter since then. I need people to connect with this story emotionally or your goddamn Christmas Festival will look like a half-assed Easter egg hunt in a trailer park. I'm not going to apologize for doing my job."

"Your job involves taking advantage of real people. I'm not letting you turn *my town* and *my citizens* into a bunch of pitiable victims."

"You'd better back up right now, Noah, if you value that pretty nose of yours," Cat fumed. She drilled a finger into his chest. "I'm giving your neighbors a safe space to tell their story and giving complete strangers the opportunity to care."

"Don't dress it up, Cat. You work for reality television. You're one step up from an ambulance-chasing personal injury lawyer promising his clients a fortune for their slip and fall."

"What is your problem, Yates?" she snarled.

They were so close he could smell her shampoo, something citrusy.

"My problem is you drag my daughter on set—without my permission—and expose her to the sordid drama—"

"Oh, you want to talk about kids absorbing things? Great. Yeah, kids are always absorbing what's around them, and you know what's around Sara? You telling your daughter her interests aren't good enough."

Noah saw red around the edges of his vision. "You're going to want to tread lightly," he said, his tone icy.

But Cat wasn't one to take cues. No, she was one to throw a canister of gasoline on a fire just to watch the explosion.

"No, I think *you* are. If you keep steering your daughter away from what she enjoys, what's important to her, what do you think the outcome is going to be? 'Gee thanks, Dad, for never supporting my interests. I'm so glad I became an insurance adjuster and married an asshole who thinks he knows what's best for me.'"

"I'm not taking parenting advice from a reality TV star! And I don't appreciate you filling her head with fantasies of fame and glamour." Noah's voice was low enough to be a growl.

"Glamour?" Cat spat out. She ripped the cap off her head. "I have mud in my hair. I've been working since five this morning, dragging debris out of your fucking park so your town can have its Christmas. I have bags under my eyes from dealing with production issues until all hours of the night because you're trying your damnedest to make this as difficult as possible. I've got an entire crew of landscapers down with the twenty-four-hour bug, and I have to find another ten grand in the budget to get April the tree house she and your daughter have always wanted."

That finger was back, and it was drilling a hole into his chest.

"I haven't done laundry in a fucking week, and these jeans are going to disintegrate at any given moment. I didn't fill your daughter's head with glitz and glamour, you fucking asshole. I filled it with the rewards of hard work and what being a strong, independent fucking woman means. Now get the fuck out of my way before I really tell you what I think."

With less than half a second to decide, Noah wisely stepped aside. Cat stormed past him down the sidewalk. She whirled around and opened her mouth as if to give him one final parting shot, then closed it again. She settled for an obstinate middle finger and a glare hot enough to burn down his world before stalking off down the block.

Noah heard a low whistle behind him. Still shell-shocked, he turned. Drake Mackenrowe looked out of place leaning against a minivan in a flannel that must have been sewn on him. "You sure pissed her off." He stated the obvious with a blinding grin.

"She's not going to come back here with a weapon or anything, is she?" Noah asked, feeling just a little like he wanted to limp off to lick his wounds.

Drake laughed. "No, man. Her verbal skills are usually the first line of defense, and if a solid warning doesn't work, she'll go with a right hook."

Noah shook his head, processing. His brain was reeling from a confrontation that had gone decisively in Cat's favor.

A now fresh-faced April skipped out onto the porch. "Hi, Noah! Where's Cat?"

The resilience of children, Noah sighed to himself.

Sara peeped between parked cars. "Dad? Can I come back and hang out if we're not leaving yet?" Sara's question was teetering on whining.

The Hais' front door opened again, and Jasper and Kathy

appeared. Of course they had been there for the filming. Noah swiped a hand over his face and found he was sweating in the chilly air.

"Oh, hey, Noah! Mind if we steal Sara for dinner tonight?" Kathy asked. "Jasper's parents are cooking up a feast, and we need more mouths or we'll be bringing fifty pounds of leftovers back to your house with us."

April and Sara embraced as if it had been weeks, not minutes, since they'd seen each other. "Please, Dad?" Sara begged.

"Yeah, please, Mr. Yates?" April added her sad puppy eyes to the equation.

"Hi, Drake," Sara said slyly.

"Hey, cutie," Drake said with a grin designed to devastate preteens.

Sara and April giggled in response.

"Have you guys seen Cat?" Jasper asked. "We were going to ask her if she wanted to join us since shooting's done for the day. We all worked up an appetite, didn't we?"

"Dad, you should have seen it," Sara said, bouncing on her toes at his side. "Cat and Drake were all like 'show us your house,' and April got to give the tour, and Kathy and Jasper were on camera too. It was *so* cool!"

"You seemed pretty upset there," Noah prodded April. He couldn't have completely misread the situation, could he?

April nodded earnestly. "It's hard to see our home in such disrepair and seeing Mom and Dad worry. But Cat's right, it's only stuff. And stuff is fixable. And even though it's okay to feel downtrodden, it's better to do something about it. She's going to help us, and I'm going to help someone else."

"Cat calls it paying it forward." Sara nodded.

Everyone calls it that, Noah wanted to point out.

"Noah, would you like to join us for dinner?" Kathy offered, a hand on each girl's shoulder.

"Uh." He shoved his hands in his pockets. "Thanks, but I've got some work to do tonight." Still a little dazed, he watched them walk down the block to Jasper's sedan, a tight little group made somehow brighter and more hopeful than they had been this morning.

He had a feeling that Cat was the orchestrator of that turnaround.

"You okay, man?" Drake asked. "You look like you could use a beer."

CHAPTER
17

S o you two are dating, right?" Noah asked for the third time.
Drake shook his head and grinned. His gleaming white
teeth were blinding in the near dark of the Workshop, Merry's
one and only bar. It was always darker than midnight inside the
bar, but that didn't stop the dozen or so female patrons from
sending admiring glances Drake's way.

"No, man. Well, not now. I don't know if we were before or
not." Drake shrugged his massive shoulders as if dating or not
dating a gorgeous, fiery TV star didn't really matter.

"Wait, how do you not know if you're dating?" Noah was
feeling a pleasant warmth from the third beer that had magically
appeared in front of him.

Drake shrugged. "In our profession, you can not be dating
a lot of people. It's a busy lifestyle. Never in one place for very
long, and just when you get comfortable in the off-season, it's
time to start shooting the next season. Cat and I 'dated' very

briefly a couple of years ago. But neither one of us was invested enough to start changing our work schedules around."

"So you're exes, and you work together?" Noah was determined to figure this out. He'd assumed, from their greeting, that Drake and Cat were together and was surprised to find out that wasn't the case. He wasn't sure why it mattered so much. He was probably just trying to get to know his enemy better, he decided.

"I guess so. I think of us more as friends. She's awesome. No one can outwork her. This industry isn't usually very friendly to women, but Cat demands better. There's a lot more there than just a great face and sexy body, and she doesn't let anyone forget it."

"Well, which one of you two nobs do I have to blame for awakening the dragon?" Henry, Cat's assistant, slid onto the unoccupied stool to Noah's left. The sleeves of his oxford were precisely rolled up to his elbows to show off the cuffs. He rested his head in his hands for the briefest of moments.

Guiltily, Noah raised his hand.

"Yeah, that'd be him," Drake tattled. "I had nothing to do with it."

Henry paused long enough to give the brunette next to him an appreciative glance before raising a finger to catch the bartender's eye. "Long Island iced tea, strongest you've got."

Drake whistled. "That bad, huh?"

"If you find a drink with more alcohol in it, I'll order it."

"She taking her mad out on you?" Noah asked sympathetically.

Henry gave him a rueful look. "No, man. Cat's not like that. She just doubles down harder. You piss her off, and she's going to work her ass off to make you look like a twat. Pardon my British. She's going to run herself into the ground if I can't get a decent meal in her and six or seven hours of sleep."

The bartender set the tall glass in front of him, and Noah watched Henry down half of it. He felt every female eye in the bar was zeroed in on them.

"You set him straight yet?" Henry asked Drake.

"We haven't gotten past the 'are you dating' portion of the evening."

"Set me straight about what?"

"We've all picked up on the fact that you don't like Cat," Henry began.

"It's not that I don't like Cat," Noah argued. But it was. He didn't like what she stood for. And he didn't like how often he found himself thinking of her. And he *really* didn't like how every time he saw her, his focus zeroed in on her like she was the only colorful thing in a world of grayscale.

"Yes, it is," Drake countered. "But the thing is, you don't know her."

"You got the wrong impression," Henry joined in. "And you don't like to be wrong so you're ignoring all evidence to the contrary."

"I like to think that I'm open-minded."

Drake gave him a sideways glance. "You do realize that your nickname in town is Mr. No, right?"

"You try managing the annual budget for a town that thinks installing a six-figure ice skating rink in the middle of town for six weeks of use would be a great investment," Noah argued. It was tough being the voice of reason, but that was what they'd hired him for. It was his job to protect his town whether they liked his methods or not.

Drake held up his palms. "I'm not saying you are Mr. No. I'm saying that's how you're perceived, and perceptions can be wrong. Including your own."

"She plays for the camera."

"That doesn't mean she's pandering. It means she's a smart businesswoman. Cat's doing what works. She's done her research. She's put in the time. She knows this business inside and out. That's why she's producing now. She knows more than any of the last five producers I've worked with. And don't even get me started on how tireless she is in front of the camera. Do you have any idea how exhausting it is to be 'on' all the time?"

Noah did not.

The bartender dropped drink tokens in front of each of them.

"Who are these from?" Noah asked, frowning at his.

The bartender shrugged. "Take your pick."

Drake grinned. Henry straightened his tie. "I quite like this town."

"Consider yourself a good-looking novelty. We don't get a lot of people like you here," Noah quipped.

"What? Black?"

Noah spit out his sip of beer in cartoon fashion. "Jesus, no! I meant style." He pointed at the man's orange-and-purple-checkered shirt that, on anyone else, would have looked like Skittles vomit.

Drake guffawed, drawing even more appreciative glances and a handful of longing sighs. The women of Merry were going to combust before Christmas Eve.

"I'm just messing with you. Let me ask you this, Noah," Henry said, steering the conversation back on track. "In your job, do you ever find yourself saying or doing something that you wouldn't in other circumstances?"

Noah had a feeling he knew where this was going. "Maybe."

"Because if you said or did what you wanted to, things wouldn't go the way you needed them to?"

Noah thought back to the reindeer streetlights. "Also maybe."

"So you assess the situation, determine what needs to happen, and then make adjustments, correct?"

Noah nodded. "Yeah, but I'm a human being. She's some perfect blond robot from the future designed to sell us something."

"We're all selling something, man," Drake cut in. "Even you."

"Okay, fine. She's a smart businesswoman. What about the fact that she emotionally blackmailed me into saying yes to the show?"

Henry's lips quirked in the closest expression to a smile the stoic Brit seemed to have. "She gets shit done with single-minded focus. You were standing in your own way, and she simply removed your head from your arse."

"I didn't want a bunch of TV cameras coming in here and painting Merry as a town of pathetic victims who can't help themselves. The last time she was here, the whole town was in an uproar over her and her brother. Kids were cutting school to watch filming. Grown men were begging to volunteer so they could stand next to her on camera. Oh, *and* she got into a bar fight in this very establishment."

"She wouldn't start a fight without a good reason," Drake said firmly.

"That was before my time. What did she say happened?" Henry asked, leaning in, his glass nearly empty.

"That's the thing. I don't know. I came straight home from a vacation I shouldn't have taken with a TV show coming to town. They wouldn't even let me talk to her. I went down to the set after news spread to straighten it out. And they said she was 'busy.' But she was sleeping off a hangover in her trailer."

Henry and Drake shrugged at each other. "That part sounds like her," Drake admitted affably.

"She works hard and plays just as hard," Henry agreed. "Not often, but every once in a while, she lets loose. In those instances, I keep my phone on in case bail is required."

"How is that responsible?" Noah demanded, frustrated.

"Who says anyone has to be responsible one hundred percent of the time?" Henry argued. "I'd like to see anyone work as hard as she does, deal with as much shit as she does, and not cut loose every once in a while. You forget how to have fun, and you're forgetting how to live."

Noah didn't like that that particular sentiment struck a big, fat chord with him.

When was the last time he'd cut loose, had a little fun? He couldn't remember the last date he'd been on. The last time he'd laughed really hard. Hell, the last hangover he'd suffered through. He couldn't recall anything other than working, nagging Sara about her homework, and sitting down with a good book in recent months, maybe years.

"The point is, man, you're way wrong about Cat. You can't go around treating her like some gold-digging ratings skank," Drake said, signaling for another round.

"I know gold-digging ratings skanks," Henry announced. "And Cat is not one of them."

"Ah. Good ol' Meeghan Traxx." Drake shuddered. "How is our favorite shrewish psychopath?"

"I wouldn't know, thankfully," Henry said primly. "Meeghan is my former employer," he explained to Noah.

"Meeghan?"

Henry took a fortifying gulp of his drink. "She is the meanest, most vapid, selfish, monstrous 'person'—and I use that term very loosely—on the planet. You look at Cat like she's a Meeghan. Meeghan is the kind of person who will do anything to get what she wants. She's had more plastic surgery than all seasons of *Botched* combined. The Botox she gets every month is a serious danger to the rest of us mere mortals because her face is so frozen we can't tell when she's about to freak out and get out of her way. She's a hell hound."

Drake shook his head. "In just one shining example of the kind of person Traxx is, she tried to ruin Cat's sister-in-law's career because Meeghan wanted Gannon for herself. She showed up on the set of their show during filming after he and Paige started dating and kissed him on camera like they were together. Then she went after Paige on a red carpet on camera. Her nails are like talons, man."

"She sharpens them that way on purpose. She likes to dig them into her assistants." Henry held up his wrist. "She drew blood my first week on the job. Thankfully, she made the fatal error of going ballistic on me in public. Cat's agent just happened to be in the restaurant, knew that Cat would enjoy a chance to stick it to the harpy asshole, and texted her. The next day, Cat offered me a job and doubled my salary. I walked out of Meeghan's penthouse with both middle fingers flying. She threw a Baccarat vase at me. I will owe Catalina King until I go to the grave."

"You realize that you both sound like you're in love with her," Noah pointed out.

They shrugged again, not overly perturbed by the observation. "I think most people are half in love with her. She's pretty fucking awesome," Drake said.

"You'd have to be more than a bit daft to not love her," Henry agreed.

"And you want me to join Team Cat?"

"You don't have to love her like the rest of us. We'd just appreciate it if you'd appreciate her a bit more," Henry told him.

"Did you know she donated her entire salary back to the budget? Didn't you wonder how you were getting an entire landscaping revamp in the park?" Drake asked. "Even with sponsorships, that shit ain't cheap, my friend."

"I'm sure she's still getting something out of it," Noah said stubbornly. "I mean, her family's company is getting paid to be here."

"No, the crew is getting paid through Kings Construction—despite their resistance. But the company is getting nothing," Henry insisted.

"Why would she do that?"

"She cares, man," Drake said, lifting his beer.

"Did you know that her pet project that she's got in the works is a trade school for women to learn not just a job but how to run a business?" Henry added. "She's ready to start looking for a physical location, but she put it on hold for Merry."

"A trade school?" Noah asked.

"Sure. Electric, HVAC, plumbing, contracting. Accounting, payroll, marketing. And then a small business incubator with resources for women who want to start their own businesses," Drake said. "We talked about it last night. She's passionate as hell about it, and I couldn't help but get excited."

Last night? Noah wondered if not dating included hooking up with a non-ex.

"That's a hell of an idea," Noah admitted, brushing the thought aside. Cat could hook up with whomever she chose. It was none of his business.

"She's full of them." Henry nodded. "Did you know she showed up here the morning after the storm so she could convince the network to do the special here instead of some done-to-death neighbor-versus-neighbor decorating contest?"

"Cat was *here*?"

"She got worried when she couldn't get through to the Hais. Came up here with a field producer and shot footage for ten hours so the network couldn't say no. Rumor has it she even spent some time on a rescue boat."

Noah was shaking his head. "That can't be true."

Drake grinned. "Face it, man. She's not the person you thought she was."

"She cares. Deeply. And she's going to do everything in her power to make sure the people of Merry get their Christmas," Henry added.

Noah scraped a hand through his hair. Could he have been this wrong about her? Could his stubborn, immobile moral code be flawed? He thought about what she said about Sara. Was his dedication to responsibility, his need for control, really cutting him off from life? When had his world gotten so damn small?

"You look a little sick. You want some wings?" Drake offered.

Noah tried to remember the last time he'd had anything deep fried and coated with blue cheese.

"Yeah. You know what? I do want wings."

CHAPTER
18

Cat dragged the heavy glass door open and ushered
Paige inside, leaving the late autumn chill outside. The
Workshop was the only bar within ten miles of Merry, and Cat
was in desperate need of a good buzz. She'd invited her mom
and Paige along to keep her from buying a carton of eggs and
going to town on Noah's house on her way back to her trailer.

In any other town in the world, the bar would be decorated
with neon beer signs and flat-screens with football on them.
In Merry, the top shelf liquor was framed by a light-up Santa's
sleigh. There was a scrap of a dance floor in the corner painted
in candy cane stripes. Regular patrons could purchase their
own mugs, etched with their official elf names. All servers wore
Santa hats.

It was both ridiculous and charming.

"I'm getting a cosmo," Angela announced, rubbing her
palms together in anticipation. "I'm sorry you had a bad day,

sweetie, but I'm glad I get to be part of the 'blowing off steam' portion of the evening."

Cat should have been dead on her feet after a full day of filming. Reggie's on-camera interview and the footage from the diner rocked. She knew because she watched the playback before they started the shoot at the Hais'. The shoot that Noah had crashed with his piss-poor attitude and head-up-his-ass judgment had gone well too. Viewers were going to get one hell of a before and after with all the feels.

Speaking of feels, she was still mad. *Seething mad.* And that temper had given her a second wind. She'd made an impromptu visit to the engineering office Jasper Hai worked for and—through eyelash fluttering and a few subtle threats that came across as flirting to the uninitiated—had gotten a new sponsor for the damn tree house *and* planted the seed for bringing Jasper back to work full-time.

"The audience would love to see what a good company does to support their employees when they need it most."

Then she'd stormed back to her trailer and revamped the call sheets for tomorrow with Henry. In addition to demo day on three sites, they'd be digging through the park's storage building to see how damaged the Christmas decorations were. She had six calls to return about her school and an entire line of new products to approve for next fall's clothing line.

But she couldn't stop thinking about how much she wanted to break Noah Yates's nose.

In a flash of self-preservation, she'd called on her estrogen posse to support her…and keep her from doing something dumb enough to go to jail over.

Paige spotted an empty high-top table in the corner and led the way. The back wall was lit with one of those snowflake laser lights that made it look like a pink indoor blizzard was happening.

Cat slid onto the barstool and rubbed the back of her neck. There was a ball of tension there that she knew wouldn't be dislodged by a fun fling or overdoing it on liquor. No. The only thing that would dissolve it was running over Noah Yates in the middle of the street.

"So let's talk about why you look like you want to murder someone," Paige suggested, shrugging out of her coat.

Angela, Cat's sweet, Italian mother, leaned in. "You just tell me who it is. We've got connections, you know."

Those connections included a baker cousin in Jersey and a small-time bookie in Queens.

"Believe me, Mom. If I wanted this guy to disappear, I'd want the satisfaction of doing it with my bare hands."

A waitress in a green elf dress and Santa hat approached. "You ladies picked the right night. We've got three of the handsomest devils enjoying themselves at the bar tonight."

Cat craned her neck. She wasn't interested in a hookup tonight, but that didn't mean she didn't want to enjoy the view.

"Damn it!" she hissed, grabbing a menu and holding it over her face.

"Oh! It's Drake and Henry and…oh." Paige nervously moved Cat's utensils out of her reach. "We can go somewhere else."

"Where the hell else are we going to drink? The parking lot of a liquor store?" Cat hissed. She was going to have to talk to Drake and Henry about where their loyalties lay. Cat rolled her shoulders and shook her head. "No. We're staying. He can leave."

They ordered their drinks, cosmos all around plus a double shot of Jameson for Cat, and Cat busied herself shooting daggers in Noah's general direction.

Angela put her feet on the rungs of her stool and stood to get a better look. "Oh, is that Noah?" she asked.

Cat yanked her back down. "Mom!"

"What? He doesn't look like a hell beast. He's very good-looking. The glasses make him look like an intellectual."

"Hell beasts don't have to be ugly. It's what's on the inside that's a rotting smorgasbord of asshole."

Paige's eyebrows winged up her forehead, and she sent Angela a meaningful look.

"What?" Cat demanded. "Do you *know* what he said to me?"

"No," Angela answered. "The only thing we've pried out of you is 'rotting smorgasbord of asshole.'"

"He comes storming up to the Hai house. I'm sitting outside with April and Sara after April got a little teary-eyed inside. He asked *if I like making little girls cry*. He acted like I'd just given both girls breakdowns and salaciously filmed it for a salivating audience of soulless sadists."

"You get really descriptive when you're mad and sober," Paige observed. "And your alliteration is spot-on."

"Don't make me add you to my hit-and-run list," Cat warned.

"Why was he in your face?" her mother asked.

"He thought I made April cry on camera until I pointed out that there were no cameras outside. Duh. Then he launched into another tirade about me being a shining beacon of everything that's wrong in this universe. And I finally let him have it. Verbally at least, because I'm a fucking lady."

The waitress returned with their drinks. "You three ladies are lu-u-ucky. Courtesy of Drake 'Hottie' Mackenrowe."

Cat glanced toward the bar. Drake and Henry waved cheerfully. Noah just stared.

Paige and Angela raised their glasses in a thank-you. Cat stared back at Noah, willing him to read her mind.

Fuck. You.

He raised an eyebrow, and the corner of his mouth quirked. Cat's eyes narrowed. *How dare he look so calm, so pleasant.*

Paige pulled out her phone.

"What are you doing?" Cat hissed.

"I'm texting Drake and telling him not to let Noah come over here or Cat will gut him like a fish in front of all these witnesses and we're going to have to drive really far in the dead of the night to hide the body."

Drake held up his phone. Message received.

Cat turned her attention back to the table. "So anyway, he's there yelling at me on the sidewalk. And I lost it. It was a long day of filming, and then we walk through a house that barely two years ago we renovated to perfection. And now it's moldy and muddy and completely unlivable. I wanted to cry with April."

Angela reached out and squeezed her hand. "Honey. You're my daughter, and if you want me to go over there and slap the glasses off that incredibly handsome man, I will do it."

Cat considered it briefly. But as entertaining as it would be to see, she preferred to fight her own battles. And do her own slapping.

"Thanks, Mom. If you don't mind, I'll keep that offer on the table for now."

Angela nodded. "You just tell me where and when, and I will be there to slap the crap out of anyone you want."

"Ah, family," Paige sighed. "So what else went down outside? We all heard the yelling."

"Oh!" Cat gave the table a resounding slap hard enough to rattle the drinks. "Get this! He compares *me* to one of those sleazebag ambulance chasers and accuses me of *kidnapping* his daughter and exposing her to 'sordid drama'!"

"Well, that's ridiculous. Sara's mother handed her over and

obviously let him know since he knew where to find you and Sara," Paige pointed out.

"Thank you," Cat said, gesturing wildly enough that her mother picked up her drink and cradled it to her chest. "Exactly what I was thinking."

"Do you think he has something going on up here that would prevent him from recognizing your generosity and brilliance?" Angela asked, twirling a finger around her ear.

"You mean like a brain tumor?" Paige asked loyally.

"That's got to be it. No other explanation," Angela announced. She drained her drink and held the empty glass aloft as their server walked by.

Like magic, the server arrived with three fresh drinks a moment later. "This round is on Noah, our very sexy, very single city manager."

Cat pushed the drink away. Why in the hell would the man who accused her of being the Antichrist to human decency buy her a drink? Was it a liquid middle finger?

"What is wrong with you? Catalina King does not turn down free drinks," Paige said, pushing the drink back at her.

"It's probably poisoned."

"I hate to point this out and make you think that I'm being disloyal, and I hope you know if you need help hiding his body, you can count on me, but…"

Cat gave Paige a cool glare, daring her to say anything in Noah's favor.

"I'm wondering if maybe we should try to keep the peace. We're going to be here until Christmas. That's five weeks that could be beyond miserable if we give Noah any reason at all to make things difficult for us here."

Cat gnawed on her lip. Backing down from a fight was not in the King nature.

"How about you just keep him far, far away from me, and he'll live to be an asshole another day?"

"I feel like I should go talk to him and find out just what his problem with my daughter is," Angela mused out loud.

"No talking to him," Cat ordered. "I will drink this drink instead of throwing it in his face, but no one is going to engage Noah in anything other than hand-to-hand combat." She grabbed at the server's arm as the woman swung past the table. "Another Jameson, please."

"Question from the peanut gallery," Paige said as she raised her hand. "Why does Noah get under your skin like that? You're used to being underestimated. And, if I may point out, you usually revel in it."

Cat pointed a rigid index finger at Paige. "Don't say it." She could hear her friend's thoughts clear as a bell.

"Maybe there's sparks flying because there's some kind of attraction going on," Angela said, fluffing her dark hair.

"Mom!"

"Paige is right," Angela continued, immune to Cat's sharp tone. "You usually let this stuff roll right off your back and then crush the undeserving, underestimating ass like a cockroach under your heel. You never waste time stewing about it."

Cat drummed her fingers on the table. "I'm not stewing."

"Maybe not stewing," Paige said in a way that made Cat think stewing was exactly what she meant. "But there's something about this guy that gets to you. And all we're saying is what if it's not hate?"

"Oh, so I'm supposed to accept this asshole yelling obscenities at me in the street as flirting?"

"Point taken." Paige nodded graciously. "I think your mom and I are just wondering if there's something else there besides abject hate."

"Not on *this* side, I can assure you," Cat said, swigging back her cosmo and letting the vodka do its thing. She had very strong feelings for Noah. Murderously strong. And she wasn't interested in psychoanalyzing exactly why he got to her.

The server dropped off her Jameson and wisely retreated without any comment.

"Excuse me." A gritty voice interrupted Cat's mental gymnastics. The man was in his fifties. He had a broad, flat nose. A hefty beer belly strained the seams of his shirt and suspenders.

"Well, if it isn't my old friend…"

"Regis," the man supplied, dipping his head in an awkward half bow.

Paige was already sliding off her stool as if to intervene.

"Refresh my memory, Regis," Cat said slyly. "How did we meet last time?"

The man's already ruddy cheeks took on a ruby-red hue. He cleared his throat. "Well, as best as I can recollect, we met right here on the dance floor."

"Mm-hmm. And how did our introduction go?" Cat tapped a finger to her chin, knowing full well how it went.

"Well, ma'am. I had gotten a little handsy, and you fairly warned me before punching me square in the face."

"That does sound familiar. How are your hands now?" Cat asked.

Paige choked on her cosmo. "Went down the wrong pipe. Sorry," she gasped.

"These hands don't wander anymore. I can promise you that. I was feeling particularly low that day, had too much to drink, and acted a fool," Regis announced. "But thanks to that bell ringer, I've cleaned up my act."

"Well, I am happy to hear that, Regis," Cat said.

"I was wondering if I could buy you ladies a round as an apology?"

Cat eyed her companions. "Apology drinks accepted."

CHAPTER

19

Cat was at the bottom of her third cosmo and feeling no pain. She'd given up not staring and watched Noah watch her. The Workshop was busy, crowded and noisy with neighbors finally able to blow off a little steam now that the figurative cavalry had arrived with hope for the future. Her mother and Paige were exchanging stories about Gabby's day, but Cat had trouble dragging her blurry focus away from those green eyes across the bar.

When Cat finally returned her attention to her empty glass and its "Nothing Says Christmas Like Merry" cocktail napkin, Noah rose from his stool and shrugged into his wool coat. He shook hands with Henry and then Drake and headed for the door. He stopped at nearly every table between the bar and the door, exchanging greetings, shaking hands. And when he got to the door, his eyes found hers.

Was she imagining the subtle nod? The pointed look?

Noah Yates was inviting her outside. Perhaps she *would* have the opportunity to kick his ass in an alley tonight. She'd save the hit-and-run for when she was sober.

"Excuse me, ladies," Cat said, sliding off her stool. She didn't bother taking her coat. She didn't need witnesses. She headed in the direction of the restrooms and then doubled back toward the front door when she was sure Paige and Angela were distracted.

The night sky was a navy-blue carpet of stars in the crisp cold. Cat crossed her arms over her chest and stared up. The noise and company of the bar behind her, nothing but the silence of a winter night in front of her.

"Hey." Noah leaned against the brick facade, hands shoved in his coat pockets. The word came out in a cloud of breath.

"Hey yourself."

"Got a minute?" he asked.

She couldn't read him. Cat didn't sense any indications of the righteous anger he'd hurled at her earlier in the day. But he wasn't exactly friendly either.

"Depends."

The door to the bar opened behind Cat, and a couple, laughing and handsy, stumbled out onto the sidewalk. Noah nodded his head toward the skinny stretch of alley next to the bar, and Cat followed him.

"Why were you having drinks with my friends?" she demanded once the darkness of the alley closed around them.

"They were attempting to educate me."

"Oh? On what?"

"You." He listed a bit to one side.

Noah Yates has a buzz going.

"What *ezatly* about me?" *Okay, maybe Noah isn't the only one a few sheets to the wind.*

"They think I'm wrong about you."

"You *are* wrong about me. Su-u-uper wrong." To emphasize her point, she stabbed a finger in the direction of his chest. It caught him at the base of the throat.

Noah made a grab for her stabbing hand. "I'm starting to wonder," he admitted.

He hadn't put his gloves on, and his hand was warm over hers.

She leaned in to bring his face into focus. His glasses were a little cockeyed on the bridge of his nose. "You make me want to maim you."

"Yeah? Well, right back atcha," Noah said, his green eyes narrowing in the dim light of the alley.

"I don't like your attitude. Like not at *all*," Cat insisted.

"You know what else I want to do besides maim you?" Noah asked. He leaned in like he was about to tell her a secret.

Cat, through her cosmo fog, could smell his soap. The sliver of air between them was charged. She could imagine the sound of the slap, the feel of his stubbled jaw under her open palm as it cracked across his face.

"What?"

"I think I wanna kiss you."

"Well, that's a stupid—"

The rest of her words were lost as if they'd been wiped clean from her brain. His lips, firm and warm, pressed against hers, shocking the breath and thoughts right out of her. Noah was warm and hard everywhere. And Cat realized she was noticing this because she'd splayed her hands across his chest under his jacket.

He spun her so her back was to the alley wall. Cold brick bit into her back, but the rest of her was overheating. Tilting his head, he changed the angle of the kiss, and when Cat opened her mouth to tell him this was the worst idea in the history of stupidity, he took possession.

His tongue swept into her mouth, rendering her completely stupid. He stroked her tongue with a rough lap of his own, and she moaned deep in her throat. Noah leaned into her, his hips pinning her to the wall. She couldn't get enough air to breathe or she would have gasped when he ground his rigid length against her. Noah Yates was either packing heat or he had an entirely different kind of weapon holstered in his pants.

Impatient and ready to take this bad choice to the next level, Cat yanked Noah's shirt out of his waistband and slid her hands underneath. His skin was hot to the touch. She felt muscle and heat and just the right dusting of hair.

"Ah, fuck," Noah breathed. He dove back into the kiss and, holding her in place with his hips, shoved his hands under her sweater.

Cat murmured a string of yeses as those big hands skimmed up the sides of her waist and around the front to cup her breasts through her bra.

"Need more," he murmured. He pulled one hand out from under her shirt and fisted it in her hair. He forced her head back, bruising her lips with his as he slid under the graphite satin cup of her bra.

When his palm met skin, when it dragged ever so lightly across the pebbled point of her nipple, Cat gave an honest-to-God whimper.

The rumble in his chest was so primal, so alpha, so beyond the cool, controlled Noah that she knew.

Without thinking, Cat hooked one leg over his slim hips, angling for more friction right where she needed it most.

He obliged, grinding and thrusting against her. He tightened his grip on her hair, and the shock of it blazed through her roots. He stopped kissing her but didn't move away. So close their lips were still brushing, she breathed him in as his hard-on begged to be freed. She couldn't look away from those eyes as his fingers closed over her nipple, tugging and pulling until she worried her knees would buckle.

Intimacy, raw and spontaneous, stripped her bare under that heated gaze. Oh yes, there were sparks here.

"This is the stupidest thing…" she whispered, lips brushing over his with the words. Regardless of the idiocy, Cat shoved her hand between their bodies and gripped his cock through his pants. Oh God. She wanted to be on a first-name basis with this particular part of Noah's anatomy.

Noah gritted his teeth at her touch. "The stupidest," he agreed, even as he pumped his cock against her hand.

"I don't even like you," Cat admitted, biting his lower lip hard.

He winced, tweaking the tip of her breast hard enough to make her yelp.

His expression turned predatory. "It's not that I don't like you. It's that I don't trust you."

"Which means fucking in an alley on a cold winter night would be astronomically stupid."

"You're drunk," he reminded her.

"You're no pillar of sobriety either," she pointed out.

"I hate your smart mouth," he hissed, kissing her again until her knee buckled. She wanted the layers of denim and cotton gone, wanted him dragging the swollen head of his dick through her slick folds before slamming into her and ridding her of the ache at her core that threatened to drive her mad.

"I hate you," she shot back.

He bit her on the neck and then sucked away the sting of his teeth.

"I don't know what this is," she said, clawing at his belt.

"Hurry up before we come to our senses."

Cat's fingers fumbled with the buckle. "Why are you wearing so many damn clothes?" It wasn't cold anymore. The heat they were throwing off was enough to chase the winter from the alley.

"Cat?" Her name called from the front of the building reached them both.

"Fuck, fuck, fuck," Cat chanted. "It's Paige."

Noah jumped back and tried to shove his shirt back into his waistband.

"Just close your coat, genius," Cat hissed as she tried to put her boob back in her bra.

"Cat? Oh, uh…" Paige trailed off as she peered into the alley. "Is everything okay?"

"Everything's fine," Cat said, clearing her throat and crossing her arms over her chest. "We're just telling each other how much we hate each other."

"Lovely." Even drunk, Paige had better judgment than Cat. "Why don't you two call it a night? And we'll clear the air tomorrow?"

Noah was still staring at Cat as if she were dessert.

"Yeah. Sure. Fine with me." He rubbed the back of his neck with the hand that had moments ago been clutching her breast.

Cat wet her lips and watched Noah's eyes narrow in on her mouth.

"Whatever." She shrugged. When she pushed past Noah, she made sure to drag her knuckles over his still ragingly hard dick.

She heard Paige saying something to Noah, but the blood pumping in her ears muffled the words. She'd just made out with her nemesis. She'd been ready to drop to her knees in an alley to take her mortal enemy's cock out of his pants and—

"You okay, Cat?" Paige asked, jogging to catch up with her. "That looked like a pretty intense argument back there."

145

"Intense," Cat agreed.

"We're really going to have to find a way for you two to keep the peace if we want this show to happen," Paige reminded her. The only hint at her lack of sobriety was the way she closed one eye to better focus on Cat's face.

"You're such a weird drunk," Cat commented.

Paige gave an unladylike snort. "Me? You're usually the one who ends up riding some guy like a bronco bull on the dance floor."

"Yeah. That's what normal drunk people do." Normal drunk people, however, did not kiss the ever-living shit out of a man whose sole purpose in life appeared to be driving her crazy. What had she been thinking? *What was in those cosmos? Inhibition relaxers?*

CHAPTER
20

N oah woke the next morning with a dull headache, an unsettled stomach, and a vague sense of disappointment. His two self-induced orgasms the night before had done nothing to get Catalina King and her breathy declarations of every dirty thing she wanted to do to him out of his head. They'd just left him feeling embarrassed.

He'd *kissed* her. More than kissed her. He'd tried to devour her in an alley in front of a recycling bin. And not ten minutes before, he'd been quite convinced that the roiling of his blood every time he saw her was just run-of-the-mill distaste.

He started the first pot of coffee in the peace of his quiet kitchen. On mornings when Sara wasn't here, he tried to be up and out the door before any of his guests invaded the kitchen. Now, he was alone with his thoughts.

And in the hungover light of day, his choices the night before didn't look any better. He'd been four seconds away from tearing the jeans off Cat and banging her against the wall. It wasn't that Drake and Henry's schooling had done it either. No, that kind of buildup must have been burning bright long before anyone told him Cat wasn't the devil herself.

Noah didn't like strong feelings. He wasn't comfortable with anything that pushed him out of his safety zone. Not extreme anger or fear or now the hazy blaze of lust. He liked being on an even keel. It was safer there. A therapist would probably say that stemmed from his childhood. But he didn't have time for therapists or dwelling on the past. He could only do his best to make sure his daughter never suffered a second of the fear or dread or desperate hunger he'd known as normal.

He glanced at his watch and poured his first cup of coffee. He double-checked his bag for his laptop, charger, office keys, phone, and wallet. He'd left his car downtown. Five beers and two shots were too many drinks for him to get behind the wheel. Plus, he'd hoped the bitingly cold air would clear his head from the fog of Cat's body responding with abandon to his.

Would he see her today? Would she remember? Would it happen again?

He'd half expected her to text him the night before. Maybe chalking it up to high tensions and alcohol. Maybe firmly stating it would never happen again. Maybe questioning if it would be the worst thing in the world to let it happen again…

Flashes of teeth and tongues and hands played on a disjointed track through his aching head. And he was hard again. Annoyed, Noah adjusted himself. He couldn't remember the last time a fantasy had gotten him in its grips like this.

He picked up his gym bag, slung his messenger bag over his shoulder, and grabbed his to-go mug.

For better or worse, he was ready for the day.

An hour split between trying not to vomit on the treadmill and free weights, another cup of coffee and a bagel from Reggie's temporary stand, and Noah found himself in his office still swamped in thoughts of last night. Was Cat really the woman Drake and Henry painted her to be? If she was, did that make his physical attraction to her less shocking?

He shook the mouse to wake up his desktop computer. As it lumbered into functionality, he put his voicemail box on speakerphone. He was into his fourth message when he realized he'd zoned out again and had to replay them from the beginning.

Noah forced himself to focus, taking careful notes the second time through. Then came the ocean of emails that washed into his inbox every morning like the tide. Along with the standard city manager stuff, now he was awash in media requests to comment on the Christmas special and the town's recovery. Then there was the recovery itself. Email chains dragged back and forth between himself and dozens of other government officials, private contractors, and nonprofits.

It was his first major disaster in Merry and hopefully his last.

He opened his calendar on the computer. Today he had a meeting with the water and sewer authority and the council meeting. He needed to update his budget report and was thankful that they were at least seeing some immediate cash from the rental of the old high school. When all this was said and done, he wanted to give some serious thought to permanently leasing the building.

A calendar alert on his phone popped up. Sara had a geography test today. He typed out a text wishing her luck, adding that he hoped she'd studied. He paused, thought better of it, and then deleted the fatherly warning, replacing it with an invitation for ice cream later. His stomach, still recovering from wings and way too much beer, rolled over at the thought. But Sara would enjoy it, so he'd pray he could leave his indigestion and poor choices behind him by the time she got out of school.

"Good morning, Mr. Yates!" Carolanne, his part-time assistant since he started as city manager seven years ago, looked as though she'd studied 1950s secretary fashion and planned her look accordingly. Her hair, a not-found-in-nature red, was teased into a bouffant that added another three inches to her petite five feet one inch. Today she wore a yellow-and-black dress with a ribbon around her middle. She resembled a bumblebee, the way she buzzed into his office carting the mail.

"Morning, Carolanne," Noah said, wincing at the volume of her tone. He rubbed his forehead and wished he'd thought to down an aspirin or seven before leaving the house. Humming some Christmas carol, she set about firing up the ancient coffee maker and opening the envelopes and packages with exuberance.

Noah rubbed his temples and considered throwing up.

There was a knock that had him opening one eye.

"Good morning, Noah!" Rubin Turnbar and Imani Greene, two of the most excitable town council members, practically skipped into Noah's office.

"Morning. What can I do for you two?" Noah asked, hoping he didn't look as hungover as he felt.

Rubin and Imani shared a conspiratorial look. They were an odd pairing, a dry cleaner and a dance instructor with a twenty-year age difference between them. Rubin and his wife were staunch conservatives in every sense of the word, but he'd bonded with Imani and her pottery-making wife. The foursome enjoyed a weekly dinner together in town where they brainstormed ways to make Merry even merrier.

"Well," Imani began gleefully. "Since the Reno and Realty Network seems to be picking up the tab for a lot of the cleanup and renovations around town, Rubin and I would like to put these back on the table for discussion."

She handed Noah a printout and he found himself staring at a pole-mounted light-up reindeer. *Rudolph just wouldn't die.*

Noah had yet to break it to the council that the five-foot snowflakes that had adorned Merry's downtown streetlamps for the last fifteen years had met their bitter end in three feet of mud and icy water.

"These are five hundred dollars apiece," Noah noted. Doing the math made the dull throb of his headache even worse.

"A bargain," Rubin said and nodded enthusiastically. Clearly the man didn't know what bargain meant.

"They're LED," Imani said, tapping the picture with a long purple fingernail.

"And the noses light up red," Rubin announced.

Oh, well then. That's worth the fifteen grand right there, Noah thought miserably.

"They are certainly festive," Noah agreed, clearing his throat. "How about you leave this with me, and I'll look into them?" he suggested.

"Sure thing," Rubin agreed.

"Question," Imani added. "Do you know if the show plans to do the downtown window competition?"

Noah rubbed his forehead. "I can check on that and get back to you."

"Great! Because my students came up with the perfect idea for a mural," Imani chirped.

"Oh, I don't think it can be better than what Elizabeth and I came up with," Rubin warned.

Imani gave him a level look. "Twenty bucks."

Rubin offered his hand. "I'll take that bet, and I'll be taking your money."

"Please! You're comparing the creativity of dancers to dry cleaners?" Imani snorted.

Noah thought about reminding them that they didn't even know if the annual window painting contest was on and decided he didn't have the energy. Imani and Rubin left, too busy trash-talking to say goodbye.

Noah took the moment of peace to put his head down on his desk. He had nearly twenty seconds of time to lament his beverage choices from the night before when another knock sounded.

A sallow-looking Paige winced at the decibel of her knuckles on wood. She cleared her throat. "Got a minute?"

Noah gestured toward his visitor's chair. His eyelids went from half-mast to wide open when Cat slunk in. She was wearing oversize sunglasses and a hat as if hiding from the paparazzi. He wanted those glasses off. Wanted to know if she was looking at him, thinking about last night. One night, one—well, several—kisses, and he was already looking at her differently. He knew what the satin skin of her stomach felt like under his hands. Knew how she tasted. Knew the weight of her breasts as they filled his palms.

And now he was nauseated *and* hard.

Paige and Cat wearily took their seats, and Paige produced three sports drinks and a bottle of ibuprofen from her bag. With gratitude, Noah pounced on the tablets she doled out and knocked them back with a swig of hot-pink liquid.

"Ungh," Cat groaned, following suit. She pulled off her glasses and rubbed her slim hands over her face. Those gray-green eyes had enough red around them to make Noah wince. "Yeah? Well, you're not looking so hot this morning either," Cat grumbled.

Paige held up a hand. "Hang on. Before we head back down Scream at Each Other Lane, I'd like to broker a truce."

Cat met Noah's gaze. There was a lot being said by those bloodshot eyes. They had more complicated problems now than just intensely disliking each other.

"What would this truce look like?" Noah asked diplomatically.

"Frankly, I'd love to say that we can just allow you two to avoid each other. But we all know that's not a possibility. There's too much work to be done, and, Noah, we need you on our side. I hope you can believe that we're not here to exploit anyone. And if you and Cat can agree to be civil to each other, I think we'll all be better off."

"Agreed," Cat said, catching Paige and Noah off guard. "What?"

"I agree as well," Noah announced.

Cat arched an eyebrow at him and studied his face.

"Okay, I thought that would be a lot harder," Paige admitted.

Cat gave a one-shouldered shrug. "I've got enough shit to do without worrying about verbally sparring with you or running into you in dark alleys for a…fight."

Noah was smart enough that he could tease apart that coded message.

It wasn't like he *wanted* last night to happen again—even though it was all he'd thought about in the last eleven hours since it happened. What he did want was to know what Cat thought about it.

But the bleary-eyed stare she leveled at him wasn't giving him any clues.

"Right. So no more fighting in alleys or otherwise?" Noah ventured.

Cat nodded. "Because it's a very, very bad idea."

"Terrible," Noah agreed. "From now on, we'll be strictly professional." Now why was it as soon as the words left his mouth, Noah pictured Cat panting as she attacked his belt buckle, her lips swollen by an assault from his own mouth?

His expression must have given away a hint of where his mind had wandered because Cat's eyes widened, and she gave him a subtle shake of her head. *Never again*, she mouthed.

Subject closed.

"Uh, okay. Well, I'm pleasantly surprised and confused," Paige cut in. "So, uh, we're going to go now and demolish a large portion of your town."

"Good. Great." Noah felt his head bobbing as if he had no control over it. "Let me know if there's anything you…uh… need."

"We won't need anything," Cat promised. "Let's go sledge-hammer some crap."

"Actually, we do," Paige countered. "Noah, since you're the town figurehead, we really could use you on camera when we go through the park storage. Maybe give us some backstories on some of the ruined pieces. It'll give our designers some ideas on what items need to be replaced and which ones we should try to salvage."

"On camera?" Noah absolutely hated the idea. Standing next to Cat pretending not to think of the insane mistake they'd nearly made the night before for a national audience? Pass.

"I don't think—"

"It would be you and Drake, and I was thinking Sara might also like to be part of the scene. She's sweet and smart, and I think an audience would really connect with a kid whose known nothing but Merry's Christmases," Paige put in.

Sara would murder him on the spot if she ever found

out he passed up a chance for her to be on TV with Drake Mackenrowe. *Shit.*

"Um, I guess so," Noah said reluctantly. "Just Drake?" he clarified.

Cat rolled her eyes, then winced.

"Cat's shooting the demo at Reggie's at the same time," Paige told him.

He stared at the swatch of tan skin at the base of Cat's throat visible above the top button of her plaid shirt. There was a small bruise peeking out above her collar. Noah swallowed hard, knowing he'd put that mark on her.

Cat coughed into her sports drink.

Paige patted her on the back.

"Down the wrong hatch," Cat gasped weakly. She glared at Noah.

Stop it, she mouthed when Paige bent to dig through her purse.

Stop what? he mouthed back.

You know what!

Paige sat up swiftly, phone in hand, and then clutched her head. "Ooof. A little too fast. So I'll email the releases over to you, and we'll need you at the park at four. Plan for about two hours."

Cat glared at him and shoved her sunglasses back on. So the kiss and ensuing second base hadn't mellowed Cat one iota. Well, he wasn't going to let it affect him either. As far as he was concerned, he'd pretend like he had no idea just how spectacular Catalina King's breasts were.

"That's fine."

Cat snatched the paper Imani had given him off his desk. "Are these for streetlights?" she asked, peering at the glowing reindeer over the tops of her sunglasses.

"A request from the city council. And looking at the astronomical price tag, yet another no from me."

"You don't like them?" Cat asked.

"Besides them being incredibly gaudy, I don't like the idea of wasting a huge chunk of the budget on reindeer. Even if their noses do light up. Now if you two will excuse me, I've got a town to run, and you've got one to rebuild."

"Thanks for your time, Noah," Paige said, offering him a friendly grin.

Cat grunted and headed for the door.

"I appreciate you both being willing to put aside your personal differences," Paige said pointedly as she slung her bag over her shoulder.

Cat paused midstride, sighed as if the words pained her. "Bye, Noah."

"Bye, Cat."

CHAPTER
21

Five weeks to Christmas Eve

Temperatures dropped and spirits rose as mid-November marched out of town. Progress was humming along on the job sites scattered around Merry. As word spread, more volunteers came out of the woodwork, demanding to help. On the weekends, the town's population swelled with drywallers, plumbers, and contractors giving up their days off to lend a hand.

And with every stranger who showed up to make a difference, Merry got just a little brighter.

Cat decided the best way to uphold the truce—and not to remind herself what Noah's tongue tasted like—was to avoid him like the drunk, shirtless guy with his face painted blue in the nosebleed section of every sporting event ever. She chalked that night up to too much alcohol and judgment-clouding rage. It was the only explanation for why she had allowed her sworn enemy to get a good handful of her tits while she gripped his hard-on like a baton.

Of course, alcohol did not explain why she'd been getting herself off to the very vibrant memory of being slammed up against a cold brick wall and consumed. Every night. She was starting to worry she might lose flexion in her wrist if she didn't chill the fuck out soon.

Cat zipped up her fleece and dragged on a knit hat that would have her hairstylist fussing over her before the next take. "How's it looking?" she asked, shouldering in next to Paige at the monitor. Paige was dressed like a kid ready for a snow day in a parka, fleece-lined pants, and giant mittens that she could pry open in case she actually needed the use of her fingers.

"Good. Really good. You and Drake look good together on camera. Should keep the rumors flying about you two."

Cat studied the image. Her bronze hair and subtle makeup made her look like the girl next door as she stared up into Drake's handsome face. His height, that thick golden mane, and the killer grin had ladies swooning from episode one. His perfectly tailored flannels and tight jeans didn't hurt either.

"He's really loosened up," Cat noted as Drake delivered a line of dialogue on the screen.

Paige nodded. "He's definitely learning from you, and it helps to have the story editors on hand providing a guide."

Drake strolled through the tent, mug of coffee in one hand and a hard-boiled egg in the other. His earmuffs were ridiculous, but if anyone could pull them off, it was Drake.

"We ready to roll?" he asked, taking a bite of the egg.

It was the one unattractive thing about Drake Mackenrowe. His paleo diet that did his body so much good required him to snack incessantly on things like beef jerky and hard-boiled eggs. His breath on set made Cat extremely happy that she didn't have to kiss him for the cameras.

She couldn't help but compare kissing Drake to Noah's

performance. It was no contest. Noah Yates knew how to kiss a woman like he was tasting her soul. It was almost a week later, and she was still retreating to that night in her head six or seven times a day. She'd lost her damn mind, and she worried that there was a very tiny sliver of her that wouldn't mind losing it again to see if it felt the same.

Thankfully, she had no time to track him down and climb him like a tree. Between shooting and production duties, she was spread dangerously thin. If it weren't for her mother sending a steady stream of leftovers to set with Paige, Cat would be collapsing into bed without dinner most nights.

Her phone vibrated in her back pocket, and she tugged it out. It was Lorinda, her partner for all intents and purposes when it came to the school, she noted with a quick stab of guilt. The woman was as excited about Cat's plan for a school as she was. Enough so that she'd signed on the dotted line to become the superintendent. She'd shuffled a facilities manager Cat's way and had taken Cat's rough research on educational tracks and dug in with both hands. She'd also taken over the grant writing when she'd discovered just how truly awful Cat's writing style was.

They were almost close enough that they should be choosing a location, and now everything was at a standstill while Cat's time was taken up by Merry.

"Hey, Lorinda. How's it going?" Cat asked.

"Cat, I have the best, most amazing news. Just incredible. I'm so excited." Lorinda was not an effusive, excitable person. Only something really big could have her utilizing so many adjectives.

Cat laughed. "What is it?"

"We got the Oppenwick grant."

Cat gripped her phone hard with her gloved hand. "What

did you say? Because it sounds like we got the Oppenwick grant."

"Three million dollars, Cat. Three freaking million dollars!"

"Are you fucking kidding me?" Cat screamed, jumping up and down and ignoring the stares.

"I am not freaking kidding you! They absolutely loved the idea, the curricula, the small business development center. Everything."

Cat doubled over and was surprised to find tears clouding her eyes. "This is really happening?"

"We are going to educate the hell out of a lot of women," Lorinda announced.

"Oh my God. We need a location. We need staff. We need students."

"We need to circulate a summary of the goals and objectives and timelines and then get everyone committed to the project on at least a video, preferably a face-to-face if you can swing it."

They ran through the list of giant whopping to-dos as a few stray tears worked their way free from Cat's eyes. It was happening. She was really doing this. This was something that was just hers. It wasn't the family business. It wasn't a TV show with her brother. This school was *her* baby!

"I had an idea on how to choose a location," Lorinda said, regaining a small semblance of composure.

"What? Tell me. I'm open to anything."

"What if we make it like a grant? Have communities apply to become the home of King Tech. We'll accept entries and choose the winner based on things like community need, proximity to urban centers, percentage of unemployment."

"First of all, King Tech? Isn't it hugely obnoxious to name a school after myself? Second, I love the idea. It will save us from months of cold research, and we'll be able to narrow it down to a community that would benefit from the school. You're a damn genius, Lorinda."

"We're going to need you to spread the word. You know, utilize that celebrity."

"I'll put it on the blog and have my agent distribute some press releases," Cat decided. She covered the phone and bellowed for Henry.

"Let's pull the trigger on this. That way, we can get a jump on this in the new year," Lorinda said.

"Perfect. I'll get the releases drafted, and you figure out how to spend three million dollars."

Cat hung up and, spirit soaring, pumped her arms into the air.

"Good news?" Paige asked mildly.

Cat grabbed her sister-in-law by the face and placed a smacking kiss on her mouth. "I fucking love you and your sarcasm!"

"You shrieked like a banshee?" Henry said, shuffling over in fleecy leather moccasins and a very stylish navy wool coat.

Cat grabbed him and kissed him. "I fucking love your British ass!"

Henry sputtered and blinked.

She grabbed the next available body by the biceps and reeled him in. She realized her mistake a split second before her lips met Noah's, but it still didn't stop her from planting one on him. She was too happy to hate.

"I even fucking love your grumpy ass!" she said. She pretended that this particular chaste kiss felt exactly the same as the others. That there was no shock of carnal desire singing through her veins at just the brush of his lips against hers. It was the first physical contact they'd had since *that night*. And just like *that night*, this was a mistake. She made a move to step back, but he held her wrist.

He reached out, and before either one of them knew what was happening, Noah thumbed away a tear that had escaped down her cheek. That gentle, purposeful touch, the seriousness in his eyes had her heart tripping over a beat.

Silence. For one intimate, spontaneous moment, it was just Noah looking into her. A connection so strong she felt like she could reach out and touch it.

"Cat, you're killing me here. Why do you love us again?" Paige demanded.

Cat stepped back from the pull of Noah. "We're building a school!"

"You got the grant?" Henry asked, calmly slipping his phone from his pocket.

Cat launched herself at him and grabbed him by the shoulders. "Yes, my British crumpet. We got the mother of grants!"

She could still feel the weight of Noah's gaze on her as she trembled from head to toe with joy.

Drake poked his head out of the craft service tent. "What's all the racket?"

"Cat got her grant," Henry called out.

"No shit?" Drake whooped and caught her in three steps, swinging her around in a wide circle. "That's my girl!"

Cat was dizzy enough that it took her several seconds to realize Noah was gone.

"Tonight, we celebrate!" she announced.

———

Trailer Town, as it was affectionately known by its temporary residents, was hopping. After knocking off shooting for the day at a reasonable hour, Cat organized a progressive drinker. It was like a progressive dinner, only with less food and more alcohol. They started off with champagne toasts to Cat's awesomeness in Drake's luxury RV.

Still high from the day's win, Cat felt the flush on her cheeks that had nothing to do with alcohol. She had a strict rule for overdoing it only once during a shoot, and she'd already used up that freebie. Besides, she'd just added an entire mountain range of work to her already steep to-do list. Every spare second of her days would be focused on tackling the next steps.

They were crowded around Drake's dining table and spilling into the bump-out living room, laughing about the last toast, when a production assistant shyly raised her glass. "To Cat, for being the kind of role model we can all look up to," she said, blushing furiously.

"To Cat!" the rest of the crowd echoed.

Cat smiled and gave the girl's hand an appreciative squeeze.

"Are you going to teach?"

"When does the school open?"

"Are you offering financial aid?"

"Will any of the instructors be men?"

Cat's head spun with the questions she hadn't answered for herself yet.

"Guys!" she laughed. "Let's talk about something else. Who else has good news?"

It turned out everyone did. Sound guy Eddie's girlfriend was *not* pregnant. Story editor Noelle had just wrapped up online classes to earn her bachelor's in creative writing and scored a date with a cute local. Gaile, a camerawoman with twenty years in the industry, announced that her mom's biopsy came back negative. Flynn had managed his handy little hammer trick on camera today, making Gannon buy lunch for everyone. And Drake—dear, handsome Drake—everything was always good in his universe. He had a line of area rugs coming out with a high-end retailer in the new year, and he'd wrangled a new, fat contract with the network.

Henry, the workaholic, pushed a bottle of water and some printouts at her. "New Duluth ads for your approval." At her behest, the company had happily created a campaign using real female blue-collar workers.

"Loving this," she said, tapping the group work wear photo. Cat stood in the center, arms around the women closest to her. They were all laughing. There was a feeling of motion and joy and confidence, a rainbow of ethnicities and shapes and sizes.

"I'll let them know," Henry announced crisply. "I gave your call sheet updates to Maria, posted your new blog, scheduled your next four Instagram posts, made some notes on the press release about the school location contest, and talked to your website designer about building an online application for interested communities to use. All information will be organized in a database and ranked."

Cat blinked. She considered herself a hard worker, but Henry could out-efficient her any day of the week. She grabbed his wrist. "Never, ever leave me, Henry."

That got her the tiniest hint of a smile out of the man.

"You also have a FaceTime workout with your trainer at five thirty tomorrow morning. All body weight so you can do it in your trailer."

"And I'm back to not liking you." She employed a personal trainer whenever she was in the city to prevent any damage from too many meals on the road. Nicki was a sadistic bitch who took great joy in making Cat beg for mercy. Cat had never finished a workout with Nicki without ending up on her back in a puddle of sweat, staring up at the ceiling wondering what happened to her.

"I knew you'd be pleased," Henry said, heavy on the sarcasm. He shrugged out of his coat and pushed up the sleeves of his red cashmere turtleneck. "Where's the wine?" he demanded.

Drake leaned in over the back of the banquette between Cat and Phil, a short, Black, wiry cameraman who spoke so softly his nickname was What. "Hope you don't mind, but I invited Noah."

Cat spun around so fast she thought she might have given herself whiplash. "And why did you think that was a good idea?"

Drake gave an elegant shrug and that playboy smile. "He's a nice guy. And I get the feeling he's a little overworked and wound too tight. Thought he could use the chance to blow off some steam."

"Did you tell him I'd be here?"

"I did warn him that his nemesis was in residence tonight."

"And he's still coming?" Well, points for Noah for holding up his end of the truce.

"Didn't seem to throw him too much."

"Ugh," Cat grunted. "Well, keep him away from me. And tell him to bring pizza."

CHAPTER

22

Noah felt stupid carrying two pizzas and wandering through the rows of trailers, listening for the sounds of a party. He wasn't even sure what had made him decide to come. Besides the fact that Sara was at her mother's and he was currently in limbo after submitting over a dozen aid applications and facing an evening of small talk in his own living room with a basketball game on.

Besides, Drake had insisted. And the truce was still on. And if Noah was being completely honest with himself, he wanted to see Cat again. She'd kissed him today, knowing it was him. And though it had been the kind of kiss she'd just given her sister-in-law, it had stirred his blood yet again. And he'd left before he could yank her out of Drake's arms and resume their alleyway make-out session.

So here he was, standing outside a monstrous RV that sounded like it was hosting a frat party and debating if he should knock.

He gave the door a kick with his foot.

"Noah." Henry, glass of red wine in hand, greeted him warmly when he pried open the inner door. "Come join the festivities."

Noah was relieved of the pizzas and handed a beer in the span of three seconds before Drake dragged him into the fray.

"Hey, man. Good to see you."

"Thanks for the invite." It was a chaotic circus inside the trailer. There were twenty people crammed into the kitchen/dining/living space, all laughing and talking at the same time. It felt like he'd just walked in on someone's raucous family dinner.

He flashed back to his mother's quiet, stifling Thanksgiving meals. As much as it crushed him to be without Sara on the holiday, he'd been the one to suggest that Mellody take Sara to her family's meal. At least Sara wouldn't have the same childhood shadows that he had.

"Guys, do you all know Noah?" Drake yelled above the general volume.

"Hi, Noah!"

"Hi…everyone." Noah raised his beer.

"Noah's turn to give a toast to Cat!" A girl with cotton-candy-pink highlights—dear lord, please don't ever let Sara meet this woman—clapped her hands together.

He spotted her then. Crammed in between production and construction crews at the dining table, laughing. She'd washed off the camera makeup and, barefaced, looked so pretty he wondered why she ever bothered covering it all up. She was wearing a long-sleeve Kings Construction T-shirt that had seen at least a million washings. Her hair, still holding the curl from shooting, was pulled into a high ponytail.

The joy he'd seen exploding out of her this afternoon was still there, crackling visibly under the surface. It had been something to behold. Noah wasn't used to overly emotional reactions to anything...unless they originated from a twelve-year-old who thought he was being "soooo unfaaaaair."

It drew him in. That brightness. He was pulled toward it like it was a magnetic force. She was so unlike anyone else he'd ever known. Anything he was used to. Even though he knew she'd undoubtedly rake him over the coals, he just wanted to see that brightness again.

Cat stared at him, more amused than angry for the moment. "I would love to hear a toast from Noah," she purred.

Danger! Danger! His inner fight-or-flight instincts warned him. But Noah was feeling a little reckless tonight.

He cleared his throat. "To Catalina King, a memorable woman."

"To Cat!" the misfit crowd echoed.

Cat's lips, pink and glossed, curved up. "That's the nicest thing you've ever said to me, Yates."

"Don't let it go to your head," he cautioned and was rewarded with an eye roll.

"Where's Sara tonight?" she asked, sliding closer to the bearded guy with the nose ring as someone levered Noah into a seat at the end of the table.

Was she asking to show off the fact that she could recall his daughter's name? Or did she actually care? "She's at her mother's, hopefully studying for her biology quiz."

"Hmm" was Cat's only response.

The volume picked back up, and Noah felt himself drawn into a few conversations at the same time. What were the Patriots' Super Bowl chances? Nil, since he was a hardcore Jets fan. Where did the pizza come from? Because it was awesome. A little place called Pranav's Pizza run by an Indian man and his Italian wife. The curry chicken pie was to die for. Was he putting his money on Cat for the most epic Christmas Festival in the history of Merry?

"Noah's reserving judgment on that one," Cat answered for him with an arch of her eyebrow.

"If she delivers what she says she can," Noah ventured, "it would be a festival for the history books."

"And I will proudly rub your face in it."

"Aww, look at you two getting along so nicely," Henry said over the rim of his wineglass. "Paige would be so proud."

There was a thump at the RV door and a disjointed chorus of "Come in." The man who wedged his way inside was broad and tall and vaguely annoyed. He wore his dark hair cut short and was sporting a Kings Construction hoodie that stretched across his chest. His frown transformed into a crooked grin when Cat whistled from where she was holding court.

"Gannon King is in the house!" Cat crowed.

Noah made a mental note to keep his mind clear of all things Cat naked related while in the presence of Gannon. He'd never had a brother, but he imagined there was some sort of telepathy that would alert them to impure thoughts about their sisters.

"Yeah, yeah," Gannon grumbled. "I'm the life of the party." He snagged a beer out of Drake's fridge.

"Where's my Gabby girl?" Cat asked, crawling over laps to hug her brother.

"Snoring in bed. Paige is ready to drop too. But I couldn't not celebrate you going back to school."

They clinked drinks and shared a one-armed hug.

"Proud of you, Cat. This is a big deal."

Noah watched as color creeped up Cat's cheeks. "Aww. Shut up." She wiggled out from under Gannon's arm, and Noah wondered if she was actually embarrassed by the praise. The Cat he assumed he knew would bask in the limelight.

"You want pizza? Noah brought some." Cat made the offer to Gannon. The way she said his name so casually as if he hadn't had his tongue halfway down her throat a week ago flustered Noah. And then he remembered he wasn't supposed to be thinking those thoughts.

What was he doing here?

"I think I met you unofficially back when we were here shooting the first time," Gannon said, offering a hand.

Noah shook it. "Right. Yeah. It's good to have you back."

"Glad we could lend a hand. We're making some good progress on the residential side. I haven't checked out Reggie's diner yet, but the contractor on that job mentioned things are on schedule."

Noah nodded. "Reggie's excited that he should be able to reopen after Thanksgiving."

"Should be a good episode," Gannon predicted. "You getting used to TV crews all over town yet?"

"Nope. I walked into the grocery store yesterday, and there was a camera crew following Mrs. Pringle around in her scooter."

"Couple more weeks, and we'll be out of your hair."

Funny how that didn't sound as good now that he'd tasted Cat.

"Time to progress," Cat called over the ruckus.

Drinks were finished with enthusiasm, cups and bottles piled into the sink.

"Let's go, Yates," Cat said, giving him a push toward the door. Noah couldn't help but wonder if Cat too felt the frisson of electricity when she touched him.

They filed out into the cold night. Fall had surrendered to an early winter. Not that Noah minded. Growing up in Merry, winter was required to be your favorite season.

They piled into a smaller, less-new RV, the quarters close enough to resemble a sardine can, but no one seemed to mind.

"Damn it, Eddie! Where are the snacks?" Cat demanded from the depths of the tiny refrigerator.

The booing was unanimous.

"That's what you get for working me late," Eddie snapped back good-naturedly.

They'd already devoured the pizza, and finding a restaurant that was open at this time in Merry wasn't going to happen.

"Ugh. Fine. I'll hit the grocery store. But that means I'm getting things I like," Cat announced.

"Someone better go with her," a production assistant joked.

"It's literally fifty feet away."

"Yeah, but we want beer *and* snacks," Eddie called out. "You'll need extra hands."

"I'll go," Noah volunteered.

He wasn't sure who was more surprised, Cat or him.

"Are you two going to need a babysitter?" Drake teased.

"I'm not helping either one of you with the body," Henry chimed in.

"So dramatic," Cat complained. "Two adults who don't like each other can go to the grocery store without committing a murder."

"Not when one of those adults is you," Gannon pointed out.

Cat flipped her brother the bird and stuck her tongue out.

Gannon reciprocated by rubbing his eye with his middle finger. "Oh, sorry. I seem to have something in my eye."

"I'm surrounded by comedians," Cat complained and wedged her way through the crowd toward the door. "Let's go, Yates."

CHAPTER
23

"You guys are like one big, messy family," Noah noted as he closed the RV door behind them while Cat zipped her jacket up to her chin.

She laughed, a silvery cloud of breath escaping with it. "We are family. You spend this much time with each other, and you end up bonding whether you want to or not."

"You don't seem to mind," he pointed out.

She shrugged, stuffing her hands in her pockets. "I love my job, and I couldn't do that job without those yahoos in there. They're very dear to me."

They set off across the parking lot.

"I'm surprised at how much they seem to care."

"Jesus, Noah. Do you realize how snotty you sound right now? *Of course* they care. They're human beings."

"That came out wrong. Sort of. I wasn't expecting this when you forced me into filming."

"I told you we wouldn't screw you over," Cat reminded him smugly.

"Yeah, but how was I supposed to know I can trust that? You can't expect me to believe that every crew would come in here and care."

"No, of course not. Not all teams are equal. Mine just happens to be pretty damn superior in every way."

"So far, they seem great."

"You are wound so tightly I'm amazed you haven't popped a vein. Why are you always waiting for something bad to happen?"

Cat was prodding at a sore spot that he'd only just become aware of. "I'm not that bad."

She jumped, landing with both feet on the mat in front of the automatic door. The doors slid open. "When's the last time you had any fun at all?" she asked, shoving a cart at him.

"Six nights ago, in the alley."

"Hmm." The look she leveled at him gave nothing away. "I was wondering if you'd bring that up. I couldn't decide if you were going to bring it up and apologize or pretend that it never happened."

She led the way toward the snack aisle. Noah leaned on the handle and followed her. The store was all but deserted after eleven.

"Besides some ill-advised second basing, what else do you do for fun?" Cat asked, tossing a bag of tortilla chips and a jar of queso into the cart.

"I've been busy lately."

"Basketball on the weekends with the guys?"

He shook his head. "Nope."

"Whiskey club?"

"Huh-uh."

"Book club? Darts? Karaoke? Running five-Ks? Collecting baseball cards?"

"All nos," Noah admitted.

Cat snapped her fingers. "Ballroom dancing?"

Noah grabbed a bag of pretzels and tossed it into the cart. "Do I look like the ballroom dancing type?"

Cat shrugged. "I haven't seen you fall on your face yet. I bet you could show a girl a nice time on the dance floor."

Cat King was flirting with him. *Flirting.* Another area he was pathetically rusty in.

"I read. I learn to make meals that Sara finds on Pinterest. And I work out." And when he said it like that, he couldn't have sounded more boring if he were a coma patient.

"Noah, you have to have some fun. Otherwise you're just a tax-paying robot." She stopped in front of the cookie section and groaned. "I want all these."

"You can't get them all."

She pointed a finger in his face. "See? That right there is Mr. Responsibility. I'm not actually going to buy all of them, but you telling me I can't have them makes that option even more attractive."

"You're like a teenage rebel. No one needs thirty-six different kinds of cookies."

Defiantly, Cat dropped four packs into the cart.

"You're being ridiculous."

"Look, I'm just trying to help you out here. You use that attitude and logic on Sara when she's a teenager, and you're going to push her into the arms of an irresistible bad boy who's one in-school suspension away from getting kicked out."

"Why do you insist on giving me parenting advice? You have zero children."

"You're missing out on the best part of being a parent." Cat threw two packs of Oreos into the cart.

"What's the best part of parenting?" Noah asked wearily.

Cat knocked a bag of chewy chocolate chip cookies into the cart. "Watching them turn into their own people."

She sounded like his ex-wife.

"What do you suggest I do?" he asked, half afraid of the answer.

"Maybe take a step back on the 'do this, do that' stuff and see what she decides on her own. Maybe lighten up a little."

"You say lighten up now, but wait until you're in charge of making sure another human being not only stays alive but turns out to be a good person," he argued.

"Get in the cart, Noah."

He blinked. "I beg your pardon."

Cat nudged the cart into him. "Get in the cart."

"*In* the cart?"

"I'm showing you how to lighten up. Now, get your ass in the cart."

He stared at her, trying to comprehend what she was saying. "I'm not—"

"The store is empty. No one will see their city manager acting a fool. You can't be worried about my opinion of you because I already think you're a stuffed shirt with an attitude problem. And I double dog dare you."

Feeling like an idiot, Noah swung a leg into the cart. "Is this even going to hold me?" he muttered.

"Quit stalling." Cat shoved the cookies and chips out of his way and crossed her arms over her chest.

He clambered the rest of the way in and sat, his knees hiked up to his chin. "Yay. This is so much fun I can barely contain myself," he grumbled.

She grinned. "You look ridiculous."

"I know I look ridiculous. I fail to see how this is teaching me anything valuable about lightening up."

"Hang on to your frowny face," Cat announced. She grabbed the cart handle and pushed off into a dead run.

Noah gripped the sides of the cart as they careened down the aisle.

"Wheeeeeeee!" Cat hopped onto the bar that was meant to hold twelve-packs of soda and sent them sailing. The cart, its wheels squealing in protest under its load, lumbered to the side, heading for an end cap display of salsas.

Noah was a split second away from jumping from the cart to save himself when Cat hopped off the back and dragged them to a stop. The front of the cart halted two inches from salsa destruction.

"You're insane," Noah growled.

"I had fun once. It was awful," Cat mimicked.

"Can I get out now?"

"Nope! On to the beer and ice cream." Cat took off at a jog again and Noah crashed back against the cart basket.

He felt her hop on behind him, heard her laugh as the cart wobbled its way across the back of the store. Noah twisted around to see her. She had her hands planted on the handle and was leaning forward, enjoying the apparent wind in her face. Cat made acting like an idiot look like a lot of fun.

She slowed them to a dignified crawl when the cooler section came into view.

"How come you can act like this without embarrassment, yet when someone congratulates you on your school, you look like you want the ground under you to open up?" Noah asked as they perused the ice cream selection.

"That's easy. I don't have anything tied to driving like a

madwoman around a grocery store. Nothing's riding on that. The school? That's my future and hopefully the future of hundreds of women. I was lucky. I grew up in a family that didn't care whether you had a vagina or a penis. You helped out in the family business. I had the opportunity and the expectation to learn."

"Are your parents involved in the business?" Noah asked.

Cat shook her head and handed him a pint of mint chocolate chip.

He handed it back. "No bowls. Try something handheld."

She put the ice cream back and pushed him down another cooler. "My mom worked in the office off and on. But my dad's the academic in the family. He taught high school history at a private school in Brooklyn. If you ever see a hammer in that man's hand, run the opposite way. My mom stayed home with us and helped Nonni with the books occasionally. It was my pop and nonni who were eyeing Gannon and me up to be the heirs apparent."

"How did you go from a family construction company to TV?"

Cat grinned, dumping a box of frozen Snickers into the cart. "That was my brilliant idea. When Pop died, the company was already barely scraping by. The economy sucked. No one was building or buying, and we were within months of closing the doors for good. It would have crushed Nonni. Everything they'd worked for, only to lose Pop and the business in the same year?" She shook her head.

"What did you do?"

"I got this crazy idea in the middle of the night—none of us were sleeping back then. The next morning, I took a video camera to the job site and shot some footage of Gannon arguing with me, some demo. And I sent it off to the network. Two months later, we got a call, and here we are."

"You seem like you're cut out for the work." Noah pointed at the Popsicles, and Cat tossed him a box.

"I'm choosing to take that as a compliment."

"That's how I meant it. You're very comfortable in front of the camera and very competent behind it."

"Well, aren't you just full of compliments today?" Cat mused.

"I feel like I may have misjudged you. Slightly," Noah admitted.

"Oh, you mean when you accused me of kidnapping your daughter and called me an ambulance chaser?"

Noah grimaced. He'd been an ass. There was no excuse for it.

"Hey, can we get some donuts too?" he asked, changing the subject.

———

Loaded down with six bags of groceries and beer, they trudged across the parking lot. Noah looked down Peppermint Lane, the street that bisected Main. He shook his head.

"You know, by now we'd have already started decorating the streetlights downtown," he sighed.

Cat stopped and looked into the festive-less dark with him. "This year will be different, but that doesn't have to mean worse."

He sighed. "It's more than just the traditions or the ornaments we've had for half a century. This time of year was really the only fun that I remember as a kid. Seeing it dark like this?" He shook his head. "It's like we're limping into the holidays."

Cat sighed heavily. "I was saving this as a surprise mainly to piss you off."

"What?"

"Follow me."

She led him over to a box truck parked on the outskirts of Trailer Town and put her bags down. She climbed onto the back gate of the truck and flipped the lever. Grabbing the handle, she shoved the rolling door up.

"Are those—"

"Light-up, pole-mount-ready reindeer with red noses," she confirmed.

Noah was speechless. A passing comment, an opportunity to get under his skin, and Cat had jumped on it. "You're diabolical and very generous at the same time."

She shoved her hands in her pockets and looked at the neatly stacked decorations. "I am, aren't I? So you want to put them up?"

CHAPTER

24

Who knew sneaking up ladders on Main Street at two o'clock in the morning would put a smile that big on Noah Yates's face? Cat watched as he tightened the mounting bracket on the very last gaudy reindeer on the very last lamppost.

He grinned down at her, his face awash in the white and red of Rudolph prancing midair, and Cat felt her stomach flip-flop. She should have been in bed hours ago. She'd ordered the rest of their misfit band of ninja elves to bed an hour ago so there'd be at least a few fresh faces on set when they started filming at seven.

But watching Noah enjoy a little mischievous public good was worth it.

He wasn't quite the stick-in-the-mud she'd thought him to be. There was a wound in there somewhere. One that made him embrace control and security and responsibility. Coping mechanisms of the wounded. He'd mentioned he wasn't sure if he'd ever learned how to have fun. Obviously, the man didn't know what a challenge like that did to her. Cat was already plotting.

Carefully, he climbed down the ladder and grinned up as Rudolph's nose beamed bright red. "They're hideous, aren't they?" he asked cheerfully.

"Totally," Cat agreed. "Merry is going to love them."

"Shouldn't you have filmed this? I mean, isn't that something that would look good on camera?" Noah asked.

Odds were the reindeer lights would have to come down and be remounted for the sake of the cameras, but giving Merry and Noah a little something to smile about tomorrow—later today—was worth it.

"Eh, Paige will figure it out." Cat yawned.

"I should take you home," Noah said, checking his watch and wincing at the time.

"I'm three blocks that way," Cat said. "I think I can find my way, guided by the glowing Rudolphs."

"You're not walking home by yourself."

"Why? Don't you trust the mean streets of Merry?"

"The last street crime Merry saw was three years ago. It involved hot chocolate." He fell into step beside her.

"And the crime rate skyrocketed," Cat predicted.

"The crime rate skyrocketed when you assaulted Regis in the bar when you were filming here before."

"Oh, here we go. Blaming the woman."

"You were drunk, and you broke the guy's nose," Noah argued.

"He grabbed my ass. Twice. The second time after I made it very clear that his hands had no business wandering in that direction."

"Oh." Noah looked chagrined. "I don't suppose there was a nonviolent way to have ended it?"

"Let's fast-forward a few years. Your daughter's out on the town having a good time, and some guy gets a little handsy with her. What should she do?"

"Break his fucking nose," Noah said immediately.

Cat laughed. "Now we're talking. I may blow off steam from time to time, but I'm not some hotheaded celebrity with a pack of lawyers on retainer to clean up my messes. I mean, I am a hotheaded celebrity, but I don't go looking for trouble."

"Fair enough. I'm sorry for judging you."

"Well, that's big of you." Cat grinned. "I promise you your crime rate won't explode while I'm in town this time."

"Merry's too good-natured for crime," Noah told her.

"Then why are you walking me home?"

"Maybe I don't mind spending time with you when there's no cameras around and you aren't making it your life's mission to manipulate me into a host of things I don't want to do."

"You were wrong about me, and you're going to be wrong about what I can accomplish," she said loftily. Cat enjoyed the zing of attraction that was playing between them. Would he kiss her when they got back to her trailer? Would she invite him in?

"I'm willing to admit I was most likely wrong about you. But I'm still not getting my hopes up about the festival. You're not a miracle worker."

"Oh, but I am. I'm Merry's own personal miracle." She tapped a finger to her chin. "I'm trying to decide what I want out of you when this year's Christmas Festival annihilates your best year's numbers."

He laughed softly. "I do admire your confidence. Delusional though it may be."

"You know, it's okay to believe. You don't have to constantly prepare for the worst." She said it lightly, but Cat noticed the shadow that flickered over Noah's face.

"Sometimes preparing for the worst is the only way you won't be disappointed...or hurt."

He wasn't talking about a Christmas Festival now, and he also wasn't talking about what she could or couldn't deliver. There was a sadness in Noah that she hadn't noticed before.

They walked on in silence for another block down the middle of the street at Cat's behest. Merry slept soundly around them. Clouds had rolled in, blotting out the stars as they'd worked.

"Look," she said, putting a hand on his arm. In the soft circle of light cast off from the streetlamp and in the glow of that Rudolph, they could see it. Snowflakes.

"Great. I forgot to reach out to the township to see if the trucks are running," Noah said. "We're supposed to get a couple of inches by tomorrow afternoon. I don't know how much of our salt stock was damaged by the flood. And this probably means at least a snow delay for the schools."

He reached for his phone as if he was going to solve all the problems right then and there.

She squeezed his arm. "Just shut up and look, Noah. There's magic in the first snow."

He did look but not at the snow. He was watching her.

"You're lucky there isn't more of this because I would hit you in the face with the biggest snowball I could make," Cat threatened, tilting her head to watch the flakes float down.

"That sounds like something you'd do."

She tucked her arm through his, enjoying the slight hesitation he had, and together they walked slowly down the middle of Main Street as the snow fell silently around them.

All was silent in Trailer Town. They tiptoed over cables and cords to the fold-out steps of her RV. Decision time.

Cat turned to look at Noah.

He was staring at her, softly.

"Congratulations on your school, Cat."

"Congratulations on your reindeer, Noah."

"You have snowflakes on your eyelashes," he whispered.

"So do you." She reached up toward his face, intending to wipe away the snow that was collecting in his dark hair. But he stopped her. His hand gripped the inch of wrist that was visible between sleeve and glove.

He flipped her hand palm up and traced the tattoo with his gloved finger. "Well, I'll be damned."

"What?"

"You know, don't you?"

"Know what?" Cat asked.

"We met before we met," he said, still staring at her wrist.

"Took you long enough," Cat said lightly. She tried pulling her hand away, but he held fast.

He raised his gaze to hers. "You have no idea how many times I've relived that moment. How many times I wondered if I'd ever get to meet you, thank you. How those seconds have made me start reconsidering everything in my life…"

Cat held her breath, waiting for him to finish. She wondered if he could feel her pulse fluttering at hummingbird speeds beneath his fingertips.

"Were you going to tell me?" he asked.

"I was saving it," she admitted.

"Like the reindeer?"

"I was saving it to rub in your face in the right moment. Something along the lines of 'Yeah, you know what I regret? Dragging your bedraggled ass out of the floodwaters on Mistletoe Avenue.' Boom. Mic drop. Then I'd get in a limo—because that's cooler than a production van—and drive away, and you'd spend the rest of your life regretting being such a dick."

"You've put a lot of thought into this."

"That fantasy kept me warm during several cold nights."

"Any other fantasies keep you warm at night? No. Wait. You're pushing me off-balance as usual. There's something I need to say to you."

"You don't have to be dramatic about it." Cat was suddenly antsy. She didn't want to know what Noah wanted to say. She wanted to go back to the flirting, the lightness.

"You saved my life, Cat." She started to argue, but Noah clapped a hand over her mouth. "Shut up, Cat. You saved my life, and then you let me act like an ass."

She grinned against his hand.

"You never once educated me on the fact that you showed up here and dragged my friends and neighbors—and me—out of raging floodwaters."

Cat pried his hand off her mouth. "I wasn't the only one out there on a boat. So don't make me doing it some kind of heroic feat. I was a regular person doing what regular people—including yourself—do."

"I kissed you when I thought I didn't like you," Noah said.

"Yeah? So?"

"So what am I going to do now that I know I owe my life to you?"

"Noah, I'm the TV star here. I'm the one who's supposed to be melodramatic. You would have popped up ten feet away from the boat, and we still would have hauled you aboard."

He shook his head. "Let me thank you, Cat."

Cat stepped up onto the first step leading up to her trailer so they were eye to eye. She gripped him by the shoulders and pulled him in a half step closer.

"No. I'm not going to let you thank me. But I am going to let you kiss me. And then I'm going to send you home because my sadistic trainer is calling me in three hours for a workout to ensure I don't start busting out the seams of my jeans."

"You're one hell of a woman, Catalina King."

"Don't I know it," she quipped.

And then he was kissing her. Her eyelids fluttered closed. The firm, warm pressure of his lips to hers sent a welcome wave of heat rushing through her. Her frozen toes uncurled in her sneakers, and she leaned into the kiss. She purred. He growled. And then he was parting her lips with his tongue. She tasted him, the beer, the pizza, the raw heat simmering under his surface. She let him be the aggressor…at least until she couldn't take it anymore.

As his tongue stroked its way rhythmically in and out of her mouth, she lost the ability to just be. She needed to participate, control. She needed to win. She dove into him, showing him just how she liked to be kissed.

Her gloved fingers dug into the lapels of his coat, holding him against her even as she pulled back.

"Are you kissing me because you think you owe me?" Cat asked.

"I'm kissing you because I want to."

"Good answer." Cat couldn't quite catch her breath. She was shoving her hands under his coat, desperate for skin, for heat, for the feel of him against her, when he stopped her. He grabbed her wrists and reluctantly dragged himself away from her mouth.

"Trainer. Five a.m.," Noah reminded her.

"Right. Trainer," Cat breathed.

"I'm not done thanking you," he warned her.

"I'm not done kissing you."

He took her hand in his, turned it palm up, and placed a gentle kiss to the tattoo over her racing pulse. Cat had never in her life swooned over a man before. Maybe a new power tool or a supremely perfect pair of stilettos. But never a man. This was new.

"Good night, Catalina."

"Good night, Noah."

CHAPTER

25

"I got it," Noah called over his shoulder as he hustled out of his bustling kitchen and down the hallway toward his front door. There was a heated argument about Canadian bacon and omelets happening between families behind him, and after another sleepless night thinking about Catalina King, he was happy to avoid the conflict.

It was a snow day, as predicted, and Merry's second in a week when another storm rolled through right behind the first. While his daughter had shoved her arms into the air in a victorious V when he told her she could go back to bed, Noah battled the old, familiar sickness that gnawed at his gut.

Snow days for Noah as a kid weren't a cause for celebration. Staying home, away from his only escape? The reality of not being able to escape to school made him feel scared and sick. Even as an adult, he was surprised that the same emotions could take hold. It gave him joy, fast and heady, to see his daughter growing up without that sick slide of fear. And maybe someday he'd forgive his past and move on.

But for now, he'd hide his discomfort, his bad memories. And he'd be the doting dad, making sure his daughter never had cause for the ice block in her stomach.

He wrenched open the front door, desperate for a snow day distraction.

The snowball hit him squarely in the chest.

Noah stood, blinking down at the snowy impact on his T-shirt.

"You have five minutes to get ready," Cat announced, hefting another snowball.

Noah wedged the door between them, peering around the corner. "Five minutes for what?"

"You and Sara. Warm, preferably waterproof clothes. Five minutes. Go!"

He stared at her, attempting to formulate words. She was wearing a knit hat in cobalt blue that stood out against the honey blond of her hair. Her parka was zipped to the neck and hid the tattoo that had changed his life on her wrist. Her mittens were thick and matched the hat. She had knee-high snow boots on.

"Come on!" she said, hauling back as if to throw her reserve snowball in his face.

It was better than an omelet fight, Noah decided. "Sara! Find your ski pants!" he yelled and jogged up the stairs.

He left the front door open so Cat could come in if she so desired.

"Sara!" he yelled again, barreling into her room.

"Geez, Dad. It's a snow day. Can't a girl get some extra sleep?" she asked, giving him a disgruntled look from under her comforter.

"Cat's here. She wants us in snow clothes in—"

"Four minutes," Cat yelled from the foyer.

Sara went from sleepy preteen to energized kid in half a second flat. She threw her comforter on the floor "Hi, Cat!" she yelled.

"Hi, Sara! Hurry up, Yateses! Get a move on," Cat bellowed.

Sara giggled hysterically and dove for her clothes.

Noah dug through his closet until he found his never-worn ski pants, some old snow boots, and a thermal shirt.

He felt like an idiot, speed dressing without any idea where Cat was taking them. Knowing her, she probably wanted to film some kind of orchestrated snowball fight. Or she could be driving them into the middle of nowhere to do shots and snowshoe. Wait, scratch that. She wouldn't ask Sara to do shots.

He fumbled with the laces on his left boot and scanned the room for his winter coat, the one he saved for shoveling snow and fighting off the biting cold at midwinter ribbon-cutting ceremonies.

"Let's go! Bus is leaving," Cat called.

"Hurry up, Dad!" Sara grinned as she ran past his doorway, and Noah felt his heart lighten.

He dashed down the stairs after her, still fumbling for his gloves.

They met in the doorway. Cat grinned at him, and Noah felt a warm rush wash through his veins. She looked like an angelic devil, beautiful and up to no good.

She slapped a cafeteria tray to his chest. "Let's go, Mr. Manager." She handed another one to Sara.

Sara frowned at it. "Are we eating at a cafeteria?"

"O ye of little imagination," Cat teased. She led the way off the porch and down the sidewalk. "Follow me, my little snow bunnies."

The hill in front of the old high school was carved with tracks. There were two dozen kids in snow gear zooming down the fresh white carpet of snow and trudging back up to do it again. Another group, with a mix of parents, was building what looked like a snow fort or igloo. Still others were working on a Calvin and Hobbes–worthy snowman army.

"Voilà," Cat announced, sweeping her arms out to encompass the chaos.

"What is this?" Noah asked in wonder.

"*This* is how you do a snow day," Cat insisted. "We're going tray sledding, and then I assume we're going to kick the as—uh, butts of everyone else on the hill in an epic snowball fight of doom."

"Race you to the top," Sara squealed and started sprinting for the hill.

Cat laughed. "Come on, Noah. You can't let her beat you. It'll give her unrealistic expectations of her own greatness."

It took him a full second to move his feet. A full second of doubt and delight and everything in between. But the shove he gave Cat that had her falling on her ass in the snow gave him the momentum to follow his daughter's footprints up the hill.

She almost beat him, but he'd gotten a good grip on her hood and yanked her backward into the snow.

"In your face," he called over his shoulder as he ran the last ten feet to the top.

"Dad!" Sara yelped. But it wasn't anger or adolescent annoyance in her tone. It was sheer delight.

Noah jogged back down and hauled her out of the snow and, still laughing, climbed back to the top.

Cat, brushing snow out of her hair, joined them. "Nice move, Yates." She grinned. "You're more competitive than I gave you credit for."

"So we're sledding on food trays?" Sara demanded.

"Yep," Cat said, dropping hers on the sparkling white at her feet. "I found a whole stash of these in the old kitchen," she told Noah.

Noah planted his in the snow next to hers. "I'm going to sink like a rock," he predicted.

"Then I guess we'll beat you to the bottom," Cat shot back with a wink.

"Yeah! We're going to annihilate you!" Sara chirped.

Noah rolled his eyes. "You've been hanging around April too much, Lady Vocabulary."

"Psht! Is that the best trash talk you've got?" Sara demanded.

"No. But I don't need trash talk when I can do this!" Noah jumped onto his tray, scooted forward, and felt the slip and slide of the tray on the hard crust of snow beneath him. His legs were too long. His heels kept digging into the snow in front of him, stopping him short.

He pulled his feet up onto the tray and scooted forward again. It wasn't the most graceful exit.

"We can't let him win!" Sara yelled from behind him as he coasted down the hill at a less-than-respectable speed.

"I'll give you a push," Cat promised.

Then he heard Sara's "Wheeeeeeee!" and a pink blur flew by him on his right.

"Geez, Sara, be careful!" he called after her.

Cat appeared on his left. She latched onto his arm, using her momentum to pull him faster toward the bottom.

Sara tipped over off the tray and lay on her back, staring up at the cloudless blue sky.

"Sara! Are you okay?" Noah demanded as he and Cat came to a skidding halt next to her. He scrambled off the tray and landed on his knees next to his daughter.

She sat up, grinning, and hit him in the face with a lump of snow. "I win!"

Cat joined in on the fun and scooped a handful of snow down the neck of his jacket.

"No ganging up on me!" Noah yelped.

"Sorry, Mr. Manager. You don't make the snow day rules," Cat announced cheerfully.

It was self-defense, pure and simple, that had him tackling her to the ground. Sara howled with laughter when Cat came up spitting snow.

She laughed, a sound that went straight to his soul. Sitting there, her perfect ass in eight inches of snow that sparkled like diamonds under a blue-skied sunny day. And Noah felt his heart take a hit. A hard one.

He didn't have time to dwell on it though. Cat King was not one to back down from a challenge. She launched herself at him, and together they rolled the last few feet to the bottom of the hill. Kids laughed and yelled around them. The snow was blindingly brilliant and icy beneath them. But Noah had eyes only for Cat. Those mischievous hazel eyes, the gray and the green, sparkled with fun. Her lips were spread wide in a genuine grin, reserved for real life only.

He felt like a king, a god, a hero for making her smile like that.

"Dad!" Sara called. "Let's do that again!"

"You heard the boss," Noah said, tickling Cat through her winter layers. "Let's do that again."

"There are a couple of things I wouldn't mind doing again with you," Cat whispered.

Noah felt his temperature rise high enough to melt the snow beneath them.

"There might be a few things I wouldn't mind experiencing for the first time with you," he admitted breathlessly.

"Hmm," Cat said.

The snowball hit Cat in the face and dripped onto Noah's.

"Hey!" Cat shouted, but Sara was running in the opposite direction, laughing like a loon.

Cat jumped to her feet and dragged Noah up. "Pardon me, I have to murder your daughter."

He watched the woman who saved his life chase, then tackle the girl who grew his heart.

"Happy snow day, Noah!" Paige, balancing a pink bundle on her hip, waved cheerily. Gannon, in sweatpants and a ski jacket, made faces at the baby in his wife's arms.

"Happy snow day," Noah answered, tromping down to meet them.

"I see my sister is asserting her dominance over the youth of Merry," Gannon said dryly, jutting his chin in Cat's direction.

Noah watched her push Sara facedown in the snow and then fire a warning snowball at a group of preteen boys who had declared war.

"The kids seem to like her," Noah observed.

"That's because she is one," Gannon said dryly. "They recognize her as one of their own, don't they, Gabby girl?" Gannon grabbed the baby out of Paige's arms and tossed her into the air.

The delighted squeal made them all laugh.

"Good lord, Gannon. Please don't drop her," Paige said, shaking her head.

"I'll never let her fall," Gannon promised. And Noah knew exactly what the man meant. There was something about being a father that had opened doors in his heart that he didn't even know existed. And sometimes, when he couldn't sleep, he wondered just why those same doors didn't open for his own father.

"No work today?" Noah asked Paige. The TV crew seemed to be working twenty-four seven since arriving in town.

Paige shook her head. "Snow messed with our shooting plans. The trades are all doing the stuff that no one likes to see on TV. We've got a few cameras out shooting B-roll. But we get the day off. And we're going to enjoy it since we probably won't have another one on this shoot."

"Well, welcome to Merry's snow day," Noah said, waving his arm at the growing crowd on the hill. Parents with toboggans and kids with disk saucers zoomed down the hill in a delighted cacophony of laughter and screams.

The igloo fort was almost done, and the stockpile of snowballs was being distributed to key points on the hill.

"Looks like Merry knows how to celebrate." Paige grinned. "Do you mind if I have a camera come over and shoot some of this?"

"Did Cat orchestrate this just so you could film it?" He guessed it wasn't that bad if everyone was having so much fun. And how many of them would really mind being on TV? But still, it lost a bit of the magic, thinking that it was orchestrated to look good on TV.

"Huh?" Paige asked, watching Gannon help Gabby wade through the snow. "Oh no. She just called and said she had a new use for cafeteria trays, and here we are. But you've got to admit, this is a pretty spectacular example of Merry's holiday fun."

He heard the jingle then.

"Oh my God. What is that?" Paige asked, her blue eyes lighting up under the red of her wool cap.

"That, my poor deprived director, is a gourmet hot chocolate truck," Noah announced. "Want some?"

"More than I've ever wanted anything from a truck in my entire life!"

Noah led the way to Elva Janerly's renovated ice cream truck. The smells of chocolate, vanilla, and melted marshmallow wafted out of the truck's open window.

Kids clamored for their place in line.

Cat sidled up next to Noah, her cheeks flushed from the cold and snow.

"Is this the famous hot chocolate I've been hearing about for weeks now?"

"It is indeed," Noah announced. "Elva must have gotten the truck back from the garage."

Cat craned her neck to peer past the dozen kids in line in front of them. "Ugh. This is going to take forever." She cupped her hands over her mouth. "Hey, guys! Snowman making contest happening right now at the bottom of the hill. Winner gets a free hot chocolate!"

Like magic, the kids whooped and dashed out of line in a mad rush to create an award-winning snowman.

"Nice work, Cat," Paige praised.

Cat stepped up to the window. "Elva, I'd like to buy these snow monsters a drink."

Elva, a stern-looking woman in her late fifties, leaned through the window conspiratorially. A stout New Englander, she was more often found frowning and squinting at the sun than smiling. But the woman had the best hot chocolate recipes on the East Coast. She made a fortune every Christmas Festival and had magazines and food bloggers begging for her recipes.

"Would you be wanting the regular hot chocolate or the special hot chocolate?" she asked, producing two metal flasks from beneath the counter.

Cat looked at Noah and grinned. Noah bit back his instinctive reply. Of course, Elva was breaking who knew how many regulations by not having a liquor license. But was it really a battle he felt he needed to win today?

"What the hell." Noah shrugged. "It's a snow day. We'll take the special. Just make sure none of the kids get one."

Elva tossed off a salute. "You got it, boss."

Gannon joined them with Gabby riding on his shoulders. The little girl yanked his cap off his head and threw it in the snow, giggling at her own joke.

"Give me that beautiful little girl," Cat demanded, reaching up to pluck the baby off Gannon's shoulders. "Who's the best niece in the whole universe?" Cat asked, nuzzling Gabby's chubby cheek.

The little girl grabbed a fistful of Cat's braided hair.

"Ouch!"

Gabby laughed and pulled again. Cat freed her hair from those tiny fingers and held the little girl over her head. She brought her down to give her a noisy kiss on the cheek before holding her aloft again.

Gabby squealed with delight.

Gannon slung his arm over Paige's shoulders and snatched the phone out of her hand. "Work can wait for an hour," he reminded her, tucking the phone into his jacket pocket. Paige frowned up at him but let her husband kiss away her annoyance.

"Drinks up," Elva announced.

Cat turned to Noah. "Here. Take this," she ordered, depositing the baby in his arms.

Noah looked down into the blue, blue eyes of Ms. Gabby King. She frowned up at him, assessing his worthiness to hold her. He crossed his eyes and stuck out his tongue, and she grudgingly gave a tiny baby chuckle.

He did it again, this time throwing in a pair of duck lips for kicks. Gabby squealed and made a grab for his face. He avoided her tiny talon-like fingers and jostled her higher up his chest. She laughed the baby belly laugh that had melted him hearing it from Sara for the first time.

Had he held a baby since his own? He'd felt both powerful and powerless staring down at the tiny creature he'd help make and who had enslaved his heart simply by existing.

Gabby leaned in, resting her forehead against his. He could feel her breath on his face. She stared him down, blue eyes wide. Finally, she squished his cheeks between her chubby little hands and laughed at some inside joke that he would never understand.

CHAPTER
26

Cat watched Noah juggle her niece, making the little girl roar with laughter in her snowsuit. It made her feel warm inside to see him enjoying himself like that, and maybe, just maybe, it was pretty sexy watching him expertly handle a baby. Ugh. Thinking with her ovaries would get her nowhere.

Kids weren't on her radar. Neither were serious relationships. She had nothing against either and hoped to one day enjoy both. But right now, her life was exactly perfect, and she wasn't willing to give that up. Not for a wiggly little girl who cooed and crowed. And not for a stubble-jawed, hometown hero of a man who was beaming at her like this was the best day of his life.

Cat heard the throat clearing and shot her sister-in-law a glare. Paige smirked. Great, now she'd been busted swooning over a hot guy and a baby. This was only going to strengthen Paige's "You're attracted to each other" argument.

Cat shoved a hot chocolate into Paige's hands. "Shut up."

Gannon took Gabby back from Noah, and Cat handed him his drink.

"This is the best snow day I've ever had," he admitted, closing his eyes on his first sip. "Mmm, Bailey's and... whiskey?"

"She'll never tell," Cat predicted, eyeballing Elva and wondering if the woman would be up for an on-camera interview during the Christmas Festival.

"Thanks for this, Cat," Noah said, gesturing toward the hill. It was populated by sled tracks and half-made snowmen. The people of Merry had shrugged off their worries for a day and embraced the early winter storm.

"You've got a great town here, Noah," Cat answered. She felt awkward. As if she didn't know what to do with herself when he was looking at her with that soft, warm expression on his handsome face. "What?" she snapped.

He raised an eyebrow at her. "Am I making you nervous with my effusive praise?"

"You're doing it on purpose!" Cat gasped.

"I don't want to be the only one here feeling all off-center and weird," he argued.

Cat threw her head back and closed her eyes. "Maybe we should stop playing games for, like, five seconds?" she suggested.

"What do you think will happen if we do that?" Noah asked pointedly.

"Are you afraid to find out?" She didn't like being the one off-balance.

"Terrified. But I think I need to know. I need to get my hands on you, Cat, and find out."

She sucked in a breath.

"Hi, guys!" A figure clad in purple trudged toward them,

and Cat noted Noah's furtive glance in her direction. He raised his hand lamely.

"That's Mellody, my ex-wife," he murmured to Cat, a strained smile plastered to his face.

"I realize that," she answered dryly. "We've met before. Remember when I kidnapped your daughter?"

"Oh right. Right." Noah bobbed his head. "Yeah. Okay. I've just...I've never been caught flirting with someone by her before."

"Ah," Cat said with understanding. She didn't have any experience with divorce, but ending a life shared with someone had the potential to be complicated and messy—another reason to be very choosy when it came to potential life partners.

"Hey, Mellody," Cat greeted.

"Please, tell me that's spiked hot chocolate," Mellody demanded, reaching for Noah's cup.

Noah held it out of her reach. "Back off, lady. You didn't get this in the divorce."

Cat blinked and then smothered a laugh when Mellody burst out laughing. "Okay, that's the first divorce joke you've been able to make. It's a snow day miracle, and for that, I'll buy my own!"

Mellody mimed her order to Elva and gave the woman a thumbs-up when she flashed the flasks. "So Sara texted and invited me to join the snow fun. I hope you don't mind," Mellody told Noah.

"Oh, uh, no. Not at all." He was shaking his head so hard Cat wondered if he'd end up straining his neck.

"The more the merrier," Cat cut in. "Besides, we need help judging the snowman contest. How are your snow architectural skills?"

CHAPTER
27

Four weeks to Christmas Eve

It was Thanksgiving Day, and Cat was knee-deep in a dirt pit. The pit had, until recently, been home to the gigantic hemlock that the citizens of Merry had been decking out with miles of Christmas lights for the past fifty years. Now all that was left was a frozen hole in the ground where the toppled tree had once lived.

The landscapers were busy giving her the bad news that there was no way in hell that a replacement tree could be planted. Too cold. Not enough time for roots to establish themselves. Blah blah blah.

Cat wasn't interested in what couldn't be done. She only had time for solutions. And walking this frozen mud pit had given her one hell of an idea for a solution. She just needed a welder and several extra thousand dollars in the budget.

She flexed her fingers in her fleece-lined gloves. Winter had moved in and decided to never leave Merry from the feel of the wind as it bit through her layers.

"Okay, Lorenzo," she sighed, already mentally calculating how to bring her new vision to life. "Don't worry about this for now. What I do want to focus on is the river wall and the swale for drainage."

They walked and talked, Lorenzo filling her in on their progress so far. That was one lucky thing about this damn hurricane and its timing. Cat had her pick of landscaping crews since it was between the demands of summer and the winter holiday decorating season. In less than a month, they'd cleared all the debris from the park and begun re-laying sidewalks that had met with unfortunate flood damage. Tons of mulch had already been distributed, and if they had to plant fake poinsettias and Christmas trees in the gutted flower beds, so be it.

Visitors to this year's Christmas Festival would be getting an eyeful of freaking Christmas spirit if it killed her.

Lorenzo wrapped up his report, and Cat nodded with satisfaction. "You guys are killing it. Keep it up. I'll make sure you get the new shooting schedule for the weekend."

"Appreciate it." Lorenzo nodded, his hands shoved in the pockets of his coveralls. He was a Mainer by birth, so twenty degrees felt balmy to him.

"Might as well take your guys home. Enjoy some family time," she said, glancing at her watch. It was already three in the afternoon. Any other year, and she would have been holding her hands over her stomach and whining about how she shouldn't have hit the stuffing so hard.

But not this year. Her mother was "throwing together" a Thanksgiving meal in the rental house. It wouldn't be the same. Not without Nonni and everyone crowding around the dining table as they had for generations. But it was what they had to do if they wanted Merry to have the merriest Christmas to date.

Dinner at seven.

That would give her enough time for a quick shower and a chance to peruse the latest entries into the school location contest. Lorinda's idea for the location contest had gone better than expected. Apparently, a trade school for women was big news. Cat had taken time out of her schedule two days ago to video chat with the hosts of a New York morning show about the initiative. In those forty-eight hours since, traffic to the website Henry had set up exploded. She even had a few applications for the school's location already as well as dozens of information requests by potential students.

Cat flexed her fingers in her pockets as she headed back toward the street where her truck was parked. She could feel the momentum building. There was a point in every project where the flow seemed to take over. But she felt like Merry and the school were warring for her attention, and she wasn't sure which one needed to take precedence.

If she were being honest with herself, Cat knew she was spreading herself too thin. She needed a little time off to recuperate, get her head on straight, and come back at both projects full steam. An outsider would suggest that she delegate. But when she was the one with the vision, it was too time-consuming trying to transfer that vision to someone else.

She hauled herself behind the wheel and cranked the heat. A little vacation would be nice. She closed her eyes and leaned against the headrest. Maybe a nice tropical island. White sand beaches. A hammock. A pink umbrella in her drink.

The knock on her window scared the hell out of her.

Drake was grinning at her. "Nap time?" he asked when she rolled down the window.

"Har. As if we have time."

"Just wrapped shooting at Mrs. Pringle's." Paige had assigned Drake to Mrs. Pringle's because the woman absolutely adored handsome men. Cat had seen some of the footage with the duo's banter and agreed it had been a solid-gold decision.

"How's it coming?"

"Got the occupancy permit ten minutes ago." Drake grinned.

"Awesome," Cat sighed. They'd shoot a reveal at Mrs. Pringle's and one at the diner this week. Despite the mountain of work yet to be done, they were on schedule. "Are you coming to dinner tonight?" she asked.

Drake's family lived in sunny Southern California, and due to the shooting schedule, he wasn't able to join them this year.

He bobbed his head, grinned. "That was the plan. But something came up."

"What came up?" If Paige or Jayla had tried to sneak in an extra scene to film on Thanks-fucking-giving Day, Cat was going to murder someone.

"I don't know exactly what it is, but you and I have been invited to the fire station."

"The fire station?" Cat repeated. She scrubbed a hand over her face. God, she was tired. She wanted a shower, a nap, and coffee and then an entire vat of gravy. But if Merry's firefighters wanted her there, she would be. Part of the success of her shows was that Cat made sure those towns knew they were important to her. She wasn't just in town to smile for the cameras and then hide in her trailer. She had their backs. She wanted good things for them. That was why people talked to her, opened up, shared things they wouldn't necessarily share. It made for good TV and good karma.

"Okay. To the fire station. Want a ride?"

———

Cat frowned at the cars lining the street outside Merry's brick fire station. Half of the building was the oversize garage for the two trucks and ambulance that served the community. The other half was a two-story structure that housed the fire hall, where community breakfasts and food drives were held. It was the heart of the community.

Cat wondered if they should add a food drive to the show. *Maybe for the Christmas Eve park reveal? Merry giving back, paying it forward.*

She was so lost in thought that it took her a full second to realize what she was seeing when Drake opened the glass door for her.

The fire hall with its ugly drop ceilings and even uglier wood paneling was filled with folding tables and chairs, all occupied by production staff, contractors, and Merry residents.

"Surprise!"

Cat clapped a hand over her mouth.

"You didn't think we'd let you skip Thanksgiving, did you?" Noah asked, appearing at her side. He wore charcoal-gray trousers and a navy pullover that hugged a chest more defined than a desk jockey nerd's had any right to be.

"You did this?" she asked. The scents of turkey and mashed potatoes and gravy were thick enough to fog the windows from the inside.

"Merry did this," Noah corrected her. "One more surprise, a little speech, and then you can attack that stuffing," he promised.

"Another surprise?" Cat parroted.

Noah pointed over her shoulder. There at the corner table were her parents, Gannon, Paige, Gabby in a high chair, and beside her—

"Nonni!" Cat flung herself at the tiny woman. Her

grandmother's cloud of white hair smelled just as it always had: Shalimar and baby powder.

Nonni's strong fingers dug into Cat's shoulders, pulling her closer. "You didn't think I'd miss a family Thanksgiving, did you?" she chided Cat.

"No, ma'am." Cat grinned down at the woman who had put her on this path. "How did you get here?"

"Your father picked me up this morning and drove like a demon to get back here."

Nonni loved her son-in-law but found his driving skills left much to be desired. She found anyone who drove above forty miles an hour to be a terror on the road.

"I can't believe you're here."

"Believe it," Nonni commanded. Her spine of steel was evident even in her diminutive stature. She gave Cat another squeeze. "Now, that handsome man has his words to say and then we eat." Nonni nodded in Noah's direction.

With the help of Reggie—festive in a turkey sweater— drumming on one of the tables, Noah quieted the room.

"I'd like to thank everyone who turned out for this meal today. This year, we've become more than a community. After the storm, we became family."

Cat saw him wink at Sara, who was sitting between Mellody and another older, unsmiling woman. She had lines carved into her blank face. The man on Mellody's left had his arm around her.

"That family has grown to include our friends from the Reno and Realty Network," Noah continued.

Spontaneous applause burst forth, and Cat slid into a chair next to her father.

"Now, you may not know that I wasn't a fan of the idea of allowing the network to film their Christmas special here," Noah said.

Several sarcastic gasps filled the air, and Cat laughed. Mr. No's reputation was widely known.

"Ha ha." Noah took the ribbing in stride. "Believe it or not, I'm not always right. So I'd like to thank Cat and Drake and their team for riding to our rescue and putting our town back together. I have a feeling this Christmas, with their help, is going to be the most memorable one Merry has ever seen."

The applause kicked up again, and Cat joined in. It was true. She'd do whatever it took to make sure this town got their Christmas.

"So for their time, their attention to detail, their genuine caring, I'd like to thank you all for spending your Thanksgiving with us. We're honored to have you." Noah raised a plastic cup of Sprite. "Happy Thanksgiving." He said it to the room, but his eyes were on Cat. She felt the familiar warm flush roll through her body.

When he looked at her like that... Well, it wasn't safe to think those thoughts when Nonni was sitting near her. Nothing got past her grandmother.

The toast echoed around the room, and cheers rose up when the first dishes of food appeared.

They dined family-style on turkey and ham, roasted vegetables, stuffing, and enough mashed potatoes and gravy to fill a community swimming pool. Cat's plate was never empty and neither was her heart. The people she cared most about were in this room, and there was nowhere else she'd rather be.

CHAPTER
28

Somewhere between the best slice of pumpkin pie Cat had ever had and the worst cup of coffee, Sara popped up at her elbow. "Hi, Cat!"

"Hey, Sara. Guys, this is Noah's daughter, Sara." Cat made the introductions to her parents and grandmother.

"My grandma is here too," Sara said. "I'll go get her!" She skipped over to the table and pulled the woman in the gray dress out of her chair. It looked like she rose with great reluctance. Her hair was streaked with gray, her face bare and lined. Her forearms seemed painfully thin.

"Grandma, this is my friend Cat and her family." Sara made the introductions like a pro. "This is my grandma, Louisa."

"It's nice to meet you, Louisa," Cat said, offering her hand.

Louisa stared blankly at it for several seconds before accepting it limply. The skin of her hand was paper thin. "Hello," she whispered, her eyes flat and dark, looking everywhere but at them.

"Sara," Mellody said, appearing at the table. "Why don't we let Grandma get back to her pie?" she suggested cheerfully.

Louisa gave them a ghost of a nod and left.

"Cat, this is my husband-to-be, Ricky," Mellody announced, drawing the man in the argyle sweater to her side.

"It's nice to meet you, Ricky," Cat said, offering her hand.

He shook it warmly. "Great to meet you."

Cat made the introductions around the table. "It's really nice of you to give up your own plans with your family to spend Thanksgiving with us," she told Mellody.

"Merry is family, and best of all, I didn't have to cook or clean up." Mellody grinned. "Best holiday ever." She snuggled into Ricky's side.

"Shall we check out the pie, babe?" Ricky asked.

"We shall." Mellody waved her goodbye as they made their way over to the dessert table.

Cat watched them go, curious whether Louisa was Mellody's or Noah's mother. Whoever she was, it seemed that the will to live had left her long before. Cat rubbed at the goose bumps on her arms. She felt as if she'd just crossed paths with a ghost.

Cat rejoined her family's conversation and listened to Gannon and Paige banter about work and babies. Her parents doted on each other and little Gabby. Nonni struck up a flirtatious conversation with Drake and Henry.

It felt so good, so right, being in this funny little fire hall on a holiday like today. Outside the brick walls, a town was on its way to being rebuilt, and spirits and expectations were rising. She wouldn't let them down.

Cat grabbed her Styrofoam cup and headed over to the coffee table.

"That stuff will scrape the lining off your intestines," Noah warned, nodding at the thermos.

"I've had worse," Cat said, filling her cup. "Not much worse, but worse." She turned to study him as he filled his own cup. "Thank you for this," Cat said, gesturing around the room that was full to bursting. "You gave my guys a family holiday even without their families."

Noah shrugged. "After everything that they've done for us, what kind of town would Merry be if we didn't give back?" He looked relaxed, happy.

"Well, thank you anyway. This was a really sweet, unexpected gesture."

"I had to make up a little bit for being such an ass," Noah teased. "I mean, you did save my life and all."

"Ah yes. And now I'll be saving your town," Cat said airily. "However will you thank me for all my goodness?"

He eyed her long and hard. "I can think of a few ways," he ventured.

Noah Yates was flirting with her. Suggestively.

"What kind of ways?" Cat asked, testing him by stepping a half step closer. She watched his reflexive nervous glance toward his ex-wife and snickered.

"What?" Noah asked.

"You look like you're looking to Mellody for permission to flirt with me," Cat pointed out.

"I'm a little rusty when it comes to flirting," Noah admitted. "And I still feel new at this whole divorce thing."

"Do you still love her?" Cat asked, kicking herself for asking a question she didn't really want the answer to.

"Of course," Noah said, looking perplexed.

"Oh." It was the only word she could manage. Noah was still in love with Mellody? How had she gotten her wires so crossed?

Embarrassed and more than a little devastated, Cat turned her focus on the dessert table. Dozens of homemade pies, cakes, and candies were lined up. A smorgasbord of goodies.

"Where'd you go, Cat?" Noah asked. His fingers closed around her arm just above the elbow, a warm, hard pressure.

"Oh, ah, I was just thinking about how much work I need to get through after dinner." She gave a careless shrug of her shoulders. Careless. Right. She didn't care if Noah was still carrying a torch for his ex-wife. The ex-wife who was counting down the days to her wedding. Maybe Noah was lining Cat up as a rebound? But Catalina King was no man's rebound. "You look like you're enjoying yourself," Cat said, changing the subject, casually sipping the sludge-like coffee.

He leaned in conspiratorially and pointed at his table. "I am. I never get Sara for Thanksgiving. It's too…depressing at my mother's. So Mellody and I agreed that it's better for Sara to spend it with her family instead. It's usually just me and my mother, sitting quietly, staring into space for two hours with a meal that we reheat from a grocery store."

"That's…awful," Cat managed. So the ghost of a woman was Noah's mother after all. A thousand questions landed at the tip of her tongue. What about his father? Was his mother always so cold, empty? What was his childhood like? He'd made allusions to the fact that it hadn't been a happy one. She wondered how much of his overprotectiveness now was due to the way he was brought up.

"But with this Merry-wide Thanksgiving celebration? It was something Sara would hate to miss, so Mellody generously offered to share her today."

"You two seem to have a really good relationship," Cat said, feeling like she was choking on the words.

"It's getting better again," Noah agreed. "I'm happy about

that. Anyway, enough about me. How are things going with the school? Are you getting a lot of submissions in the location contest?"

Cat nodded mutely. She felt tongue-tied and brain freezy. He'd yanked the rug out from under her feet with his declaration of love for his ex-wife. Moments earlier, she'd been debating whether she should invite him home with her tonight so she could finally peel off all those layers of clothes and get a close-up look at the muscled physique she'd felt every time they'd touched. She'd wanted to kiss him again, dizzyingly, brashly.

But Cat was no second fiddle no matter how attracted she was to someone.

"Uh, yeah," she said, still nodding. "I need to go over the latest submissions, but it looks like we've got a couple possibilities that would be a good fit for us."

"Pretty exciting," Noah prodded.

"Yep. Yeah. Sure is," Cat said without the enthusiasm. She shook herself. She was a woman to be lusted after. She was not a pouter. If Noah Yates had his stubborn head shoved up his own ass that far that he couldn't see the amazingness that was right in front of him? Well then, he didn't deserve to see her naked.

She squared her shoulders. "Well, I'd better go share my Thanksgiving thankfulness. Uh, thanks again for this, Noah. It was really thoughtful of you."

She left him alone by the motor oil coffee and plopped down at the first table she found with an empty seat.

CHAPTER
29

Noah raised his fist, ready to knock, and then shoved it back in his pocket. He walked away, shaking his head. He was an idiot. And in this case, he didn't know exactly what idiotic thing he'd done or said, but it had been enough to get Cat to stop flirting with him and become desperate to get away from him.

He paced back to the trailer door. He could hear the TV on inside. Or was that voices? Maybe she had someone in there with her. Maybe she had a boyfriend, and he'd been misreading everything since day one…or whatever day he'd decided he wasn't going to keep fighting this attraction to her.

Maybe it wasn't a boyfriend. Maybe it was a hookup.

Oh God. He paced to the back of the trailer. Was he coming here for a hookup? Or was this something more? Why would Cat be up for something more? She had a life in New York. She had a TV show. A glamorous, busy schedule that didn't leave room for a torrid, long-distance affair with a boring Connecticut city manager or being a stepmother to a twelve-year-old.

Noah tripped over a cable running beneath two trailers. Well, that had mentally escalated quickly. He rubbed the back of his neck. He went from thinking about having sex with Cat to thinking about having a life with Cat.

See? His inner conscience blared at him. He wasn't cut out for flings or one-night stands. He was a boring, monogamous guy who just wanted to settle down and build a boring, stable, predictable life around himself.

Definitely an idiot. He needed to leave. Thank God he hadn't humiliated himself by knocking. Noah wasn't exactly sure what he'd planned to do once she'd answered. Demand to know why she got weird at the dinner? Start taking his clothes off in hopes that she'd follow his lead? Break into a dissertation on all the reasons they would be better off not having sex?

He hated that he went stone-hard the second he thought "sex" and "Cat" in the same sentence. He was no better than a teenager.

Yeah, he was going home to take a cold shower and let this thing die a natural, uncomplicated death.

"You're wearing a ditch in the asphalt." Cat's calm observation came from where she leaned against the doorway of her trailer.

"Oh, I was just, uh…" *What? Inspecting the parking lot? Looking for permits?*

"You might as well come in, Noah, before you freeze to death trying to come up with a lie."

Cat stepped back from the door, and Noah felt that he had no choice but to follow her inside. He shut the door behind him with a bang and was relieved to note that it was the TV

215

he'd heard and not the dulcet tones of some Latin lover Cat had flown in to satisfy her needs. She was watching a Christmas movie.

A tiny fiber-optic tree was plugged in in the corner, shifting from pink to blue to green.

"Why do you look sick and mad?" Cat asked, flopping down on the small couch.

She was wearing a tight white tank with nothing, zip, zero underneath it. The thin straps looked like they might break under the strain of her very visible, very full breasts. He'd never wanted to touch anything so much in his entire life. He'd slide his palms up over her stomach to the lower curve—

He was instantly harder than he could ever remember being.

She wore cropped sweatpants that ended just below the knee. There was an inch of skin visible between the waistband of her pants and the hem of her tank top. And Noah wanted to run his tongue around it.

Her face was bare, hair piled on top of her head, and she was surrounded by papers, a laptop, and a tablet.

"Yoo-hoo?" Cat snapped her fingers, and Noah woke from his breast-induced trance.

"Sorry. What?"

She looked amused. A woman like Cat would be used to having men slobber over her. It was part of the job, wasn't it? Being attractive, being a brand. He hated that he was just one more man lusting after her. He wanted more than that for them both.

"I was asking what you're doing here," Cat reminded him.

"Why did you close up at the fire hall?" He blurted the question out, forgetting each and every carefully crafted segue he'd worked on in his head since she walked away from him.

"Noah, you can't be serious."

"We were flirting, talking. And then you just clammed up and walked away," he argued.

"Yes, we were flirting, and I was thinking about inviting you over tonight so I could run my tongue over every inch of your body."

Noah's knees buckled, and he slid bonelessly into one of the chairs around her minuscule dining table.

"Wh-what?"

"Oh, but that was before you confessed to still being in love with your ex-wife."

Noah blinked. He wasn't sure if he'd been struck dumb by Cat's breasts or her announcement about her intended plans regarding her tongue. But either way, he had no idea what she was talking about.

"I'm in love with Mellody?" he asked.

"Yeah. You already told me," Cat said, leveling those pretty hazel eyes at him.

"That's—that is not what I meant or said. You asked…" He brought his fingertips to his eyeballs behind the lenses of his glasses. If he kept his eyes closed, he wouldn't be hypnotized by those breasts that seemed to be begging for his hands, his mouth. "You asked if I still loved Mellody."

"Yep," Cat said, clearly not thrilled with the outcome.

"I said yes."

"Oh, I remember very clearly," Cat said, picking up the remote and flipping through the channels as if she didn't have any stake in the conversation.

"You didn't ask if I was *in* love with her," Noah pointed out, rising out of the chair.

Cat's eyes narrowed. "What's the difference?"

Could the woman really know so little about love? he wondered. "You love your nonni, right?"

"Uh, *duh*." Cat rolled her eyes at the stupidity of his question.

"But you're not *in* love with her...although I could see why anyone would be. She's a firecracker." He was digressing and forced himself to reel it in. "What I'm saying is, I love my ex-wife as the co-parent of my daughter and within the awkward friendship we've been cobbling together since the divorce."

Cat blinked, frowned. "Well, why in the hell didn't you say it that way in the first place?" she demanded.

"I don't know if you've noticed, but you get me a little tongue-tied when you look directly at me," Noah pointed out.

"Don't be ridiculous."

"I'm serious, Cat. You're the color in a gray day. I don't know how else to describe it. I look at you, and I see all this passion and joy and fun and excitement. I've never met anyone like you. Including my ex-wife, who I care for and respect but have no desire to be married to anymore," he clarified.

Noah didn't know how he'd expected Cat to respond, but it certainly wasn't jumping into his arms and locking her legs around his waist.

"Let's try less talking," Cat suggested, a millimeter away from his mouth. "Less room for misunderstanding."

He gave his assent by gripping her sweatpant-clad ass and squeezing.

She brought her mouth crashing into his in a tangle of teeth and tongue and want. Blindly, Noah stumbled forward, pressing her against the entertainment center cabinet.

She tasted like danger. And for once in his life, Noah wanted to slide a toe over the line onto the wild side. He squeezed her hips, her ass, yanking her tight against him. She responded with a muffled moan against his mouth.

Noah whirled and pressed her hard against the closed door, losing himself in a ravenous kiss. The way she moved against him, writhing and sliding. The sexy noises that clawed their way up from the back of her throat. He wasn't going home tonight. Unless she wasn't sure…

"Are you sure about this, Cat?" he murmured, his lips dancing over hers.

"Stop. Overthinking. And have sex with me." She shoved her fingers into his hair and gripped hard.

He felt the shock of pain, saw stars behind his eyes. And then lost his damn mind.

He spun them, desperate to lose the layers that separated them. He stumbled against the dining table and spread Cat on it as if she were a feast ready for the sampling. She wouldn't let him pull back, her fingers digging into his shoulders, her thighs holding him in a death grip.

Noah shoved a hand under her tank, reveling in the smooth flat of her stomach. The warmth, the silky texture of her bare skin finally beneath his. It was an exquisite torture being so close to her yet still not close enough.

"Lose your shirt, Noah," Cat commanded.

Happy to oblige, he reached behind his head and dragged the pullover off.

"So much better." She reared up to rain kisses and bites across his chest. "So built," she murmured.

"Back at you," Noah said, sliding both hands under her shirt and yanking it up and over. "Fuck. I don't know if I can survive this." Reverently, he trailed his hands higher over the ridges of ribs to the swell of her perfect breasts.

"They're not going to break," Cat said breathlessly as Noah splayed his fingers over the heavy bottom curve of each breast.

"No, but they deserve to be savored," he promised.

"I don't know if I can handle savoring," Cat warned him, a hitch in her voice as his palms blazed a trail to her pebbled nipples. She dropped her head back onto the table with a *thunk*. "Oh God."

Noah took his time lowering his mouth to her. He dropped a circle of kisses around one pink, aching point.

"Killing me," Cat groaned.

Finally, Noah gave in to the desire to taste. He lapped at her nipple with the flat of his tongue. Her hips bucked against him, lining his throbbing cock with the wet that seeped through the cotton of her pants. He flexed, testing.

"Noah!"

"I've barely touched you, tasted you yet," Noah teased.

"Touch and taste faster, or I'll make you," she threatened.

CHAPTER
30

Ignoring her warning, Noah leisurely sucked her other nipple into his mouth. Cat bowed off the table and used her nails to carve shallow trenches into his shoulders. She wanted to take and take and shove him off that precipice of control so Noah would free-fall with her. She couldn't handle the measured worship of her body by his.

It was doing things to her heart, her head. Confusing her.

Sex in Cat's world was simple, physical, enjoyable. But this? What Noah was doing to her with just his mouth? It was something that walked the razor's edge of pleasure and torture.

There was a power struggle happening right here on her dining room table, and she was losing. She was melting under his soft kisses and gentle hands.

His erection was evident under the zipper of his pants. The fabric strained around the demanding column of steel.

His mouth was working its way across her ribs and over her

stomach. He slipped his fingers into the waistband of her pants, and she heard the murmur of approval when those fingertips didn't find any barriers underneath.

He slid the pants down her thighs, taking his time to enjoy the skin-to-skin contact. His fingers blazed hot, bright paths down the backs of her thighs, her knees, her calves. He knelt before her and Cat felt the anticipation that ached inside her echo hollowly.

With the finesse of a man who had all the time in the world, Noah brought his lips to the inside of her knee. The shock of it, the neediness that bloomed within her, heightened every sensation. She was beyond sensitive, beyond primed.

Gently, he pressed her legs open wider until they hooked on opposite corners of the table. Vulnerable, spread bare before him, Cat watched him.

He was studying her body as if it were a fine work of art. Something to be appreciated, admired. The touch of his fingers stroking inside her thighs was driving her to madness. She needed him inside her, filling her, stretching her.

And just when she thought she might die from need on the table, she felt the tip of his tongue trace its way around her smooth folds. Still, he wasn't touching her where she needed it most. But he couldn't possibly hold out much longer, and then he'd give her what she craved.

"Noah!" His name was a strangled gasp forced from her throat. One stroke of his tongue from her aching center through her sex and over her clit delivered a creeping blackness at the edges of her vision.

Reflexively she tried to close her legs. But Noah's big hands closed over her thighs, spreading her open. He stroked her again with his magical, glorious mouth. Lapping at her, tasting, teasing. Cat's legs quivered at the knife's edge of pleasure that was cutting her to ribbons.

"So beautiful. So perfect," he whispered against her as his mouth worked her closer and closer to release.

Noah was destroying her cell by cell. Cat couldn't move, much less participate, dragging him over the edge for a fast fuck that she so enjoyed. She couldn't do anything but lie there and take layer after layer of silky pleasure that his mouth dealt her.

She could feel the tightening, the drawing in of her muscles as they begged for an orgasm she knew she'd never forget. The tingling began in the soles of her feet and sparked all the way up her spine.

"N-Noah," she gasped.

Knowing her body with an impossibly intimate knowledge, Noah drove two fingers into her tight sheath. The invasion of his flesh against hers, the skillful stroke of his tongue, sent Cat spiraling into the abyss. Colors, pinks and reds and golds, danced before her eyes as her muscles pulled him deeper and deeper. She went blind and deaf. Cat could only feel as each explosion traveled the entire length of her body and back again to her throbbing core.

She gasped, words failing her as Noah gentled his mouth against her tiny bud of nerves.

Thoughts, wild and terrifying, careened through her mind. She pushed them aside and focused on the only one that mattered. *More.*

She levered up off the table and pushed Noah all the way to the floor.

"Cat, let me—"

She wasn't letting Noah anything at this point. Her legs were so weak her thighs were trembling.

"My turn," she argued, her throat raw from her cries.

She undid his belt and zipper in record time, even with the

postorgasmic tremors in her fingers. The fabric of his pants was smooth and soft beneath her hands.

She felt Noah's reluctance at her haste, but she wanted him out of his comfort zone just as he'd dragged her out of hers. She wanted to show him the mind-clearing elation of fast and hard.

She worked his pants down his thighs to his ankles, and leaving his boots on, she crawled up his body, pausing to bite his inner thigh hard.

His cock jerked before her eyes, and his guttural groan was fucking music to her ears. She hadn't even touched him yet, and precum was leaking from the crown of his—as predicted—impressive cock.

She fisted a hand around the root, and Noah's feet scrabbled for purchase on the wood paneled floor as if he were trying to escape.

"Uh-uh," Cat tutted, brushing a feather-like kiss over the swollen head.

The cords of his neck stood out as he fought back the urges she was desperate to free.

"My turn now," she said, her confidence returning with the control she'd wrested back.

"Cat—" Her name sounded like a warning, but he knew Cat didn't think much of the rules. Or he should have known.

She made sure Noah was looking at her when she wet her lips. His erection jerked in response against her hand. She gave him no time to anticipate before drawing her lips around his crown and sliding down the length. There was too much of him to go far, but when she hit the back of her throat, Noah's hips flexed up before he could fight the urge.

This was where Cat liked to be: in charge.

She lost herself in the rhythm, the slick slide of her mouth over and around the thick column of aching arousal. He was pulling at her hair, oblivious to the pain he caused, and she liked it. Faster, pushing him closer and closer to that razor-thin edge between controlled and wild. Between principled and primitive.

She needed him like that. Shredded control, driven by desire.

He was fucking her mouth now with shallow pumps of his hips, and she let him draw himself closer to the line. Brazenly, she reached down and cupped his balls.

He growled, a rumble that wrenched its way free from his chest. This time, when he pulled her hair, it was to drag her off his cock and up his body. He rolled them across the floor. The metal seams between the wood of the kitchen floor and the rug of the living room bit into Cat's back and shoulders. But she didn't care. Not with Noah ranging himself over her. Not with the head of his penis prodding at her begging entrance.

She was light-headed with want. But somewhere inside, a tiny shred of logic lived. "Condom," she breathed.

He swore and wrestled with one of the pockets of his pants.

Cat was barely breathing now, but the sound of foil tearing made her open her eyes. She watched him roll it down his thick length. Their gazes met as he fisted his erection, pumping it. His free hand closed over one of her breasts.

Cat used her legs to draw him back into position. "Now, Noah," she demanded. There was no time for teasing games. Just a desperate drive for release. He lined himself up, pressed gently, and Cat opened for him. "Jesus, Noah. Now!"

And then he was pushing his way into her body, stretching and sliding until he was fully surrounded by her.

Cat cried out. The shock of the pleasure, of the edge of pain from being so full. Roughly, Noah clapped a hand over her mouth.

This. This was how Cat wanted it. Wild and fast, unthinking.

Hand in place, Noah withdrew too slowly. She could feel every ridge, every vein of his dick as he left her body. She hooked her heels around his back and begged him to come back.

He slammed into her, hitting bottom. Cat felt her shoulders bite into the carpet.

"Yes," she hissed against his hand.

"Open your eyes, Cat," Noah commanded. No hint of the good-natured man now. Just a beast ready to lose himself in an ancient rhythm.

She did as she was told, fighting against the intimacy that connected them. He withdrew again, and just as Cat's breath hitched, he pushed back in, harder, faster. She couldn't tear her gaze away from his face. His jaw was set with tension, the hollows of his cheeks standing out. And the guttural grunts he released every time he bottomed out inside her had her tender muscles gripping his erection harder.

She was supposed to be in control here, setting the speed, demanding the wild. But she felt her tethers on him snapping, her control dissolving every time he slammed into her.

He pushed off with his feet, digging into the floor. She heard a crack, a thump, and she couldn't have cared less what had just smashed to the floor because Noah was fucking her hard enough that they were moving across the floor from kitchen to living room on the power of his thrusts alone.

"I want to feel you come on my cock, Cat," he told her. "I want to feel every squeeze of your tight, hot pussy until you make me come inside you."

Cat couldn't answer him. Couldn't process the filthy promises her mild-mannered, tightly wound Noah was making as he raked himself in and out of her. She was already near another release when he leaned down between their bodies and lapped at her breast.

She answered him the only way she could, by squeezing those secret muscles, clamping around him like a vise.

"Mmmm," he rasped. "I knew I'd love fucking you, Cat." Even as he spoke those harsh words, he threaded his fingers with hers and squeezed. Reassuring her, promising her they were in this together.

And it was that promise that triggered her building orgasm. In one glorious rush, Cat felt herself tense and close around him as Noah drove his cock into her and held. Her cry was muffled by his hand. Her fingers gripped his as he pulled out and rocked back into her, timing his thrusts with the powerful waves of her release.

"Oh my God," she chanted against his hand as her body trembled and shivered and sparkled through every detonation. "Noah." She repeated his name over and over again, and with one more hungry squeeze, she felt him stiffen and jerk inside her.

He released her mouth and blindly reached for her wrist. Pulling it to his mouth, Noah laid his lips over her tattoo as he came, and Cat felt her heart explode into a thousand shards.

He groaned, a gravel-laden gasp from the gut. Cat watched him, felt him as he came deep inside her, branding her, using her body to ride out every shuddering burst of his orgasm.

She didn't know if it was his pleasure-ravaged face or the feel of his cock throbbing in her as it emptied itself into her, but she came again, a softer, more delicate climax that warmed every cell in her body. It felt like coming home.

CHAPTER
31

"Are you alive?" Cat prodded Noah in the shoulder. She wasn't sure how long they'd lain like this, tangled together in a heap on the floor. Frankly, she wasn't sure what year it was. She couldn't even scroll back through her memory banks to compare any of her earlier sexual escapades to what clearly was the mamma jamma of all orgasmic experiences.

Her body was loose and lazy, her mind virtually blank. Cat was left with only two coherent thoughts:

First, Noah Yates was the king of orgasms.

Second, her dining room table was broken.

One of them, in the throes of passion, had kicked the leg and dislodged it from the table, which now leaned precariously without the support.

Noah stirred and shifted the weight that was holding her fast to the floor.

"Mmm?"

Cat poked him in the ribs. "Hello?"

"Think I'm in a sex coma," Noah muttered against her shoulder.

A sex coma. That was about as perfect a description as possible for their current scenario. Her heart rate had yet to return to normal, still revved from the adrenaline and perhaps from the swirl of fear he'd stirred in her.

Cat liked it fast, fun. No time to think or linger. But he'd taken her beyond that. He'd taken her to a space where all she could do was feel. And the tenderness with which he stared into her eyes, her soul? It was enough to stir some anxiety.

Noah was complicated. He was a father, a reluctant part of the show, and he made her feel things she wasn't interested in feeling. Cat wasn't willing to make room for complicated. Noah was a long-term monogamous guy. He studied risk and chose the safest route. He'd expect a relationship. A real one. Not just a "Hey, I'm in town" booty text.

Noah needed someone who'd be home every day by 5:05 p.m. Someone who would be around on the weekends. Someone to go to the movies with on a Wednesday.

But Cat loved her life, ridiculous schedule and all. She loved the business, the importance and necessity of what she was doing. She loved not having to check in with someone if she was running late. If she wanted to spend an extra weekend on a shoot, she didn't have to confer with anyone else's schedule. She enjoyed the jet-setting life, the frantic rush, the intense time frames of television. Didn't she?

God, a handful of orgasms, and she was already anticipating a marriage proposal from the man. She was short on sleep and brain cells. *Could sex kill brain cells?*

Cat scrambled for an excuse to send him home, to give

herself a little distance to find her balance. But the sex coma left her brain mushy.

"Want some water?" Noah murmured, lips brushing the tender skin of her neck.

"Yeah," she croaked. Anything to get his hot skin off hers.

Noah pushed himself up, and Cat pretended not to notice the bulge of biceps, the ridges of abs. Stripping off the pants bunched around his feet, Noah padded naked to her minuscule kitchen and opened the fridge. "Jesus, Cat," he called. "You've got three bottles of water, half a green juice, and some wilted lettuce in here. How do you survive?"

"I do just fine. Water me," she ordered, working her way into a sitting position. She grabbed a shirt off the floor and dragged it on over her head. If she wasn't naked, there wouldn't be a reason for him to stick around. She stumbled to the couch and flopped down on the cushion.

His ass is a fine specimen of male asses, she thought, cocking her head to admire its firm symmetry. She'd admired it before in Dockers and jeans, but it was even more spectacular without any adornments.

"Do you work out?" she asked before her brain caught up with her mouth.

Noah returned to her, water bottles in hand, and gracefully sank onto the cushion next to her. He opened a bottle and handed it to her. "I go to the gym," he said, guzzling his own water.

"It shows," Cat said, letting her gaze appreciatively wander the rest of his body. She liked that he was confident enough to not immediately reach for his pants in the corner or his underwear, wherever the hell they were.

"We're making small talk now?" Noah asked, eyeing her. "After that?"

Cat felt embarrassed over her embarrassment. He had her off-kilter. It reminded her of when she and Gannon were kids playing baseball in the neighborhood. In their infinite nine-year-old wisdom, they'd put their foreheads on the end of the bat and spun and spun until they couldn't run a straight line.

That was how she felt now. Dizzy and giddy and not completely in control.

"An observation isn't small talk," Cat argued.

"Hmm," Noah responded. He was watching her with something warm, something possessive in those sharp green eyes. His hair was a mess from her demanding fingers pulling on it. He looked so relaxed, so happy and confident. All Cat wanted to do was curl up in his lap and fall asleep. But that wasn't how she rolled. Not even close.

"Well, I've got an early morning," she began.

"Ask me to stay, Cat." He gave the order calmly, quietly.

She blinked, opened her mouth to argue. But her body didn't want her to argue. Her body wanted to curl up next to Noah's heat, wanted to wake up to that soft look and those strong hands.

But damn it, her body also wanted pizza and a Jack and Coke and deep-fried Snickers. Her body did not rule her mind.

"Stay with me. Please." The words were out of her mouth before she could corral her traitorous urges.

He pulled her back against him, his lean, hard body cradling hers. Cat resisted the urge to relax, but his heat and the gentle stroke of his hand over the curve of her hip were impossible to fight.

"I have questions," she said into the dark.

"Okay," Noah sighed indulgently into her hair. "Fire away."

"Your mother. Why is she...the way she is? And why is the Christmas Festival so important to you personally?"

He took another breath, let it out slowly as if he were carefully choosing his words. "My dad was an alcoholic gambler. But I didn't know that until years later. All I knew when I was five or six was that he scared me. There was never enough food. Never any money. The house was never warm enough in the winter. My mother was never happy. They fought a lot at night. He'd disappear for days at a time."

Cat sat up to look at him. This was not what she'd expected.

Noah swallowed hard and then gave a wry smile.

"One day, he was supposed to be watching me while my mom went to the grocery store. He thought I was making too much noise. So he...he, uh, locked me in the basement. When my mother came home, he was passed out drunk, and she thought I'd wandered away. The cops were called, but it took a while before they finally found me."

"How long were you down there?" Cat asked quietly.

"Six hours." There was no amusement in Noah's dry laugh.

She reached out and interlaced her fingers with his. Just a touch. A friendly reminder that the past was where it should be. Far, far behind him.

Cat swore under her breath. "You could have just said 'none of your business, nosy.'"

He gave her a crooked grin and adjusted his glasses. "After what we just experienced right there," he said, pointing to the floor, "you want to start drawing boundaries?"

"I don't want you to feel obligated to tell me...anything," Cat began. "It's just—I mean I know it has to be hard for you, and we didn't exactly get off to the best start."

"I think we've more than made up for that," Noah countered. "I guess I just want you to know. That's why the festival is so important to me. Cat, that was the only time of year I could really escape. When that tree was lit the day after

232

Thanksgiving every year, when the whole town was decked out in lights and tinsel, I had a place to go every day after school besides home. I helped out wherever I could just so I wouldn't have to go home. And the people of Merry let me. I manned the hot chocolate stand. I swept sidewalks. I wrapped gifts. They fed me, paid me. Even when they didn't have to."

He cleared his throat, his voice thick with emotion. "I went to every tree lighting. Ada Romanski—she was the last city manager—she'd give a little speech and then push the button that lit the tree, and I thought it was the coolest job in the world. I wanted that job. Sometimes in the summer when my parents were fighting or when there wasn't enough to eat, I'd go to bed, and I'd dream about those lights."

Cat blinked back a hot rush of tears. "Jesus," she breathed. "Is your dad still alive? Because I'm all for driving to his shithole apartment—because I know an asshole like that doesn't have a house—and kicking his ass."

"He left when I was a teenager. Went to work and just never came back. It was a relief to me at first. He wasn't around to tell me what a disappointment I was or how pathetic I was. But then reality set in. Mom didn't work, never had. And we went from barely scraping by to heads underwater."

Cat squeezed his hand, her heart breaking to bits over the little boy who dreamed of Christmas lights.

"The only things I had in those days were school and the Christmas Festival. Two bright, shiny things that I could hang on to to get me through the rest of it. The fights, the never having enough, the never being good enough. So I worked hard, got some scholarships, and decided I'd spend my life giving back to the town that had given me so much. And my mother? By the time he left, there wasn't much left of her. She moved, a couple miles outside town. Neither one of us could stand the sight of that house anymore. But she just gave up a long time ago."

Cat dropped her head back and stared up at the ceiling. "Noah, this explains so much."

"Like what?"

"You're not an asshole. You're scarred."

"I'm not scarred," he argued. "It was decades ago. I'm over it. I should be over it."

Cat cupped his chin with her free hand. "Listen to me. There's a difference between being scarred and being a victim. You took what was a terrible childhood, and you made sure your daughter would never feel any of those things. She'd never be hungry or cold or scared."

"A lot of good it did her. She wants to be a celebrity and have pink hair. Next, she's going to be telling me she doesn't want to go to college."

She gave his grizzled chin an affectionate squeeze. "Stop. You didn't have control when you were a kid. Your parents weren't responsible enough to provide the stability and security you needed to feel safe. It's why you're Mr. No now. Why you were such a dick about the show."

"I wouldn't say I was a dick—"

"Totally a dick."

"Fine. I was a dick," he conceded. "I just… Things need to be safe, tidy, secure. I'm in charge of the livelihood of this town, and I take that very seriously. I don't want to let anyone down or make a bad decision that would hurt people."

"So you play it safe," Cat said, filling in the blank.

"Sometimes maybe a little too safe," he admitted. He picked up her hand and traced the tattoo with the tip of his finger. "I'm unnaturally good at assessing risks. And you're a huge one."

She grinned. "How am I risky? I'm light, I'm fun, I don't require constant care and attention."

"Oh, you're risky. I could fall for you, and you could just walk out of my life onto the next job, the next guy, the next adventure. And I'd just be left remembering."

———

Cat woke with his sleep-hardened cock buried at the base of her spine. Even in his sleep, Noah was shifting against her, greedy for more friction.

Her body felt sore and well used from last night, and yet… there was a sharp yearning for *more*. She'd thought getting it out of their system at least once would dull the need she felt. But now she feared she may have only awoken the dragon. The intimacy? That was too much. But the outcome. Dear, sweet baby Jesus, she'd never experienced anything like that in her entire sexual history.

It was ironic to get to thirty-two only to realize how sorely she'd been deprived. She wanted more. More of his rough words, more of his body worshipping her own. More of that edge of pain mixed with a pleasure that threatened to drown her. And yet her heart ached for him, for that little boy hungry for love and safety. She'd misjudged him on so many levels.

His arm was thrown over her waist, hand gripping her breast. She felt her nipple pebble against his palm, seeking, needing. Noah flexed against her ass again, and Cat felt a shiver of desire snake through her.

She closed a hand over his as it gripped her breast and kneaded.

"Mmm," he murmured against her hair. She waited for him to wake and was rewarded with a more conscious thrust at her back.

Cat reached behind her between their bodies and trailed her fingers over his hard-on. He pulled his hips back, giving her room to wrap her hand around him. One pump of her tight hand was all it took to feel moisture pooling at his tip.

She heard the sigh resonate in his chest, and his cock twitched in her hand. He was beyond ready for her. But she wasn't ready for the intimacy, the rawness they'd shared last night. It felt too…serious. Too intense. She wanted to show Noah fun, not turn him into a sex slave soul mate.

Cat rolled onto her stomach, knees pushing her ass in the air. It was all the invitation Noah needed.

"Condom," he demanded in a sleep-roughened voice.

She pointed to the nightstand, and he ripped the drawer off its tracks in his hurry.

Like a Pavlovian experiment, Cat felt herself go wet at the sound of the foil between his very capable fingers. There'd be no finesse here, just a sleepy morning fuck that woke and warmed their bodies. No staring into each other's eyes and guessing the other's secrets. No unsettling yearnings for something so much more.

Cat buried her face in her pillow when Noah notched himself into place. He stayed there for just a moment, one inch inside her, igniting a fire that threatened to burn them both to the ground. Smoothing his hands up her back and around her sides, he leaned forward just slightly to cup her breasts and slide another inch deeper into her.

She could barely hold back the cry. It wasn't deep enough. She wasn't full enough. She was desperate for it. For him.

She flexed her hips backward against him, and he allowed her another inch. Cat took a shaky breath. Her fingers held the sheets in a death grip. Noah stroked up her spine and back down, a gentle yet stirring touch. Everywhere he touched her,

her skin felt a thousand degrees warmer. Her ass cheeks, the backs of her thighs, her spine, and now her breasts again. He kneaded them with his firm fingers and without warning used his grip to yank her backward onto his cock.

Cat cried out into the pillow. Her muscles were already dancing and sparking with an impossibly swift build toward orgasm.

"Damn it, baby. You're so wet," he groaned, fingers flexing into her soft flesh. "I haven't even touched you yet."

Noah took his time sliding out of her, and Cat immediately felt bereft, empty. When he sank into her again, she could feel his body coiling against hers. The need that she was fighting was present in him too. Instinct was driving them in one direction and one direction only. *Fulfillment.*

He started a leisurely pace that had Cat writhing against him, needing more. This slow, sweet slide of his body against hers, the gentle stroke of his hands, were doing things to her heart. She felt warm, open, worshipped.

He was making this too serious, too intense.

Cat pressed herself up onto her hands and flipped her hair. She stared at him over her shoulder. She caught his eye and gave him a dirty grin. "Fuck me, Noah."

The second those words were out of her mouth, Noah clamped his hands on her hips and drove into her like a man on a mission. Stroking in and out of her, his measured pace tripped and then stumbled into brutal speed. Mindless with it, Cat curved her spine to change the angle.

"God, yes," she murmured.

His fingers dug in, bruising the soft flesh at her hips, but Cat didn't care. She wanted more of those soft grunts that were spilling from him. Wanted the stab of his fingers. Wanted the feeling of being impaled as he bottomed out inside her.

Harder and harder he thrust into her, his hips pistoning against her. He held her in place with hard hands.

Her breasts swayed with the thrusts, nipples dragging across the soft sheets and sparking her arousal.

She was mumbling nonsense. Begging for what they both knew he'd deliver.

"I want to come, Noah." She shouted the request.

He shoved her shoulders down so only her ass was in the air and then slid his hands down to tug at her nipples.

"Touch yourself, Cat. Come on me. Make me feel it."

His fingers pulled on nipples in a concerted rhythm like twin mouths. Cat slid her hand between her legs where their bodies joined.

Nothing mattered. Not time, not call sheets, not even Christmas. Just this.

Cat was an expert on her body. She knew just what pressure was needed. She used her fingers to rub and stroke her way to the top.

"Noah," she gasped.

"I feel you, baby. Let it go. Need to feel you—"

The first delicious squeeze of her orgasm cut him off. Noah gritted out a sound of pleasure as Cat closed around him.

"Fuck, baby. Yes."

His fingers never stopped their pulls at her nipples, and Cat felt her body slide into heaven between the strokes of his cock inside her and the tugs at her breasts. She closed over him again and again, riding out a blissful, soul-shattering release that left her weak-kneed and shaking.

She heard him, the guttural grunt of the build to his own climax.

"Come on me," she heard herself say.

She didn't need to say it twice. Noah was pulling out of

her and dragging off the condom. Cat reached between her legs to cup his balls and peered over her shoulder. She didn't want to miss a second of this fantasy she'd had for a straight month.

He fisted his cock, primed it once, and growled.

"Come for me, Noah," Cat instructed.

He stared into her eyes, a madman out of control, as he dragged his hand down the length of his shaft.

"Faster," Cat whispered, enthralled.

Noah obeyed, never breaking eye contact. The grip on his cock looked almost painful. Cat forgot for a moment that she had the soft cushion of his balls in her palm. Remembering, she tugged them down, palming them.

Noah's nostrils flared, his green eyes hooded. Cat suddenly felt the sensation that she was his prey, not his tormentor.

"Harder, Noah." She squeezed his balls, hard, saw the wince, but his hand sped up, jacking his erection harder, faster, until his jaw locked tight and his breath stopped. Then suddenly his free hand was between her legs, fingers pressing on her clit, dancing over its slick surface.

Cat cried out as the sneaky bastard shoved her into another orgasm. She felt the first hot rope of his release land on her back, dripping down the curve of her ass. Cat forced her eyes open to watch as they came together. She felt imprinted, branded, engraved, as Noah grunted softly at each pump of his fist. Cat sobbed her way through the orgasm that wrung her out, destroying her ability to think.

CHAPTER
32

Noah practically floated from his desk to the ancient coffee maker in his office. He actually had to look down to make sure his feet were touching the ground…and not tripping over rain-catching Christmas tins. There they were, rooted to the creaky hardwood floor in his sensible brown loafers. His entire body felt lighter as if, through some sort of new age orgasm therapy, Cat had somehow burned off the mists dragging at him for the past several decades.

Last night had been…magical. And then this morning was dark magic.

He sat back down, forgetting to pour himself a cup of coffee. He'd never in his life felt this kind of satisfaction after sex. Sure, he'd enjoyed his short list of partners, and he was fairly certain they'd enjoyed themselves. But last night? Nothing held a candle to Cat underneath him screaming his name, her teeth biting into his palm.

"Whoa. Down, boy," he cautioned himself as he felt his cock stirring. That particular body part should be comatose right now. Yet just a second of reminiscing brought it stirring back to life. Such was the spell Catalina King had cast on him.

He glanced down at his empty mug and stood back up, returning to the coffee maker. He felt like he owed Cat a gift of gratitude. Not anything that would make her feel like a prostitute taking payment for sexual favors. But something sincere, thoughtful.

He poured and sat, frowning at his email inbox that was filled to the brim.

Flowers seemed too...predictable. Too presumptuous. They hadn't discussed whether this would happen again. Whether they were seeing each other. Noah frowned fiercely at his coffee. They also hadn't discussed whether this was monogamous or not. As much fun as he was having letting her shove him outside his comfort zone, he wasn't about to share her. And if that was what she wanted, well, it was a deal breaker.

Noah mentally kicked himself. One night—and early morning—of sex, and he was fantasizing about a relationship. He needed to calm the hell down. They had time to figure out if there was groundwork for a future.

He sipped his coffee and smiled at absolutely nothing. His jaw was starting to hurt from beaming. Carolanne had stared at him suspiciously until he sent her out to the post office just so he could bask alone.

Drumming his fingers on the desk, Noah decided he'd text Henry. Who better to know the way to Cat's heart than her assistant?

Noah: Got any ideas for gifts for your boss?

The response came swiftly, as Noah knew it would. Henry's phone was never out of his hand.

Henry: What kind of gift? Sorry for revoking your building permits gift? Thanks for rebuilding my town gift?
Noah: Something more...personal.

He could practically hear Henry's gleeful laughter.

Henry: I wondered why she was smiling so much today. Starting to freak me out.

Crap. He may have just opened a can of gossip worms on set.

Noah: I'm not confirming or denying anything that she wouldn't want anyone else to know.
Henry: I'm a vault, my friend. Let's meet for lunch and we'll chat.

With a hopeful heart, Noah turned his attention to his inbox and began working his way cheerfully through his never-ending to-do list.

———

Noah felt like he was back at the scene of the crime when Henry let him into Cat's trailer.

"Like I said, man, Cat's a practical woman," Henry explained. "She's not really the wine and roses type. If you can find a way to be useful to her? That's the best way to get to her."

Noah looked around the living space. It was still crowded with papers and electronic devices that she'd been in the middle of before he'd interrupted her with his libido the night before. The sad Christmas tree in the corner blinked on and off.

"She a fan of Christmas?" Noah asked, jutting his chin toward the tree.

"Oh yeah. Huge fan. That's why she was so keen on Merry in the first place."

Noah nodded and filed the information away.

"Whoa. What happened here?" Henry asked, eyeing the broken leg of the dining table.

Noah turned his back on Henry so he wouldn't see the guilt on his face.

He opened the refrigerator and found it bare except for the wilted lettuce he'd noticed last night. "Not very well-stocked."

"She tries to eat well on the road, so it's usually to-go salads or craft service stuff," Henry explained.

They wandered down the skinny hallway to the bedroom. Noah hadn't noticed the dirty clothes in piles around the bed last night or this morning. He'd been too busy being balls deep in heaven.

Henry wrinkled his nose and picked up a tank top that was draped over a cabinet door and tossed it into a pile of like clothes.

Cat must have left in a hurry this morning, Noah noted. The bed looked as if a sex tornado had whirled through. And there were two distinct head dents in the pillow.

Henry cleared his throat. "Looks like *someone* had some fun last night."

"Yeah, uh, thanks for giving me some ideas," Noah announced, suddenly in a hurry to get away from the all-knowing Henry. He wasn't by any means ready to have a conversation about what had happened last night. At least not without talking to Cat about how seriously he was taking it.

He'd trusted her enough with his story, one that was widely known around town but never discussed. Sara had no idea who her grandfather was or what kind of childhood Noah had. cat had listened and been angry for him. And it felt like there was something more there than just sexual attraction. Whatever it was, he wanted more.

She dazzled him. She made him *feel*. Made him want to walk away from steady, from secure, and play on the wild side.

This was his shot at some temporary but memorable-for-the-rest-of-his-life fun. He was throwing his hat into the ring to claim the rest of her time here in Merry. He just hoped Cat wouldn't kick his ass for it.

CHAPTER
33

Cat's attention was wrested back to the present by Paige's whistle. "Welcome back," Paige said. "Where'd you go?"

"Huh?" Cat mumbled, searching the recesses of her mind for a plausible lie. It was the third time in this shoot that she'd spaced out.

"You okay?" Drake asked. He'd been feeding her the same line for ten minutes now inside Reggie's nearly completed diner, and Cat just couldn't get the response right. It was like their roles were reversed.

Cat rolled her shoulders and dragged her mind out of her bed, where Noah had ranged over her and driven her to madness. She slapped a smile on her face. "Just didn't get enough coffee this morning." Lies. She'd had three cups so far. Nothing was dragging her mind away from last night…and this morning.

She felt like she was reliving some life-altering experience, and that terrified her down to her pretty pink toenails. Fun. *It was supposed to be fun.*

"Can someone get Cat a coffee so we can wrap this before midnight?" Paige called into her headset.

An espresso magically appeared in front of her moments later, and Cat took a swig.

"Sorry, guys. I'm good. I swear. Where were we?"

"Drake is explaining to you why he chose stainless steel for the diner counter and the backsplash," Paige reminded her, settling back in her chair behind the camera.

"Right, right. Okay. I'm good."

"Rolling."

They started over from the mark, and this time Cat nailed the required interest in Drake's explanation. It was a bit of TV magic. Drake hadn't picked the counters. Cat had. But it would be more entertaining for the viewers if they split up the projects and ribbed each other along the way. Drake was used to having a team of high-end designers on hand to help shape projects on his show. Cat, on the other hand, was a veritable control freak. Her vision was law. It required an exhausting amount of prep and research before shooting started, but until someone else proved they could do it better, Cat was happy to hang on to the responsibility.

Reggie's diner was coming together in a wild melding of traditional diner architecture and Jamaican flavor. She'd kept things simple and modern with the stainless counter and open kitchen. Part of the charm of Reggie's was listening to the reggae that blared from his radio by the grill and hearing the waitresses shout at the cooks. The booths and stools were new and boasted turquoise cushions. She'd squeezed in one extra table and two stools at the counter. Room for more paying customers.

The second register and sales system were cordoned off in

the old storage corner. The metal exterior had held up well to the mud and water, but the innards had been a disaster. New black-and-white-checkered flooring had gone down two days ago, and the tile workers were finishing the wall the booths butted against.

They'd brought in a Jamaican-born mural artist to paint the far wall. A Caribbean beach scene with palm trees and hammocks. Cat could almost hear the steel drum band. Back in the kitchen, she'd reorganized the storage and given Reggie all new appliances. The reveal was being shot this afternoon, and tomorrow they'd shoot the reopening. Postproduction would have one hell of a time cobbling together an entire episode in such a short time, but the story editor had been dictator-ish about sequences, so it was still doable.

Next on deck was Mrs. Pringle's house and the Hais'. Cat had a few furniture pieces and knickknacks she needed for both projects. She'd need to carve out some time to shop. Maybe she could take a crew with her and head to one of Merry's antique shops?

Maybe Noah would like to go with her. They could grab dinner—

"Fuck," Cat muttered.

Paige pulled off her headset. "Cut."

"Shit. Sorry, Paige," Cat said, scrubbing a hand over her face and immediately smudging her makeup. "Dang it!"

"Makeup!" Paige yelled. She levered herself out of her chair and latched on to Cat's arm. "How about we have a little chat for a minute. Take five!"

In all their years of working together, Paige had rarely had to remind Cat to keep it together on camera. Only during her post-birthday hangovers was that order necessary, because otherwise, Cat was a consummate professional. Or she had been until she'd consummated the hell out of Noah.

"What is going on in that brain?" Paige demanded when they stepped out the front door.

Cat looked at the anxious crowd who were hoping for a glimpse inside and dragged Paige down the block. "I did something stupid last night."

"Did you kill someone? Oh God! It's not Noah, is it? I'd feel bad about helping you hide his body. I thought you two were getting along after the whole Thanksgiving thing."

"Where do you get these ideas?" Cat grumbled.

"Is Noah alive or dead?" Paige pressed.

"Alive. At least he was when I kicked him out of my bed this morning."

"What was he doing in your—oh. Oh!"

Paige gaped at her like a betta fish in a new bowl, unsure of her new environment.

"Yeah. *Oh*." Cat shoved her hands into the pockets of her cargo pants. She'd left her coat inside and hunched her shoulders against the winter wind.

She glanced around. Christmas was slowly maneuvering its way down Main Street. With the Rudolph lights mounted on the streetlamps, businesses had begun decking their own halls with festive window displays, Christmas lights, and greenery.

It was taking shape, at least on the outside. The snow certainly helped the holiday look. They'd shoot the window painting contest this weekend and would host a ceremony mainly for the cameras, but with a little luck, they could pull in some vendors and sponsors and turn it into a shoppers' night and pre-festival celebration.

"Done processing?" Cat asked, kicking at a seam in the sidewalk.

"Almost." Paige nodded. "Almost. Okay, I'm there. You slept with Noah. Okay. So what does that mean?"

Cat gave a surly shrug. "Why does it have to mean anything? I mean, we had sex. It was great. End of story."

"Is it?" Paige asked pointedly.

"Well, I mean, I wouldn't be opposed to getting naked with him again," Cat said, still not willing to make eye contact. Paige would take one look at her and *know*. This didn't feel like just a quick, fun fling like she'd enjoyed before. No, this felt more important. Scarier.

"So the sex was adequate?" Paige prodded.

"Adequate times a million." Okay, maybe Cat could brag just a little without letting Paige know how terrified she'd been of losing her soul to Noah Yates as he whispered dirty little secrets into her ear while he moved in her.

"So good then?"

Cat dragged her hands through her hair, instantly ruining the "effortless" tail the stylist had spent thirty minutes on that morning. "Like so much better than good I can't even find the words."

"Oooooh." Paige dragged out the syllable in understanding.

"Yeah. That's why my head is…" Cat gestured into the distance. "I'm orgasm drunk."

Paige nodded approvingly. "Nice job, Noah."

"Oh my God. You have no idea."

"I probably do, but since my husband is your brother, you don't want the details. By the way, Gannon is insanely insatiable in bed."

"Gross. So what do I do now? How do I go back to being normal?" Cat asked. She needed sister-in-law wisdom and needed it stat.

"Are you going to get orgasm drunk with him again?" Paige asked.

Cat brought her shoulders to her ears. "I don't know!

I mean, we're in town, and there's not much else to do at night…but is he really the fling kind of guy? I mean, he's got a daughter, and what if it gets out around town that we're… uh…banging? Like is Sara going to be embarrassed and grossed out? Are people going to think he's an idiot for rolling around naked with me since we all know it can't last?" She saw the thought flash through Paige's blue eyes and held up a hand. "Uh-uh. It can't work," Cat said firmly. "I'm not getting in a long-distance relationship at this point in my life. Noah's entire life is here, and asking him and Sara and, hell, Mellody and her future husband because they're a co-parenting unit to give all that up and move to New York or better yet follow me around the country? Stupid and not happening."

"And staying here isn't an option?"

"I have a school to build, a show to host, a life too big for Merry. Besides, aren't I supposed to be fake dating Drake for ratings?"

"Oh please. Don't pull that crap with me." Paige gave her the stop-throwing-your-peas-on-the-floor look that Cat had seen her give Gabby only yesterday. "You really think that I would force you to fake a relationship? Have you completely forgotten the disaster on *Kings* when they started miking me and making Gannon and I look all hot and heavy for each other?"

"You *were* hot and heavy for each other," Cat pointed out.

"You know I would never ask you to fake a relationship. If you choose to, that's fine, but don't use that as an excuse to hide from your feelings for Noah."

"Who says I have feelings?"

"The fact that we're having this conversation!"

"Fair enough." Cat was yelling. "So what do I do? Give me some married lady, smart woman wisdom here."

"I guess you find out if Noah's okay with some short-term naked fun and go from there," Paige suggested.

Cat nodded. "Good idea. That I can work with. How do I find that out?"

Paige laughed. "When's the last time you were in a relationship?"

"I don't know. I guess Drake?"

Paige scoffed. "Please, that was just a two-month-long booty call. There was no relationship there."

Cat frowned and dug her way back through her sexual history. "I guess it was Miguel?"

Paige frowned. "I don't remember him."

"That's because I dated him my senior year of high school. He took me to prom. I gave him his first blow job." Cat smiled fondly at the memory.

"You're a piece of work." Paige shook her head.

"My blow jobs are masterpieces," Cat insisted.

"You're thirty-how-old, and you've never been in a relationship?"

"Do I look like I would even want to make the time?" Cat argued. "I love my life just as it is."

"Then maybe you should let Noah walk away unscathed from this," Paige suggested. "He's divorced. You already know he does the relationship thing. What if he gets attached and then we pack up and drive on back to the city?"

"Noah isn't some sad puppy who'd run after my truck as I leave town," Cat insisted. She rubbed a hand over her heart, which had inexplicably started to ache. She'd felt it, that connection between them. It was why she tried to make their second time more impersonal, but she'd fucked that up too. Watching him over her shoulder. She'd felt their connection in her blood when they came together. It wasn't just another fling. But it couldn't be a relationship.

251

CHAPTER
34

Cat let herself into her trailer and face-planted on the couch. The long days of filming hadn't always bothered her, certainly not when the ratings for the first two episodes were sky-high. But this show was more hands-on than most, and the lack of sleep from the night before caught up with her by noon. She'd had a ridiculous amount of caffeine that had decided to abandon her system all at once, leaving her weak and shaky.

It was the only explanation for how filming with Reggie had gone.

Reggie's reveal had gone well. The man had cried standing in the middle of his kitchen, clutching the new spatula Cat had engraved with the Jamaican flag.

Then of course, Cat had cried. Something she rarely did on camera. Drake was already gracefully swiping errant tears from his gorgeous cheekbones, something both the female and gay viewership would swoon over when the show aired.

But no one needed to see her wipe snot on her sleeve every ten seconds. Cat chalked it up to the lack of sleep and the rawness she still felt. Noah had done something to her. He'd stripped her bare with a wild tenderness that she'd never known, never expected. And now her soul was just a little rough around the edges from it.

He'd texted her twice today. Sweet little messages.

Noah: Thinking about you and smiling like an idiot.
Noah: I have rug burn on my knees. I'll treasure it until it scabs off and leaves gross scars.

She'd read them and smiled. But she hadn't responded. She didn't want to set a precedent there. Didn't want him to start thinking of this...whatever it was as a relationship.

She sniffed the cushion under her face, wondering what the clean, pine scent was. It sure as hell wasn't her. After the diner shoot, she'd hopped in with a paint crew at the Hai house and then driven thirty miles to a welder's shop for her top secret special project that was going to be even better than she'd hoped.

She needed a shower and dinner, which she'd forgotten to ask Henry to order.

Ugh. Maybe she'd just skip it. Maybe she'd just go to bed, catch up on the sleep she'd missed, and start fresh and focused tomorrow.

But that fresh pine scent teased her until she picked her face up off the cushion. Her sad little fiber optic Christmas tree had been replaced with a live one, decked with lights. There were three boxes of ornaments—silly reindeer and snowmen—stacked up under the tree.

She frowned at the five feet of tree, its colorful lights

glowing cheerfully in the corner. There was an envelope stashed in the branches. She rose, plucked it from the tree.

To keep you in the Christmas mood.

Noah

She fought against the flutter in her stomach at his handwriting. Noah had gotten her a real live Christmas tree.

Cat glanced around the rest of the living space. It was neater than usual. She didn't let Henry fuss with her private space. He had enough on his plate, and everything about Cat's life was temporary enough that a little mess didn't drive her too batty.

But things had definitely been picked up, rearranged. Pillows were fluffed. Her blanket was folded. And the dining room table had been repaired.

Cat stalked into the kitchen, flustered. One night of stellar orgasms, and the man thought he had the right to paw through her personal things? She yanked open the refrigerator door, desperate for water or wine.

It was stocked. Salad fixings, cold grilled chicken, neat containers of black beans and vegetables. Everything she'd need for chicken salads. There were a dozen bottles of water neatly lining the top shelf. She grabbed the first one and the note stuck to it.

To keep your energy up.

Noah

Damn it! Cat wrenched open the bottle of water and drank deeply. She could have stocked her own fridge if she wanted to. Or at least had Henry do it. She didn't need a keeper.

The bedroom smelled of fresh linens, and there was a week's worth of clean laundry neatly folded on top of her precisely made bed. The man had stolen and washed her dirty underwear. It should have creeped her out. But the practicality of it made her heart soften, just a little. She had clean jeans to wear tomorrow, dinner tonight, and Noah had left a goddamn chocolate heart with another note on her pillow.

I have Sara tonight, but I wanted you to know I'm still thinking about last night.

Noah

Cat rubbed absently at the ache in her chest. He wasn't making it easy to keep things simple, uncomplicated. And she had no idea how to handle it. Could she just avoid him until the end of the shoot?

She wandered back out to the living area, weighing her options, and spotted them. The papers she'd scattered near and far. Every application in her school location search. She'd been knee-deep in applicants when Noah had come not knocking last night.

Those dozens of applications were now in a neat, thick stack with a slew of color-coded sticky notes. Curious, she picked them up.

Population too small.
    Geography a hindrance.
    Employment rate high. Good for them, but not a good fit.

Baffled, Cat flopped down on the couch, clutching the paperwork. She'd been trying to make the same assessments for a week. And Noah just breezed into her personal space and helped himself?

She glanced at the handwritten note paper-clipped to the top of the stack.

Cat,

After a cursory glance, I don't think any of these applicants are ideal for what you have planned. Just my two cents. And if you want my opinion—which you haven't asked for—I'd recommend that you keep looking. The right location is out there.

Noah

It was the same conclusion she'd been dancing around last night. Either the physical location wasn't right, zoning laws were too strict, or the local economy was already more than stable. She wanted to bring this school to a community that needed it, that would embrace it. But at least it was a start. She still had another month before the application process expired. She'd find it.

She traced a finger over Noah's hastily scrawled signature and, with a sigh, pulled out her phone. She snapped a picture of the stack of papers, the Christmas tree in the background.

Cat: I see I had a helpful elf here today.

When he didn't respond immediately, Cat opened the boxes of ornaments. She took her time, hanging them in a pattern for best coverage. And while she did, she wondered how Noah knew she'd want to decorate the tree herself.

Her phone buzzed from the couch cushion.

Noah: Santa and his elves work twenty-four seven in Merry this time of year.

Cat smiled despite herself. The man had gone out and figured out how to do the nicest thing possible: save her time.

Cat: Well, please tell them I appreciate it.

Noah responded with a picture of his rug burn on one knee.

Noah: Not as much as I do.

She laughed and before she could think better of it, shucked off her shirt. She'd earned her own rug burn on her lower back over her hip bones. She snapped the picture over her shoulder and fired it off to him.

Noah: You're literally killing me. How am I supposed to focus on Sara's essay on M. C. Escher now?
Cat: From what I can recall, you're quite attentive. I'm sure you won't have any problems.
Noah: The Hais are moving back into their house this week.
Cat: I'm aware.

They'd film for a day at the Hais. It would air as the next-to-last episode of the show.

Noah: They're spending the weekend with Jasper's parents, and Sara stays with her mom...

Cat paused and chewed on her lip.

Cat: Is that so?

Noah: How would you feel about spending the night here? With me. My shower is bigger than yours. And my couch is bigger than the Barbie furniture in your trailer.

Cat: Tempting.

It was. *He* was. And she wasn't sure how she felt about that.

CHAPTER
35

Three weeks to Christmas Eve

It was after ten when Cat slipped onto Noah's porch under the cover of shadows and knocked softly. She leaned against the clapboard siding and stared out at the darkened neighborhood. They had three weeks before Christmas Eve. Three episodes had already aired, and people were talking about the show and not just speculating about her and Drake now. Best of all, a few more advertisers were on board. And she was riding the fine line between adrenaline and exhaustion.

The applications for the school were trickling in, still without a standout location. And with the grant money burning a hole, Cat was anxious to give the project her full focus. But that meant leaving Merry. Leaving Noah.

The door opened, and there he was. Hair disheveled, worn college T-shirt, and bare feet sticking out of those easy access sweatpants she found so sexy. He shoved his glasses back up the bridge of his nose and grinned at her.

Cat forgot all about her exhaustion and pushed him backward into the house, hands flat on his chest. Noah pulled her into his arms, spinning them, and kicked the door closed. One-handed, he flipped the dead bolt.

"Bed?" she breathed when his mouth closed over hers.

She was already revved, ready for him. "I'm two floors up," Noah said, biting at her lower lip.

"Couch first then," Cat said, slipping her fingers into the stretchy waistband of his pants and pulling him toward the family room.

It was much the same as the last time she'd seen it except there was a fat tree crammed into the corner. It was covered in a hodgepodge of handmade ornaments, obviously family favorites, and glass bulbs. There was a lopsided plastic star perched atop the tree. A trio of candles blazed in the front window. Homey. Cozy.

"Boots. Pants. Lose 'em," Noah ordered, his mouth busying itself against hers, his tongue a tempting devil that swept between her lips to taste her.

Cat heeled off her work boots, letting them land with twin *thunks* on the living room rug. Noah was too impatient to wait for Cat to get to her jeans and helped himself to her button and zipper. The denim bunched and slid down her legs until she was free.

Cat backed Noah up to the worn, comfortable couch, pressing him down.

"Do you want a drink?" he asked as he freed her from her coat and pulled her down to straddle him.

She swiped the hat off her head and threw it into a dark corner of the room. "Sure. After."

His fingers opened her fleece vest and slid it from her shoulders. "How many damn layers?" he murmured as Cat shoved her hands into his hair.

Cat kissed him hard. "Three more." She shucked the thermal shirt off over her head, leaving him to stroke over the silky fabric of her tank top. "Two more," she whispered.

Noah slid his hands under the hem and skimmed upward, drawing the tank with him.

"Last one," she promised.

He yanked at her bra, a simple sports design, and unceremoniously discarded it.

He paused for a breath, admiring the view of her bare breasts just inches from his face. Cat felt his erection lengthen beneath her. Then his hands, those rough and ready palms, were on her, drawing out the winter's cold and replacing it with a heat warm enough to scorch her. He leaned in, his tongue darting out to taste the tip of the breast closest to him.

Cat dropped her head back, her hair tickling her back, and sighed. Noah closed his mouth over the pink bud. The windows inches behind the couch fogged as Cat's breath grew ragged. She rolled her hips against him, grinding against the cock that was straining against his sweatpants. He took a handful of both breasts and worshipped them one at a time with his busy mouth.

With some minor gymnastics, Cat managed to force his pants down a few inches, just enough to free his hard-on. It jutted proudly, arching away from the flat lines of Noah's stomach. Cat didn't bother taking a moment to admire it. She pounced, gripping him firmly at the root. Noah groaned against her breast, the vibrations surrounding her aching nipple and tingling her to her core.

"I love when you touch me." His voice was a gravel road on a Sunday drive.

Cat pumped up his shaft, brushing her thumb across the tip. She felt powerful as Noah collapsed back against the couch, his hands seeking purchase on the curves of her hips.

"I can see that," she teased, stroking up the column of hot, smooth flesh.

His eyes were clamped shut, his jaw tight as if the pleasure she doled out was more torture than rapture. She loved watching him react to her. Increasing her pace, Cat gripped him tighter and lifted onto her knees.

"Hold this," she ordered, pulling her simple gray briefs to one side. Noah's finger snaked in and hooked the material. Wickedly, he brushed his thumb over the lips of her sex, and Cat's breath caught in her throat.

She was the one in charge. *She* was the captain of this ship. Brushing aside his exploring digit, Cat brought the crown of his cock to the gap in her folds. She pleasured them both that way, hard, tight strokes that brushed her bud of nerves, which was already begging for more.

She needed the control. Needed the anchor it gave her so she wouldn't be swept away like last time. This was temporary. A fling, an affair. And she needed to be able to walk away from it, from him, heart intact.

Noah's fingers dug bruises into the flesh of her hip. "Cat." Her name from his lips made her toes curl with pleasure. There was so much in that one word. Need, desire, an ache, an echo of something so much deeper than she expected. It jettisoned her away from her anxieties, from her agenda. Nothing else mattered.

Cat made a grab for the jeans she'd flung on the end of the sofa and fumbled through the pockets before finding the condom she'd stashed there. The foil crinkled between her fingers as she worked it open. She couldn't wait. She'd wanted to torture Noah to the edge before riding him into oblivion, but she couldn't take the empty ache in the depths of her core. He'd fill it. He'd fill her.

She rolled the condom on, sliding it down his thickness, and Noah groaned. Still holding her underwear to the side, he lined himself up with her entrance. She wasn't ready for him, wet but still so tight. As she slid down to sheath him, that edge between pleasure and pain cut at her with silver blades. Pain, fullness, and all-consuming pleasure. She was stretched tight around him and still hadn't taken all of him in.

Noah gripped her by the hips and, with one hard yank, settled himself all the way inside her, her ass resting against his thighs. She was stretched beyond her limits, and it took more than a deep breath and then another to let herself start to relax around him.

He was panting beneath her—they both were—as if they'd run a mile at a flat-out sprint.

"God, did you get bigger since last time?" Cat gritted out.

"Just relax," he ordered, breath ragged. "Relax and give me a minute, or I'm going to fuck you too hard before you're ready and you won't be able to walk tomorrow."

It was the threat that did it. Cat never backed down from a challenge. She wanted that feeling, that soreness tomorrow. Wanted to be reminded of Noah every time she took a step.

"Do it," she begged. "Take me that way."

She didn't need to say it twice. With his grip painful on her hips, he guided her up and slammed her down on his cock, jarring her.

She cried out. "Again."

"Are you sure?" he asked, whispering the words.

"So sure. Need you."

This time, he held her in the air, biceps straining, and he pumped his hips into her from below. The steady slap of warm flesh, the catch of breath, the cries of pleasure and pain. It all filled the room in a music unlike any other.

"God. Yes. This," Cat demanded, leaning into him. He closed his mouth over one of her nipples and sucked hard. She saw stars.

"Christ, I need more," he rasped. He rose, plucking her off his dick. He slid free, and Cat stared at the evidence of her own arousal coating his wrapped cock. He pushed her, draping her facedown over the hefty ottoman. "Tell me if this isn't okay," he warned her as he settled between her spread legs.

She accepted his weight against her and wriggled her ass. She was open, needy, more than a little desperate.

"So very okay."

He slapped at her ass, the flat of his palm connecting with the round of her curves. She yelped, and he groaned deep and guttural.

"Fuck." He drew the word out as he pushed his way into her. Cat felt the sharp ache as he hit bottom. "Am I hurting you?"

She shook her head, not trusting her voice. She didn't need soft, tender words. She needed his body bruising and using hers. He shifted against her, pushing off from the floor and powering into her, again and again, biology urging him on. Cat felt every inch of him as he drove into her and dragged himself out. She'd wanted to dominate him tonight, yet once again she found herself giving over to the moment, the craving to be taken.

This wasn't her thing. She shouldn't be feeling the edge of release already teasing her spine. Shouldn't be shuddering as an orgasm built so quickly she feared she wouldn't survive it. Noah shifted just a bit and pressed her thighs apart, opening her lips to bare her clit against the ottoman's hideous plaid upholstery.

His next thrust dragged her clitoris and nipples against the material, and Cat cried out. The friction of the fabric, the depth of his thrusts, those short grunts of pleasure that worked themselves out of his throat. It all worked together in a symphony that carried her to a crescendo. It slammed into her, through her, molten like lava, fast like electricity. And Noah never slowed. He fucked her fast and rough through the shudders of pleasure that erupted in wave after wave.

"Noah!" She shouted his name as he owned her body.

His thrusts slowed, and he went stock-still in her, every muscle, every cell tensed against her. The guttural, primitive noise came from his chest as Cat felt his cock pulse inside her. He fought it, the release that was inevitable.

"I need to see you, Cat. I want to see you, taste you, when I come."

She was too weak to answer. He pulled out of her, and despite the climax that had left her wrecked a moment ago, she ached for more.

He pulled her up and arranged her on the couch, pillows at her back, legs open. When he ranged himself over her, Cat felt her breath catch. Was there anything in this world more lust-worthy than a naked Noah Yates professing all the ways he was going to take her? Desire, hard and dark, crystallized in his eyes. And when he pressed her thighs farther apart and lowered himself between them, she felt the promised ache of soreness.

"Hold on to me," he ordered.

She obliged, gripping his shoulders and pulling him to her.

"Fuck me, Noah. Hard. I want to feel you come."

Surprising her with tenderness, Noah leaned down to nuzzle one breast and then the other. His teeth grazed her nipple, and Cat sucked in a breath.

"God, you're built," he murmured, tongue brushing the sensitive tip. "I could do this all day." The rough flat of his tongue dragged over her peak.

"No complaints here," she gasped.

"I'd come too fast if I let you keep riding me," he confessed. "Just watching your perfect tits puts me on the edge."

Cat bucked against his hips. "Noah. Please?"

He probed at her core, and Cat relaxed her muscles, open and ready. The pulls from his mouth on her breast were echoing in her core.

"Once I start, I'm not going to be able to stop, baby." He gave a testing push of his hips. "Once I'm inside you, I'm going to fuck you until I can't stop coming. Until I fill you with everything I've got."

"Jesus, Noah." Cat wrapped her legs higher up his hips.

He gave her other nipple a lazy stroke with the flat of his tongue. "Don't you love the anticipation?" His lips hovered over the bud that strained toward his mouth like a flower reaching for the sun. "It's like Christmas Eve."

When his lips closed over her bud, Cat cried out, and he slid into her in one powerful thrust. Her breast popped free from his mouth. And Noah let himself off the leash. It was what she wanted. Noah Yates beyond control. But she'd failed to anticipate being there herself. His hips slammed into her, his cock riding her slickness home. Cat could do nothing but hang on for dear life. The power in him, the rocketing of his thrusts into her core. She was dizzy with need, with desire.

"I'm never going to get enough of you, Cat." He was panting, breathless, hammering into her with the single-minded ferocity of an animal.

She felt the sparks in her fingertips and toes. Felt the molten glow, volcanic as it began to move through her body. "Noah?"

"Come, Cat. Come on my cock. Milk it for me."

How could a man so reserved, so responsible, turn into an animal, primitive and dangerous and dirty?

Her arms were vises holding him against her. Noah lifted her hips, adjusting the angle, and dragged the crown of his cock over that secret place of wanton pleasure, that bundle of nerves that turned detonator.

"Yes." Cat hissed out the word.

"I can feel you, baby. I can feel you," he chanted. "Don't hold back."

Cat squeezed her muscles around him, his erection brushing exactly the right spot again.

"Fuck." Noah murmured as his thrusts changed, wild and powerful, taking what he claimed. It sparked bright, hot. She closed around him in involuntary pleasure, shouting his name. He was there with her, coming hard, loud. She gripped him with those hungry squeezes and felt him pour himself into her. Again and again until he collapsed on top of her, pressing her into the pillows beneath.

CHAPTER
36

They were still intertwined, Noah still inside Cat, when the knob of the front door jiggled. It had the same effect on his heart rate as an unexpected gunshot.

Noah jumped up, desperately searching for his pants as they both heard Sara calling from the front porch. "Dad! Are you there? I forgot my history book!"

He yanked his T-shirt over his head and dragged Cat up off the couch.

"You need to hide," he hissed.

She blinked those cool hazel eyes. "What? Excuse me?"

"I haven't told her that we're…whatever. I don't want her to get the wrong impression." He pushed the naked Cat toward the kitchen, picking up articles of clothing as they went.

"Dad?" Sara called from the front door, ringing the bell and knocking.

"Where exactly am I supposed to hide?" Cat demanded. Her body was flush with marks from his mouth, his hands.

"It's a big house. Pick a spot." Noah shoved her down the hallway, and when he was sure she was out of sight, he opened the door as casually as possible.

Mellody took one look at him and clapped a hand over her mouth, her shoulders shaking with suppressed laughter. He didn't feel an ounce of amusement at her coughing fit.

"Geez, Dad. You never lock the door. Why's your shirt on backward?" Sara asked as she brushed past him. "I forgot my history book, and I've got this essay due on Monday." She took the stairs two at a time.

He looked at his ex-wife and opened his mouth. But there were no words.

"Looks like we caught you at a bad time," Mellody said, amused.

"Maybe try texting next time," Noah suggested, spinning his shirt around. It was on straight now but inside out.

"Please tell me it's Cat," Mellody demanded.

"What makes you think—"

There was a thud from the kitchen, followed by some colorful swearing.

"Sure sounds like her," Mellody observed, wandering into the living room and picking up a size seven work boot.

"I don't know what the etiquette is for this," Noah admitted. "I don't want Sara to think..."

Mellody waved away his concerns. "Noah, you're an adult. A good one. Relax. It'll be fine."

"I don't want her to think casual sex is the right answer to—"

Sara thundered down the stairs, textbook triumphantly aloft. "Found it!"

"Great. Now let's go write an essay about Patrick Henry," Mellody said with feigned enthusiasm.

"You okay, Dad? You look kinda sweaty," Sara observed.

"All good. Everything's fine. I'm fine," Noah choked out.

"Are you sure?" Sara gave him the suspicious eye.

He felt like a teenager caught trying to sneak in after curfew.

"Hey, whose jeans are those?" Sara asked, pointing at the couch.

Mellody clamped a hand on her daughter's shoulder. "Come on, babe. Your dad looks like he could use some rest," Mellody announced, pushing Sara toward the door.

"Bye, Dad!" Sara called over her shoulder as she was hustled out of the house.

"Bye, Noah." Mellody gave him an exaggerated wink as she closed the door behind her.

"Bye," Noah said to no one.

He laid a hand over his pounding heart and took a moment to breathe. Nearly busted by a twelve-year-old. That was something new and horrific for him.

He didn't want Sara to get the impression that casual sex was a good, safe option. He'd prefer if she stuck with abstinence until around thirty. People tended to make better choices after thirty. Himself for instance. He'd just hooked up with Catalina King, the sexiest woman on the planet…who, judging from the noise, was hiding in his pantry.

He pulled the door open, and Cat hid behind an outstretched T-shirt.

"It's me," he said, wondering if the situation was actually funny or if he was just hysterical.

Cat glared at him. "Are they gone?" she asked. Her underwear was on backward. Her thermal shirt gave enough away for Noah to notice she hadn't found her bra in the living room, and he counted his lucky stars that Sara hadn't spotted it. Her hair was a wild mess of finger-combed snarls.

"They're gone."

She pushed past him, muttering about pants and boots.

"Cat, where are you going?"

She whirled on him in the hallway. "I don't hide, Noah. I'm not something to be ashamed of."

She yanked her jeans off the sofa and pulled them on with violence.

"Hang on!"

She grabbed a boot and Noah wrestled it out of her grip. She couldn't very well leave the house with no shoes.

"Gimme the boot, Noah," she ordered.

"Sit your ass down first and talk," he countered.

"You want to talk? Okay. I get that you're not ready to discuss this with Sara, I do. But you made me feel cheap. Like I was something to be ashamed of. I am *neither* of those things. Now give me the fucking boot."

She reached for it, off-balance, and Noah pushed her onto the couch. With no other options, he lay on top of her, pinning her.

"Noah! I swear to God—"

He clamped a hand over her mouth. "Shut up a second, will you? Christ, Cat. How could you think for a second that I think you're something to be ashamed of?"

"You made me hide in the pantry." She said it as if he were half deaf and a whole lot stupid.

"Sara is twelve years old. She's never met anyone that I've… dated." He was at a loss to describe just exactly what he and Cat were doing. "I haven't done much…dating. So I don't know what's acceptable to expose a child to. And you know me. I always err on the side of caution."

Cat went still beneath him, and tentatively, Noah removed his hand. "Fine," she said coolly.

The strength she possessed in that long, lean body always surprised him as it did now when she managed to shove him off her and onto the floor. She pulled on her jeans with temper and snatched her bra out from under the coffee table.

"I didn't realize you had such issues with casual sex," she snapped out.

She wasn't fighting fair when she shucked off her shirt and dragged on her sports bra.

Frustrated, Noah shoved his hands in his hair. "Just because I don't want Sara to think that it's okay. That's what upsets you?"

She gave him a long look. This one wasn't cool. There was fire behind those eyes.

She shoved a foot into a boot. "What are we doing here, Noah?" she asked, reaching for the laces.

"Having mind-boggling sex. Enjoying each other."

"Having mind-boggling *casual* sex," she pointed out, lacing the boot and searching for its mate.

"I'm new at the whole casual sex thing."

"That's the point. You're not a casual sex kinda guy, and I'm not a serious relationship kind of girl."

"I'm trying—"

"Maybe we shouldn't be trying. You obviously have some kind of judgment about the way I choose to live my life. And it's not like I'm going to be here much longer."

Noah was at a loss. He didn't understand how he could go from feeling sated and whole to panicked. It slid through his gut like ice. "I don't want you to go." He wasn't just talking about tonight.

"And I don't want to be in a relationship. I'm not going to make room for something like that right now. So I guess we're at an impasse."

She made it to the door before he gathered his wits. He

grabbed her by the arm and spun her around. And when she wouldn't stop struggling against him, he pressed her to the door and did the only thing that came naturally. He kissed her.

She went stock-still beneath him, and then her mouth came to life. She ravaged him. She reached into his body and grabbed on to his soul, and he let her. Their tongues tangled, teeth dragging, breath sighing.

He was hard again and oh so desperate for what only Cat could give him.

And then she was pushing him back a step. He let her this time. He needed the space, the air.

"I'm not going to let you make me feel bad about how I live my life. I choose what sexual relationships I want to have. And five minutes ago, you were at the top of that list. But there's no room on that list for someone who doesn't respect me," Cat said quietly.

"Cat, just because I don't want Sara to—"

Cat cut him off. "I have to go."

And just like that, she slipped out the door, leaving Noah alone in his big, empty house.

CHAPTER

37

What exactly did he say again?" Paige asked, guzzling a coffee and staring at Cat. They were huddled together over the playback monitor under a tent that offered zero protection from the icy fingers of winter that danced down Mistletoe Avenue.

She looked confused, which was not where Cat wanted Paige to be. She wanted her firmly in her camp, irate at the insinuation that had been so natural to Noah it had flown over his head.

"It wasn't necessarily what he said. It was the *way* he said it. As if Sara knowing he was having sex with me would be worse than nuclear war. He was implying that I'm a slut."

Her sister-in-law raised a finger, and Cat knew she wouldn't like the words that would follow. "Let's examine that," Paige said.

"Stop being documentary director Paige, and be best friend Paige," Cat ordered.

"First of all, if Noah said or did anything to hurt you, I'm first in line with the baseball bat for the Noah piñata."

"Thank you," Cat said, raising her hands to the sky.

"Now that the figurative Noah bashing is over, let's look at his reaction from his side."

Cat rolled her eyes and crossed her arms over her chest.

"Don't get defensive," Paige told her. "Noah's a single dad with a twelve-year-old girl. Do you remember what you were like at twelve?"

Cat shrugged. "Awesome."

"Of course you were. You were what? Playing baseball? Following your grandfather around job sites?"

"Yeah, so?"

"Great. What about thirteen and fourteen?"

Cat couldn't stop the nostalgic grin. "Boys. I discovered boys."

"Aha!" Paige was triumphant. "And how many good decisions did you make at that age?"

Cat wrinkled her nose, remembering the incredibly stupid make-out sessions, the desperate love notes, the heady delight of a new crush. "Pass."

"I figured." Paige grinned. "As a mother of a new human being, I'm dreading those years. Your body is coming of age, but your brain is light-years behind. You don't understand consequences. You aren't capable of predicting the outcomes of your decisions. Parents spend those years trying to prevent you from making any kind of decision that could have life-altering complications."

Cat slumped in her parka. She hated when Paige made sense.

"Now, you, my beautiful, talented, smart, hard-working sister-in-law, make choices that fit your life. You enjoy a healthy and safe sex life that doesn't require the boundaries of marriage. You have your healthy, safe sex with single men who respect you and vice versa. There's absolutely nothing wrong with that, and anyone who tries to shame you for it is jealous. But the difference is, you're thirty-two. Not twelve."

"I have the ability to pick the right partners because my hormones aren't careening around in my head, begging me to do really stupid things." Cat kicked at a rock.

"Exactly. Sara's a smart kid, but she's about to be a *hormonal* smart kid, and parents will do whatever it takes to keep those hormones away from decisions. Religion, scare tactics, shaming. And maybe it's not the best way." Paige shrugged. "But when you're in charge of keeping another human being alive and on track, you do what you have to do."

"What are you and Gan going to do when Gabby hits the teenage years?" Cat asked, a half smile at the thought of her brother with a teenage daughter.

"Move to an uninhabited island?" Paige joked.

"Ha. But seriously?" Cat asked. Paige was a fierce feminist, and there was no way she didn't have a color-coded binder with life lessons according to developmental stage.

"I want Gabby to grow up knowing what she does with her body is ultimately her choice, and I want her to make smart choices and have the inalienable right to say no."

"So you have no idea," Cat supplied.

"None at all. I'm hoping to keep her a toddler for the next decade until I can figure it out."

Cat laughed and bumped Paige's shoulder. "You and Gannon will be just fine."

"And you and Noah could be more than fine if you let it happen," Paige said pointedly.

"What's that supposed to mean?"

"I say this with love. I think you're looking for an out because your feelings for Noah and your spectacular casual sex are bigger than you expected."

Cat scoffed even as the bells inside her head began ringing a warning. *Ding ding ding.*

"Agree to disagree," she said. "Now that the venting is over with, let's figure out how to film this reveal."

———

Cat smiled and delivered charming lines on command for the cameras for the rest of the day as Drake was mercilessly flirted with by the enigmatic Mrs. Pringle. For a grandmotherly figure in a wheelchair, the woman had some serious cougar running through her veins.

Drake, blushing constantly, didn't seem to mind the attention. Cat's instincts had been correct. Putting him on camera with the flirtatious Mrs. Pringle equaled TV ratings gold. They were adorable, and when Drake revealed the secret updates they'd done to make the woman's kitchen more wheelchair friendly, she kissed him on the mouth. Cat was pretty sure Mrs. Pringle had slipped her costar the tongue too.

Filming kept her out of her head where she wanted to wallow. *Is Paige right?* Cat wondered, turning it over in her head as she climbed into the makeup trailer to freshen up her face. Was she looking for an out with Noah? Sex with him couldn't even be classified as mere sex. Her extensive experience in that particular area informed her that there was something much bigger at stake every time he put his hands on her.

She'd never felt so consumed, so connected. When Noah was inside her, they were one. Not just two healthy adults having fun. He was stealing pieces of her soul, and she was letting him.

It was terrifying.

Cat flopped down in the makeup chair and frowned at her appearance. She looked tired. Ragged. Not like the glowing TV personality she was required to be.

She couldn't afford to be distracted. Not now. Not within striking distance of the highest ratings for a holiday special the network had ever seen. Not with her school being this close to becoming a reality. She was used to a million miles an hour. Used to being home less than she was on the road. Used to finding a new adventure around every corner.

"You look tired." Drake made the announcement as Archie, the makeup artist, attacked the circles under Cat's eyes for the second time in two hours. Drake looked annoyingly handsome in flannel. His hair was styled with one careless shove of his hand.

"Gee, thanks. You look chubby and balding," Cat shot back.

Drake ran a hand over his washboard abs. "Are you hangry? Because if you are, I can share my special paleo salted caramel brownies from Mrs. Pringle. I'd prefer not to, but I'm willing." He shook the plastic-wrapped chocolate in her face.

Cat gave him a tired smile. "Sorry for biting your head off. I'm not hungry."

"You don't have to do everything alone, you know," Drake pointed out, dropping the paper plate of brownies on the makeup table.

Cat opened one eye. "What's that supposed to mean?" she demanded, sliding right back into irritated.

"You're trying to juggle thirty-six full-time jobs," Drake pointed out, biting into one of said brownies. "You're not getting enough sleep. You're getting pissy. You're spacing out." He counted off the list of offenses on brownie-colored fingers.

"Okay! Okay! I get it. I'm a broody asshole."

"You could make things a lot easier on yourself by leaning just a little. You don't have to shoot every single scene. You don't have to coordinate every day's shooting schedule. You don't have to single-handedly build your school brick by brick."

Cat yawned despite herself. She was fucking exhausted.

"I get what you're saying, but it's just faster if I do it myself."

"To a point. Then there's the point where you end up suffering 'dehydration and exhaustion.'" Drake added air quotes. Dehydration and exhaustion were the industry's pretty code words for breakdowns and overdoses.

"I'm not going to crash," Cat insisted carefully. Archie was lining her lips again, and she couldn't move them.

"You've got Paige and me and Gannon and Henry, hell, even Noah. We're a team. Use us," Drake said.

She opened her mouth to argue with him. Noah was not a teammate. But Drake was faster than her denial and stuffed a tiny corner of delicious dessert past her lips.

"Eat your chocolate and stop thinking you can't rely on us." Drake sauntered off, leaving every female in a ten-yard radius staring after him.

Reflexively Cat checked her phone. Only she wasn't looking at Instagram or her blog or Facebook. She was checking to see if Noah had texted her. He had a half dozen times after she left his house. He'd also called twice. But she'd ignored them all. She didn't want an apology from a man who didn't know what he was apologizing for.

It looked as though he'd gotten the message. There were no texts or missed calls from Noah.

CHAPTER
38

Noah swore and sucked his smarting thumb into his mouth.

"Come on, Yates. I expect that from Jasper, not you. I don't need to be babysitting two unhandymen," Gannon joked between short bursts of the nail gun that he didn't trust either of them to run.

Noah couldn't figure out how he'd ended up here. The woman who'd brought him to a shattering orgasm had skipped out on him without an explanation, and now he was working ten feet off the ground, trying not to break his thumb with a hammer as he "helped" his apparently ex-lover's twin brother and Jasper add the finishing touches to a tree house.

He'd given up trying to understand and just went with it.

Sara had questioned him about his morose attitude when she'd gotten home from her weekend at her mother's. He'd been at a loss there too, so he'd lied. She'd given him the same look Mellody used to give him when he wasn't articulating his feelings. Then she'd sighed heavily and said, "Okay. If you want to talk to me about it, I'm here for you."

When had his daughter turned into an adult?

He hung the framed picture of Sara and April from first grade, arms around each other at a school picnic and grinning in little girl delight, on the wooden post. Why couldn't things just stay the same? Why did everything have to change and get so complicated? Why wouldn't Cat talk to him?

"Hey, if you're done moping over there, you can help Jasper paint the trim," Gannon said, pointing at the spare paintbrush.

Noah crossed to the paint can and stared blankly at the brush.

"I know that look," Jasper said wisely. "It's a woman. I get that deer-in-headlights look when Kathy's mad."

"Definitely not talking about women," Gannon insisted. "We're just working on a tree house, not talking about my sister."

"Well, since you brought her up..."

Gannon, on his knees on the floor, hung his head. "Please don't make me do this, Yates. I'm begging you, man."

Noah glanced at the nail gun in Gannon's hand. "Uh, maybe you want to put that down?" he suggested.

Gannon rolled his eyes heavenward and closed them as if he were praying for patience. "Paige texted and said you and Cat are fighting." He sounded as if he'd rather be discussing women's menstrual cycles.

Noah would too.

"Is it fighting if she's freezing me out?" he asked.

Gannon swore under his breath. "Listen, man, I'm her brother, and *I* barely understand her."

"So what do I do? Just let it go? Let her just walk half-naked out of my house and never talk to her again."

"For fuck's sake, man! That's my sister!" Gannon looked a little green.

"Sorry. I'm just…" He was tied up in a million fucking knots. Cat took him by the hand and dragged him to heaven in bed and then acted like he'd punched a pony in the face.

"Women," Jasper said with a shake of his head. "I wish I could tell you it gets easier, but Kathy and I've been married fourteen years, and I still have no idea what goes on in her head."

Noah dipped the brush in the paint and slapped it against the window trim.

"Just *try* talking to her, okay? Leave the rest of us out of it, and go talk to her," Gannon pleaded.

"I've tried! She won't return my calls. She's ignoring my texts."

Gannon muttered something about the things he did for his wife under his breath. "Look, Noah. You seem like a nice guy. If you want to pursue something with Cat, pursue it. Make her give you a firm no if that's not what she wants. And then don't talk to me about it ever again."

"It seems like the only time she wants to talk is after—"

"Shut the fuck up, Yates! Are you trying to get me to throw you through the window?"

"Dude," Jasper whispered on Noah's left. "Don't poke the bear, man."

"Sorry. I'm sorry. I'm just…stupid and confused."

"Look, just talk to this woman who I'm pretending is not my twin sister. Okay? Do us all a favor, and lock her in a closet until she talks. And then don't give me a status update."

"Got it. Okay. Thanks." Noah bobbed his head. Talk to her. He could do that. Somehow. Merry wasn't that big. She couldn't hide from him forever.

"Great. Awesome. Now, can we please finish this goddamn tree house before filming?" Gannon demanded.

Noah dipped the paintbrush back in the can, feeling marginally more hopeful.

———

That evening, covered in paint and nursing a few splinters, Noah wandered toward home. His shoulders hunched against the cold. He'd grown up here, so Merry's icy winters were nothing new. But when he felt cold on the inside, no number of thermal layers could warm him up.

It was ridiculous. He was an adult, damn it. And so was Cat. He'd just go talk to her, clear the air.

He spun around and headed in the opposite direction. He'd just knock on Cat's door and very calmly explain to her…something.

He was still working it out in his head when he spotted her ducking out of a production van and heading into Trailer Town. She saw him, and they eyed each other across the expanse of asphalt for a moment before she jerked her head toward an empty box truck next to the RVs.

Her face was unreadable. But Noah was committed. He climbed into the cab on the passenger side as she slid in behind the wheel on the opposite side. They closed their doors and then there was silence. The cab light slowly dimmed. It smelled like stale cigarettes and dust inside.

"You hurt my feelings," she announced without preamble.

All his prepared explanations vanished. "I'm sorry, Cat. I swear I didn't mean to hurt you—"

She cut him off. "Yeah. I know. I'm not really here for an apology. The point is, I *let* you hurt my feelings. I thought you were slut shaming me by not wanting Sara to know about me."

Noah's open mouth closed with a snap. "Huh?" he managed.

"I realize that probably wasn't the message you were trying to send me."

"Absolutely not."

"Good. Okay then." She nodded briskly. All business.

"Is there anything else you want to say?" he prodded, seeing the indecision in her eyes.

She took a breath. "I only do casual because, well, because it fits my schedule, my life. You make me wonder if maybe that's not all I want. With you. And I'm not really ready to consider that possibility. Because it can't be. I'm not staying here, and I don't know when I'm going to be ready to find a permanent home and stay put. I literally don't know where I'll be living next year. And it wouldn't be fair to ask you to wait for me to figure out when I'd like to settle down."

He nodded and then, at a loss for words, kept on nodding.

"Anyway, I get that you're not comfortable with Sara knowing about us. I'm not a parent. You are. I get the need for secrecy. So…that's it."

She leaned toward him, pressed a chaste kiss on his mouth, and turned to open her door.

Noah thanked his reflexes for being faster than his wits. He grabbed her wrist and dragged her back across the bench seat. The kiss he gave her was anything but chaste, reminding them both of what was at stake. The heat, that glorious burst of flames that leaped to life when her lips moved hungrily under his, was all they needed to know.

He pulled back and searched her face, those swollen lips, her half-closed hazel eyes. "Tell me what you want now. What can we have now?"

"Fun," she suggested. "Let's just have fun. I like it. You need it. Everyone wins."

"Fun?" he repeated.

She gave him a little smile. "Don't look at me like I'm speaking Russian. Fun. Naked fun."

"And will we be having this naked fun with anyone else?" he pressed.

Her eyes widened, sparking with annoyance. "No! Exclusive fun only for both of us."

"I'm fine with exclusive naked fun," Noah said, threading his fingers through her hair. She closed her eyes.

"And it can be secret exclusive naked fun," Cat offered. "That way, you don't have to start a safe casual sex conversation with Sara."

"I'd be eternally grateful for being able to put off that conversation for as long as possible," Noah admitted.

"And think of it this way," Cat added cheerfully. "I'll ease you into a fun-loving lifestyle, and by the time I'm gone, Merry will be calling you Mr. Fun instead of Mr. No."

Noah laughed. "I don't see that happening," he answered dryly.

"Never underestimate me, Noah." Cat winked at him in the darkness.

"I find it hard to believe that anyone bothers doing that where you're concerned."

She grabbed him by the coat and kissed him. It escalated into wandering hands and whispered promises as the windows fogged around them.

"Come home with me," he demanded, breaking the kiss.

She shook her head. "You have Sara tonight," Cat reminded him.

"Tomorrow then. I'll meet you."

Again, she shook her head, but this time there was a smile playing on her swollen lips. "Filming at the Hais' all day. That is, *if* you guys managed to finish the tree house."

Noah proudly held up his paint-splattered hands. "Done with the splinters to prove it."

"Poor baby." Cat gave his palm a tender kiss.

He reached for her hand, placed his lips against her tattoo. Homage paid.

"I should go," she said, and he heard the regret in her tone. "I have a lot of work to catch up on. I've been ignoring social media and emails and pretty much everything."

"Maybe I can call you later?" he suggested.

"Maybe you can," she agreed with the flirty smile that made him feel like he was a king.

She flipped that long honeyed-blond hair over her shoulder and smiled shyly at him as she opened the truck door. Catalina King looked at him like she had a schoolgirl crush.

Noah watched her slip out of the truck, then walked the rest of the way home with a spring in his step.

———

"You're acting weird again." Sara frowned at him.

Noah stopped midwhistle as he chopped fresh parsley.

"No, I'm not," he insisted.

"Dad, you've been moping around here for two days, and now it's all singing and whistling." She eyed him from across the counter. "You're acting like LauraBeth Fidowski when she and Tommy Bigelow get into a fight and make up."

"LauraBeth is dating a sophomore?" Noah wasn't a fan of this news.

Sara groaned. "Trust you to completely miss my point. You're such a dad!"

Noah decided to take it as a compliment. "What was your point again?" Noah asked, shoveling up a mound of parsley and sprinkling it over top of the two bowls of spicy tortilla soup.

"I'm wondering why you're acting like an eighth grader who keeps breaking up with and getting back together with her tenth-grade boyfriend."

"Hmm," Noah hummed. He was starting to learn that his knee-jerk response didn't get him very far with his daughter.

Sara heaved another sigh and carted the plates to the table. Dinners were quieter with just the two of them in the house. He hated to admit it, but at times, it had been nice to have a crowd under his roof.

"Don't you prefer me in a better mood?" Noah asked, sidestepping her question.

"I like knowing *why* you're in the mood you're in. I value predictability."

Well, that was a new one.

"You value predictability?" Noah parroted.

"In some ways, all kids do," she insisted wisely.

"Huh. Well, I'll try to be more predictable," Noah promised.

Sara dipped her spoon into her soup and muttered about parents being "so weird."

CHAPTER
39

Cat hurried down the sidewalk as quietly as she could. It was nearly midnight, and snow flurries were dancing on the night air. Filming had given way to two conference calls, a quick sit-down with the story editor, and then rewriting the call sheets for tomorrow. She and Drake were going to have to sit down for another round of one-on-ones to round out the Hai episode. She'd barely made a dent in her miles-long social media notifications, but she wanted Noah. Wanted his arms around her. Wanted to hear that slow, dependable beat of his heart.

She'd texted him, booty called him if she was being honest, which Cat always tried to be with herself. Of course, booty calls weren't supposed to spend the night wrapped up in each other like lovers. It was just how they ended up after… It was how she hoped they'd end up tonight. She loved waking up and feeling his heart beat. Trying to wriggle away only to have his grip tighten on her. Even in his sleep, he wanted to keep her close. It made her feel...treasured.

They were sneaking around like teenagers. And Cat loved it. Just yesterday, she'd ducked into her trailer for a snack and a nap and found Noah on his lunch break waiting for her. Naked. They were both late getting back to work, and Cat couldn't seem to wipe the smug smile off her face for the rest of the day.

Two days before that, a chance run-in at the grocery store led to some heavy petting in the parking lot. They'd had to duck down beneath the windows of Cat's truck, giggling, when Velma Murdock wandered by, consulting her shopping list. Every night that Noah spent in her trailer, he arrived under the cover of darkness and crept out before dawn. And when Sara was with Mellody, Cat sprawled, sated and smiling, across Noah's big bed.

No one was any the wiser, at least not that they'd let on. And in a town of Merry's size, if there was news, everyone knew it by lunchtime. They were careful to remain professional around others. But alone? There were no rules, no barriers, no strings.

They'd seemed to settle into a limbo of relying entirely on the present, never discussing the future.

It was just the way Cat liked it. She'd be leaving soon enough and didn't want anything complicating that. She couldn't imagine moving on to the next project while her heart was still with the last. It wasn't how she worked, how she lived. Newer was better, more exciting. There was always another adventure around the next corner. She just needed to keep turning corners to find them.

As her days in Merry ticked down, she had to admit there was a pull here. The town, the people, Noah. Cat couldn't remember feeling more at home anywhere else besides her grandmother's kitchen.

A dog barked from a second-floor apartment over the dry cleaners, and Cat pulled the wool cap lower. She was a spy, a ninja of the night. Meeting her secret lover for a midnight tryst. The image made her smile.

She was two blocks from Noah's house. Noah's warm, childless house. With his comfortable couch, his big-screen TV, his rumpled bed, his warm, capable hands…

She was daydreaming. That was why she didn't see it coming, the arm that snaked out from the alleyway, hooking around her waist and pulling her into the dark.

She didn't need to see his face. Her body recognized Noah's, even under all the layers.

"Are you mugging me?" she asked, slyly pressing her cold face to his neck.

"I'm walking you home." The words came out in a silvery cloud, and she could feel the heat of his breath against her face.

What was it about the man that made her feel…happy? A warm Sunday kind of happiness. Soft glowing embers and meaningful smiles. He was her warm, safe place. Temporarily, of course.

"I know where you live," Cat teased.

"We're secret lovers," Noah insisted. "You need my help sneaking over the fence in the backyard so no one sees us."

"Why don't we just go in the front door?" Cat asked.

"I saw Mrs. Appleby's blinds twitching since nine tonight. I think she's watching, waiting."

Cat laughed, and they started down the alley. "Well, we can't get caught. I never got caught. It would ruin my perfect streak."

"You snuck out when you were a kid?"

Cat slipped her arm through Noah's in the privacy of the dark night. "I was very stealthy."

"Did you meet boyfriends after curfew?" Noah asked.

"On occasion." Rules of good conduct held no allure for Cat, not now and not when she was a teenager.

"I want to be impressed, but all I can imagine is the fresh hell I'll be living with Sara in a few years."

Cat rested her head on his shoulder as they walked. "She's a good kid and comes from two great parents. I think you'll all survive."

"I appreciate your vote of confidence."

"Do you wish you'd grown up differently?" Cat asked.

Noah scanned the night quietly. She could hear his wheels turning, weighing his answer.

"If I could go back and have two parents who came to my baseball games and cheered. A dad who took me fishing. Food on the table every night. Heat in the winter. Clothes when they were needed. If I could have all that and still end up right here, right now, I would wish it."

Cat rubbed his arm with her hand. "But since you can't?"

He looked down at her, his eyes sparkling in the light of the lone streetlamp. "There's nowhere else I'd rather be. Except maybe in my bed with you."

"I hate that you had to grow up that way, Noah." The pain of knowing that he'd suffered, that he'd been scared and unprotected, welled up in her unexpectedly. "You deserved better."

He stopped, pulled her around to face him. "I wouldn't change anything, Cat. Not since it brought me right here."

Using the thumb of his glove, he brushed snowflakes off her eyelashes.

"Do me a favor, Noah?" Cat breathed.

"Anything."

"Kiss me right here, right now." She wanted to remember this. The feeling that it was just the two of them in the whole world under a sky of stars and snowflakes.

Understanding what she was asking, he lowered his lips to her gently, softly. They melted, melded like metal. Warm and sweet. Noah's lips moved over hers until she opened to him. Cat fisted her mittened hands on to the lapels of his jacket as he brazenly, tenderly left a mark on her heart.

There was something about this man, this night, this town that had worked its way under her skin to swim through her veins.

Tenderly, he tasted her as if he had all the time in the world to sample and tease.

She breathed him in, his air, his scent, his flavor. Inhaling Noah.

It was a mistake. She shouldn't have asked for this. Should have kept it light. But the kiss was the light, a new kind of illumination that warmed her and guided her.

CHAPTER

40

"My dad wants to invite you to dinner tonight," Sara announced, sliding into the diner booth across from Cat.

Cat's wrap fell from her hands onto the plate. She'd scored an honest-to-goodness lunch break that had landed the first official "Cat Wrap" in her freezing cold hands and had been busy warming herself up remembering each and every orgasmic detail with Noah the night before. At least she had been before she was interrupted by the man's daughter.

"Uh. Huh?" Cat wiped her mouth with a napkin and prayed she didn't look like she'd been fantasizing about Sara's dad naked.

"Dinner. Our house tonight," Sara repeated.

"Is there a special occasion?" Cat asked, feeling like she was missing an essential piece of information. April Hai peered around the end of the counter at them, holding a to-go bag.

Sara shrugged. "I aced my earth sciences test?"

"Congratulations?"

"Thanks. Bring some wine for you and my dad."

"Oh, uh, sure. Okay," Cat said, baffled. They were supposed to be keeping this…romance a secret. Sara wasn't supposed to know that her father was doing the horizontal mambo with Cat. "What time should I be there?"

"Eight," Sara said decisively. "We're having salmon."

"Okay. I'll see you at eight," Cat said.

Sara grinned. "Awesome! See ya tonight, Cat!" She turned and scampered off, grabbing April's arm and dragging her friend off to giggle somewhere about twelve-year-old things.

Cat shook her head and picked up her truly excellent chicken wrap. *Kids.*

———

She meant to text Noah to confirm but got sucked into watching playback, and by the time she slipped away, she barely had enough time to shower and change. For the first time in her life, Cat wasn't sure what to wear. What did the woman secretly sleeping with a twelve-year-old's father wear to a family dinner?

She finally settled on jeans and an emerald-green sweater with a V-neck. She pulled on a pair of suede booties and braided her still damp hair over her shoulder. Stylish, but not too sexy, she decided, studying herself in the mirror. Now she just had to remember not to grab Noah's crotch or straddle him at the dinner table, and everything would be fine.

Since the night was cold as hell and she was already running close to late, Cat drove the six blocks to Noah's. She grabbed the wine Henry had selected and hurried up the porch steps. After a brief moment of debate of knocking or ringing the bell, she stabbed the bell with her gloved finger.

She heard yelling and footsteps, and then Noah was opening the door.

"Hi," she said breathlessly. He looked tousled and tasty. His hair was ruffled. He was wearing jeans and a T-shirt and was barefoot. She was definitely overdressed.

"Hey." Noah's face went through a range of emotion. Excitement, pleasure, lust, and then confusion. "What are you doing here?" he asked quietly, stepping out onto the porch with her.

"I'm here for dinner," Cat reminded him. "Did I get the time wrong?"

"Dinner?" he repeated, blinking.

"Oh good! You're here," Sara called from the foyer. "Geez, Dad, let her in before she freezes."

Wordlessly, Noah stepped aside, and Sara pulled Cat inside.

"I hope you're a good cook, because we're just getting started," Sara said, practically dragging Cat's coat off her shoulders.

"Uh, your dad didn't seem to know that I was coming to dinner," Cat pointed out.

Sara wrenched the bottle of wine away from Cat and handed it over to Noah. "Here, Dad. Go open this."

"You want to explain why you're inviting dinner guests over without telling me first?" Noah asked.

Sara rolled her eyes and ignored their questions. "Cat, take your shoes off. Dad, open the wine. Then we'll chat."

They both watched as Sara bopped back to the kitchen where a cheery pop song was playing.

"What's happening?" Cat whispered.

"I think we're being played," Noah whispered back. "You look incredible by the way. I've missed you."

Cat reached out to hold on to his arm while she pulled off her boots. "I might have missed you too."

"What are you wearing under that sweater?" Noah asked, peering down the neckline of her shirt.

"I don't think you're going to find out tonight," Cat said, nodding toward the kitchen.

"Dad! Wine!" Sara yelled from the depths of the house.

"We'd better get back there," he said, giving her subtle cleavage another look of longing.

"I feel like we're walking into a trap."

"Oh, we most certainly are. Welcome to parenting."

Sara had three salmon filets on a baking sheet. She was dressing them with salt and pepper. There were two empty wineglasses and a corkscrew on the counter.

"Cat, do you want to do something with these tomatoes and asparagus?" Sara asked, jutting her chin toward the pile of produce next to the cutting board. "I printed out a recipe you can follow."

Cat padded over to the veggies. "Recipe," she scoffed. "My nonni would slap me upside the head if she saw me using one. Just point me in the direction of your balsamic vinegar."

Sara pointed, and Noah poured, and an eighties rock tune came on.

"Come on, Dad! It's your jam," Sara announced.

Noah shook his head, cheeks going a bit pink. "Nope. Not happening."

"He does an air guitar solo that any other time I can't get him to stop. Now suddenly he's embarrassed," Sara explained, shaking her head.

"Oh, I need to see this air guitar solo," Cat insisted.

"No way."

"It's AC/DC. I'll drum," she offered.

It took a full glass of wine and a replay before Noah reluctantly performed. Cat laughed with Sara until her face hurt.

While the salmon and veggies baked, Sara took Cat up to her bedroom to ask her advice on decor.

It was a typical pink bedroom littered with clothing and magazines and stuffed animals. The perfect cross section of childhood and the teen years.

"Dad said I can repaint and stuff, but I'm not sure what I'm going for," Sara mused, picking up a ragged stuffed dog and tucking it into a bin on the wall. "I like some of these ideas," she said, pulling up Pinterest on her tablet.

"So I see color, fun, but more grown-up," Cat said, studying the space and the pins. Two large windows overlooked the street. "That wall over there in a teal or a turquoise. And you need a new bed. You've got room in here for a queen. One of the ones with the upholstered headboards."

"Um, that sounds awesome," Sara decided, flopping onto her pink comforter.

"And you need better clothing organization," Cat said, toeing a pile of crumpled T-shirts and leggings in front of the dresser.

Sara giggled. "That's what my parents say too."

"If you're into fashion, you have to treat your clothing well," Cat pointed out.

"Okay, okay. I'll clean up. But look. I found this rug that I love, but it's got all these reds and oranges," Sara said, pulling out her cell phone and calling up the picture.

"Oh, yeah, definitely." Cat nodded. "That would look great with a dark teal wall. You could leave everything else white, walls, bedding. Maybe do something funky with the bedside lamps."

"That sounds awesome," Sara said. "I hope Dad will be okay with it. Sometimes I don't think he wants me to grow up."

Cat gave the girl a smile. "Sometimes parents have trouble with that," she admitted.

"But you wouldn't." Sara said it as if she was sure of it. "You see growing up as an adventure, not something to be protected from."

"Uhhh…" Cat wasn't sure how to respond to that.

"I think you're good for my dad," Sara continued.

They heard the beeping of the timer followed by Noah's call for kitchen aid.

"Good, I'm starving," Sara said, bounding past Cat and heading for the stairs. "Hey, Dad! Cat gave me some ideas for my room!"

"Can we still afford to send you to college?"

Cat wandered down to the kitchen where Sara was plating up the food.

"What happened? Any hints about what's going on?" Noah whispered without moving his lips.

Cat shook her head. "Huh-uh. Not yet," she whispered back.

"Come on, guys. Dinner's ready," Sara announced.

They sat cozily around the dining table. There was a small fake Christmas tree in the corner casting a soft glow. Candles in pine and cookie scents flickered on the mantel over yet another fireplace. Sara had switched the playlist to an instrumental Christmas station and dimmed the lights.

It was cozy, romantic. And Cat was starting to get an inkling of exactly what Sara was up to.

Cat had just speared her salmon filet when Sara leaned back in her chair.

"So I'm sure you're wondering why we're here tonight," she began as if she'd been addressing boards of directors since she was a toddler.

"I think that's a safe assumption," Noah said, sampling a bite of the asparagus.

"I know what you guys are doing," Sara announced.

Noah choked on his asparagus and reached blindly for his water glass. Sara waited until his coughing fit eased.

"What exactly do you think we're doing?" Noah asked, clearing his throat and looking wild-eyed at Cat across the table.

"I know you're dating. I know you think you're hiding it, but honestly, Dad, you're terrible at hiding things. And I don't see the point in you pretending you're not really into Cat. She's pretty awesome."

"Thank you?" Cat said, picking up her wineglass, desperate for an alcoholic buoy.

"You're welcome." Sara nodded primly. "Mom's getting remarried. It would be nice to see you move on too, Dad."

"Sara, Cat and I…we…a relationship isn't really…" Noah gave up his stumbling and looked beseechingly at Cat.

"Your dad and I are in very different places in our lives, and while we're enjoying spending time together, the potential for a future relationship just isn't there," Cat said.

Sara nodded as if the information wasn't new to her. She looked down at her napkin. "I get that. But I think you're both doing yourself a disservice by automatically discounting the idea of a relationship."

Noah frowned at Sara. "Are you reading from notes?" he demanded.

Sara snatched the scrap of paper away out of his reach. "April helped. So sue me."

"April knows?" Noah asked.

"Dad, everyone knows. You two make goo-goo eyes at each other constantly. I'm surprised you thought you were being sneaky."

"Everyone knows?" Cat repeated.

Sara shrugged. "Merry is small. People talk *a lot*. Especially when someone sees you getting out of a truck with steamed-up windows. What I'm trying to say is don't think you have to hide your 'whatever you want to call it' from me. I like you, Cat. And I think you two could make each other very happy *if* you give yourselves the opportunity to do so."

Cat looked down at her lap. "That's very sweet, Sara, but my life doesn't exactly allow me to settle down in one place for longer than a week at a time. I have a place in Brooklyn that I see three months out of the year. I've got projects that require extensive travel, and I'll probably end up moving wherever my school is built. You and your dad, your lives are here. It wouldn't be fair of me to ask either one of you to pack up and follow me around."

She felt Noah's gaze heavy on her. Maybe they hadn't pushed this discussion this far before, but it was something they were both aware of. They both knew there was no future here. Just fun. And disappointing a twelve-year-old made Cat feel like a monster. She didn't want to feel guilty for choosing herself over Noah. But damn it, that was what she wanted in life. She shouldn't have to feel guilty for choosing what was best for her. That was *why* she was single.

"What I'm hearing are a lot of problems and no solutions," Sara said as she steepled her fingers. Now the kid sounded like Mini Noah.

"Sara, this is something that is really between Cat and me," Noah reminded her.

Sara rolled her eyes. "Dad, you make it everyone's business when you're mooning over each other and then sneaking into alleys to make out."

Cat covered her eyes with a hand. "Ah, crap."

"Look, what you two decide to do is your choice. All I'm trying to do is save you the energy of pretending to hide it and asking that you at least consider what a future together could look like."

CHAPTER

41

I feel like I just sat through a three-day interrogation in the desert," Cat said, collapsing on a stool in the kitchen.

Sara was upstairs doing her homework and video chatting with April, leaving the mess to the "grown-ups." She'd gone without a fuss, and Noah considered that a victory.

He slid the last of the plates into the dishwasher and shook his head. "When did she get to be so damn smart? It feels like yesterday she was throwing herself on the floor and screaming because the pictures in her book were upside down because she was holding it upside down."

It hurt him to think that his little girl worried that he was lonely.

He wasn't even sure if that was true. Before Cat, his life was…quiet. And now? Everything was so much brighter, busier, louder. And he didn't mind it.

Cat laughed. "She seems to have gotten wiser since then."

"Apparently I haven't. I thought we were pulling one over on everyone," Noah admitted. He topped off Cat's wineglass and slid it toward her.

"It's kind of weird knowing that your neighbors are basically watching our every move," Cat said, wrinkling her nose.

"Goes with the territory in a small town."

"Do you think she's going to expect a report from us on all the reasons a permanent relationship won't work?" Cat asked, leaning against the counter next to him.

They were barefoot, relaxing after cleaning up from dinner. It was such a normal scene for so many couples around the world. But for them? They were just playing at a relationship. Noah cleared his throat. "I'm sure. With footnotes."

He felt…disappointed. It wasn't that he'd been planning to spend the rest of his life with Cat. They were both aware of the temporariness of their situation. However, it still sucked to hear her say the words, to know that she wasn't even willing to consider it.

Cat's eyes narrowed over her glass. "What's wrong?"

Noah topped off his own glass and avoided eye contact. "Nothing. Just surprised at how grown-up Sara's become without me noticing."

"She's smart," Cat commented, nudging him companionably with her elbow. "And she's got a great eye. The designs she was thinking for her room? There's talent there. As a nonparent offering unasked-for advice, I'd recommend that you support her interest in fashion marketing."

"As a parent accepting unasked-for advice from a nonparent, I'll take that into consideration," he said, raising his glass.

She clinked her glass to his, and Noah felt a war of wants. Wanting to kiss her as if it were the most natural thing in the world and wanting to back away and figure out if it was too late to protect his heart.

"A friend of a friend in Manhattan runs this immersive summer camp kind of experience for teens. They basically act as lowly gophers for whatever fashion house is hottest that season. Long hours, no pay. She's too young now, but if she's still interested in a few years, it would probably help Sara decide whether it's something she wants to pursue."

"Will we still be in touch in a few years?" Noah asked. He was surprised at the bitterness that colored the words.

Cat frowned. "Noah, you and Sara are special to me. Just because there's no future doesn't mean it has to end badly. I couldn't stand that."

Noah's heart sank as he realized that no matter how this ended, he'd be the crushed and broken one. Cat would move on to the next project, the next excitement. He'd be left here picking up the slivers of his heart.

It was a joke. And he was the punchline.

Cat would be gone, and in a few short years, he'd also have to face the fact that Sara would be growing up, moving on, building her own life.

Noah stared skeptically at his glass of wine. He wished it was scotch. A bottle of it.

CHAPTER
42

Two weeks to Christmas Eve

Cat's foot twitched in Noah's lap when he tickled her bare sole. "Focus, Yates," Cat ordered from her end of the couch. They were both wading through opposite halves of a stack of papers.

He handed her another application. "Maybe pile."

Cat dropped it onto the stack on the coffee table and groaned. "Who knew it would be so hard to find a location for a school?"

"Literally anyone who ever tried to start one themselves," Noah said mildly.

"We've got a hundred definitely nopes and, like, six maybes," Cat lamented. "And not one of them feels right."

"You may need to visit the ones at the top," Noah mused, flipping over another application. "Nope pile."

She tossed it onto the growing mound on the floor.

"I can't start hiring staff until we know where this damn building is going to be."

"And you can't wait until you have a building to start hiring staff," Noah said, familiar with Cat's cyclical frustration. "Now drink your wine and keep reading."

Dutifully, Cat picked up her wine and cocked her head. "What would you say to canning the research for the night and just pretending we're normal people who order pizza, watch TV, and have sex?"

Noah tossed his stash of carefully organized papers in the air, and Cat laughed.

"You're dying to pick them up, aren't you?" she accused.

"It's killing me. Please pretend you don't see me putting them back in order." He shuffled and stacked and placed them neatly on the end table.

Cat laughed again. "I'll order the pizza."

"You're actually going to eat a slice and not just shovel salad into your face and whine about how good my pizza smells, right?" Noah asked as he organized Cat's paperwork.

"I'm not filming tomorrow, so I think I can afford a slice, maybe even *two*," Cat said with a wink.

Playfully, Noah clutched his heart. "Well, in that case, order a large."

She took her wine and headed into the kitchen. She pulled the short stack of takeout menus out of the last drawer of the peninsula that also housed flashlights and leftover cat treats from furry flood victim Felipe's stay. Cat pawed through Noah's bulletin board by the door until she found a coupon.

Noah appreciated frugality. A leftover, she assumed, from his childhood. Sometimes she pictured him, a little boy, going to bed hungry in a cold house with thin walls. His only escape from the constant fear was his town's Christmas Festival.

This year would be one for the record books, she promised herself. She'd been determined to make it big first to prove him wrong, then to prove herself right. Now, she just wanted to give Noah a gift that he would appreciate all the way down from his city manager practicality to his little boy holiday joy. She wanted that for him. And she'd be lying if she pretended that a part of her didn't want him to always associate her with the festival. After this year, memories of Cat King would be so wrapped up in the Christmas Festival, Noah would never be able to separate them.

That was a kind of fame that Cat could really embrace. Being unforgettable to a man like Noah.

She dialed the pizza place and ordered what had become their usual. A grilled chicken salad and sausage and pepper pizza. They'd fight over the remote. Cat usually watched competitors' shows for research while Noah preferred documentaries on the History Channel. Each proclaimed the other didn't know what entertainment was.

"Pizza will be here in twenty," Cat told Noah when he entered the kitchen. He pressed a kiss to her cheek and reached around her for the refrigerator.

"Hmm, not enough time to get you naked."

She laughed and twined her arms around his neck. "There's always time for you to get me naked."

He picked her up and settled her on the counter. "Naked yes. But fully exploring your nakedness? No."

"After pizza and *Property Rehab*," Cat offered.

"After pizza and *Submarines of the Pacific*," Noah countered.

"Hmm, I wish Sara was here as a tiebreaker." Cat had been joining Noah and Sara for dinners regularly, to the girl's delight. Sara's entertainment choices ran toward binge-watching sitcoms. "That reminds me, Henry passed along some crazy recipe his mother always made him growing up. I thought we could try making it and invite him over so he could tell us how horribly we failed."

"Sara cooking dinner for a handsome British guy?" Noah mused. "Sounds like a father's worst nightmare."

"Oh, then we definitely have to invite Drake too," Cat teased.

Noah grimaced. "Put it on the calendar. I'm sure you'll be Sara's favorite human in the world for another week if you pull that off."

"Hey, have you ever thought about redoing your kitchen?" Cat asked, running her fingers through his hair. She liked it messy.

"No, but I can see your wheels turning every time you're in here."

Cat grinned. "Guilty as charged. Don't take offense. I do it to every room I'm in."

"What would you do in here?"

"I'd kill this peninsula," she said, slapping the counter she sat on. "Put in an island, a huge one, running length-wise. Bar stools. Black leathered granite. Extend the cabinets on to this wall." She pointed.

"What? No walk-in pantry?" Noah teased.

"I'm trying to reconfigure that too-tiny-to-be-usable powder room and the space under the stairs into something workable."

"Your brain is a wonder," Noah said, placing a kiss to the corner of her mouth.

"I like your house, Noah. Your kid too," Cat admitted.

"I like having you in my house, around my kid."

"I'm going to miss this," she said, feeling a pang of sadness. "When we wrap filming next week, when I'm on the road. I'm going to miss nights like this."

"You say that like you're confessing some deep, dark secret," Noah said, rubbing his thumb across her lips.

"I love my life," Cat said. She was reminding herself as much as him. "I love the hustle and the travel and the cameras."

"But you like this too," he pointed out.

She nodded. "I like you a lot, Noah. More than I've ever liked anyone else." She needed him to know that.

"What's not to like about a stick-in-the-mud city manager who tried to throw you out of town?"

"You're a good, kind, smart, sexy, attentive, interesting man, Noah Yates. Don't sell yourself short."

"You're kind of okay yourself," Noah teased.

The doorbell rang, cutting her off before she could make him understand just how serious she was.

CHAPTER

43

"I f you keep frowning like that, you're going to need to buy stock in BOTOX," Henry said, handing her a bottle of water with a straw so she could sip without ruining her makeup. Cat slapped a demonic fake smile on her face as she scrolled through her phone as Elton the hairstylist fortified her high ponytail with enough hair spray to freeze a woolly mammoth in place.

"I'm not frowning, I'm concentrating," she told Henry with a haughty look.

"Wrinkles," he said, tapping her forehead between her eyebrows.

"Don't you have some lunch to order and fetch for your evil boss or something?" Cat asked pointedly.

"Grilled chicken salad heavy on the veg and unsweetened green tea are already on order. And if you're a good girl, there's a tiny bowl of squash soup in it for you."

Cat was a sucker for squash soup. "Consider my frowning finished. What else is happening?"

Henry pulled out his phone and scrolled through notes. "I took a run at your email backlog and flagged everything that needs a personal response. I proofed your next two blogs for this week and got in touch with the jeweler for those earrings everyone was asking about. She gave us a coupon code to use on the blog."

"Nice," Cat said, only half listening.

It was strange, this feeling of disconnect she had staring at those little red icons declaring she had four hundred new followers, thousands of new likes. They had entertained and sustained her before when shoots went long or she got a little lonely so far away from her family.

Before Merry, showing up on set to shoot had been the highlight of her day. Now, with Gannon and Paige and her parents nearby, with Noah and Sara and the Hais, she found herself looking forward to the end of the day. To washing off the makeup and grabbing a glass of wine with loved ones...and liked ones.

Cat brushed it aside, chalking up the uncharacteristic sentimentality to the holidays. She was about to embark on the most important project of her life. She'd been dreaming about starting a school like this since she was the only girl in shop class in junior high.

Henry was still plowing through their combined to-do lists when Maria, a newbie production assistant, appeared.

"Ready to roll in five," Maria told Cat.

The Hai reveal was finally here, and energy on set was nearing Red Bull danger zones. Cat could hear the rumbles of the crowd just outside the makeup trailer. The postproduction team was having aneurysms about turning around an episode in barely enough time to shoot one, but Cat had faith that they'd deliver. They had to. It was the next-to-last show to air before the live Christmas Eve finale in two weeks, which would be an even more complicated production nightmare.

Half the town had turned out on the street and sidewalks to watch the action.

Cat slipped out of the stylist's cape and pulled on her down vest. Henry slung her parka over his shoulder. They'd be shooting outside first to make the most of the light, which meant the front of the house reveal and the tree house. Between takes, she'd be cuddling with a portable heater until they could get inside where she'd sweat through her layers with the press of dozens of crew squishing themselves into corners to shoot.

"You ready?" Drake asked, meeting her outside the makeup trailer.

Cat nodded. "Let's knock their socks off."

April, in a red dress with green and red leggings that Sara had picked out, hopped from one foot to the other in front of her parents, who looked damp-eyed already.

"Who's the first to cry?" Drake asked, nodding at the family.

"Oh, my money's on you today." Cat grinned. "I saw those baby blues glistening when Mrs. Pringle was singing your praises."

Drake gave her a nudge with his shoulder. "Shut up."

Cat waved to Sara, who was standing behind the wooden barricade in the street keeping the crowd at bay. She was holding a sign that said *Welcome Home, Hais*. Noah, handsome as always in his black wool coat, gave Cat an anything but innocent smile.

Cat pulled out her phone and stabbed out a text.

Cat: Have time to get naked tonight?

She arched an eyebrow at him as she hit Send and enjoyed watching him fumble through his pockets for his phone. When he managed to free it from his coat pocket, Cat swore she saw steam coming off his head.

Noah: You're killing me. I'm handing Sara over to Mel at eight.

Cat felt the slow burn of anticipation ignite.

Cat: Maybe I'll sneak into your bedroom after curfew?

He looked up at her, heat in his gaze, and Cat grinned wickedly. She winked at him and then waved to the rest of the crowd. Usually reveal crowds were full of strangers, but not in Merry. Rubin and Elizabeth Turnbar held up a sign thanking the show for "cleaning up Merry." It had their dry cleaning logo on it. Elroy Leakhart, the school principal, was trying to keep twenty-five high school seniors in line, nervously mopping at his forehead with a handkerchief. Freddy and Frieda Fawkes made a rare appearance together with Sadie, chief of emergency services, who finally looked as if she was getting regular sleep.

Cat and Drake shuffled over to Paige and the production team. "You all ready to make people happy?" Cat quipped. It was the question she always asked before the reveal on her own show.

Her team put down their energy drinks and coffees and put their hands in.

"One, two, three, Hais!"

The crowd, already primed for excitement, cheered.

Cat and Drake took their places on the Hais' new front porch.

"Cue the limo," Paige called into her headset.

"I still say she cried first," Drake insisted.

Cat laughed and threw a companionable arm around her costar. "It's hard to stay dry-eyed when a twelve-year-old is sobbing over her brand-new tree house."

"You did, you heartless monster," Drake said, accepting the bottle of water Henry handed him.

Henry gave Cat a bottle of water and slapped a twenty into her hand. "Remind me never to bet against you again," he grumbled.

Cat smugly tucked the twenty into her back pocket. "When are you boys going to learn that I know everything?"

Still muttering, they walked off, leaving her to bask in the victory of not only a win but a really good day of filming. The Hais were home again. Jasper's boss had popped in to announce that Jasper's job would once again be full-time. And April had freaking loved the tree house. The kid had been speechless, her Scrabble-winning vocabulary deserting her as she clambered up the ladder sobbing.

It had been an excellent day. And it would get even more excellent if she could spend the night naked with Noah.

"Hey, Cat!"

The voice of the daughter of the man she'd just been fantasizing about doing filthy things to jarred her awake.

"Hi, Sar. Did you see the tree house?" Cat asked, slinging an arm around Sara's shoulders.

"Oh my god. Seriously the coolest thing ever. I can't wait 'til summer so we can have sleepovers in it," Sara announced.

"Your dad helped build it." Cat couldn't seem to resist throwing out a comment about Noah. It gave her a special little thrill to say his name to others. To be proud of him and to share that pride with someone who loved him.

"That's so cool! He's, like, the best, isn't he?"

Cat nodded slowly. "He is indeed."

"Are you spending the night since I'm at my mom's?" Sara asked.

"Uh, I feel like it would be weird if I answered that question."

"Then we'll both just pretend like I don't know that you'll be there."

"I can live with that," Cat decided.

Sara left her to explore the house with April, and Cat sat down on the front porch for a moment of peace. Sure, dozens of people carting equipment bustled past her, but she'd gotten adept at finding quiet moments to herself on set over the past several years.

This had been her life for so long now, had altered the course of her life really. Five or six years ago, she'd been focused on how to keep the doors of her grandfather's business open. Then life had thrown her a curveball. Reality TV was meant to be a temporary solution. But she was *good* at it. She enjoyed it. And sometimes you just had to take a swing at those curveballs to find what you were meant to do.

She spotted Noah talking to her parents at a makeshift coffee station Reggie had set up for them. Her mom beamed up at her father as he told some ridiculous story or another, Gabby balanced on his hip. Noah's laugh boomed. He didn't laugh often enough in her opinion. She found herself doing and saying things just to tease that laugh out of him. He was so serious, and she had a feeling that scared little boy was still inside him somewhere, hoping for something better.

She felt tears prick at her eyes and forced herself to look away.

Cat didn't know where these urges kept coming from. She wanted Noah happy. That was normal, healthy even.

What wasn't was the fact that she kept thinking of all the ways she could push him in that direction. Ways she could make him laugh. How she could make him smile that unguarded, delighted smile.

But she wasn't going to be here much longer. And sooner or later, it would be someone else making him laugh, someone else dragging him out of his responsible shell for fun, someone else talking to Sara about boys and school.

Her phone vibrated in the pocket of her coat. Cat pulled it out and raised an eyebrow when she saw her agent's name on her screen. She debated letting it go to voicemail. She should be celebrating a reveal that would be ratings gold. But Marta never wasted time. There was a reason for the call.

With a sigh, she swiped to answer. "Hey, Marta," Cat answered. "What's going on?"

"Are you sitting down?" Marta demanded, no nonsense.

"As a matter of fact, I am."

"I just got off the phone with a VP over at Reno and Realty. They're interested in your school."

Cat snorted. "Of course they are, now that it's getting play in the media."

"They want to shoot a show around your inaugural class. Early talks now, but they're throwing around some huge numbers for you and for the school."

Cat gripped the phone harder. "What about my show?"

"Tentatively the reno show would shift to a spring through summer shoot. There would be some overlap at the beginning and the end of the season, so you'd be flying back and forth."

Cat pressed a hand to her forehead. "Back and forth from where?"

"The network is ramping up production on the West Coast. They've got some ideas for locations in LA."

"Locations for my school? In LA?" Cat felt like she was parroting everything Marta was telling her.

"You'd be giving up some freedom on choosing the location, and the network wants a say in key staff at the school. They want personalities. But they're talking serious money. You'd have yourself a state-of-the-art facility."

"What about curriculum control?" Cat asked.

"That's still in your court. They're not as interested in what's being taught as in how it's taught and who it's taught to."

"They're not picking the students."

"They'd keep your criteria in mind," Marta said in Hollywood backhand. "But personality and appeal would be factors for the show. Executive producer credit is yours, of course. And you'd have the freedom to choose your crew. And, Cat, the money they're talking? Scholarships. Equipment. Salaries."

Cat could see it as Marta spoke. Hadn't she been thinking of filming it anyway as a documentary with Paige?

"This is a once-in-a-lifetime chance, Cat," Marta reminded her. "You'd be able to write your ticket beyond reality TV after this."

Cat's gaze tracked to her parents and Noah. He was juggling Gabby on his hip as she played with his scarf. "I need to think about it." The words were out of her mouth before her brain caught up to them.

"I'll have them put something down on paper, a place to start negotiations," Marta said briskly.

Cat could hear the click of a keyboard on Marta's end of the call as the woman prepared a battle plan.

"Uh, great. Thanks." Her voice sounded flat. Foreign to her own ears.

"I'll try to nail them down and get something to you in the next week or two," Marta promised. "Take care and keep those ratings up in Merry. Every little bit will help when we go into negotiations."

"Will do." Cat laughed weakly and disconnected.

Why did she feel like she had a ball of lead sitting in her gut? This was literally her dream being handed to her on a silver platter. At least it had been eight weeks ago. Things hadn't changed since then, had they?

She'd be filming year-round. Living full-time on the West Coast and crisscrossing the country four months out of the year. Sure, she'd have to give up some control. LA was not the economically depressed location she was hoping for. But she'd stick to her guns when it came to the quality of the instructors. She wouldn't let a production company choose her students. That was what negotiations were for.

It was what she wanted. Wasn't it?

"Cat!" Her mother waved.

Cat waved back numbly.

She'd put this away for now, think about it later with a clearer head. For now, she'd celebrate a job well done.

CHAPTER
44

One week to Christmas Eve

Cat peered into Noah's office. He was alone, focused on his laptop, muttering to himself. She loved watching him focus on a problem. He approached everything with seriousness and logic, carefully weighing options.

He'd been invaluable helping her narrow down potential locations for her school, though if she took the network's offer, all their work would be moot. She'd be setting up shop in LA. But it was pointless to mention it to anyone until she saw the official offer, so she'd just obsess about it internally until she saw what they'd given her agent.

The only time she wasn't obsessing about whether she should say yes was when she was naked under or over Noah, chanting the word. Last night, they'd spent a particularly adventurous hour in the back seat of Noah's SUV after dropping Sara off for Elf Camp—a Merry tradition where junior high schoolers helped elementary students shop for their family members in the dollar store equivalent of Santa's Workshop.

Giddy as teenagers, they'd shed their clothing and set that fogged-window SUV to rocking. She couldn't tell for sure, but she thought there might be the slightest hint of a hickey poking out above the collar of Noah's button-down.

Cat knocked on the open door, breaking his concentration. "It's time," she said with mock solemnity. The advertising dollars had kicked in, and with a week to spare, Cat was squeezing in the new roof on town hall.

Noah rose, accidentally kicking over a bucket behind his desk. "Sorry. New leak," he said sheepishly.

He was so fucking cute in his jeans and leather boots, the neat knot of his tie visible over his sweater. His glasses were askew, which meant he'd been rubbing his eyes. Noah's dark hair was mussed, and Cat smothered the urge to further muss it. Because she knew once she got started on him, she wouldn't be able to stop. Even after having him inside her groaning out her name as they came together on the cold leather of his back seat less than twelve hours ago, she was primed for another go.

"I don't see why I can't work in here while the roof is redone," he said, frown lines appearing between his eyes as he packed his laptop and folders into his messenger bag. He was loosening up, marginally, but Cat was starting to find Noah's natural resistance to change a little adorable. It was as if he thought he actually had a choice.

"Noah," Cat said, stepping into the room. The closer she got to him, the brighter the electricity between them sparked. He closed the flap on his bag and took the long way around his desk, keeping the furniture between them. "It's going to be dirty and loud and very, very messy."

He tripped on a lump in the carpet, and Cat smiled,

showing her teeth. Carolanne was long gone for the day. It was just the two of them. And if the tension in the room was any indication, they were both thinking about last night.

"Still. I could just move into an office downstairs."

Cat shook her head. "The whole building is being checked over by an architectural engineer to make sure there aren't bigger problems than your Swiss cheese roof. It's easier if the building is empty. You'll be back to your musty, moldy cell in no time."

Noah skirted around her. "It's not that bad," he said. A floorboard groaned out its protest under his foot.

"This place is a fire trap," Cat insisted.

"Hey, I don't go around dissing your office, do I?"

"My office is the dining table in an RV."

"Well, you don't see me pointing out its many flaws."

"Like the fact that it's missing a leg because you fucked me too hard on it?" Cat shot back. He blushed. An honest-to-goodness blush.

"Jesus, Cat!"

"Aww, loosen up, cutie." Cat slapped him on the ass and had the satisfaction of watching him jump away from her hand.

"Catalina," he said, his tone full of warning. "If I didn't have a meeting in five minutes, you'd be in big trouble."

She laughed and pushed him toward the stairs. "Naked and bent over your desk trouble?" she whispered in his ear as they descended.

His sharp intake of breath was reward enough.

"You're evil. Pure evil," he muttered under his breath.

"You love it. Now give me your key, and have a good meeting." She paused to tuck his office key into her pocket and then sneaked a quick peck on his cheek. "Bye, Noah."

"We'll revisit this desk thing," he promised on his way down.

———

She was feeling playful, Cat thought as she steered her pickup off the highway in the direction of the rental house her parents were sharing with Gannon and Paige. Being sneaky had that effect on her. Poor Noah. He had no idea she'd been lying her ass off to him. And wouldn't he be surprised? Hopefully he'd take the gift as it was meant. As a thank-you for their time together. He'd been more special to her than anyone outside her own immediate family.

It was bittersweet. Knowing that the end was looming. That in just a matter of days, she'd be packing her bag and driving away from him.

The thought, the visualization of the actual moment, had Cat slamming on the brakes and swinging off the road onto the snowy shoulder. Her breath caught in her throat. What the hell was that? That white-hot blast of…pain? Fear? Regret?

It was temporary. She knew that, had preferred that, had made it abundantly clear.

"What the hell is wrong with me?" Cat muttered. She flipped the visor down and studied her reflection. Her mother could always tell when something wasn't quite right, and if Cat didn't want to face an Angela King inquisition, she'd better get some color back in her cheeks.

Consciously, she relaxed her face, draining the tension out of the muscles. She smiled with forced cheer. She'd been smiling on command for nearly five years now and had mastered faux sincerity.

She took another deep breath to slow her heart rate.

"I've just been working too much. I'll take a few weeks off in January, get my head on straight, and—"

And what? Move across the country? Away from her family? Her home? Noah?

"Sweet baby Jesus, woman. Get it together," Cat told her reflection. She slammed the visor up and pulled back onto the road. "Everything is fine. I'm happy. I'm excited. I'm just fine."

———

"What's the matter?"

The first words out of her mother's mouth told Cat she wasn't as skilled an actress as she thought.

"Geez, Mom. Hello to you too," Cat said, pressing a kiss to her mother's cheek before unwinding the evergreen and navy scarf from her neck.

"Stir this and tell me what's wrong," her mother ordered, pointing at the pot on the stove. A stew, thick and savory, simmered within.

Cat grabbed the spoon and dutifully went to work. "Nothing's wrong. Can you give me the recipe for this? Sara would love—"

She wouldn't be seeing Sara again either. Sure, maybe on her annual pilgrimage to visit the Hais, but would Cat even have that opportunity next year?

"Who's Sara?" her mother demanded, dressing the baby greens with her homemade vinaigrette.

"Noah's daughter."

"Why do you sound like you're choking when you say his name?"

"Geez, Mom. I don't know."

"Are you in love with him?" Angela was relentless.

"Mom!"

Her mother shrugged. "What? One minute, I see stars in your eyes. The next, you're moping around like when you didn't magically sprout boobs at thirteen."

They had thankfully made a spectacular appearance at sixteen, making the year of her driver's license one of the most entertaining.

"I like him. A lot," Cat admitted. "Sara too. They're good people."

"So marry the guy."

"Marriage is not the answer to literally every problem in the world," Cat argued.

"It worked for your father and me," Angela pointed out smugly. "And just look at your brother and that wife of his."

"Speaking of, where are they?"

"Gannon and Paige took Gabby to see Santa at the mall. They want to test her out with the big guy before she has a meltdown on camera on Christmas Eve."

Gannon's little cherub sitting on Santa's lap had been Cat's personal brainstorm. Viewers would eat that shit up with a spoon.

"It'll be funnier if she cries," Cat said.

"If she takes after your brother, she will." Angela grinned. "Every year until he turned seven. Hysterics."

"I think we should remind him of that tonight," Cat decided.

"I already pulled all the pictures. They're on the table."

"Diabolical. That's where I get it from," Cat told her.

Her mother bumped Cat in the hip as she picked the colander of green beans out of the sink. "Now, back to you and Noah."

Cat dropped her head back and growled at the ceiling.

"Might as well talk now before your father wakes up from his nap and you have to discuss your sex life in front of him."

"Do you ever regret not having a career?" Cat asked suddenly.

"I worked in Pop's office off and on for years."

"Yeah, but when you were growing up, what did you want to be?"

"An equestrian, a librarian, and then in my teenage years, I thought about physical therapy."

"Do you regret not going for it?"

Angela dropped the beans into the strainer over the boiling water and wiped her hands on the towel stuffed in the waistband of her slim black jeans.

"You mean, do I regret focusing on family over a career?"

"Yeah. That."

"Of course not. You and your brother would have wrecked the house and set each other on fire if I hadn't been around."

"Har. Har."

"I see your face. You're thinking it has to be one or the other: career or love. Why do you think you have to choose?"

"Mom, I can't see where things go with Noah and be traveling for the next however many years."

"You film how many months out of the year? And with the school, aren't you looking for a more permanent place?"

"The network made me an offer," Cat confessed. "A really good one."

Angela lifted the green beans out of the water and drained the pot. "What kind of offer?"

"They'd invest in my school. Set it up in LA. Base a show around it. I could still do my show too. But I'd be based out of LA and traveling the rest of the time."

"*Los Angeles?*" There was clearly an opinion behind the near shriek. Her mom wasn't one to withhold her opinions. So Cat waited her out. "What would you be giving up by taking the deal?" Angela finally asked.

"The network would want to make certain calls on staffing.

They want to pick the students too because of the show, but Marta drew the line in the sand there. I hadn't considered the West Coast. It's not ideal. But the money they're willing to throw at this? It would mean better equipment, maybe more qualified staff. Both could impact the learning experience for students."

"And Noah?" Her mother prodded.

"I'd be living in LA. It wouldn't be fair to ask him to come with me or wait for me."

"So either this opportunity or this relationship?" Angela sighed. "You think you can't have both, but you're wrong. You're smarter than that, Cat."

"I don't even know if things would work out between us. I mean, we're so different. He's got a kid, a great one. But he can't just pick up and fly to Texas or Washington or Idaho with me."

"Do you love him?" Angela asked again.

"Geez, Mom. Don't you think that's something I should talk to him about first?" Did she? Was that the feeling that kept fluttering through her chest? She wanted to protect him from his past, wanted to make him laugh every day, wanted to go to him for advice and tell him good news. She wanted to lean on him when she was tired and cook more barefoot dinners with him and Sara. Was that love?

"Do you want to know what I think or not?"

"By all means. Tell me," Cat said, frustrated.

"I think life just threw you a curve, and it's up to you to decide whether to go for it. Figure out your top two priorities, and then figure out how to make at least one of them work. Go with your gut. No one's going to be able to tell you what the right choice is."

"It would be a hell of a lot easier if someone would," Cat grumbled.

"You wouldn't believe them anyway."

"Yeah, well, I get that from you."

"You're only looking at the obstacles. You gotta start looking at solutions if you want it to work. Though why you wouldn't want to lock down that sexy hunk of man is beyond me." Angela sighed. "You know, I've always had a thing for glasses. I was so excited when your father got his first pair of cheaters. You're lucky you didn't end up with a baby brother or sister that night."

"Oh my God, *Mother*."

Angela grinned and laid a hand on Cat's arm. "Fine. One last thing, and then I'll shut up. It drives me batty to hear your generation going on and on and on about balance. There's no life-work balance. Okay? Get it? It's *all* life. You get the same twenty-four hours as the next girl. Fill yours with what you love."

Cat blinked, processing.

"There's my girls," Pete King boomed as he shuffled into the kitchen.

"Hi, Dad," Cat said, offering him a kiss on the cheek and a squeeze around the middle.

"Your daughter's considering a move to California," Angela said with the accusing tone of an Italian mother.

"California, eh?" her father said, scratching his belly. "What's for dinner tonight, my angel?"

Angela slapped at his hand. "Your daughter wants to move across the country, and you want to know what's for dinner? This family!"

"Who's moving across the country?" Gannon, Gabby bundled in his arms, marched into the already crowded kitchen with Paige on his heels.

"Your sister!"

Gannon leveled a look at Cat. "And you didn't think we'd want to know?" he demanded.

Paige peered over his shoulder. "Why don't we open some wine and get our daughter a snack before we jump all over your sister," she suggested.

"How did it go with Santa Claus?" Pete asked, swooping in to steal Gabby from her father's arms.

"Perfect." Paige grinned. "She screamed like a banshee until Gannon jumped over the fence to save her."

CHAPTER
45

One day to Christmas Eve

The eve of Christmas Eve found Noah playing host to half the men of Merry. Cat had arranged a spa afternoon for the women including Sara, Paige, Angela, Kathy, and April. She'd also thoughtfully included Mellody in the mix, and off they all went, chauffeured by Pete King to do God knew what with their hair and nails.

"We have to look good, Dad. The finale's live," Sara had explained the night before as she and Cat browsed nail art on Pinterest.

Noah was well aware of the finale and exactly what it meant. The excitement of finally opening the Christmas Festival was dampened to ashes by the thought that his time with Cat was coming to an end. Sara seemed to have accepted it. Now if only he could force himself to do the same...

The idea of moping around alone was enough to have him

throw out a half-assed invitation to the men who would be abandoned for spa day.

Gannon brought Gabby and cannoli. Drake and Henry brought beer, a lot of it. Jasper brought sausages. Ricky—because if Cat was kind enough to include his ex-wife, Noah didn't have much of a choice in extending an invitation to his ex-wife's fiancé—arrived with two dozen deviled eggs, a bottle of vodka, and Mellody's famous brownies.

Noah called in an obscenely large order of wings and cued up college football on the living room and kitchen TVs while everyone talked around him.

"Man, you look morose," Henry observed, popping the top on a fancy pale ale. He propped a hip against the countertop and pointed at Noah with the bottle. "Bit of a letdown, isn't it?"

"What is?" Drake asked, sidling into the conversation and shoving a deviled egg into his mouth.

"Noah here preparing to miss us."

"And by *us*, you mean Cat," Drake corrected his friend.

"Can we *not* revisit that train wreck of a conversation?" Gannon growled, pulling Gabby's chubby little hands away from the vodka and lemonades he was mixing. Noah's mixer supply was limited to whatever Sara brought home from the grocery store. So it was either blue sports drink or lemonade… or straight vodka.

"I'm not talking about anything," Noah said, holding up his hands.

"Here." Gannon thrust a drink at him. "Drink this and keep not talking."

Noah drank like a man walking through the Sahara.

"She's something though," Jasper said, blissfully unconcerned by Gannon's discomfort. "I mean, it would be hard not to fall for Cat. Even my wife has a crush on her."

"We're not talking about my sister and anyone having any kind of feelings for her," Gannon cut in.

"So what are you going to do?" Henry asked Noah.

"Do?"

"You know, the grand gesture. How are you going to tell her how you feel and that you want her to stay or you want to go with her?"

"Guys, neither of those things are options. My life is here in Merry. Sara's here. Mellody and Ricky are here. My job. Everything."

"We'd work something out with you, man," Ricky promised amiably.

"Then ask her to stay," Drake said with a shrug.

"Her entire life is…well, everywhere but here. She travels all the time. She works long hours when she's filming. And she's only going to get busier."

"Yeah, even if she does make the move to LA, I don't see her slowing down any time soon," Gannon said.

Noah blinked. "LA?"

"Oh, for fuck's sake. Why can't you two just get your heads out of your asses and talk to each other?" Gannon groaned, exasperated.

"Ffff. Ffff." Gabby was gleefully trying to eke out her first four-letter word.

"Nobody react," Gannon ordered. "Just insert 'funky' into the conversation every other sentence, and we'll be fine. Be cool about it." He was sweating though.

"When in the *funk* did Cat decide she was moving to LA?" Noah demanded.

Drake and Henry looked just as surprised. Ricky and Jasper were too busy in an apparent head-to-head egg-eating contest to react.

"I don't know, man. I don't think she's decided yet. The offer's on the table. The network wants her to build her school there and turn it into a show." Gannon was backing toward the door to the living room.

"Well, now you *have* to make a grand gesture," Drake insisted. "You can't just let her jet off to the other side of the country when you're in love with her."

"I didn't say I was—"

Gannon, Jasper, and Ricky burst out laughing. "Ah, funk. It's so cute when they try to fight it," Jasper said, slapping the countertop.

"It's written all over my stupid funky face, isn't it?" Noah sighed.

"Oh, totally."

"Funk yeah."

"Uh-huh."

"Ffffff."

Then why hadn't Cat noticed? Or had she, and she was too busy crafting an exit strategy to react?

Noah took a gulp of his second drink. It wasn't awful. Not like the clawing panic in the back of his throat. He was in love, and the woman who'd turned his life upside down was going to walk out of it tomorrow night and never come back. Unless...

He pulled a chair out from the breakfast table and sat. "She saved my life. Did she tell you?"

"Are we talking metaphorically here?" Ricky asked, pulling another beer out of the fridge.

Noah shook his head. "She was here in the flood. Pulled my ass out of the water when I went under."

"She funking did what?" Gannon choked on a sausage.

Henry took Gabby from him, and Drake slapped him on

the back until he stopped coughing. He washed down the rest of the sausage with an entire vodka lemonade.

"She came here to prove to the network that this would be a better holiday special than some decorating contest. And while she was here, she climbed aboard some guy's fishing boat and started pulling people out of their houses."

Gannon shook his head. "She said she gave a ride to a few people, not saved actual lives. Between my wife, my sister, and my daughter, I'm going to die young." He took a long pull of beer.

"One of a kind, man," Henry said, jiggling Gabby on his hip.

"I hope you don't mind if I weigh in here," Ricky said, brushing brownie crumbs off the front of his sweater vest. "But if a woman waltzes into your life, saves it, and then changes it, you're totally funked."

"I am totally funked." Noah nodded. "What the funk do I have to offer her that would be better than LA?"

"If any of you assholes say 'cock,' I'm going to murder you all," Gannon cut in. "I don't want to hear it about my sister."

"No one say 'cock,'" Henry cautioned. "I don't feel like getting murdered before Noah's grand gesture."

"Stop saying 'grand gesture,'" Noah said, picking up another vodka lemonade. They were tasting better and better. And every one of them helped dull the panic and nausea just a little more.

The doorbell rang.

"Wings!"

They trooped to the door as a pack, scaring the hell out of the delivery kid.

"Uh, here you go, Mr. Yates," he said, holding up two bags of to-go containers.

Noah's guests pounced and stripped the guy of his food like a vulture with roadkill.

"Thanks, Edmund."

"You having a going-away party?" he asked.

"Let me ask you something, Edmund. Can I call you Edmund?"

"That's what my mom calls me." The boy's voice cracked. Puberty was never kind to teenage boys.

"Edmund, if you were in love with a beautiful woman who was leaving town in less than forty-eight hours, what would you do?"

"Uh, well, I guess write her a song?"

"A song?"

Edmund's head bobbed. "I play a mean accordion. Do you need me to serenade anyone? My rates are reasonable."

"Thanks, Edmund. I'll, uh, let you know."

Noah handed over the bills and closed the door. He pushed his glasses up his nose and listened to the wing unloading chaos coming from the kitchen.

He wasn't a risk-taker, Noah thought. But he'd had plenty of missed opportunities in life that he'd lived to regret. Was he prepared to add Cat to that list?

CHAPTER
46

Cat relaxed as a woman with the shoulders of a linebacker and soothing magic fingers rubbed creamy crap over her face. She felt like she'd run a marathon. Between finalizing tomorrow's filming locations with Paige, installing and covering her supercool present to Merry, and taking care of her secret project, she was beat.

A swarthy masseuse named Teddy had worked out the kinks in her back and shoulders. Her nails were a pretty, festive plum, and after the facial and blowout, she'd be camera ready for tomorrow.

"This. Is. The. Best." Sara sighed across the room. She was sporting new caramel highlights that were probably going to make Noah lose his shit because of how grown-up they made her look. She and April had gone for matching red glitter nail polish. Perfect for the Christmas reveal.

"Mmm," Cat's mother purred as Teddy worked on a delicate spot on the arch of her foot.

Paige, Kathy, and Mellody were animatedly discussing Mellody and Ricky's upcoming wedding.

"You're all set here," Magic Fingers announced in a thick Austrian accent. "Don't move."

The woman shoved a warm towel around Cat's neck and lumbered out the door. Cat could appreciate efficiency over friendliness. Especially when the results spoke for themselves. She'd been pampered to within an inch of her life and was content to just sit.

Her phone buzzed in her lap. Cracking one eye open, she held the phone aloft.

Noah: We've had some drinks.

The attached picture made her grin wide enough to crack the facial and get antioxidants in her mouth. One of Gabby's socked feet poked out from under the coffee table as did most of Drake's lower body. Gannon was sound asleep, mouth open on the couch, while a grinning Henry carefully dotted his face with stickers. Ricky was either dancing in front of the TV or having some sort of seizure.

Cat quickly snapped a selfie and sent it back.

Cat: I'm busy getting beautiful.
Noah: Waste of time. You're already beautiful. The most beautiful. Is that mayonnaise?
Cat: It's not mayonnaise. It's something very expensive and French sounding.
Noah: Have I mentioned I had some drinks?
Cat: You may have said something about that.
Noah: I'm probably going to ask you to stay tomorrow even though I know the answer's no. But I hate

surprises, so I thought I'd warn you anyway. Also, there were drinks.

Cat didn't know how to respond. He'd gotten attached, just as she'd feared. And damn if he wasn't the only one. She loved Noah's grumpy predictability. His sexy nerd glasses. His unfaltering devotion to his daughter. His drive to do the best for everyone.

And just what the hell was she supposed to do about it?

———

By the time the spa circus rolled up to Noah's front door, they'd all been primped and polished to a new shine. They piled out of the SUV and trooped up the steps to the front door. A now mostly sober Noah opened the door with an enthusiastic flourish. "Ladies!"

Cat patted him on the cheek as she walked past him into the foyer. The living room was full of men. Sound asleep men. Gabby was sitting on Gannon's lap happily watching creepy puppets sing on TV while her dad snored.

"Oh my," Paige sighed. "Looks like you guys had a big day." She picked Gabby up and pressed a kiss to Gannon's forehead.

Gannon pulled her down to sprawl on top of him.

"Hey now, sister present," Cat said, pretending to gag.

"This is nothing compared to what I had to listen to today." Gannon yawned. "Come on, wife. Let's go home and do bad things to each other."

"Ffffffck." Gabby chirped, clapping her hands together.

"What was that that just came out of my sweet child's mouth?" Paige asked sharply.

"She said *funk*," Drake said, his head popping up from the pillow.

"Clearly," Henry agreed from his position on the floor.

"Definitely did not say 'fuck,'" Ricky announced.

Jasper kicked Ricky in the shin.

"Ouch!"

Cat smothered a laugh and watched Noah try not to flip out over Sara's hair.

The party over, they left in families and twosomes, carting leftovers and kids until it was just the two of them.

Noah slipped his arm around Cat's shoulder as they waved Sara, Mellody, and Ricky off. And by the time the headlights came on in Mellody's car, Noah was dragging Cat back inside.

He kissed her, and she tasted sweetness.

"Don't you think we should talk?" she asked.

"Talk later." He bent low, tossing her over his shoulder and heading for the stairs. Cat shrieked as he jogged up them, his shoulder shoving its way into her solar plexus with every bounce. He tossed her with less ceremony and more enthusiasm onto the mattress.

Laughing, she bounced once against the wall of pillows. "Just how many drinks have you had?"

"Why?" Noah asked, kicking off his slippers and yanking his T-shirt over his head.

"Because there are rules about taking advantage of partners when they're inebriated," Cat reminded him.

"You're a really good person, you know that?" Noah insisted as he unzipped his jeans.

Cat bit her lip as they slipped low over his hips, offering a view of that V of muscles she loved to bite.

"I am pretty great," she agreed.

"It's no wonder I'm in love with you," he said conversationally.

Cat blinked.

With jeans low on his hips, Noah crossed to the dresser. He opened a drawer with a flourish and pulled out a matchbook. Striking one, he lit the two pillar candles in front of the mirror.

"Noah." She said his name softly, not even sure of what she could or should say next.

"It's funny how you can go through life and be as careful as possible, follow all the rules, and then *bam*!" He plugged something into the wall, and the floor lit up. He'd strung Christmas lights over every piece of furniture and the floor the whole way around the room. "Anyway." He hooked his thumbs into his jeans and slid them down his thighs. "I'm going to ask you to stay tomorrow. And I'm giving you a heads-up on that because I want you to really think about it."

He was hard already, a spectacular specimen in the soft glow of Christmas lights.

He crawled up the foot of the bed toward her. Cat felt her breath catch in her throat at the beautiful man who loved her, covering her body with his. He pressed her into the mattress with his weight.

"Tonight, I'm either going to convince you to stay or give you a memory that will stay with you forever."

"And ruin me for other men," Cat guessed.

"That too," Noah said, cupping her chin in his hand. "I love you, Catalina King. I didn't mean to, and I'm not sure how it happened. But I'd be a fool if I just let you walk away."

His mouth finally shut the hell up and got to work brushing soft kisses over her mouth, her nose, her eyelids. Together, they wrestled her shirt free and then her pants. He stroked her, every inch of her massaged, oiled body, igniting wants so terrifying that Cat wished she could forget them.

Her bra seemed to disintegrate, her underwear evaporated, and then it was just skin against skin. He kissed her from forehead to toes and back again, unhurried despite her begging him for more, despite how his hard-on throbbed against her. He tickled and teased her with his tongue, stroking between those slick lips at the apex of her thighs until she trembled over the edge into a breathtakingly beautiful orgasm. It was like having the sun rise in her body, bit by bit, flooding her with light.

When she moved to take control, to touch him back, Noah cuffed her hands over her head. "Just take."

It was an order she'd obey this time. Every cell in her body tingled, primed for more pleasure.

He settled himself between her legs, lazily rolling on a condom, pausing to lap at both breasts until she was writhing again. Helpless, vulnerable, deprived, she opened for him, tempting him with rolls of her hips.

When she felt like she'd die if he didn't slide home into her body, she begged him tearfully to fill her. And he did. One languorous push, and he was sheathed inside her. Whole. Full. Joined. Her body recognized his as part of itself.

And the glow began to build all over again.

Slowly, languidly, he circled his hips. This wasn't the fast, reckless sex she'd preferred in a past life. This was love in physical form. Worshipping each other. Carrying each other to an unexplored heaven.

Tears leaked from beneath her lashes at the beauty of it. And the smart bastard knew that she'd never forget this moment. Never forget their connection. She would come, exploding around him like a supernova, and she'd never be able to move on.

She squeezed him tight between her thighs. "Noah. Wait."

He stopped, still as a statue even as his cock twitched inside her in protest. "What's wrong? Did I hurt you?"

She shook her head. "If we're going to make this the most

memorable experience in the history of sex, I want you to come inside me."

"Anything you want," Noah agreed.

"Without the condom."

His body coiled tightly against her. "Are you sure?" His voice was gruff.

She'd never not used a condom. Never in her sixteen years of having sex.

"I'm sure." She was. She wanted there to be nothing between them this time.

Noah braced himself on one arm, gently pulling out of her. She heard the slick slide of the condom coming off. Felt him positioned at her entrance. Nothing but heat between them now.

"Really sure?" he asked again.

"Positive," she breathed.

And with that affirmation, Noah drove into her in one exquisite thrust.

They cried out together, and Cat clung to him as he began to move in her. Different from before. So much more.

Noah groaned against her throat, and she knew he felt it too. That connection that perhaps she'd hidden from, ignored. There was no denying it, not like this.

He moved in her, slow, measured strokes that made her lose her mind. She flowed with him, letting him carry her closer and closer to the sun.

He whispered dark promises of love in her ear. Cat dug her nails into his shoulders when the first flutter of release awakened.

"Noah!"

"I'm here. I'm with you," he promised.

She jumped, open-armed, into the sun, letting it blaze

within until she was sure they both would burn up. But he was there with her, his cock releasing his orgasm into her very core. Wave for wave, they met each other eagerly, desperately.

CHAPTER
47

C at paced back and forth in front of the cameras, ignoring the amused looks Eddie the sound guy was shooting her.

"Chill, babe," Drake said, pressing a bottle of water into her hand.

"I'm so fucking nervous. What if they don't like it? And why the hell do we have to film this?" She sent an anxious glance over her shoulder to where Noah and a couple dozen Merriers were laughing and joking around the coffee and cookie table.

"They're going to love it. It's incredible," Drake promised.

"And we have to film it because it's gold, Cat," Paige said, giving her a sympathetic smile. "If you wouldn't have been so thoughtful and awesome, we could have brushed all this under the rug."

"So helpful. Thanks," Cat snapped back.

Paige laid a hand on her shoulder. "You're going to be just

fine. And your second surprise is a camera-free event. So maybe you should be worrying about that one."

"And now I'm doubly panicking." Cat chugged her water, let Archie touch up her lipstick, and pasted on a dazzling for-the-cameras smile. "Let's just get this shit over with."

"That's the spirit!" Drake slapped her on the shoulder.

They found their marks, and Cat wished she was standing anywhere but here for this particular reveal. Her gynecologist's office. Jury duty. She'd thought it was a good idea, symbolic of the town, of their resilience and traditions. Now it seemed stupid. Really stupid. And they were going to hate it. They'd probably pelt her with burned Christmas cookies. The ultimate insult.

"Rolling."

Cat automatically shifted gears from doubting human to charming show host. "When Merry lost their official Christmas tree, an eighty-year-old pine they've decorated every Christmas for the past five decades, we knew we had to find a way to replace it."

Drake smoothly took the next line while Cat stared at Noah. She was worried most about his reaction. Traditions were important to him. Hopefully this wasn't too much of a departure.

"We give you Merry's new Christmas tree. One that you can light for the next fifty years." Cat's delivery was strong even though her stomach was a roiling mess of nerves. The crane driver perfectly executed the tarp drop revealing the surprise beneath.

The crowd gasped, then broke into spontaneous applause, and Cat watched as Noah covered his mouth with his hand. No one was laughing or throwing shards of Christmas cookies her way.

The bronze statue rose twenty-five feet in the air, its sinuous metal twists reminiscent of the branches of a perfectly shaped evergreen. It rose proud and strong, firmly rooted to the earth yet reaching for the sky.

The metalwork firm she'd commissioned had outdone themselves. It was beautiful, strong, and absolutely perfect.

"Noah?" Cat called. "Can you come here, please?"

He looked over his shoulder as if expecting there to be another Noah behind him. Cat crooked her finger at him, and he obeyed. Reluctant as ever to be on camera, he shoved his hands in his pockets, but there was only joy in his green eyes.

"Could you do us a favor and push this button?" Cat asked, handing him the slim remote.

He cast a glance at the cameras. "Uh, sure." Deftly, he stabbed at the button with his gloved finger, and the crowd erupted again as the statue glowed to life.

Thousands of tiny fiber-optic lights dotted the surface of the metal, making it look like it was made from stars. It would be spectacular at night.

"I hope you like it," Cat said softly. She was speaking directly to Noah, but it was everyone else who reacted. They mobbed her and Drake, a town-wide hug. Dozens of people laughing and hugging and thanking them.

The cameras gently pushed their way into the fray to capture the moment.

"Got it in one," Paige yelled. "Let's set up for one-on-ones." This time, it was the crew who cheered.

Cat ducked through the crowd and slipped an arm through Noah's. "Got a minute?" she whispered in his ear.

"I've got all the time in the world for you...at least until the end of the night," he answered quietly.

"I need to show you something." She guided him around

the far side of the tree, away from the crowds and cameras and crew.

Running a finger over one of the curving branches, she found what she was looking for.

"Here. Read this," she said, guiding him to the branch.

Noah leaned in, frowned at the tiny type. "For the boy who dreamed of the light," he read aloud.

Cat bit her lip and watched a wave of emotions pass over his face. Those green eyes misted behind his glasses.

"For me?" He whispered the words, running his finger over and over the engraving.

She nodded, not trusting her voice.

He shoved his glasses up, wiped at his eyes.

Cat cleared her throat. "We were going to do another tree. But the timing was bad, and I wanted you to have something more. Something you could count on forever."

"Stay." He said it, staring at the statue before shifting his gaze to her. "Stay here, Cat. Make a home with me. A family. Whatever you want. Just stay."

Cat opened her mouth, took a step toward him.

But Jayla was already bustling around the statue. "Let's go, King! We need Noah for a one-on-one, and we need a couple of pictures of you and Drake in front of the tree."

"Yeah, in a sec—"

"Cat!" Paige called. "We've got an issue."

"Shit. Noah. Hold that thought."

She left him there, next to his tree.

———

Cat found a bubble, a pocket of quiet in the blazing, celebratory bustle of North Pole Park. It was nearing midnight, and the band was showing no signs of slowing down. Neither were the crowds. They should have thinned out hours ago, families heading home to wake early to celebrate Santa's visit. But instead, they clung to Merry, moved by the holiday spirit.

Just a few more minutes.

Just one more hot chocolate.

Just one more dance.

They'd arrived in droves. Even more than she'd expected, and she'd set very high expectations. They'd seen the show, or they'd come to Merry as a child, or they were here every year. Thousands of families listening to Christmas carols, kids sitting on Santa's lap, adults enjoying spiked hot chocolate while their sons and daughters raced through the holiday in Santa's village obstacle course.

The snow that had started to fall during the official tree lighting was gently blanketing the park in white. The promise of a new day, a fresh start.

She'd done it. Exactly what she set out to do and so much more.

Cat stroked her hand over the bronze of the sculpture. It was smooth and cold to the touch but oh so strong. It would stand for decades. Permanent and rooted in the community. It belonged here, standing for something. She felt the lump in her throat return.

Her family, all of them, were clustered around a park bench. Nonni was holding the sleeping Gabby wrapped in a plaid blanket. Gannon, his arm slung around Paige's waist, gazed into his wife's eyes as they swayed to the music, and Cat felt a punch to the gut at the unconditional, raw love she saw radiate from them. Her parents, just a step away, had their arms wrapped around each other like teenagers, looking on with something like satisfaction.

Sara and April dashed past her, soft pretzels clutched in

their gloved hands. A pack of their classmates giggled on their heels. Sara waved and blew Cat a kiss.

And there was Noah, hands in his pockets, watching her quietly from the other side of the tree. A yearning so intense it felt like it was cracking her heart open swept through her.

So *this* was love. And wasn't that ridiculous to finally know it *now*?

When had it all changed? When had her goals shifted from big and sweeping, from spotlights and followers, to this? Tight circles. Intertwined roots. Family. Community.

He rounded the twists and tangles of metal, slow and steady—that was her Noah. Cat held her breath. She wanted to fold herself into his arms and press her face into his chest. But they needed to talk. There was so much to say.

"You did it," Noah said, tilting his head toward the band and dance floor still crowded with couples in winter coats and boots. People whirled around, blurs of color and laughter, in time to a particularly energetic version of "Jingle Bell Rock."

A ghost of a smile played on her lips. "I told you I would."

"This is the part where you're supposed to rub my face in the fact that I ever doubted you," he said, nudging her boot with his.

Cat crossed her arms over her chest so she wouldn't climb into his arms. "Oh, I prefer to let the results speak for themselves. It makes the disbelievers feel like bigger assholes."

He smiled, warm and sweet, and Cat melted to her toes.

"You told me you were a miracle worker, and I didn't believe you. Not even after you saved my life." Noah's hand snaked out and grabbed her wrist, pulling her in.

Cat glanced around. "There's an audience," she whispered.

"I'm okay with that. Besides, there's something I need to tell you, and I want to make sure you hear me."

Cat bit her lip, her pulse thrumming in her throat. "Noah, I need to tell you—"

"Cat. What I'm trying to say here is *I'm* perfect for you. *I'm* what you're looking for. I know it's crazy. I know it's not what we talked about. But I would spend the rest of my life regretting it if I let you walk away. Stay. Or I'll go with you. Logistically, it would be more complicated. Sara, Mellody and Ricky, April and her parents, they'd all have to come with us. But I will find a way, Cat."

"Noah—"

"Don't say no. Since you came into my life, I've started saying yes, and it feels so damn good."

"Noah, stop." Cat held up her mittened hand. "I need to show you something."

CHAPTER

48

"You're dragging me somewhere private so you don't crush me in front of my town, aren't you?" Noah demanded as Cat pulled him up the stairs to his office.

"Don't be so dramatic," she sighed, pulling the key out of her pocket. She pushed it into the lock. "Now, tell me what time it is."

Impatient, Noah glanced at his watch. "Almost midnight."

"Good enough. Merry Christmas, Noah." Cat pushed the door open and stepped aside.

Noah frowned and reached for the light switch as he crossed the threshold.

"What the hell? I thought you were redoing the roof?"

She'd gutted his office from leaky ceiling to creaky floor with her own money. The floors, sanded and stained, gleamed a deep caramel. A huge rug, from Drake's new collection, covered the floor. The walls were painted a deep navy, the shoulder-height wainscoting stained dark to match the built-ins behind the desk.

The big walnut desk was Cat's pride and joy. She'd made it herself with a guiding hand from Gannon, of course. Simple, classic, durable. Like the man who would sit behind it.

Noah wandered, open-mouthed, picking up trinkets, running his hands over new wood. "How? How did you ever do all this?"

Cat shrugged. "I'm a miracle worker, remember?"

His face lit up. "A new coffee maker?"

Cat laughed. Trust Noah to be impressed by the mundane/functional/efficient.

"I can't believe you did this."

"For you," Cat added. "I did this for you."

He moved behind the desk, trailing a palm over the silk-smooth surface before sinking down into the leather chair. "This is too much."

"This was supposed to be a goodbye present," Cat said, swallowing hard.

She saw the pain, the sharp edge of it in his eyes, and pressed on.

"After we started…getting to know each other…" She shook her head and tried to clear the emotion from her throat. "I just… You're the best person I know. You work hard. You try hard. You want to fix everything and protect everyone. You could have gone a hundred different directions because of your father. But you became this quiet, steady hero, and I just wanted you to have something really, really great before I packed up and left town."

"Before you moved on," he added quietly. He fidgeted with a pen she'd left on the desk blotter.

She nodded. "Yeah. But somewhere along the line, this stopped being a goodbye present. It became a present present."

"A present present?"

"Shut up, Noah. I'm not good at this, and if you keep interrupting me, it's going to come out so much worse."

He held up his hands.

Cat cleared her throat again. The clock tower chimed midnight, and they listened to every bong of the bell. It rang clear and sweet. And on the twelfth strike, Cat could hear the distant notes of "Auld Lang Syne."

"What I'm choking on here is that I love you, and I wanted to tell you, but I didn't want you to get attached, get hurt. The network offered me a new show if I move the school to LA."

Noah's shoulders sagged. "I know. Gannon told me."

Cat held up her hand. "You know how badly I want that school."

He nodded.

"So you can imagine how much I must love you, because I turned them down this morning. If I have to choose between you and my school, it's going to be you. I'll figure something out eventually. But I'm not walking away from you, from Sara, from this ridiculously festive town."

"What are you saying, Cat?"

"I'm saying that I'm choosing you. You're my dream come true, not some bricks and mortar. Not another TV show. It's you that I want more than all the rest. You taught me that it's okay to lean, and I didn't even realize how hard I was leaning on you."

"You can always lean on me, Cat."

"I love you. I fucking love you, and if you don't say it back right now, I'm going to die in your new office, and I'll haunt you here for the rest of your days." The tears threatened to spill forth in a never-ending flood.

"Cat." Noah pushed away from the desk and rose.

"Say the words, Noah." She was trembling as if an earthquake had occurred within the confines of her body.

"Shut up, Cat." Noah reached into his jacket pocket and pulled out a slim stack of folded papers. "First this. Here."

"What's this?" She opened them. "Oh my God." She couldn't breathe. Couldn't even think.

"It's Merry's application to be considered as the future site of your school."

"I can see that," she said, her voice strained with emotion. She blinked as her vision blurred.

Noah took a deep breath. "We're perfect for you, Cat. We're exactly what you're looking for. We even have the building."

"The old high school." Cat nodded blindly, not trusting herself to look up at him, the papers swimming in front of her eyes.

"You don't have to have one or the other. I want you to have both. Here. With me."

She launched herself at him, catching him by surprise so that he stumbled back against the desk. She was crying now, ugly, loud sobs, and she didn't even care.

He banded his arms around her, holding her to him. "I'm going to wake up any second now and realize this is all a dream."

Cat shook her head and cupped his face. "Oh, it's real. I promise you that."

His hands, large and warm, caressed her back. "What did I ever do to be so lucky as to have Cat King crying all over me on Christmas Day?"

Cat hiccupped against him. "Yeah, well, don't get used to it, okay?"

He nudged her chin up so she could look at him. "I love you, Catalina."

She sniffled as the tears fell hot on her cheeks.

"I love you so damn much, Noah."

He picked her up and spun her around until she was giddy. Lights danced red and green outside the windows as Main Street celebrated.

"You're probably going to have to marry me," she told him.

"I think I can handle that," Noah teased.

"How is this going to work?" Cat asked, grasping his hand. She needed solutions to the hundreds of questions she had. Where would they live? She still had another year in her contract with the network. How would she honor that? Would she have to give up her celebrity?

"We have options," Noah promised her. "What's important is that we weigh the pros and cons and—"

"You're so hot when you're responsible."

"Bottom line is we'll make it work. I'm willing to do whatever it takes, Cat. That includes being on the road with you if you want me there. Or I can live with you part-time in Brooklyn. We'll find what works for us."

"What about Sara? We should talk to her—"

On cue, Noah's phone rang in his pocket. He pulled it out, held it up.

Sara Yates is calling.

"She's expecting a yes," Noah informed her.

Cat snatched the phone out of his hands. "What is my future stepdaughter doing up so late on Christmas Eve?" she demanded.

Sara's shriek was ear-splitting. "She's staying!" Sara shouted.

Cat could hear a crowd both through the phone and the office windows. She dashed to the window, dragging Noah with her, and pulled up the blinds.

There on the street below was the better part of the entire population of Merry and her crew.

Sara was waving from the center of it all, flanked by the Kings. An accordion player wheezed out the notes to "I'll Be Home for Christmas."

Cat waved back, tears flowing like a river. Noah pulled the phone out of her hand and closed the blinds.

He cupped her face in his hands, those strong, kind, capable hands. The kiss was everything. Tender and possessive. Sweet and swoon-worthy. Cat was right where she was meant to be. In the arms of the man who believed in her.

Noah pulled back, stroked his thumb over her damp cheek.

"Merry Christmas, Cat."

EPILOGUE

The Engagement

Almost one year later

Cat King slid behind the wheel of her SUV and cranked the seat heater to full-on toasty ass. The end of November in Connecticut apparently meant frostbitten butt cheeks. The walk from the train to her parked car had frozen the blood in her veins. She couldn't wait to get home to Noah and that thick quilt on the couch, a fire in the fireplace, and a movie that they'd argue about.

She was hours past dinner, but there were leftovers from yesterday's Thanksgiving feast.

Cat salivated, thinking about a plate of turkey and mashed potatoes and her mother's gravy. They'd hosted, she and Noah. The big old house on the hill in Merry was the perfect spot for their families to sprawl out and gorge themselves on every carb known to man. Her parents, her nonni, Gannon and Paige, and two-year-old Gabby—who was as fiercely independent as her mother. "No, me!" was Gabby's mantra. Mellody, Noah's ex-wife, and her husband, Ricky, and Noah's ex-in-laws joined them too. Even Noah's mother had made an appearance. The woman had showed a little life, laughing at Sara and Gabby's game of hide-and-seek.

One big, happy, blurred-lines family. Cat loved it.

The day had left her with some things she needed to discuss with Noah. Some big, important things.

But it was hard to carve out time for big, important discussions when Cat's school was slated to admit its first students the first week of January. She and the smarter, more experienced team she'd surrounded herself with had worked their asses off to bring this idea to reality.

In six weeks, fifty-five women of varying ages and backgrounds would be shuffling into Merry's old high school. The building had been renovated to within an inch of its life and was now a small but state-of-the-art facility just waiting to educate its students on the ins and outs of several different trades. The small business arm of the school had already unofficially opened for consulting, and with Noah's invaluable help there, they were already making a difference.

Cat's Bluetooth signaled an incoming call from Sara Yates.

"Hey, babe. How was your Black Friday?" Cat greeted Noah's daughter.

"Oh my God, Cat! I got the UGGs you saw for sixty percent off!"

"The double coupon worked?" Cat asked gleefully.

"Yep! I'm never taking them off," Sara announced. "I'm wearing these forever and ever and ever. Oh, I also got a ton of Christmas shopping done, and I may have found something pretty for you."

"Gimme!" Cat teased. Between she and Sara, they were going to drive Noah bonkers before Christmas.

"You have to wait until Christmas morning like a good Dad's girlfriend."

Cat groaned. "I hate waiting."

"Are we still going for a Christmas tree tomorrow?" Sara asked hopefully.

"Definitely. And I'm thinking we should maybe get two. One for the family room and one for the front window in the nook upstairs."

"Two trees? Best. Christmas. Ever."

It would be. Cat was sure of it.

She heard Sara cover the phone and murmur something. "Mom and Ricky say hi and thanks for yesterday. They're still in food comas."

"Hi, Mellody and Ricky," Cat called.

"How did it go in the city today? Good meetings?" Sara asked.

"We added a dozen new products to the clothing line, and the teasers for next season look awesome," Cat told her. "Then I hung out with Grumpy Gannon for a few hours, figuring out holiday bonuses for the crew."

"Business is booming," Sara chirped. The girl was fascinated by all things fashion and glamour but had expanded her interest to include the business end of things, thanks to Cat's influence.

At thirteen, Sara was rapidly turning into a short adult. Cat loved it. Noah was terrified by it but fighting the urge to smother the independence out of his daughter.

"Oh, and one more thing," Sara said. "There was a mitten tree in one of the stores. You know the kind with kids' names and stuff they need?"

"Uh-huh," Cat said, heading toward Merry. "Yeah."

"So I kind of went super crazy and grabbed, like, a dozen mittens. Wanna help me shop?"

Cat grinned in the dark, proud of her sort of stepdaughter's big, shiny heart. Noah would bust buttons over this. Sara didn't know about Noah's childhood. The neglect, the hunger, the cold. And she'd never know what those things felt like because Noah was the kind of father, the kind of *man*, who would do anything to keep someone else from hurting.

Knowing that Sara had those same tendencies? Well, that was the whipped cream on a slice of homemade pumpkin pie.

"Kid, you know it. Trees tomorrow, and we'll start a shopping list!"

"You're the best," Sara said emphatically. "Okay, I'm going to go beat Mom and Ricky at blackjack."

"We'll pick you up tomorrow," Cat promised. "Love you."

"Love you!"

Cat hung up, feeling that warm and fuzzy sensation in her chest that she got every time Sara or Gabby said "I love you." Those two girls made her life more. More colorful. More crazy. More everything.

She took the exit toward Merry and cranked the Christmas tunes on the car stereo. Living in the Christmas capital of the country hadn't yet dulled her love of Bing Crosby and all his cronies.

She took the turn onto Main Street and shook her head at the holiday spectacle before her. Never in a million years had she thought that Catalina King would be happy to settle down in a small town. She had big dreams of success. She still had them but now knew that no success would fill her with the feelings that having Noah in her life did. So she'd adapted. And now she called Merry, Connecticut, home.

And it fit her like a custom-made mitten. She knew that right now, at ten o'clock at night, Freddy Fawkes, co-owner of the Merry and Bright Café, was working on a crossword puzzle and watching the *Jeopardy* episode his wife, Frieda, had DVR'd for him. She knew that Rubin Turnbar, Merry's dry-cleaning mogul, had personally overseen the installation of the Rudolph streetlights today.

She missed this place like crazy when she traveled for filming in the summer. But they made it work. Noah was with her nearly every weekend, and Sara was able to tag along too. And any time Cat wasn't shooting, she was on a plane back to Merry for a few days of normal.

It was a good life that she'd built here with a man who she loved. And to her way of thinking, it was time to make it permanent.

Cat was singing along to "White Christmas" when the next call came in. Noah Yates.

"How's the sexiest city manager in the country?" Cat asked, answering the call with a smile.

"Oh, you know. Just awesome and sexy as usual. Where are you?" he demanded.

"Just pulled into town. Miss me?"

"Every second you were gone. Can you meet me at the park? I think there's something wrong with the switch for the tree. I want to get the bugs worked out before the official lighting tomorrow."

"Shit. I tested them myself. They should be fine!"

"I'm pushing the button. Repeatedly. No lights."

"Damn it. Maybe the remote got wet. I'm two seconds away. I'll fix it," she promised. The tree and its lights were some of the most meaningful things to Noah during the holiday season, though she had a feeling the very naughty Mrs. Claus lingerie she'd squirreled away under the bed would be coming in a close second when she donned it for him on Christmas Eve.

To Noah, the lighting of the Christmas tree had been a

bright and shining reprieve from a childhood of never enough. The Christmas magic had been his home when the roof his father put over his head would never be. And the tree, that skyscraping sculpture of fanciful bronze, stood for something good, something beautiful, something permanent.

For the boy who dreamed of Christmas lights.

Come hell or high water, Noah's tree would light, damn it. Cat would make sure of it.

She eased to the curb in front of the park behind Noah's SUV. She saw him under the streetlights, the light glinting off his glasses. He had his hands in the pockets of his gray wool coat. Even now, nearly a year after they'd made a commitment to each other, she still got a rush when she saw him. *That in itself is a kind of magic*, she thought.

Handsome, kind, sneaky funny, and oh so smart. Noah Yates was her best friend, her favorite person to argue with, and her biggest fan.

She slid out of the vehicle and jogged over. His arms opened for her, and she was finally home.

He swept her up in those strong arms and swung her around in a tight little circle. "Is it stupid that I missed you since you left this morning?"

"Very few things that you do are stupid," Cat said, leaning up for a kiss when he dropped her back to the earth.

Noah pulled back at the last second, and her lips missed their mark, catching him on his scruffy jaw. "Business first," he insisted with a wink.

"You and your lights," Cat teased. "Let me see the remote."

"I left it by the tree." He draped his arm around her shoulder, pulling her into his side as they walked down the winding path. He towed her in the direction of the tree. The tree she'd made for him. "How did everything go today?"

"Good. Really good. The business is doing well, and the network didn't have a hemorrhage when I told them I wanted to only do eight episodes next year."

He squeezed her shoulder through the down of her coat. "Are you sure you're okay with cutting back? You don't have to do that for me or Sara. We'll make it work."

"It was hard being on the road last summer. I want more time with you," Cat said. She cleared her throat, gearing up to have *the talk*. "In fact, I'd like to talk to you about something important."

"Uh-huh. Sure. In a minute. Now, where did I put that remote?" Noah asked, glancing around in the dark, the sculpture rising from the ground in front of them.

Cat sighed and reached for her phone. "Here. Let me at least turn on the flashlight," she offered. Apparently, no conversation would happen before she fixed Noah's damn lights.

"Hang on. Ha! I knew I kept it close." Noah triumphantly fished the remote out of his pocket. He handed it over. "Here, Catalina King. Light up my world."

She rolled her eyes at her sappy-ass boyfriend and turned to face the tree. "Are you sure you weren't just pushing the wrong button?" she asked, ribbing him. She stabbed the button.

The tree lit up just as it should, thousands of lights twinkling to life.

She whirled around to taunt him. "Ha! I knew it wasn't— Holy shit."

The semicircle of pines they'd planted this spring were lit too. Only instead of the pretty white lights she'd helped string two days ago, a colorful message glowed from their branches.

Will you marry me?

"What is that? Who's it for? Is someone proposing tomorrow?" Cat's mind was racing, and it was sprinting full speed toward a conclusion she was terrified might not be real.

"Someone's proposing," Noah agreed. "But it's not for tomorrow. It's for right now."

"Right now, me and you right now? Or right now two other people who are about to walk over here?"

"You and me, Cat," Noah said earnestly. "Your mind is a wonder, as is your ability to jump to conclusions. Just one of the reasons I want forever with you. I've thought it through. I've looked at it from all the angles. I love every bit of you exactly the way you are. You drive me nuts. You push my buttons. And you put my pieces back together. I've never been happier. You're it for me. And I hope I'm it for you."

"Jesus, Noah." He could have sneezed, and the breeze would have knocked her down. Her knees were buckling as her brain scrambled to catch up with what was happening. She was supposed to bring it up, talk him into it. It was how she worked. How *they* worked. It always took weeks, months even, to get him heading in the right direction. How did he get there before her?

"I know you're not big on tradition. But I am. And I want this with you. I want to see my ring on your finger. I want to call you my wife. I want you to be Sara's stepmom. I want more of this last year."

She couldn't breathe. She was going to fucking hyperventilate.

"I'm going to take your momentary speechlessness and do this right," Noah told her, sinking down onto the frozen ground on one knee. From his other jacket pocket, he withdrew a small jeweler's box. "The diamond is Nonni's. She wanted you to have it, but the setting is new. Something a little flashier, a little more dramatic. A little more you."

He was offering her everything: family, roots, tradition in a package that suited her down to the ground.

"Baby, stop crying."

"I *can't*," Cat wailed. "I love you so much and Sara so much and this damn town so much. I was just thinking on the way home—this is home. I've never had home before. I've had my place or my parents' place or Nonni's. But this is home. You're home. Now, put that damn ring on my finger, and kiss me hard, Noah."

He obliged, sliding the platinum band on her shaking finger. Noah didn't stand fast enough for her liking, so she hauled him to his feet and threw her arms around him with so much force that it took them both back down to the ground. She kissed him hard enough, long enough, that the cold ground ceased to be a factor.

"Is. This. A. Yes?" Noah laughed between kisses.

"Hell yes, it's a yes."

He kissed her again, sealing the deal. Those firm, familiar lips that drove her crazy in oh so many beautiful ways tempted and teased her. She felt something featherlight and soft graze her cheek.

"It's snowing," she whispered, looking up at the night sky.

Noah stroked a hand over her cheek.

It was a night like this a year ago, under the first snowfall of the year, that Noah had first spotted her tattoo—that tiny hammer etched on the inside of her wrist—and figured out exactly who she was. The snowflakes laid the white blanket of a brand-new beginning for them that night. And again tonight.

"I love you, Noah. So much more than I ever knew was possible."

"You're my miracle, Cat. You saved my Christmas and gave me the lights."

Later that night, Cat lay sated and loose in Noah's arms. They were curled on the couch under the big patchwork quilt. The glow from the fireplace and the curtain of still falling snow through the windows gave the room a soft, cozy magic. Their clothing, long ago discarded, was scattered across the floor. Music, low and Christmassy, spilled quietly from the speaker on the bookcase.

They'd cleared the space in the corner for the tree—Cat hadn't yet broken the news that there'd be two—and stacked the boxes and tubs of ornaments in front of the TV.

Noah snored softly behind her, spooning her body with his own. His arm was heavy over her ribs, his hand fisted between her breasts. She loved the feel of him, skin to skin, heat to heat. Heart to heart.

Cat held out her hand, admiring the glitter and glint of diamonds. It was a promise of forever together. And she was ready.

Now, she just needed to figure out when to drop the bomb on Noah about wanting a kid or two...

BONUS EPILOGUE

A few years later

"Put the paintbrush down or we're going to be late," Noah admonished. He grabbed the brush out of Cat's hand and moved in for a kiss when she opened her mouth to complain.

"I just have one more wall to go," she argued, reaching for the brush her husband held over his head.

"You have thirty minutes to shower and change."

"I miss having wardrobe and makeup," Cat sighed.

"You'll have them back in a few months," Noah said, stripping her out of her paint splattered T-shirt. "But for now, you have fifty-five young women waiting for you to send them off into the world with words of wisdom."

Cat wrapped her arms around Noah's neck. Obligingly he carried her into the bathroom that way. He leaned into the shower and twisted the knob to scalding.

"Where are the boys?" Cat asked.

"Sara and your parents are entertaining them outside...or

at least trying to prevent them from burning down the house. Gannon and Paige will meet us at the school."

"Nonni too?"

Noah unbuttoned her denim shorts. "Nonni too," he promised.

"What about your mom?" she asked.

"She's getting her hair done, and she'll meet us there. Are you nervous?" Noah asked.

"No," she said. "Yes. Maybe? Excited. Very, very excited. I can't believe it's here."

"The first graduating class of King Technical Institute. It's a huge deal. For them and you." Noah cupped her jaw. "I think you can afford to take the afternoon off your current project and bask a little bit."

Cat looked over his shoulder at their new master suite. She'd taken over the third floor of the house, opening it up into one large room with spacious en suite and two gargantuan walk-in closets. She'd whitewashed the floors and was in the midst of painting the brick and plaster walls the same. Color came from the bedding and pillows stacked high on the high-backed king bed. There were plants in every window, books and photos carefully organized on the low shelves. And the fireplace was ready for chilly fall nights. It was peaceful.

Except for when the kids and cats—Felipe had showed up one night with a girlfriend and they'd never left—snuck in...

Sara and the twins were one floor below them. And there was invariably someone in one of the guest rooms.

It was home. And though Cat's list of projects for the house might never end, every coat of paint, every new appliance, every opened wall made it more theirs. And every root that she and Noah planted in Merry erased a shadow from his eyes.

His mother, Nana now, had finally begun her own healing after Cat tricked her into a therapist's office two years ago.

"How's your speech?" Noah asked, pushing her toward the shower.

"Will you read it? It's on the dresser." She pointed to her tablet.

Noah used the opportunity to drop a kiss on the inside of her wrist over the tattoo that he regularly worshipped. "Confession. I snuck a peek at it last night when you fell asleep. It's perfect."

Cat brightened. "Are you sure? You'd tell me if it wasn't?"

Noah grinned, and the boyishness of it melted her. She hadn't managed to build an immunity to him. Not yet, after three years of marriage, of kids and pets and projects. He and their boys traveled with her when she filmed in the late spring and early summer. Sara joined them most weeks, sometimes with Mellody and Ricky, sometimes with April.

Cat paused just outside the tile shower. The steam billowed around her. "I'm not dreaming, am I? This is all real?"

Noah's smile was soft, knowing. "Reality check. You're still a TV celebrity, albeit only for a few months a year. We have three children who seem to have made it their life's purpose to drive us insane. Because of you, we're about to watch several dozen young women graduate from a school you envisioned and built. And your husband still thinks you're the most beautiful, exasperating, determined woman in the history of the world."

Cat fished her fingers into the neck of Noah's T-shirt. "You know, I hate to use this gigantic shower all by myself…"

"Catalina King, are you trying to tempt me with sex while your parents deal with Ms. Teenager and Double Trouble downstairs?"

"Is it working?"

The shoe Noah shucked off bounced off the wall behind him with a celebratory *thud*.

MR.
FIXER UPPER

Paige St. James crossed her long legs restlessly under the glossy wood of the conference table. She wasn't cut out for marathon meetings with multipage agendas. The longer the suit with the receding hairline and the PowerPoint presentation droned on, the antsier she felt. She had things to do, and listening to a bunch of network drones salivate over how to milk more ratings out of an already hit show didn't get her any further down her to-do list.

"What we really need is to see some emotion out of Gannon," the suit announced. The next slide appeared with Gannon King's sex god face and a bar graph. Paige was pretty sure none of the handful of women in the room were looking at the graph. "That's what the female demographic is clamoring for."

"To be clear, you're not talking about his usual emotion. Correct?" Eddie Garraza, the man on her right, was the executive producer and ringleader of the three-ring circus known as the reality show *Kings of Construction*. In a room full of designer suits and shoes that cost more than most people's first cars, Eddie was wearing his trademark khakis and rumpled button-down. His trusty moccasins tapped an incessant beat under the table.

Paige hid her snicker behind a cough.

Gannon King's usual emotion was fiery temper that singed anyone within a forty-foot radius. A builder by trade, he was an artist with woodwork, producing furniture pieces that were one-of-a-kind works of art. The female viewership worshipped Gannon's shirtless physique, but Paige saved her lust for the furniture, not the man. With that talent came a passionate, argumentative, stubborn attitude that often held up shoots and pissed Paige off.

"We want to see the human side of him. Cat plays great in the ratings, but Gannon needs to soften up a little. Viewers will eat it up."

Cat King was Gannon's equally attractive and talented twin sister. Younger by two minutes, she shared Gannon's long-lashed hazel eyes but had miles of California blond tresses where her brother had dark hair usually worn shaved short. Where he was abrasive, Cat was smooth. Where Gannon argued, she orchestrated compromise. Without their uncanny family resemblance, it would be difficult to make the familial connection by behavior alone.

"Paige." The man in the too tight Hugo Boss—Raymond? Ralph?—gestured at her with the presentation remote. "You've gotten into a few skirmishes with Gannon. We're looking to you to rile him up and catch him on camera. You know he's a softie for kids. See if you can push him over the edge there. There's a five-thousand-dollar bonus in it for you if there's tears from him."

She gave a nod, acknowledging that she'd heard the man

without actually agreeing to anything. It was true. There had been more than a few on-set arguments between them in season one of the home renovation reality show. Gannon seemed to instinctively know what buttons to push to send her into an internal maelstrom. Given the instant success the show had been, the network had ordered a twelve-episode second season, which would give her plenty of time to get into it with the brash host.

If she were that kind of field producer.

But as much as she needed an extra $5,000, she wasn't going to set up Gannon and push him over the edge or stir up his emotions for fun. He might be an asshole, but he was an extremely talented asshole. And in her heart of hearts, his open hatred of "network bullshit" was something that she could respect.

Not that she'd ever tell him that.

Eddie jabbed her under the table with the capped end of his ballpoint pen. "We'll do our best," Eddie told Raymond-Ralph, his face a perfect poker mask while Paige's fingers flew over the laptop, making notes.

Behind the same wire-rimmed glasses he'd worn since the mid-1990s, Eddie never gave up what he was thinking with unnecessary facial expressions or body language. He spoke plainly and knew when a battle wasn't worth fighting. That was why, in an industry of perpetual youth chasers, Eddie rocked a head of fluffy silver hair and had never been near a Botox needle.

The presentation moved on, and Paige's gaze wandered to the view of New York through the wall of glass. They were downtown, six floors up at the production company's headquarters. Summit-Wingenroth Productions sounded like a company with a long, respectable history, but it was founded five years prior by a former reality star and made its profits churning out dozens of barely unscripted shows for the networks.

Kings was the only show in the company's lengthy credits that Paige could stomach. They helped people, and that—to her—was the endgame. For Summit-Wingenroth, it was a schmaltzy hook to reel in an audience and sell advertising.

The double doors to the conference room opened, drawing everyone's attention. Gannon King, larger than life, strode into the room. Cat breezed in behind her brother, smiling warmly at everyone gathered. Smoothly, Raymond or Ralph clicked to the next slide, and Gannon's face disappeared behind another chart of audience demographics. Paige turned her attention back to the laptop screen in front of her and refused to stare.

Gannon was the kind of man who wrestled your attention from you as soon as he walked into a room. Built like a Norse god, his broad shoulders and muscled pecs gave way to a taut abdomen that had Twitter lighting up every time he took his shirt off on camera. The gray Henley he wore today stretched across his chest and molded to his impressive physique. A trio of leather cords wrapped around his left wrist.

Disheveled as usual but in the careless, confident way, his hair was a little longer on top than last season. Paige bit her lip. She was a field producer, not some lovestruck teenage fan. And he was the narcissistic bane of her professional existence.

"There are our rising stars." The suit's tone had an extra layer of phony to it that had Paige barely controlling an eye roll.

"Sorry to interrupt," Cat said without a hint of apology in her tone. "But we were in the neighborhood and thought we'd stop in."

"You're welcome to join us. We were just going over the demographics."

And ways to break your brother on camera, Paige added silently.

Gannon ignored the pleasantries and stalked to the coffee station. He poured himself a mug—black—and leaned against the counter. Cat took a seat near the head of the table and stared raptly at the presenter until he turned a bright shade of fuchsia and fumbled over the word "ratings."

Paige grinned. Cat was a master at manipulating men. What looked like a pretty smile and keen interest was actually a calculated move to disarm the enemy and get her what she wanted. The more she was underestimated, the more she was able to get away with before her victims realized they'd been victimized. Paige wondered what Cat was after this time.

Still smiling, she glanced in Gannon's direction and cursed herself when she found him watching her. He must have taken her expression as an invitation because he rounded the table to take the empty seat next to her.

The denim of his worn, ripped jeans brushed her forearm as he took his seat. Paige immediately yanked her arm off the armrest and put her hand in her lap. Once seated, he shoved his long sleeves up, revealing a hint of new tattoo on his forearm, and settled in, leaning on the arm closest to her.

She could smell sawdust and noted he was wearing his scarred work boots. He had probably spent most of the morning in his workshop in Brooklyn before Cat dragged him here for whatever scheme she was cooking up.

Why did he have to be so drop-dead gorgeous and so profoundly talented? It wasn't fair.

He leaned in closer. "What's not fair?" he whispered. His breath was warm on her neck. Paige turned to look at him, finding him entirely too close. Was he a mind reader now?

He nodded toward her screen.

It's not fair. It's not fair.

Crap. Her subconscious was trying to make itself public.

Paige bit the inside of her cheek. She shrugged. "Carpal tunnel exercise." She wiggled her fingers, committing to the lie.

"Sure it is, princess."

His smirk made it clear that he wasn't fooled. And the "princess" pushed just the right buttons with her. He'd called her that ever since an unexpected downpour last season had soaked her to the bone. One of the volunteers happened to have her daughter's gym bag with her, and Paige had spent the rest of the day into the night in a pair of volleyball shorts and a bedazzled too tight T-shirt that said *Princess* across the chest. As soon as Gannon found out the nickname irked her, he became steadfast in his regular use of it.

Paige deleted the lines and tried to tune back in to the speaker, who was finally approaching the important part of the meeting. The families that would be featured on the show this season.

"Our first family for the season is the Russes." A slide showing an older couple surrounded by kids of all ages filled the screen. "Phil and Delia Russe have three kids and nine grandkids." He clicked to the next slide, which showed the exterior of a nondescript commercial building. "Twenty years ago, they opened a soup kitchen in town and have served up something like one million meals. The entire family still volunteers there." Another slide, this one showing a shabby-chic office with the Russes accepting a giant check from two men in suits. "Five years ago, they added a job placement service to the operation. So we've got formerly homeless ready to volunteer, all the kids and grandkids will be on hand, and the rest of the community is on board. It'll be a schmaltz fest. Perfect season opener."

Author's Note

Dear Reader,

Here we are again at the end of another book. This was another one that I had no intention of writing, but you made me do it! You wanted Cat's story after *Mr. Fixer Upper*, and I hope you enjoyed it. It combines some of my very favorite things: Christmas, enemies to lovers, and steamy HEAs.

I knew with Cat's background she'd need to find someone who wasn't impressed with her fame. She has enough people seeing her as just a celebrity or just another pretty face. And Cat isn't the kind of girl to fall easily. So it took Noah and his "rotting smorgasbord of asshole" to sweep her off her feet.

The flood scenes in this book were inspired by Houston as it was hit by Hurricane Harvey. I was so moved by the pictures and videos of hundreds of private citizens mobilizing to help that I wanted to pay homage to their bravery.

In the spirit of this story, I hope you have a meaningful and happy holiday season, however you choose to celebrate, and plans to make next year even better.

If you enjoyed Cat and Noah's story, please feel free to leave a glowing review of awesomeness. Want to talk more about books? I'd love to have you in my readers group, Lucy Score Binge Readers Anonymous. And if you'd like to get a heads-up on preorders and sales, please join my newsletter!

Thanks for reading. Thanks for being great.

Xoxo,

Lucy

PS: My reader group made me leave the "mamma jamma" placeholder in the book.

Acknowledgments

Joyce and Tammy, for admin-ing the hell out of Binge Readers.

Mr. Lucy for that really awesome nap last week.

Dawn and Amanda for your ability to fix my typos.

Claire and Kathryn for listening to me whine about my first draft blues (and for not slapping me).

Marissa and Andy for all those plants that "fell off the truck."

Ideology for some hella comfy sweaters that I can wear around the house without looking like I'm on Day 3 of living in my pj's.

Dark chocolate almond milk.

About the Author

Lucy Score is a #1 *New York Times, USA Today,* and *Wall Street Journal* bestselling author. She grew up in a literary family who insisted that the dinner table was for reading and earned a degree in journalism. She writes full-time from the Pennsylvania home she and Mr. Lucy share with their obnoxious cat, Cleo. When not spending hours crafting heartbreaker heroes and kick-ass heroines, Lucy can be found on the couch, in the kitchen, or at the gym. She hopes to someday write from a sailboat, ocean-front condo, or tropical island with reliable Wi-Fi.

Sign up for her newsletter and stay up on all the latest Lucy book news.
And follow her on:
Website: Lucyscore.com
Facebook at: lucyscorewrites
Instagram at: scorelucy
TikTok: @lucyferscore
Readers Group at: Lucy Score's Binge Readers Anonymous
Newsletter signup: